TUCKED AWAY

TUCKED AWAY

A NOVEL

Phyllis Rudin

INANNA poetry & fiction

Toronto, Ontario, Canada
www.inanna.ca

We gratefully acknowledge the support of the Canada Council for the Arts and the Ontario Arts Council for our publishing program. We also acknowledge the financial support of the Government of Canada.

Cover design: Val Fullard

Tucked Away is a work of fiction. All names, characters, businesses, places, events and incidents in this book are either the product of the author's imagination or used in a fictitious manner.

All trademarks and copyrights mentioned within the work are included for literary effect only and are the property of their respective owners.

Library and Archives Canada Cataloguing in Publication

Title: Tucked away : a novel / Phyllis Rudin.
Names: Rudin, Phyllis, author.
Series: Inanna poetry & fiction series.
Identifiers: Canadiana (print) 20230221998 | Canadiana (ebook) 20230222021 |
ISBN 9781771339278 (softcover) |
ISBN 9781771339285 (EPUB) | ISBN 9781771339292 (PDF)
Classification: LCC PS8635.U35 T83 2023 | DDC C813/.6—dc23

Printed and bound in Canada

Inanna Publications and Education Inc.
210 Founders College, York University
4700 Keele Street, Toronto, Ontario, Canada M3J 1P3
Telephone: (416) 736-5356 Fax: (416) 736-5765
Email: inanna.publications@inanna.ca Website: www.inanna.ca

To Ron and David

expression is the need of my soul
i was once a vers libre bard
but i died and my soul went into the body of a cockroach
it has given me a new outlook on life

i see things from the under side now

don marquis
archy and mehitabel

CHAPTER 1

CHANTAL LEFT IMPULSIVELY, if you can call impulsive a thought she'd been tossing about for months, with just the bit of savings she had stashed in her Hello Kitty bank. Even in her scramble to leave the house behind once and for all, she had enough presence of mind not to take her debit card. It was rule number one in the *Handbook for Runaways*, its importance reinforced by years of reruns of *Law & Order* and *CSI*. The card trail was how they usually tracked you down. If not that, they used the phone, its pings mouthing off your whereabouts, though parting with it was like losing a limb. She'd left them both on the kitchen counter in front of the Nespresso machine where her parents would be sure to find them, a crystal clear statement; no note required. At the time she'd been pleased by the elegance of it.

Though she had no previous experience running away from home, Chantal knew enough to travel light, just a plastic bag stuffed with the absolute essentials. There would be no gate check where she was headed, no locker to dump her belongings for pick-up at her later convenience. Whatever she brought along she would have to keep tight within reach. Who knew what types she would be rubbing up against in her new digs? If they were half as desperate as she was, they wouldn't bat an eye at swiping her bag.

Where to run to. Now that was a problem. She'd seen what she presumed were street kids before around downtown Montreal, squeegeeing, panhandling, but she'd always seen them during the day. Where they laid their heads down at night was a mystery to her. Maybe they went to a shelter of some kind, but that was a no-go for her. She

3

wasn't signing in anywhere. Some of them probably had friends they could crash with. Not Chantal. She was on her own. Entirely.

She did have half an idea tumbling around in her mind as to where she might go when she left the house; a place that would keep her dry and warm and anonymous, where she could hunker down for a while and consider her next steps. She'd been there often enough and was familiar with the layout. During the day it was bustling with shoppers and office workers. She could easily lose herself among them. At night it was calmer, concert- and moviegoers mostly, or couples out for a bite to eat, but still busy enough for her presence to go unnoticed. Surely she could find herself a secluded niche somewhere in the endless maze of corridors that made up the complex where she could bed down after-hours. It was the ideal spot, the more she thought about it. Smack in the middle of downtown, yet apart from it. In the Underground City she would be hiding in plain sight. Very civilized. Far superior to some stinking alleyway or a squat. Chantal fished her last bus ticket out of her bag and used it to take her to her intended destination, there to forge her new life off the grid.

■ ■ ■

Civilized? What had she been thinking? Chantal's early first nights in the Underground City were an experiment in terror. She staked herself out a spot among hard cases who'd lived rough for years and psychos who were off their meds. Unwittingly, she horned in on sleep-sites that others had a historical claim on. How was she, a newbie, to know that hot-air grates were reserved for homeless royalty, and she was chased from these prime spots to the most wretched where she lay rigid listening to her neighbours shout out against their private demons. The noises around her were unrelenting: coughs raucous enough to turn lungs inside out, snow-blower snores, atomic farts, hawking and spitting, and the unremitting skittering of tiny claws that she tried to convince herself belonged to cats. She negotiated her way through the drunks and the druggies and the garden-variety down-and-outers, trying to find a way to block her nostrils against the stench.

It was hell on earth, but at least she was safe.

CHAPTER 2

THE PILE OF BILLS on her desk was starting to list at an alarming angle. Whenever Daphne forgot herself and went at it too heavy-handed on her keyboard, it tilted yet another degree or two off plumb. Pulling out a desk drawer for a postage stamp or paper clip was a similarly risky move. Lately, its sense of balance was so iffy that even the pipes banging in the walls threatened to deliver the death-flick. The stack would have spilled onto the floor long ago into a great murky puddle of debt if she hadn't switched over to e-billing on as many accounts as she could in a shell game she was playing against herself. And losing.

Every morning when she settled herself in at her desk, Daphne assayed the pile. It seemed to be growing of its own accord, as if the bills had got to canoodling during the night and spawned a whole new generation while she slept. That the pile was inching inexorably upwards Daphne could live with. Just. As long as it didn't tip over. If only it stayed in the upright and locked position, she could delude herself into thinking that she was in control. As a precaution, she worked at keeping all seismic activity in the house to the minimum, every movement wrapped in cotton batting. But then her grandmother, who had never fully bought into Daphne's edict against stomping and clomping in her own home, or else had simply forgotten it, slammed the bathroom door shut with too much urgency and sent the stack tumbling.

"It was on purpose, wasn't it?" Daphne asked her. They were sitting on the front steps, nursing their smoothies. Her grandmother was a firm believer in a nightly stoop-sit. It allowed her to keep tabs on the neighbourhood where she had spent her entire life, and had the added

5

positional advantage of placing the house behind her. Not that Nora could forget the wish list of repairs her home had posted by simply facing in the opposite direction, but at least it gave her a reprieve. The paint would still be flaking off the window frames when she turned back around, the porch posts still rotting. The diagonal crack running through the brickwork that hinted at a doomed foundation wasn't going to vaporize because her eyes were focussed on the gentrifiers and their dumpsters across the street.

"Well, maybe it wasn't entirely accidental," Nora said. "But at least there was no forethought, if that earns me any forgiveness points. It was a spur-of-the-moment kind of thing."

"To get me off my ass."

"Do you have to talk to me ugly like that? Is that how I raised you? But yes, since you mention it. I thought you needed a bit of a poke. You've been too much head-in-the-sand lately. Even for you."

"Guilty as charged."

"A confession may be good for the soul, Babka, but what I want to know is, what are you planning to do?"

"I've got a plan in the works to deal with the bills. Just give me a little time to work out all the kinks."

"You've had nothing but time, and where has it gotten you?" Nora's granddaughter hadn't been vaccinated against Procrastinitis as a child. As a result, the concept of *now* was a foreign one to Daphne. She set every problem in a holding pattern, waiting for conditions to clear.

"You haven't pulled out *the road to hell is paved with good intentions* yet," Daphne said.

"I was saving that for my big finish."

"Grandma, I'm working on it. Like I said. Quit pushing me."

"Old habits are hard to break, Daff. But I'm telling you, if I could just have the satisfaction of seeing you tackle those bills and whack what you owe into submission somehow, I'd lay off pushing for the rest of my days, as God is my witness."

It wasn't entirely Daphne's fault that she was so strapped. Events conspired, as they say. In the space of one month, that same vindictive January when her part-time job on the Quik-Shred truck fizzled, some low-life at Thai Express lifted the computer bag containing her phone and splurge laptop that she'd been meaning to insure, and her landlord hiked the rent on the cell he grandiosely referred to as an apartment. She might have rebounded if only student support, her old standby, hadn't chosen that moment to dry up. She was taking so long to finish her degree that the bursary she used to count on to keep her afloat had been awarded instead to a younger, more promising grad student. Just when she needed it most, her academic security blanket had been yanked off, leaving her dangerously exposed. The resulting hypothermia was what prevented her from doing anything more with her bills than gawp at them.

Here it was already 2015, and the university still had her classed as ABD, all-but-dissertation, shunting her into a club she wasn't proud to be a member of. It had been seven years she'd been languishing there. Most of the others who had also been relegated to that student dead-letter office eventually abandoned the slog and took the job their uncle offered with Midas Muffler. Not Daphne. And it wasn't just because there was no one in her family who could offer her patronage. She had her heart set on a clean-hands profession. As well as a non-overalls profession, a non-fluorescent-vest profession, a non-hairnet profession, a non-dust-mask profession, and a sitting-down profession. After the string of blighted jobs she'd held down over the years to help her grandmother make ends meet and to put herself through school, her list of non-negotiables was long and well curated. Of all the job titles she ran through her occupational gauntlet, the only one still standing at the other end was *professor*. And so it was decided. She would teach, sit cogitating in the library, churn out books and articles, and attend conferences in places with palm trees. It was a hygienic life, a unionized life, a life safe and secure.

And she was making progress, however haltingly. Her research and fieldwork were complete, her notes organized to the max, and her bibliography beyond reproach. All she had left to do was get the words down on paper. That was the rub. If only that constipated first paragraph would squeeze itself out, then the rest of her words, she was certain, would follow along in snappy progression. Those friends of hers who were still in the game couldn't offer her much in the way of comfort. None of them seemed to share her particular problem. They tended to run off at the mouth, if that expression can justly be applied to writing, their bloated theses ringing in at 150,000 words, some of them, every paragraph of their prose so precious, they never felt moved to apply the pruning shears. Daphne, alone among them, couldn't get her writing battery to hold a charge.

Daphne was stalled on every front. Not only was she light years away from finishing her degree, she had no paying work to speak of, and her creditors were on her case, with her grandmother riding them piggyback. The stoop, as she sat there reflecting on her situation, was turning cold and unwelcoming under her tush. It seemed to her that it was sending her a message. The time had come to rise up, it said. To act.

So she did.

"Where are you going?" her grandmother asked her. Her smoothie glass, which was the arbiter of how much time she still had left to sit on the stoop prodding Daphne to take herself in hand, was still half full.

"For a run."

"At this hour? It's getting dark already. Some maniac texting won't see you and you'll get hit by a car. Don't make me have to go identify you on a gurney. Do me that favour."

"Stop your worrying. I'll stick to the sidewalk instead of the street. Just for you."

"You're all heart. You know I'm a wreck when you go out running at night. At least make sure to wear all your reflective whatevers."

"It's a promise. I'll sparkle like Tinker Bell."

Before Daphne went inside to gear up, she bent over to kiss her grandmother on the top of her head. Nora didn't return her gesture in kind. Instead, she grabbed Daphne's hand and applied a noisy raspberry to her palm. She didn't run to fancy displays of affection, Nora, not even to unfancy ones. It was a good thing Daphne was in possession of the secret decoder ring that allowed her to translate her grandmother's tart mannerisms into the emotions that hid behind them. Otherwise she might get the mistaken impression that she was unloved.

To Daphne, running had nothing to do with locomotion. She wasn't one of those jogging obsessives who lived and died over their splits or logged all their times and distances on spreadsheets. Hamstrings? She neither knew where they were nor what they did. For Daphne, the only body part that counted in running resided in her skull. She did some of her best thinking while she was out on her route, criss-crossing the corrugated streets of Montreal, hoping not to fall into a pothole and end up in China. On a good day, a run took hold of her brain and treated it to a deep cleaning, as if a cerebral hygienist were up there attacking all the crenellations with her picks, scraping out the accumulated plaque. Out on a run like that, just ask her and she could come up with a solution for world peace. Her mental leaps were worthy of Billy Elliot. But today the gods of running were in a pissy mood. Or maybe just lazy. They loaded the you're-a-leech playlist on her iPod, and set it to repeat while they put their feet up and took a nap. Even though Daphne took a dogleg over towards the expressway, hoping the roar of the transport trucks would drown out their message, it mainlined into her consciousness. How could she still be living off her grandmother when Nora could just barely afford to support herself? All the minute calculations she'd made before deciding to retire were predicated on her living solo.

Retirement hadn't even been on her grandmother's calendar when Daphne pushed the idea on her. It was meant to be a goodbye gift as Daphne was readying herself to move out. "You've worked your fingers to the bone your whole life, Grandma. You deserve a little R&R."

"I'm a tough old bird. I've still got lots of years of work left in me. The city hasn't spray-painted an orange ring around my trunk yet."

"But why keep on working?" This was the part Daphne cringed to recall. "I swear I'm not going to be one of those kids who ends up moving back into the basement."

"Your room's upstairs."

"The metaphorical basement, I mean, where deadbeat children come home to roost."

Nora let herself be convinced. After all, Daphne was educated, in university no less. She must know what was best. But then didn't her granddaughter show back up on her doorstep just a few years later with a gimme-shelter look in her eyes?

Daphne was of an age that she should have been contributing to the communal pot, bringing home some meat to add to the carrots and potatoes. She should have been easing her grandmother's money worries not compounding them. Instead, she was back in her old room, a freeloader. No way to pretty it up.

Maybe they weren't living in outright penury, but if they cut any more corners, their underwear would be showing. The latest indulgence to bite the dust were Nora's casino visits with her pal Madame Marcil from across the street. The girls' cocktails and slots nights, more cocktails than slots, amounted to Nora's only outing, the one time a month that she ever cut loose. Next, she'd have to axe the massages that allowed her blue-collar back to quit squawking for a few days running. There was no wiggle room left, and wasn't wiggling what made retirement bearable?

This evening's run, with its hectoring refrain and its guilt reverb, pushed the normally action-averse Daphne into making a move. As soon as she got back in the house, she shot off a stab-in-the-dark email that she hoped would set things rolling.

CHAPTER 3

Hmaintenance? No. Too strong. Labour intensive maybe? No, not precisely that either. Needy. Yes, that was it. Needy.

"Needy? She's more than needy." Iris seized on her husband's tepid adjective.

"How can you judge? You've never even met her."

"Who needs to meet her? Seems like I've spent the better part of our married life listening to you rattle on about her. Tell me, when was the last time a whole month went by without her sending you a dear-professor email for an appointment to discuss that moribund dissertation of hers?"

Derek buried his head back in his laptop. He knew where this was headed. He should never have read Daphne's message out loud across the breakfast table when it popped into his inbox. He hadn't meant things to escalate. Especially not before coffee.

"It's a daddy she wants," Iris said, "not an advisor. Don't say you haven't been warned." Out of her husband's menagerie of graduate students, Daphne alone piqued Iris's interest by virtue of her longevity and her over-frequent irruptions into her husband's day. "Or maybe I'm wrong," she went on, wringing the essential juices out of the subject, "not a daddy. Could be she has her eyes on you in a different capacity altogether."

Iris was stretching it with that last remark and they both knew it. He wasn't the type students had designs on. He was too stodgy by half. She was only giving his vanity a little wifely boost with the implication. Daphne's relationship with her advisor was strictly on the up and up. Laughably so. He couldn't even convince her to call him by his first name. The other students had no trouble Derek-ing him left and right, even the bottom-feeders with whom he would have preferred to keep a certain professorial distance, but Daphne held the line. He would never admit it at home, it would be handing Iris too much ammunition, but he found her deference endearing, a throwback to an earlier age, an age when he was her age.

In many ways Daphne was the ideal graduate student. It wasn't just that she was bright; there were plenty of brainiacs in her cohort, postponing the moment when they'd receive their first donkey kick by the job market. She alone had that spark professors despaired of ever finding among the bodies that clogged their classrooms. The semester when Derek had her at the seminar table with his other first year grad students for the Archaeology Methods course, it was always Daphne who zoomed in on the essentials, while the rest of them jittered around at the edges hoping they'd trip over the gist. And her research? Impeccable. She could sift through sources that a hundred pairs of eyes had already plundered and come up with a fresh take. Same story for her own work; the conclusions she drew were original, but not so out-there as to get a panel's nose out of joint. If, that is, a panel were ever in a position to peruse her dissertation, that reclusive document. Daphne was one of those students who saw the blank page as her enemy. When it came time for her to write, she froze.

In front of Iris, Derek tried to cast Daphne as a perfectionist. He had to account for her plodding progress somehow. His student suffered, he told his wife, from a deep-seated fear of getting it wrong, even though he knew that perfectionism wasn't what held her back. It was Derek's theory, one that he had been stitching together for a good while, that Daphne saw herself as an interloper on campus. She seemed always to be looking over her shoulder, fearing that someone in authority would come along and smack her down as some kind of poseur in academia. About her secret interior life he felt fairly confident in his conclusions, but about her day-to-day life, which should have been easier to decipher, he hadn't a clue.

For all that he had been meeting with her for years, he'd never gleaned all that much about it. Did she have a partner? Iris asked him. He didn't know. Whereabouts in town did she live? He didn't know. What was her background? Same again. Which way did she swing? Definitely, he didn't know. To Iris, his vast font of ignorance in his student's regard was unfathomable. You could sit next to a stranger on the two-hour Greyhound run to Ottawa and learn that much about them. "She sounds to me like your sister," she said, "so buttoned up she wouldn't tell you if it's raining outside."

Iris had a point. It wasn't normal to know so little about a person with whom he had logged so many hours. She'd always said he was born without the sociability gene. But it wasn't as if there was any dead air at his meetings with Daphne. She was hardly close-lipped. It was just that all the talk was strictly on topic, no mission creep into friends and family. Somewhere along the way, though, Derek did manage to pick up one crucial personal detail about his prize grad student.

He'd gone down to the cafeteria in the basement of his faculty building for a bagel and a double-double to get him through a department meeting when he caught sight of Daphne a few people ahead of him in line. She slid her card into the reader to pay for her doughnut but it rejected the transaction. The cashier encouraged her to try again, those readers could be temperamental, but when Daphne did, again the transaction was refused. On her third attempt the result was identical. By now the students behind her in line were starting to get antsy, their coffees were getting cold, and the cashier's smile was flatlining. Daphne rooted around in her bag but couldn't come up with enough spare change to cover what she owed. She took back her card, left the donut behind on the counter, and scuttered away. Derek couldn't even explain to himself why he did it, but he left his order behind too and followed her. She took the stairs up to the lobby and went directly to the ATM. She nudged her card into the slot for a withdrawal and it spit it back out directly. Just as she'd done downstairs in the cafeteria, she gave it a second try. This time it seemed to shoot the card out of the slot even harder, as if it were sticking its tongue out at her. She got the message.

For the first time in his university career, Derek went to his meeting un-caffeinated, but it didn't matter. His spying mission had him fully awake. Imagine being so skint you couldn't even pay for a maple-glazed. Instead of contributing to the departmental discussion on hiring priorities, he profited from his time at the meeting by cooking up ways he could help rekindle the friendship between his student and her ATM.

From that day forward, Derek made it his business to throw as many part-time jobs at Daphne as he could, a course here, a course there, anything he could scrounge up. And she never disappointed him. Unlike himself, a tin-man in front of the class, Daphne was a gifted teacher, beloved by her students for whom she made herself endlessly available. Her course evaluations for the Collecting Culture course topped the charts. The trouble was, she used these jobs that would support her writing as an excuse to put off the writing. *Catch-22* could have been the title of her biography.

Although her email didn't say it in so many words, he could tell from reading between the lines that she was fishing for a job, but there was nothing at the moment around the department as far as he knew. At least nothing he had control over. Her timing was off. All the classes were already covered. No one needed markers or invigilators. At this time of year every nickel was already locked down to a specific purpose. He dreaded having to deliver the bad news. She always had a clenched look about her as she sat in his guest chair, a look that gave him the urge to reach across his desk to squeeze her shoulder in a buck-up kind of way. But touching was a no-no, of course. He would have been more than happy to tide her over out of his own pocket, but that would be humiliating to her, not to mention inappropriate and unethical and all those other in's and un's that would end up getting him sacked. Too bad. It was just that he would have liked to see her relaxed for once. Maybe she wasn't looking for a father in him, but it struck the childless professor only now that he might have been looking for a daughter in her.

Derek caught himself remembering the first time Daphne came to his office, how she had sat on the edge of her chair in quick-getaway mode, never removing her coat, her back curved as if to make a smaller target of herself. Derek had tried to draw her out on her academic interests to discern if he would be a compatible advisor, but she preferred to let her undergraduate research thesis that she'd submitted earlier do the talking. He hadn't been sure about her at the time, even if her file spoke eloquently to her capabilities. Getting her to pipe up about anything was like pulling teeth, although the few times in their interview that he did succeed in drawing her out she spoke with quiet authority. It was his hope that having her in his class, someone who knew her subject upside down and backwards might give him some blessed relief from the mansplainers who had recently started to invade his classes like zebra mussels. If, that is, he could only get her to open up. And over time he did.

He dreaded their upcoming meeting, which he had set for that very morning to have it over and done with. For the first time in their acquaintance he would have to send Daphne home empty-handed. What would she do to get by? It worried him more than he cared to admit to himself. Straight after breakfast he packed up his computer bag to head downtown to the office. Usually the shady walk down Victoria focussed him on the day to come, but today the steep downhill had the opposite effect, the low-hanging maple branches popping all his thought bubbles so that by the time he arrived on campus he was no further ahead on the Daphne issue than when he'd left the house.

Once at the office, Derek tried to settle in at his desk, but he couldn't concentrate on the lecture he had to write. The cursor, which he normally barely registered, flashed against the white screen like a pesky eye tic, taunting him, "No fresh ideas, old man?" After fifteen minutes of this treatment, he accepted defeat and slammed his laptop shut. What he needed was some busywork to get him through the hour until his appointment with Daphne, but once he'd watered his ficus, and shaken the crumbs and dusticles out of his keyboard, he'd exhausted every opportunity his office presented. All he could think to do to pass the time was to go over to his faculty mailbox in the main departmental office to sort through the accumulated mess. Not much of any interest came by snail mail these days so it was his habit, and that of his colleagues, to let it pile up for weeks on end. Flyers for talks long past, mostly, and catalogues from publishers. Nearly all of it, once opened, was tossed directly into the giant wheeled recycling bin placed strategically beneath the mail slots. Open toss, open toss, open toss. It was a calming rhythm. But towards the bottom of the pile, in one of the manila envelopes that looked every bit as unimportant as the others, he made a surprising discovery that gave him hope. He might have a bone to throw to his favourite graduate student after all.

■ ■ ■

His poky office always depressed her. The cement block walls were painted hoodie grey and the floors were covered with industrial linoleum in the Pollock vomit pattern. It was on an interior corridor, so no windows, only fluorescents, and the suspended ceiling panels bulged damply in one corner where a rusty pipe poked through. The only splash of colour in the room came from the fire extinguisher. In fairness to Professor Séguin, he had tried to make the office look homey with some scattered bric-à-brac, but it was like trying to tart up a cubicle in a public bathroom. Daphne hoped that the university that eventually hired her would have seen all the professor movies on Netflix and would outfit her office accordingly, heavy on the oak.

Daphne had to suck up her courage before knocking. She was going to be asking him for a job. Again. Lately she'd had to pull her begging bowl out of her backpack so frequently that she was thinking of having it monogrammed. Professor Séguin was unfailingly good about her requests. He always made her feel that he was lucky she showed up when she did because, as chance would have it, he needed someone to fill in a course or sub in the lab, but she suspected that behind it all he pitied her. Nothing that he said really, just a look he gave her, as if he were withholding a sigh.

"Ms. Elman, come in. Sit down. Please."

"Hello, Professor Séguin. Thank you for meeting with me on such short notice."

"Not a problem. It's always good to catch up on your progress." The man was a saint. Maybe the others dismissed him as a fuddy-duddy, but couldn't they see? There he was, at it already, complimenting her progress, which they both knew was only measurable in negative numbers.

Daphne was trying to mould her lips into asking mode when Derek cut her off at the pass. "You couldn't have emailed me at a more opportune time," he said. "Have you seen this?" He passed a flier printed on thick glossy paper across to her and gave her a minute to look it over. "You should apply. With your background, you'd be a shoo-in. If you need me to serve as a referee, you can count on me as always. Go for it, Ms. Elman—onwards and upwards."

16

CHAPTER 4

MAYBE IT WAS because there were no distinct seasons underground, no dramatic climatic events to punctuate its calendar, that the Underground City maintenance crew got confused and started putting up the Easter display way in advance, while the world outside was still in full battle mode against snow squalls. Chantal settled herself in on a bench in Place Montréal Trust to watch. The flurry of activity distracted her and no one paid her any mind.

The Easter chick centrepiece was mammoth, rising up three stories through the atrium of the complex. To Chantal, the Godzilla-sized bird didn't have the warm and cuddly aspect the holiday demanded. Its beak was razor sharp and predatory and its claws, so cute and harmless in the itsy-bitsy version, looked like they were itching to clamp down on the bunnies scattered around at its base and squeeze the stuffing right out of them. It took the workmen more than a week to mount the full display and get it all decked out. Once it was completed Chantal found that her negative assessment did not seem to be shared by the legions of little tykes brought in by their parents for their annual ritual viewing. They gazed up at the monster chick with adoration. Chantal's gaze, though, was fixed downwards, at a different element of the display entirely.

The decoration that commanded her attention, if indeed it even qualified as a decoration, was the expanse of fabric that passed for a grassy meadow. The rectangle of material was so vast, that when the workers held it at opposite ends to stretch it taut in preparation for draping it around the chick's base, they looked like housemaids about to fold a sheet for a giant's bed. The crew positioned it carefully, ruching it strategically to camouflage all the electrical wires.

It was a luxurious, velvety piece of material of an intense golf-course green, with a nap so deep it could hold a handprint. Chantal didn't have to touch it to know it would feel as cozy and toasty warm as a weekend bathrobe. In the Underground City's shadows, where she made her home, every surface was cold and unforgiving. The thin slip of cardboard she slept on at night was as good as useless against the concrete chill. All it really did was mark out her space, and for that she was grateful. Only the most pathetic slept bareback.

Chantal never could have predicted that sleeping, or trying to, would be the low point of her daily grind, ranking even below scrounging for food, a task at which she wasn't proving particularly adept. On the face of it, eight hours of oblivion sounded like a gift, a nightly hiatus from both the horrors that drove her from home and the nagging uncertainty about where her life was headed. Except that her nights weren't restful. Far from it. She always slept with an eyelid cocked to ensure that her neighbours weren't making moves on her person or her property. She dozed, clenched and wary, and when morning came around, she felt as exhausted as she had when she turned in the night before. Sure, she was indoors, not out under the open sky, but at bedtime, when she found herself back in enforced proximity with a cast of characters who creeped her out when she was awake, let alone asleep, she would reconsider whether her move to the Underground City had really been the right way to go.

Chantal had observed in her brief time sheltering there that the Underground City could be fickle, yo-yoing between terrifying and welcoming. It left her feeling tipsy, never knowing which of its personas to trust. Right now, for instance, it was teasing her with possibility, dangling before her the gift of a little staycation beneath its Easter chick where she could snuggle under a sumptuous blanket guaranteed to blot out all her yesterdays. She should have known enough to be suspect of its generosity, she should have known enough to give all the pros and cons a serious weighing out. Instead, she jumped for it. She would treat herself to one night, or maybe more, far from the grubbies, even if she had to admit to herself that the grubbies were her peeps now.

Well after dark, once the Underground City had spat out all the stragglers and locked its doors, Chantal made her way back to the Easter display, hugging the walls all along the way to avoid the cameras and security. With no serious barriers to prevent her, she stepped right up to lift a corner of the blanket so she could scooch underneath, and she found that the cover she had been coveting from afar was as soft and cushy as she'd anticipated. She drifted off on the count of two.

Deep in a blessedly dreamless sleep, a sleep deeper than any she had experienced since running away, a sharp kick to her shoulder jerked her awake.

"Get up. You can't be here." A security guard was standing above Chantal, his hands on his hips. Her head was still so sleep-fogged it took her a minute to figure out where she was. The guard took her delay in responding amiss and gave her a second whack to move her along. It didn't work. Her mega-dose of grogginess had her limbs operating in slow motion.

"You wanna play it that way?" he said when she was too slow to rise. "Fine. You're coming with me." He bent over to grab her wrist and then yanked her to her feet. She struggled to free herself from his grip so she could make a run for it, but it wasn't a fair match. Chantal was undernourished, under-rested, and under any other measure that counted. That he would have his way was a foregone conclusion. The guard dragged her through the complex. She figured he'd shove her out into the cold at the first opportunity, leaving her to fend for herself on the streets, but he bypassed any doors leading to the outside. Instead, he led her through a narrow service corridor and paused in front of a gunmetal grey door marked *Sécurité*.

"Look," he said, turning to face her. "It doesn't have to be like this."

"What do you mean?"

"You don't have a decent place to spend the night, right?" He looked her up and down, taking in her snarled blue hair and the general overlayer of grime. "I'm telling you, there are options."

This wasn't what Chantal expected from a guy who kicked first and asked later. Here her assailant was actually a hard dude with a soft centre. He was going to try to help her out, recommend a shelter maybe, or slip her a twenty.

He unlocked the door with a key from his ring. "Just come in here with me and pay up and you'll be back under the Easter display before you know it."

"Pay up? What do you mean? I'm broke."

"Quit acting stupid. You know the way the game works. If it was money I wanted, why would I have picked you? Lucky for me you have something else I want." He smiled indulgently when Chantal let out a scream for help that rebounded unanswered along the corridor. "Knock yourself out," he said. "There's no one around to hear you."

She had enough experience underground by now to know that he was right, but her gut told her to scream, so she screamed.

"You got it out of your system now?" he said, after her latest effort came out more like a croak. "Face it. It's just you and me. Now come into my office, ma belle. See how the other half lives underground. Who knows? You might get to liking it."

Chantal ducked her head submissively. In fact, she ducked it so far down that she was able to sink her teeth into his hand without him seeing it coming. She gagged at the taste of flesh tinged with blood, bile puddling at the back of her throat. Her reflexes urged her to unclamp her jaws and spit out the chunk of rancid meat they were chomping down on, but she resisted, clinging with the fervor of a rabid dog. Chantal had no backup plan. If her bite didn't get him to let go of her wrist, he would close that door behind them, the door mockingly mislabelled *Sécurité*. It was only when her teeth penetrated deep enough to sever sinew and scrape bone that his hand sprung open, allowing her to flee. Later she would reflect on the irony that she had run away to the Underground City to escape from animals like that, only to see her destination of choice turning her into one.

CHAPTER 5

"OKAY, YOU LUMPS," Larry said. "Gimme your what-ifs. And I hope to hell they're better than last week's."

It was their third what-if meeting on the Underground City ad campaign. The first two were bombs. This was not how the work was supposed to be progressing. Gathered in the conference room were the best creative thinkers in the business, hand-scouted by him, plucked away from other agencies in Montreal that had undervalued their brilliance. The ideas should have been spewing out of them. Instead, all they'd served up so far were retreads from the company that had lost the account in the first place, the firm that had been canned because it couldn't breathe any life into the campaign. But the way things were panning out, it looked like his minions hadn't been trained in CPR either.

"So our assignment, kiddies, in case you've had a concussion since our last meeting that's knocked it out of your minds, is to pump up the Underground City. Tourisme Montréal is paying us a pretty sum to hike up the traffic down there, to plug it as an actual winter destination, so the Americanskis will come up here in droves instead of shunning us once the snow starts to fall. Keep them from automatically thinking *south*."

"As if anyone in their right mind would decide to come here instead of Saint-Lucia when it's twenty-five below."

"I read in *Métro* that Irkutsk has warmer winters than we do."

"Yeah, we're a real winter paradise."

"Even with their higher dollar, why the hell would they come up here to have the pleasure of slip-sliding around on pack ice?"

"If I may remind you," Larry butted in to get them back on track, "that's the whole point. The Underground City is indoors, not out. It's dry, it's bright, it's climate-controlled. It has everything down there, all linked up under one roof. You got your metro to run you around. You got your stores, your movies, your apartments, you got skating rinks, museums, hotels, restaurants, spas, grocery stores, libraries, hospitals. A symphony orchestra and an opera for Christ's sake. And you never have to go out in the weather. Get your stunted imaginations working on that, why don't you. That's why we're here today, isn't it? Or did I miss the memo?"

Creatives. Feh. It was like herding cats. Not for the first time did Larry wonder what ever possessed him to start his own agency. On days like this he wished he had followed his father into accountancy. Larry wasn't much of a motivator. The agency succeeded despite him. Usually he just holed up in his office with his accounts and let his hired guns do their thing. But in this case, the client was unhappy in the extreme with their thing. Unhappy enough to require his rare intervention at their meetings. His presence had its usual dampening effect. After their initial flip comments his staffers clammed up, radioing him the subliminal message that he had no business pissing in their sandbox.

Into the coordinated ringing silence, Marius, the intern, piped up. "What if we said you could live your whole life underground and get everything you ever wanted or needed?" Marius offering up an opinion was a leap of epic proportions. He'd only been with them a week and had barely mastered who took one sugar or two. Larry was as stunned as the others by his intervention. He hadn't thought the boy had much backbone in him, which was partly why he'd chosen him in the first place. When Larry launched the new firm, he had no plans for an intern, but once he discovered that all his competitors had personal stagiaires to abuse for no pay, he decided he would have to have one too.

"You hadn't started here yet when we had our earlier discussions, Marius, so you're out of the loop," Larry said, his impatience barely tamped down, "but that's essentially what the previous agency proposed. That idea never did fly which is why we inherited the campaign. To come up with something different. Snappier."

Marius still hadn't twigged that although he'd been allowed into the meeting, he wasn't officially at the grown-ups' table; he was just sitting on Larry's lap, his bare little legs dangling. The unwritten protocol that had Marius silently observing, absorbing the higher wisdom of his elders and betters had clearly shot right past him. He kept on talking as if his contributions were genuinely welcome. "But what if we made it into a challenge, a contest, kind of. Prove that someone could actually live there, never doing without anything. Like you said, it has all the essentials of life. Maybe have someone live down there for a full year, without ever coming out, not once. For prize money, let's say. You could follow them for the whole year, or maybe they could blog about it."

The flushed intern checked around the table to gauge the reaction to his idea. What he observed were frozen faces; faces out-thunk by the understaffer who barely had to shave. In his innocence he mistook the root of their glares. "It was just a thought," he added, trying to efface himself behind an almond croissant.

Larry's face, however, assumed an expression that none of the others could ever recall seeing there before. He was positively beaming. Marius bore a vague resemblance to Tintin so maybe that had coloured his boss's original estimation of the intern's intellect, or lack of one, but now he was revising his appraisal upwards.

Marc-Olivier, who fancied himself the Don Draper of the group, quickly calculated that a shifting of alliances was called for and scrambled onto the life raft with the red-haired bobble-head at its helm. "So tell us, Marius, how exactly do you see this contest playing out?"

CHAPTER 6

SUNDAYS TENDED to be the dreariest days underground, not that any other of Chantal's days could necessarily qualify as peppy. Most of the stores and offices were shuttered, the Muzak was turned off, and the lights were set low on their dimmers. The whole complex had a deflated air to it. She couldn't even treat herself to a good Sunday morning lie-in to make her day tip into Monday faster. Asleep she was easy pickings. If the security guard at the Easter display had proved anything to her it was that. Ever since that night, Chantal preferred to be a moving target, sleeping the bare minimum, wide-eyed and on-guard come dawn, lighting here and there as she came upon new safe spaces in her ramblings underground.

Starbucks was her latest retreat of choice. Chantal had no money to squander at a coffee shop, least of all such a pricey one, but occasionally she would find an empty Starbucks cup on the ground, uncrumple it, and use it to legitimize her occupation of a table. Like a Mafia don, she always sat with her back to the wall. Duly settled in, she would read all the giveaway tabloids from the rack till she had them memorized.

At the end of yet another stultifying Sunday nursing invisible coffee, Chantal made her way back to what passed for home. Many of the corridors she normally traversed during the week were blocked, with mesh gates pulled across them, forcing her to experiment with routes she had never taken before. To keep her brain cells in working order, she turned the endless detours and dead ends into a game for herself, a sort of underground Snakes and Ladders. She meandered unfocused, doubling back and changing levels as required. An aerial mapping of her circuit would have resembled the Turcot Interchange. It was while zigzagging the back roads of the Underground City, far from her normal haunts, that she found herself plunk in front of the entrance to Christ Church Cathedral. Chantal skimmed the plaque. The Anglican Cathedral, it informed her, was a neo-Gothic structure that, at over 150 years of age, was the oldest link in the Underground City chain, with stained glass windows designed by William Morris. Whoever he was. This church, she decided, seemed worth a peek. It wasn't as if she had anything better to do.

As she went in, an aged parishioner welcomed her and deposited a program in her hand. It was for an organ recital that was just about to begin. "If you've never heard Monsieur St. Laurent play," she said to Chantal, "you're in for a real treat."

Chantal didn't think that would be the case, even if the overflow crowd spoke to the truth of the woman's insider review. The organ wasn't an instrument she had ever warmed to, its music was so dour, but the concert would give her an excuse to pass some time in the splendour of the Cathedral, and for that she was willing to put up with its throbbing and bleating. She took a seat off to one side, and let the music envelop her. The concert didn't succeed in changing her opinion of organ music all that much, even if, to her inexperienced ear, the performer seemed talented enough, but she appreciated the interlude all the same. For an hour it allowed her to forget, as sleep couldn't manage to do, the depth of the mess she was in.

When the recital wound up, the organist came down from on high and accepted the applause of the audience. He was a good-looking guy, young, his head shaved, tattoos marching up and down his arms. His appearance surprised her. Somehow she'd expected a musician playing such a dowdy instrument to look like Beethoven. He took several modest bows and chatted with the admirers who clustered around him. After he'd shaken the last hands and the pews had cleared out, Chantal hung back, putting off for as long as possible the moment when she would have to head out into the underground complex for yet another bout of aimless walking. Her eyes followed the organist as he headed back to the grille that led up to the loft, closed it and locked it. Then she watched him take the key and hang it from a hook behind the door frame. That was their security system? It was like hiding the key to the front door under the mat. The organist's bike, u-locked to a column by the main doors had superior protection. The Cathedral higher-ups must have figured that an organ weighed down with 2,778 pipes, as she'd learned from reading the program, wasn't likely to go anywhere, and of course they were right. But what their lax safety measures failed to take into account was an uninvited visitor making the loft her home.

CHAPTER 7

"LUNCH?"

"No can do."

"Reason being?"

"Still pounding the pavement."

"Didn't you text me that you had a good interview for something or other yesterday?" Theo asked her.

"That's right."

"Well, if it went as well as you say, then you'll probably get it. You're not one to exaggerate. I'm betting you aced it and they call you tomorrow. Come on, Daff, why not treat yourself to some time off? Poutine at La Banquise? My treat. A celebration in advance."

"Haven't you ever heard of the evil eye?"

"Don't try to sell me on that voodoo crap again."

"I happen to come from a long line of believers in the mystic power of the jinx."

"All the way down from your grandmother, you mean. That hardly constitutes a long line."

"Long enough."

"Or a rational one."

"Don't start in on her, I'm warning you."

"Fine, fine. You don't have to bite my head off. So lunch is a *no* then."

"Yes, lunch is a *no*."

Theo's experience in job-hunting wasn't exactly extensive so he had trouble connecting with Daphne's situation. Unlike his girlfriend, he had never had to serve summer stints wilting behind the press at a dry cleaner, never had to sweep up tufts of hair from the floor at a hairdresser, or work the graveyard shift in a nursing home laundry. His parents made sure their private-school darling devoted every summer to projects that were educational or uplifting. On one summer break from Selwyn House, Theo met Jimmy Carter out building houses; he had a picture of the two of them looking manly and capable in hard hats, even though Daphne knew first-hand that he (Theo not Jimmy Carter) was barely capable of driving in a nail. Normally, Theo wore his privilege lightly, but occasionally his intense preppiness combined with his lack of any known ethnicity, the sheer white-breadedness of him, set her teeth on edge. Maybe it was jealousy. Or maybe he really was a prick. The jury was still out.

Daphne had chosen not to tell Theo what her interview was for. Spending an entire year underground as a publicity stunt sounded too cracked, as if she'd dug up the ad in *The Onion*. She didn't want to be forced to defend it to him when she herself was dubious of the whole venture. Not that she would have blamed him for ridiculing the idea; it was calling out to be mocked. But let it be later, once the whole thing had fallen flat and they could ridicule it together; not now, when she would be the butt of the joke.

What on earth had Professor Séguin been intending in bringing it to her attention, something so sci-fi, so un-scholarly? It seemed unlike him to involve her in an endeavour that fluffy, unless of course, it was meant to be a subtle jab at her lack of progress, a see-what-happens-when-you-don't-buckle-down warning, which if true would put him and her grandmother on the same page. Daphne only applied so as not to ruffle his feathers; she needed him on her side, but she assumed, even though the interview went smoothly, that she would not be getting a callback. If she wanted to see a paycheque again in the near future, she would have to go job hunting in a more orthodox venue.

■ ■ ■

Marché Jean-Talon, the public market in Little Italy, was vast, with hundreds of outdoor stalls that splayed off a central core of permanent shops that stayed open year-round. It was a market for locavores. Nearly all of the products on display were trucked in fresh every morning from Quebec farms. The zucchini blossoms and the wild garlic and the fiddleheads were pure laine. Even the honey on sale came from bees who buzzed back and forth to each other in French exclusivement. When Montreal foodies lay on their deathbeds and tried to picture heaven, what they saw was Jean Talon Market but without the parking issues.

Daphne loved the market in springtime. Hard on the heels of the winter whiteout, the kiosks with the first brave little baskets of raspberries and strawberries, the early bouquets of rhubarb, and the nubile spears of asparagus warmed her soul. When Theo called trying to lure Daphne into truancy with a free plate of poutine he caught her there, in a blitz of passing out résumés. She had already been at it for a couple of hours, stopping at every fruit and vegetable vendor, every artisanal cheese maker, every crêperie, every fishmonger, every egg man and charcutier, but even though she was using the specially pared-down version of her résumé, the one that snipped off most of her academic credentials so she wouldn't look too high and mighty to wear an apron, nobody was biting, not even the horse butcher. Before things had started going awry at the market, Daphne reckoned that the list of past jobs on her CV, three pages worth, made her look admirably versatile, but now she had to consider that instead it made her look flighty. Only the owner of the wild-mushroom booth gave her the courtesy of a semi-interview, but in the end, when she couldn't point out the difference between the wood ears and the enokis, he sent her on her way.

The intense onslaught of no's in such a short interval hit Daphne hard. If she couldn't dislodge a job here, where not much more would be required of her than making change and bagging cucumbers, then why would anyone ever want her? She knew she would come back in a few weeks to find legions of CEGEP kids manning the stands, collecting their below-minimum wage. What did they have that she didn't? She looked down the last row of kiosks that she still had to approach, a row that seemed to extend on to eternity. She couldn't summon up enough juice to put herself forward for even one more rejection. Her beloved market had beaten her into the ground.

Dragging up rue Saint-Dominique towards the metro, Daphne performed a strategic revamp of her priorities. What she needed most at that moment, she determined, wasn't a job at all, so she swatted it out of top spot. Her immediate need was for some coddling; coddling so intense it would counteract her impulse to take to her bed and assume the fetal position, her habitual response to adversity. Although Daphne's grandmother could be depended on to provide her with a bottomless cup of support, she didn't always fill the bill in the coddling department. Daphne could predict what would happen if she showed up at home jobless and blue for all her efforts. Nora would give her a brisk pep talk and spin her back around towards the front door, not expecting her back till dusk. To Nora, looking for a job was a full-time job; you didn't treat yourself to breaks. And she was probably right. But low as she was, Daphne was in the mood to talk to someone with more softness to her, someone a bit less judgmental. For this assignment no one but her mother would do.

Running there was the way to go. All the fresh air rushing past might brush off at least the outermost layer of gloom, giving her mother an easier time of it. The only glitch was that she wasn't dressed for a jog. Daphne timed a quick pit stop to the house to coincide with Nora's chair-yoga class so she could change into her running clothes without having to risk a lecture, and she made her outfit change in record time. On her way out the door, she picked up a nicely shaped stone from the front garden and then headed off in her mother's direction at a snappy pace. Theo would blast her for it, if she were to tell him, that is. Keeping things from him seemed the easier tactic lately. It was Theo's considered opinion that it was disrespectful to go running in a cemetery, to wear skimpy, sweat-drenched clothes. A cemetery, according to him, was a place that required decorum. He could be such a prig. She was just visiting her mother after all. No need to dress up.

The run was a fierce uphill. All the cemeteries in town were terraced along the shoulders of Parc Mont Royal, overlooking the city, but what they lost in accessibility they recouped in beauty. Montrealers considered the cemeteries an extension of the park and thought nothing of strolling the paths between the gravestones to commune with nature, take in the view, or to reflect on the botchery they had made of their lives. Even though Daphne had her mother's grave to account for her presence at the cemetery, she still fell in with the last bunch, she supposed.

Daphne plunked down on the grass and snuggled up against her mother's gravestone. The granite was clammy against her damp back and the rough-hewn edges of the base scraped her spine, but still she found it comforting, as if her mother were embracing her. Miriam was wholly a creature of her daughter's imagination. They had hardly been properly introduced; they just met in passing while Daphne was slipping into the world and Miriam slipping out, Daphne's birthdate on the gravestone a permanent reminder, as if she needed one. These visits to her late mother took place on no regular schedule. They waited until Daphne was so irretrievably down in the dumps that she needed someone else to dig her out. It seemed counterintuitive to rely on someone six feet under to dig *her* out, but Daphne's mother had the gift.

As a young girl, Daphne used to be tongue-tied at the cemetery. No amount of prodding could get her to open up. She would just deposit her stone, and then stand at the grave, clinging to her grandmother. It fell to Nora to report on her latest accomplishments. She was the one who told Miriam about the compliment from Mademoiselle Jocelyne when Daphne first drew within the lines, about her granddaughter tying her own shoelaces for the first time, about her learning to skate backwards, all the milestones Miriam was missing. Once Daphne gained enough confidence to speak for herself Nora didn't withdraw entirely from the scenario. Instead, she would coach her before they left the house, like the elf at Santa's Village who did the pre-interview to facilitate the eventual meeting with the man himself, coaxing out the good deeds from the chaff. Nora developed this habit of tilting the graveside conversations in an up direction because Daphne had it in her to be too hard on herself, even then. It grieved her to hear her Daphne, the best of granddaughters, treating the gravesite like a confessional, pouring out her little-girl transgressions and failings, but that developed into Daphne's ultimate pattern, even when she was old enough to go on her own.

This post-Jean-Talon visit to the cemetery, another my-life-in-ruins account, was no exception, but Miriam never thought to belittle her daughter's concerns, however hyperbolic, and that was because all of Daphne's insecurity, her tendency to think so little of herself, could be traced directly back to her, definitely not to the paternal line that bent in the wind rather than broke. Over the years she guided Daphne as best she could, drawing upon her cache of past experiences as a living breathing human. She didn't speak to her aloud so much as send out thought waves that Daphne absorbed through some cosmic intake valve.

Lately, though, Miriam was less secure in the counsel she was giving. Her shakiness started on Daphne's last birthday, which was a landmark birthday. Daphne was now older than Miriam had been when she died. It tickled the balance. How could she presume to give her daughter solid advice when her authority was so lame? It was a good thing that Miriam trusted her mother-in-law. Nora was out in the world and knew what was what, but Miriam couldn't just abdicate responsibility, handing her daughter off to Nora like a baton in a relay. It would be remiss. There was no one she could consult. All of Miriam's neighbours on the plat had died old, as was right and proper. Their visitors never leap-frogged over them in age, so even though they had plenty of opinions to sling her way, they had no real familiarity with her situation. Miriam was on her own. What she decided in the end was that a division of labour was the way to go, one that left Nora to deal with the practicalities while she handled the general perking up. Between them they'd keep their girl going. That was the theory at least. Whether the new regime helped she couldn't say for sure, but at least Daphne kept coming back to her for more.

CHAPTER 8

"SO DO YOU understand exactly what is being asked of you, Ms. Elman?" Larry said to her. Daphne had already advanced to the third and theoretically the final interview. It had all zipped along far more quickly than she'd ever imagined, her candidacy elbowing its way up and out of the slush pile, thanks no doubt to some energetic back-channelling from Professor Séguin.

"Yes, I read the dossier several times over," Daphne said. "I'm fully aware of what would be required of me."

Fully aware she might have been, but whether she could accomplish what was expected of her was another question entirely. The blog, for example. The trouble with a promo blog was that it had to be relentlessly upbeat. They were hiring a cheerleader for the Underground City but she wasn't the rah-rah type. She tried not to let her doubts leach through to her face.

"I feel compelled to ask it even so, Ms. Elman, just so there are no misunderstandings going forward. You do not have any obligations, familial or otherwise that would prevent you from living in the Underground City for one full year, never leaving it ever?" Larry spoke ponderously, trying to attach to his words their full import. For all his solemnity he might have been intoning *speak now or forever hold your peace.*

No, she had no such obligations. That was abundantly clear. The night before, in a pre-interview exercise that ended up sinking her into an epic funk, she'd totted up all her current connections. The list was so minuscule it didn't even fill up a Post-it. Her life rubbed up against so few others in any meaningful way that she could sink into the slurry of the Underground City without causing the slightest blip in the normal unfolding of the universe, even her tiny universe.

Who out there would miss her? Her grandmother, yes, but she'd slip into her old traces easily enough. Nora worried about her whether she was there or not, but when Daphne lived with her, in easy surveillance distance, the worries were magnified. Whenever Daphne was out late, Nora tossed and turned until she heard her granddaughter's key in the lock. Daphne would be doing her a favour by moving out, allowing her to sleep through the night undisturbed. Other than Nora, though, nobody of any consequence would register her absence. She had friends, yes, but they were mostly of the virtual variety, no one who would miss the smell of her perfume. Theo, well, the less said about him the better. She had to face facts. As far as the Earth was concerned, it was just humping her along as so much excess baggage.

Daphne wasn't a born loner; she was a sunny, gregarious child. The condition crept up on her. It started when she was old enough for Nora to explain to her about her parents, how, when she was no more than a baby, first her mother died, and then, soon after, her father. Daphne's take-away, upon learning that those closest to her seemed to have a habit of dropping off the edge, was that the best way not to lose anyone else was not to find anyone else, and she folded in on herself like an origami swan. Over the years, a few people did manage to sneak in past her firewall, but they tended not to hang around for long. The chill she exuded didn't encourage lingering. So if Daphne was inept in the relationship department, at least she came by it honestly, not that it was any comfort now as she sat in front of the administrator of the interview panel. When he asked her if there were any impediments to her living like a mole for a full year, she had to answer, in all mortifying truthfulness, in the negative.

Daphne presumed that her application had been well-received because of her expertise on the subject. Her research into the underground cities of Cappadocia under the direction of Professor Séguin set her up as the perfect candidate. She knew all there was to know about subterranean life. In ancient Turkey anyway. But to Daphne's way of thinking, the underground networks of Cappadocia and Montreal weren't all that much different from one another, even if their periods of peak construction were separated by millennia. They both had miles' worth of tunnels running up, down, and around, ant-colony-like, connecting shops, houses, churches, schools, and storage areas. Every day, in each network, thousands of people trundled along, going about their business, all their needs met beneath ceiling not sky. Cappadocia was Montreal's twin, minus the halogens.

It would have astonished Daphne to learn that her assumption regarding her application was way off the mark. The committee was drawn to her in the first instance because she was so completely and utterly unattached. None of the other aspirants was nearly so solitary. Their lives were complicated by all sorts of hangers-on: spouses, children, exes, infirm parents, pets. They'd never last out the year. But in Daphne they had a lone wolf. Except for some granny who was fully ambulatory—thank God—she was gloriously alone. In addition to that, she was photogenic enough, and bilingual. That she had some expertise in underground living was just frosting. Her writing sample was a bit arid for a blog—it sounded like it was meant to have footnotes—but they'd find someone to help her in buffing off her bookish edges. Yes, she was the ideal candidate. They were itching for her to sign on and make it official.

But the point had come in the interview where it all threatened to implode. "You understand," Larry said, not without a certain degree of discomfort, "that we have to have some way of proving to the Tourism Board that the chosen candidate is in fact restricting all their movements to the Underground City." Daphne nodded her comprehension. "And to do that," he said, "one of the requirements is that you'll have to be fitted with an ankle monitor." Those last two words fell out of his mouth like a couple of rotten molars. The ankle tracker had been very contentious in the committee's deliberations. Frankly, it sounded, well, pedophile-ish. But there was no way around it that they could come up with. They'd batted it about for hours. It wasn't like Tourisme Montréal would be satisfied with Daphne's solemn oath, though Larry had tried valiantly to persuade them. No, those nitwits wanted scientific confirmation that they were getting their money's worth, and in the end, Larry had to give in. "It's completely waterproof," he went on inanely, "so you can shower and swim with it. It has a slim unobtrusive design. It won't impact on your daily life in any way."

Entrapment, that's what it was. Entrapment pure and simple. They'd reeled her in with a bevy of enticements at the earlier interviews, piling them up at her feet like it was a bloody bridal shower, and now they throw this kink into the works? It shouldn't have mattered except that Daphne had always assumed that she would be able to sneak out of the Underground City on the sly once in a while. Not for any frivolous reasons; she was an honourable person. She'd just check up on her grandmother and scoot right back, no one the wiser. So much for that idea. Her future overseers had already smoked out all the escape routes and plugged them with cement.

For a millisecond Daphne was tempted to tell them where they could stick their ankle bracelet, but she wasn't the confrontational type. Besides, the perks were nothing to sneeze at; an apartment in the Underground City rent-free for the year, a monthly stipend of five thousand dollars and a bonus of twenty-five thousand dollars if she made it to the finish line. On top of that there were the other little gifties. As blog assists, they were handing over a new laptop and a real camera. Then there was an OPUS card good for unlimited travel on the metro, a free membership at the underground Y, a fat coupon book for restaurants and shops all over the network, and passes to Place des Arts and the Maison Symphonique. She'd barely have to shell out for anything.

More important than any of that, though, the contest would deprive her of the distractions that always kept her from applying herself to her dissertation. Once her underground countdown began, she would be making no more midnight trips to Fairmount for an everything bagel when her attention was flagging, no more runs past the ponds and waterfalls at Parc La Fontaine, no more trips to the Tam-Tams on a sunny Sunday afternoon to get her juices flowing amid all the stoked revellers. The Underground City in its exquisite sterility would never have the pull on her that the blood and guts city exerted. What could she do in that subterranean isolation booth other than write? At the end of the year, she'd be able to take her pages, bind them in buckram, assuming that there was a bindery underground, and plunk them down on Professor Séguin's desk. She could already hear the satisfying *thunk*.

"What's your feeling on the anklet, Ms. Elman? Is it acceptable to you?" The thought that he might have to start again at rock bottom had Larry reaching for his antacids. They had been his constant companions ever since this farkakte Underground City business started up. Marius's year-long challenge idea was a good one in theory, but it all hinged on getting the right person, and Daphne Elman was precisely that right person. The other candidates in the pool were non-starters, every last one of them, so pathetically unsuitable he'd have to send out a new call if she conked out, and that would set them back months. The timing for the campaign kickoff would be all crapped up.

Daphne weighed her options one last time until she realized that they weren't really options plural at all. In her present tapped-out circumstances, there was only one choice open to her. "Yes, I would be willing," she said. "The anklet wouldn't bother me."

Larry's relief was palpable. "In that case, welcome on board." He shoved a contract written in lawyer under her nose and she signed away 365 days of her life. At least it wasn't a leap year.

CHAPTER 9

CHANTAL WAS PASSING through the Centre de Commerce Mondial, looking for a friendly bench where she could sit and read a novel she'd gotten out of the livre-service dispenser, when she spotted a family of tourists tossing some coins into the reflecting pool. They were probably readying themselves to go back to the States and didn't want worthless Canadian change polluting their homegrown pennies and dimes. Still, she was shocked at their extravagance. These high rollers were making their wishes with loonies and toonies, push-to-the-front wishes they were, sure to be granted ahead of all the ones bankrolled on the measly nickels left by lesser families.

Chantal looked down into the pool after they'd gone and did a tally. The coins only added up to thirteen dollars, but they glistened up at her as if they were gold doubloons. If she were to fish them up, she would have enough to treat herself to the Taco-Taco platter, the one that came with extra avocado and beans, and she'd have enough leftover change to stick down her bra for a rainy, or rainier day. It wasn't really stealing, she reasoned, if idiots tossed their money away, leaving it to moulder at the bottom of a public pool. If they'd dropped it on the ground, no one would blink over her stooping to pick it up. So what was the difference? Ethically, maybe none, but perception-wise, plenty. You just didn't go trawling in pools and fountains for booty. It disrupted the lines of communication between the supplicants and the fairies, or whatever mid-level sprites had responsibility for coin-wishes.

But even if Chantal was willing to risk the bad karma, what she really hoped to avoid was attracting too much attention to herself, at least no more than her dyed-blue hair already drew. This was one of the tonier corners of the Underground City, unfrequented by the homeless. That was what originally drew her here. It had artsy affectations. Lording over the reflecting pool was a fountain dating from the eighteenth century that had been specially flown in from France to luxe up the place. The area had a hush about it, like a museum. A certain decorum was expected. In the end, though, thirteen dollars trumped decorum. In running away to the street, she had chosen to put behind her propriety and convention. She had to accept the demands of her new life.

What she was aiming for was a quick dip of the hand, in and out, an aquatic smash-and-grab, but the water was deeper than she'd gauged. She stretched out over the edge of the pool as far as she was able and still her hand couldn't reach the bottom; some chewed gum on the end of a stick would have helped. She gave it one last try, tipping precariously over the rim. The coins were nearly within reach, her fingernails brushing against them, when she felt a hand take hold of the foot she still had on the floor, and whoever belonged to that hand upended her into the water.

The surprise dunking had her gagging down water, coughing and sputtering. The water might have been shallow but she felt as if she were drowning, her saturated clothing and shoes anchoring her to the bottom. She was close enough to the edge that eventually her flailing arm banged up against the rim and she managed to haul herself out to face the music. But when she emerged from the pool, she wasn't the one being told off. A few shopkeepers were gathered around a guard, the culprit she assumed, chewing him out for turning what could have been a minor incident into a spectacle. She took advantage of the commotion and squelched her way out of there, with only four dollars to show for her trouble.

CHAPTER 10

THERE WAS SPUNK. Nora had nothing against it. There was unconventionality. Also okay in her book. But Daphne was spinning off into the lunatic fringes with this decision of hers. What was she doing signing on with this batty underground contest? She should have been focussing on her studies. She'd be a doctor if she ever got around to finishing, even if it wasn't the real kind. Instead, here she was turning herself into a novelty act.

In fact, Nora had just the sketchiest description of what her granddaughter was actually getting herself up to; they'd only touched base briefly on the phone after Daphne signed the contract. Had she really understood her to say she'd be living below ground for a year? Was that even humanly possible? She'd have to shake Daphne down for the full details over dinner. Nora called Ethel Marcil to uninvite her for their usual Tuesday night chili so she could have Daphne all to herself at the table in case things got ugly.

"She's gone off the deep end, Ethel. I pushed her so hard to get her debts paid off that she took the first wacko opportunity that came her way."

"Don't go feeling guilty, Nora. It's not your fault. She's all grown up now. Making her own decisions."

"You call this the act of a grown-up? I hardly think so."

"Daphne has a good head on her shoulders. And she has more schooling in her than the two of us put together. She must know what she's doing."

"You can't really believe that, Ethel. She's letting herself be a guinea pig. She's letting herself be used. You think these people give a damn about what happens to her? She could turn to mulch down there for all they care. If she was prepared to do something that way-out, why didn't she just sign up for one of those clinical trial things they advertise on the metro? At least they have rules, regulations. They do them in a lab. They're controlled."

"What, you'd rather she get herself pumped full of experimental drugs that would do who knows what to her body so she could get money? That would be okay with you?"

"Right this minute I'd have to say yes."

"Nora, you're looking at it all wrong. You should consider yourself lucky. You know what some young girls do to get themselves money. You've heard the buzz about Jacinthe, from around the corner? Maude-from-the-dollar-store's youngest?"

"You're saying I should be happy that she's not out turning tricks?" Ethel didn't have any kids of her own, so her shadow parenting was hit-and-miss.

"All I'm saying, Nora, is that it's honest work she's found. Give the girl a chance to explain herself during dinner."

■ ■ ■

"So, run it past me one more time, would you? Slower this time." Even though they were on to dessert Nora wasn't much clearer on her granddaughter's plans than she had been when Daphne sat down to soup. In fairness to Nora, Daphne was blathering. The combination of relief and fear that she experienced after having signed the contract left her at once elated and incoherent. She tried to get a grip on herself.

"They want to promote the Underground City as a tourist destination. Year-round. I'll blog about it. And get paid. They're going to call it *Daphne Down Under*."

Nora was a bit hazy about what blogging actually entailed, but she let it pass. She didn't want her granddaughter to start in with a lecture on twittering and hashtags and all that Internet mumbo-jumbo that she had lived without so far at no discernable detriment to her well-being. Daphne was a great one for detours.

"You wouldn't need me to come live there with you, would you, if you'll be too busy bloggating all day to take care of yourself?" Nora asked. Her negative formulation was disingenuous. Despite her deep attachment to her little house, she wanted desperately to be invited along so she could serve as her granddaughter's conduit to the outside world, but it didn't pay to look too eager.

"Nope, 'unattached people only' is how they put it."

"How can they be sure that you're not living there with anybody?"

"They do spot checks apparently. There'll be someone who's assigned to keep tabs on me."

"And you're okay with that? Being snooped on? How can you be sure that they won't be installing a nanny cam in that free apartment of yours if they're so hot on surveillance?" Daphne rolled her eyes at her grandmother's conjecture, even if it did give her a momentary twinge. "It sounds like jail to me," Nora went on. Now was not the time, Daphne judged, to mention the ankle monitor.

"You don't understand," Daphne said, holding herself a little straighter, "I'll be the Ambassadress for the Underground City." She thought that classy designation might bring her grandmother around, but it didn't seem to move her. Nora wasn't about to be swayed by any trumped-up title. The King of the Cockroaches was still a cockroach. "And I'll be making good money," Daphne added. "By the end of this year I should be well in the black. Isn't that what you wanted?"

"I thought you'd do waitressing, telemarketing, something more conventional. Go back to Boris's garage maybe. He paid you decent."

"I'm never going back there."

"Okay, okay. Sorry. Forget I ever suggested it. But locking yourself up in a tomb for a year for prize money, it's just, well, it's over-the-top is what it is. Nobody ever asked you to make yourself into a martyr. There's got to be something else out there you can do instead."

"It's not a tomb. You've been there. You know what it's like. It's more like being locked up for a year inside the West Edmonton Mall. And it's not like I won't ever be outside. The apartment they're giving me has a balcony, so I won't die of rickets or whatever from lack of sunlight. I'm not going to grow black zombie circles under my eyes."

"I don't get it. How does that even count as part of the Underground City if it has a balcony that lets you outside?"

"I already told you," Daphne said. "Any building in town that has an entrance from the Underground City counts as part of it. That's why skyscrapers count. Even the observation tower at the Big O, all however many hundreds of metres of it. As long as you can get into a building from underground, it's in."

"The whole thing still sounds crazy to me. Who in their right mind would want to live in a space that's all steel and plate glass and concrete, surrounded by stores, stores and guess what? More stores. What kind of an environment is that? It's cold. It's antiseptic. Nothing but strangers everywhere you look. I bet you too that it's lonely and dangerous in all those corridors at night, once most people have gone home from work. Anything could happen to you, alone down there." Nora scribbled in on her mental to-do list to buy her granddaughter one of those personal alarm thingamajigs they were always flogging on TV.

Truth be told, Daphne wasn't much more of a fan of the Underground City than her grandmother, but now that she owned it, she felt duty bound to defend it against belittlers. She decided to start her diplomatic duties at that moment, even before the publishing of the banns. She rebutted Nora's critiques with ease, regurgitating all the propaganda she'd absorbed in preparation for her interviews, drowning her in facts and figures. But then things got personal.

"What if you get sick?" Nora asked her.

"There are loads of medical clinics down there if I catch anything. And the super-hospital's hooked up now too, remember. I'll be able to have a heart transplant without even leaving the Underground City."

"Don't joke about such things. It attracts the evil eye," Nora said. She wasn't old-country enough to spit three times, but she entertained a healthy respect for the tradition. "And me?" she asked, pulling out her trump card. "What if *I* get sick?"

"You're not going to get sick," Daphne said, although this was a worry she secretly shared. There were no out-clauses in the contract for illness, not even if your nearest and dearest were in extremis. "Aren't you always telling me you're healthy as an ox?"

"Even oxes get sick."

"Oxen."

Nora shot her the look; the look that said "you might have all the book learning, girlie, but I'm still your grandmother and you damn well better treat me with respect." Daphne was known to lord her erudition over her grandmother on occasion. Time and again over the years Nora had stood up for herself saying that she'd come up through the School of Hard Knocks, but Daphne pooh-poohed her alma mater because it wasn't a degree-granting institution. Even though Nora was proud of Daphne's educational accomplishments, she balked when Daphne took cheap shots at her own threadbare scholarly baggage. Nora's look delivered its message.

"You know if you ever needed me, I'd be there." Daphne said in compensation, toning herself down. Sometimes her mouth got away from her. "And we'll Skype. We'll see each other, virtually anyway, all the time."

"But I'm terrible with the computer."

"It's easy. I'll show you everything you need to know. Besides, you can come over anytime and visit. Nothing's preventing you. It's not far at all."

"Far enough." Nora's loneliness before the fact was making her petulant.

"Please. Don't be like that. Be happy for me."

"I just don't want you to be made a fool of, Babka."

"Who would do that? What I'm going to be doing, it's no crazier than lots of things people have gone out and done for a year to prove some point. Remember that guy we heard about on NPR, the one who lived literally according to the bible for a year? Followed every single picayune rule? Nobody made fun of him."

"Yes, they did. He came off as a kook. But he's a professional NPR kook. He can handle it."

"I could handle it too if it came to that, but it won't. Nobody's going to make fun of me for this."

Nora was quiet for a time. In her back-and-forth reasoning she both wanted Daphne to tread her own path and didn't. She tried another tack.

"What about you and Theo? Do they allow, what are they, conjugal visits?"

"We're not conjugal, Grandma. We're just good friends. And not even so good really."

"God forbid you should get conjugal."

"Let's not go there, okay?"

Theo wasn't Nora's smartest move. It got Daphne on her muscle. Nora could never figure those two out. They were so on-again-off-again that you could blink and miss the shift. All she'd succeeded in doing by inserting Theo's name into the conversation was speeding it along to its end, an end which, since lawyers were involved, was preordained. Nora could rail all she wanted; Daphne was locked into this freakish year underground. There was nothing she could do to prevent it.

■ ■ ■

"Everybody's going to think you're a crackpot," Theo said the following evening. A theme was starting to emerge.

"What you're saying is that *you* think I'm one."

"Well, let's face it, it isn't the most rational decision you've ever come to."

"I think it is. It's perfectly rational. It gives me money, which I'm way short of, a roof over my head that isn't my grandma's, and the freedom to finish my dissertation. What in that isn't rational?"

"Seriously? You need me to tell you what's not rational? You're cutting yourself off from the world for a start, narrowing yourself."

"I'm not. I'll be more in the world that I am now, locked up in my room writing. And my world won't be narrow. Did you know that the Underground City covers more than twelve square kilometres?"

"Save the stats for your blog, Daff. You know what I mean."

"No. I'm afraid I don't. Maybe you should spell it out so I'll be sure to understand."

Theo's sensors must have been fogged over. Otherwise they would have alerted him to lighten up.

"Face facts, Daff, stick-to-it-ive-ness isn't your strong suit. You'll be climbing the walls before two months are up."

"I've stuck with you all this time, haven't I? Doesn't that show a strong degree of intestinal fortitude?"

Theo wasn't sure how seriously to take that remark, so he just blustered forward. "It's nothing but a stunt. It belongs on reality TV. How will you explain it away on your CV? It'll muck it all up."

Theo's own CV, the result of him endlessly running a lint brush over it, was pristine. The perfection of that document would net him his first position any time now. Unlike Daphne's, it was unsullied by low-level jobs. Sometimes, when she stopped to consider it, Daphne got the feeling Theo was only deigning to go out with her. She was hardly from the projects, but all her predecessors in Theo's affections had been private school princesses whose upper-crusted résumés would have made a more obvious match.

"It makes absolute sense on my CV if you'd stop to think about it," she said. "Aren't I supposed to be an expert on underground life? It fits right in. I'll be living in the field. Just think, someday I'll be known as the Margaret Mead of the Underground City. Or the Jane Goodall. One of those."

"Ha! Hardly. More like the Mike Myers."

Daphne stood up. The conversation was over. And not only the conversation. She would make her entrance to the Underground City as a free-range researcher, unencumbered by any masculine negativity. Let the games begin.

CHAPTER 11

W AS THIS WHAT parents used to feel like when they dropped their daughters off at a convent to start on the road towards their vows? The thought was absurd of course. Nora could go see her granddaughter any time she wanted, but somehow this goodbye had a different heft from their other goodbyes over the years; it had a cutting-off-from-the-world quality that those others hadn't carried.

"Don't get all overdramatic on me now," Daphne said when her grandmother revealed her cloistered vision. "It's more like dropping me off at a university residence. I'm not going off to join the army or a cult. I'm just a few kilometres away, one bus door to door."

"But I'm used to having you come home every week, make sure you're washing behind your ears."

"You'll come over here instead. You and Madame Marcil will be my first dinner guests, to break in the place once I'm settled."

"So let me help you unpack. It'll get you settled that much sooner."

"You don't need to do that. You know there's hardly anything in my suitcases."

Daphne had packed like a snowbird trainee. All her parkas, boots, gloves, and hats she'd mothballed in her grandmother's basement, irrelevancies in her new life. She'd only brought along from her closet the clothing that was not too hot, not too cold, a three-bears assortment. The kinked umbrella Daphne had been determined to keep using till it died definitively she relegated to the garbage can on her way out the door. She was ready, sartorially anyway, for her uni-seasonal life.

There was no excuse for Nora to linger. Daphne was clearly impatient to get herself moved in, and under her own steam. The apartment needed no grandmotherly attention at all, so she couldn't busy herself vacuuming up dust bunnies under the bed or organizing the cupboards. It was perfectly orderly and respectable, as Daphne had promised: a studio, fully furnished down to the dishes on the shelves and the toilet paper on the roll. If there had been any prior tenants, all evidence of their existence had been Javexed into oblivion before their arrival. The place had a hotel-suite quality to it, but Nora could find no fault beyond its impersonality, slightly mitigated though it was by the welcome bouquet of flowers from the Tourism Board that they found parked on the coffee table when they arrived.

"That's good," Nora said. "You'll need it. A nice big plant like that, it'll give off lots of oxygen."

"You mean in case my scuba gear ever fails me?"

Nora had steered them into this shtick aimed at keeping their relations as light and airy as possible and Daphne latched on with gratitude. Outwardly they now acted as if Daphne's decision to live underground was one great joke between them, a merry romp that would keep them both in stitches for the duration.

Inwardly was a different story. Daphne's conscience, normally a passive enough instrument, had lately started acting up, roused no doubt by the forthcoming change in her circumstances. It now sent regular bolts of guilt to its owner's gut. Who would shovel her grandmother out after a storm dumped thirty-five centimetres on her front walk? Who would borrow Monsieur Hamel's extension ladder when the roof drain needed un-gunking? Who would swap out the screens for the storms? These had always been Daphne's chores, even when she lived away. Around the house, she played both the strong man and the high-wire artist. She knew Nora would never hire anyone to stand in for her; she'd view it as an extravagance. Her grandmother would just tackle all the jobs on her own, laying out the welcome mat for the subsequent heart attack or broken hip that would be all Daphne's fault.

Nora, for her part, had become so shrill as the time for Daphne's departure approached that she could barely abide the sound of her own voice. She was on Daphne all the time for one thing or another. If she kept it up, her granddaughter would leave home relieved to be out of there, and that was the last thing Nora wanted. So, she forced herself to change her approach. All those worries that were at the root of her peevishness she stuck under the mattress, saving them for when she was alone in bed. Overnight they had their way with her, but before breakfast she folded them tight away with hospital corners. The new daytime tone she was able to adopt as a result was syrupy and carefree. It made her teeth tingle uncomfortably—they were more at home with vinegar and hot peppers—but at least she would no longer be pushing her granddaughter away.

Daphne initiated the hug that guided her grandmother towards the door. "I'll be fine here," she said.

"And I'll be fine there."

"So the Elman women are set then."

"The Elman women are set."

Nora handed over the foil roaster pan filled to the brim with cookies that she had been churning out over the previous week in industrial quantities—snickerdoodles, chocolate pixies, and Nutella-filled thumb-print cookies—her granddaughter's all-time favourites, the recipe cards stained to near unreadability. Nora prepared them from muscle memory. It was a coals-to-Newcastle farewell gift; you couldn't take five steps in the Underground City without tripping over a pâtisserie, but Nora wanted Daphne to have an edible buttress against homesickness. She gave a hank of her granddaughter's hair a sharp tug signifying goodbye and was gone.

■ ■ ■

Instead of heading straight home as she had originally intended, when the elevator opened its doors on the ground floor Nora made the snap decision to take a little stroll around the Underground City, make her own assessment. This move went against her instincts. She had an elemental grudge against the Underground City, one that went beyond the simple fact that it had kidnapped her granddaughter. It was the science of the place that she distrusted. What bogus principle of engineering was it, she asked herself, that was supposed to prevent the Underground City from collapsing into rubble, what with the dead weight of the entire city of Montreal perched on its head? In her imagination she could see the footings of the buildings downtown hunting around for purchase and finding nothing but air. Nora was aware that air wasn't just emptiness; it had some load-bearing qualities. Her beloved Aero bars were a good example, chocolate held up by air bubbles. But the more she considered it, her proof only went so far. Maybe air bubbles had enough oomph in them to hold up fifty grams of chocolate, but gazillions of tons of concrete? Uh-uh.

Even though Nora was an intelligent woman, she had her moments of pushback against higher learning, against facts and formulas, and she had a particular blind spot about engineers. That they managed to keep the Victoria Bridge up and the Chunnel down did nothing to efface her general contempt for the species. She'd seen all the fracking documentaries. What engineer in his right mind would choose to plunk skyscrapers on top of such a perforated foundation? A kid with a plaster of paris cross-section of downtown Montreal would get laughed out of the grade six science fair.

She did have a faint recollection of Daphne telling her that it had been done the other way round, that they had created the Underground City by tunneling under buildings that were already there, but who cared if it was chicken or egg? The simple fact remained that according to Nora's calculations the subterranean complex was living on borrowed time. She could only pray that the Underground City wouldn't take it in its mind to cave in this year of all years, and her beloved Daphne would be well out of there before her doomsday scenario played out.

The temptation to leave was nearly overwhelming. The outdoors beckoned. It was sunny and clear, light-sweater weather, a perfect day for a stroll. Daphne's apartment building was at the Chinatown end of the Underground City. If Nora exited through the double doors just ahead of her, she could go buy some veggies at the Chinese greengrocer on La Gauchetière that she favoured when she happened to be in the neighbourhood. He had all those oddball Third World lettuces that she bought on occasion to zing up her salads when she was feeling adventurous. And his prices were unbeatable. But instead, she forced herself to stay inside and do some reconnaissance, to experience first-hand the environment her granddaughter would be huckstering.

It was an uninspiring beginning. Daphne's apartment lobby opened directly into the sector of the Underground City that was home to federal government offices in Complexe Guy-Favreau. This was where you had to report to get your passport renewed or to get yourself deported. It was an immense open area, punctuated here and there by escalators, commissionaires, and fire-resistant perma-trees. It was clean, Nora gave it that much; the Underground City janitorial staff clearly knew its way around a mop. It was well-lit too, she noticed. But these were the only feeble pluses she could come up with. The place was about as interesting to look at as an airport concourse at 3:00 a.m. Daphne would have her work cut out for her trying to spin a silk purse out of this bleached-out cul-de-sac of the Underground City. And she had to do this for a full year? Her Babka would have to retrain herself to write fiction. Nora was bored already. There was nothing worth going out of your way to see here. Any tourist who stumbled in under the illusion that the Underground City was wall-to-wall bling would leave feeling conned. Big-time.

Nora reverted to plan A. She would go out in the fresh air and do her marketing, the way God intended. If He hadn't wanted mankind to be subjected to the elements, she reasoned, He would never have invented them. And once she was freed to the great outdoors, Nora would let the breeze disarrange her hair, let the street grit gum up her pores, and the car exhaust inflame her nasal passages. That was the way of the world. She was about to push on the door that would allow her to exit the complex when the shame of her disloyal impulse stayed her hand. Here she had dissed the place before even giving it a chance. She owed the Underground City more than that. After all, if her only granddaughter was devoting her life and soul to it for a year, the least Nora could do was give it a fair shake. And what was her hurry anyway? Who did she have to go home to? Nora turned her back on the exit, walked to the middle of the Guy-Favreau lobby and made a slow three-sixty, the better to get a fix on the territory. By the time she regained her equilibrium, she had come up with an assignment for herself. The *Dummies Guide* Daphne had borrowed for her from the library recommended that retirees seek out for themselves specific activities to anchor their days. Now she had hers. For today anyway. She would invest the afternoon poking around the place as if she were a bloggist like Daphne, nosing out points of interest.

Nora the Explorer took a turn away from the main lobby and headed down a narrow side corridor of shops and services that fuelled the civil servants when they were away from their desks. She spotted a dépanneur and stopped in. All her theorizing about the buoyancy of Aero bars had given her a taste for one. There was nothing like a good dose of chocolate and sugar to remove any residual crabbiness she was nursing towards the Underground City. While Nora was dithering at the candy rack between regular and mint, a steady run of office workers passed behind her, heading purposefully towards the back of the store. For such a tiny establishment, the number of customers coming in struck her as all out of proportion. Nora put her sweet tooth back on its leash and followed the crowd to see what magnet was drawing them in.

She smelled it before she saw it; a selection of steaming hot food in chafing dishes that was just being set out for the upcoming lunchtime rush. None of the Chinese specialties on offer was recognizable to her untrained eye, but if all the people she saw lining up were just the early birds making sure they had first dibs, the food here had to be good. She scratched her chocolate bar idea and decided to have a proper meal instead, tacking herself on to the back of the line that lurched along in fits and starts. When her turn came along, the woman staffing the counter explained to Nora what each hot plate contained, but even with the benefit of her thumbnail descriptions Nora was bewildered. She didn't know what went with what. To keep her dawdling customer from creating a bottleneck in the line that was now snaking as far back as the entrance to the dépanneur, the server suggested a combination of dishes that Nora might try and fixed her up a styrofoam clamshell with the assortment that they had agreed upon. Nora paid and left the dépanneur to look for a seat.

Most of the spots were already full, commandeered by secretarial types with Tupperware containers that they had heated up in their office microwaves. What with the crowds milling about and the scents duking it out in the airspace above her, the whole place now had a warmer, livelier atmosphere than she'd first attributed to it when she'd seen it in empty ballroom mode. In just the short time that Nora had spent in the takeout line it had gotten so busy that she had to walk almost to the end of the corridor before she could find a bench to call her own. She would have preferred to snag one of the tables, but they were all taken by foursomes forking up their leftovers of moussaka and peri-peri chicken. Except, that is, for the group at the table just in front of her where no eating at all was going on.

The four older Asian men seated at that table were deep into a game of mah-jong. Nora pegged them as being from the quartier, not the office towers. They weren't wearing the uniform. Instead, they were dressed in bespoke retiree, comfort clothes and sensible shoes. The *click-clack* of the tiles had a homey sound to it. Nora's mother had been an avid player, and Nora had grown up to that background music. Sometimes, when her mother had her ladies over to play, she would allow Nora to sit in for a hand before sending her off to bed. Little Nora loved everything about the game from the case, covered in hide tanned from a plastic alligator to the pearlescent Bakelite racks. She'd innocently thought the tiles genuine ivory, even though no elephants had been sacrificed in the making of her mother's humble set.

Nora tucked into her meal, which was every bit as luscious as she'd anticipated, and watched the men play. She made slow work of her lunch since she was such a klutz with her chopsticks, and before she had even felt the time pass, all the government workers had long disappeared to their desks, and she was left alone with the mah-jong players. They had taken note of her presence and could sense in her eyes a knowledge of the game, but not a word did they exchange with her. When they finally got up to leave, she followed suit. Maybe this Underground City wasn't so blah after all.

CHAPTER 12

"ABOUT YOUR BLOG. I have to say I found it...well, how can I put it, a bit on the pedantic side."

"It is not pedantic. What it is," Daphne corrected him, "is educational. I'm trying to teach people about the Underground City."

"I know. And no one at the agency is against that. It's one of the goals of the campaign. But there's educational and there's *educational*. Here, just open your ears and listen to the beginning of your blog as if you were a stranger." Marius cleared his throat elocution-wise and started to read aloud from Daphne's text on the screen.

"'Montreal's Underground City dates back to 1962. Its first modest connection linked Place Ville Marie with the Queen Elizabeth Hotel and Central Station, but since that time it has burgeoned into a sprawling network that covers over twelve square kilometres in the city's downtown core. Oxymoronically, many links in the Underground City chain are, in fact, above ground. If one were to adhere to the definition set out by Professor Andreas B. Littenberg of the University of Tübingen in his groundbreaking work, *The Nature of Underground Cities from Pre-history to 1972: A Critical Analysis*, Montreal's complex should more accurately be labelled an indoor city rather than an underground one.'

"Need I read on? I mean, just for starters, you use the term *oxymoronically*." Marius pointed at the offending word with the non-business end of his Bic. It was one of several words on the screen with a yellow comment bubble hovering above it. In fact, it was probably accurate to say that there were more words in her original text with comment bubbles than without. "Now, as a word I don't think it goes down that well with the general public. Maybe you should be pitching to more of, let's say, a middlebrow audience."

"What you really mean is a lowest-common-denominator audience. You want me to talk down to people."

"No. Not that. But let's face it, Daphne. May I call you Daphne? *Oxymoronically* doesn't exactly roll off the tongue. It's not what you'd call everyday language. Maybe you could dial things back some. Seven syllable words are a bit much for this kind of piece, don't you think? It gets in the way of the message. You have to casual it up." Marius danced his shoulders side to side a bit, hoping that they would relay the message better than his words. "And maybe deep-six the references to further reading."

"What you're saying is that I should dumb it down. I refuse to insult my audience."

"That's not what I'm saying," Marius said, although it really *was* what he was saying. "I'm just advising you to keep the vocabulary more like spoken language. More informal, colloquial." He wanted to tack on, "or you won't have an audience to insult," but he held it in. "You have to write the blog as if you're just sitting around, gabbing with your friends," but for all he knew she and her friends routinely threw around seven-syllable words when they met in a café for lattes.

This was going to be rougher than he had originally thought. When the ad agency gave Marius this assignment to knock Daphne's blog into shape, he assumed he would have to do some minor proofing and copy-editing, shuffle a few commas around, not perform major surgery. But he couldn't hold back, even if it wasn't in his nature to be critical, especially not face-to-face. This was his first real job, his first grasp at responsibility, and he didn't want to blow it. Their fates in this venture were bound. If Daphne failed in the blogosphere, then so did he.

"Also," he forced himself to go on, "you tend to be a bit harsh now and again, like this part here—" he scrolled down a bit "—about the 'over-abundance of chain restaurants'? Let's just skip over the word *plethora* in that paragraph for now. See, what you seem to be forgetting is that you're supposed to be pushing the Underground City, not critiquing it. Brutal honesty isn't what we're going for. Your blog is a public-relations vehicle."

"I refuse to intentionally mislead."

"Not mislead. But maybe you could generally just avoid writing about what you don't like, and praise what you do. How would that be for a solution?"

"I want it to be balanced."

"And the agency wants it to bring people in. That's why they're supporting you in this whole adventure, no?"

"I will not put up with censorship."

"No one's trying to censor anything. This is only a sample blog anyway, a kind of breaking-in exercise. I'm just here to help you find your blogging voice."

"I have a voice."

She had one all right and Marius sensed he would soon tire of hearing it, but he soldiered on. "Well, it's more what you'd call a scholarly voice. A journal-article voice. Too many *ergo*s and *however*s. Colons and semicolons all over the place."

"Even my choices of punctuation don't suit you?"

"Well, it is punctuated more like a legal brief. Can't you try to make the whole thing a bit—" and he knew, even based on their brief acquaintance, that this suggestion would not go over well "—bouncier?"

"Bouncy? You want bouncy?"

He might have said *jaunty* to better effect, or *less dense*. *Bouncy* sounded too cocker spaniel-ish.

"Maybe you've got a tin ear for writing," she said.

A stray tidbit left over from honours English swam up into Marius's memory from wherever it had been treading water for years.

"Isn't that what you'd call a mixed metaphor?"

"What is your background, if I may presume to ask?" Daphne said, her phrasing coming out snootier than intended.

"In terms of writing? Advertising copy mostly. Lately anyway."

"So I suppose that has trained you to be a formidable literary critic."

"I know a good blog when I see one."

They sipped their coffees in silence at the food court, watching the ebb and flow of the underground crowds, the faulty machinery of their conversation creaking and groaning.

"So I understand you're not just my blog counsellor. You're also the lucky one who they've assigned to be my factotum." Daphne's vocabulary tended to up itself when she got nervous.

Factotum? Who talked like that? Chatting with her was hard enough. What would it be like to play Scrabble with her? "Just consider me your contact person," he said. "Anything you need, anything contest-related, any issues, let me know and I'll get right back to you. I'm on call 24/7."

Though Marius knew full well that the agency had already provided her with all his co-ordinates, he handed her one of his business cards. He was inordinately proud of those cards. Embossed. The agency had furnished him with a box of five hundred and now he had passed out a grand total of two, the first one having gone to his mother.

Marius had never expected to get signed on by the agency. In the normal course of events, internships sucked in young people and spit them out three months later with a glowing letter of reference and one leg two inches shorter than the other. But Marius turned out to be the exception that proved the rule. Larry took a shine to the little-intern-that-could and put him on the payroll with special secondment to the underground contest portfolio. Marius figured that actually earning a living would be a breeze compared to the grunt work he had survived as an intern, but this Daphne person he had to deal with was hyper-prickly. She had one stinkin' blog post per day to crank out and somehow she'd mixed herself up with Tolstoy. Marius wasn't in on the negotiations that landed them with Daphne; Larry hadn't brought him up from the farm team yet. Maybe he would have voted for her too if he'd been there. Apparently, her paper credentials were exceptional. In person was another story.

As poorly as the blog dissection was going, Marius would happily have continued wallowing in the bog of vocabulary and punctuation forever as long as it meant he wouldn't have to broach the next subject on his internal agenda for this meeting, but he had deconstructed the blog until there was nothing left to target. He had no choice but to move on.

"How are you finding your apartment?"

"Completely satisfactory."

"Good. That's good. Uh, just a reminder. After today, I'll be dropping by every once in a while, just to make sure you're abiding by the contest regulations." He didn't want to say, "just to make sure you're not shacking up with anyone." He was trying to approach their relationship with délicatesse.

"I'm fully aware that it's a stipulation in the contract. I haven't forgotten. Spot inspections to make sure I'm on the straight and narrow. You won't be making me pee in a cup, will you?"

Marius was slowly coming to realize why Larry was so willing to go against CEO protocol and hire the intern to take on this job rather than assigning it to one of his more tested staffers. Invading someone's private space on an unscheduled basis was a recipe for trouble. Hiring Marius wasn't a reward for his contest brainwave; Larry needed someone to throw under the bus.

And now that the meeting was drawing to a close, Marius felt well and duly flattered. Who would have thought that there would come a time when he would look back more fondly on his days as an unpaid drudge than as a salaried probation officer–cum–grammarian. Working life was definitely not all it was cracked up to be.

CHAPTER 13

CHANTAL WAS BECOMING quite the authority on art history, specifically Canadian art history. She had started to audit courses at Dawson College, at the westernmost border of the Underground City. It was all unofficial, of course, just slipping in to lecture hall 3F.6 every Tuesday and Thursday at eleven and opening her ears and her mind. In her pre-underground life, she had never really been much of a student. She always had too much else on her plate to allow her to concentrate in school, but now she was finding that she liked the orderliness of the classes and the routine. They gave her life a semblance of normalcy. As a plus, the classes threw her up against people vaguely her own age. Not that she ever spoke to any of the other students. It was too risky under her circumstances to make connections. Whenever she entered the hall, she made it a point to leave a seat or two vacant on either side, setting herself up as passively aloof. But like most of the other students, she always gravitated to the same corner of the classroom so she got to know, by sight anyway, the cluster of students who had similar spatial inclinations.

A few weeks into the term Chantal was studying a slide of an Emily Carr landscape projected on the screen at the front of the lecture hall when she noticed that one of her fellow students seemed to have his eye on her. She didn't think she was imagining it, even if her imagination had been running on overdrive ever since she left home, seeing pursuers at every turn. She decided to test out her hunch by looking at him directly. Immediately he glanced away. But later, when she sneaked another peek, there he was, at it again, soaking her in. It gave Chantal a boost to know that she could still be considered even partway attractive in her current state of disrepair. Her clothes hadn't seen a washing machine in ages, and the soles of her shoes, what with all the miles she was putting in underground, were starting to come loose and flap like a clown's. But she discovered that one of the advantages to college classes was that lots of the students looked a bit grotty and no one seemed to think it unusual. She fit right in.

Chantal neither encouraged nor discouraged her admirer, just basked in the glow of his moony eyes. Hugo, she'd heard the others call him. He was cute in the extreme, tall and sandy-haired and abundantly pierced. His attentions gave rise to a new pattern in Chantal's nights. She let thoughts of Hugo shove her nightmares aside temporarily. In her dreams, she threaded a ribbon through one of the rings in his nose and led him away to a secret bower in the Underground City where they could be alone to explore and discover one another.

Hugo might well have been dreaming about Chantal at night as well, but during the day he was clearly too shy to approach her. Each class he sat a bit closer, as if he was working up the courage to speak to her. His progress was so painfully slow that the term would probably end and there would still be four rows separating them. Chantal knew that the wisest course would be to sit in another part of the hall or better still skip classes altogether, nip it in the bud, but it buoyed her to have someone notice her, even if her whole life underground was built around not being noticed.

Directly after class, which ended at noon, Chantal took off. She never hung around to mix with the other students who were pairing off for lunch, although she would have loved nothing more than to stick a second straw into Hugo's iced capp and sip companionably. Instead, she hightailed it over to the Eaton Centre. It was her goal to arrive there no later than twelve thirty. That's when the blood bank was at its busiest.

It was a keyhole-sized blood bank, only five chairs, but the post-donation buffet was lavish, at least by her standards, worthy of a wedding reception at the Ritz. Chantal had observed in her travels that employees from the office complexes and shops often crowded the blood bank on their lunch hour, trying to fit some charity into their working day. Often, they came in groups to give each other courage and the place was bustling, filled with laughter and bluff talk, while the blood coursed out of their arms and into the awaiting baggies. If Chantal showed up at peak time, she could slip in, stuff her face with juice and sweets from the Héma-Quebec smorgasbord, and sneak out with no one the wiser.

Chantal was in the midst of scarfing down a handful of Chips Ahoy, her favourites, when she became aware of another body horning in on her personal space. It wasn't just a random individual from the crowd brushing up against her; that wasn't the vibe she was getting. This was purposeful. Someone was closing in on her. Panic took hold of her. They'd done it; they'd tracked her down. She didn't think she'd be caught so flat-footed when the moment finally came, but today hunger had made her sloppy. All her addled brain could think to do was to give her stalker a giant shove and try to make it to the door. Once out in the Underground City, she would have the advantage, knowing the lay of the land as she did. Chantal turned to raise her hands against her aggressor, but when she saw his face, relief drained through her. It was Hugo who was standing in front of her. He must have followed her from Dawson. It was both spooky and gratifying to realize that he wanted to be near her enough to trail her. If her mouth hadn't been full, she would have treated him to a smile, presuming that she still remembered how to form one. Chantal was anxious to hear her timid Romeo's declaration, now that he'd worked up his nerve, and tipped her head up to better drink in his words. He started to talk but he was all off-script. In a bellowing voice that carried over all the racket of the room, he said to her, "You steal food from the blood bank? How low can you go?"

Silence descended on the donors and the technicians. All attention turned to Chantal, both of whose hands were crammed with evidence. What else could she do? She ran. No more Art History 205, no more undercover flirting, no more hunk-dreams, no more cookies from the sweet table. She vowed to herself as she raced away, that once she got her life righted, or rather if she got her life righted, she'd give blood every month and never eat a thing. Atonement.

CHAPTER 14

ONCE DAPHNE GOT on her high horse, she usually found it difficult to dismount. Just ask Nora. But this time around it wasn't her grandmother's fault. That honour belonged to Mr. May-I-Call-You-Daphne, that carrot-topped jingle-meister. Daphne was unaccustomed to civilians taking potshots at her intellectual output, poseurs from outside the academy. Professor Séguin always found her arguments tight as a drum, as he put it, and complimented her unstintingly about the limpidity of her prose. Every core journal in the GN478 section of the library had an article authored by her advisor. Here was a man who knew his way around a noun and an adjective. His opinion had weight. Certainly more weight than that of Marius, her blog's designated back-seat driver. On the other hand, now that she thought about it rationally in the quiet of her little studio, chivalrous as he was, maybe all the praise Professor Séguin lavished on her writing was simply his way of encouraging her to churn out more pages.

Before her meeting with Marius, Daphne had thought she'd produced an unassailable document. She had slaved over that blog post, drafting and re-drafting it so many times that, had she done it on paper, she would have laid waste to a hectare of old-growth forest. To insure its proper composition, she had consulted her three amigos: her *Roget's*, her *Chicago Manual*, and her *Fowler's*. The eight hundred words she'd come up with were bulletproof. Undeniably, the piece that resulted from her all-nighter cuddled up with her beloved reference books was cogent, it was forceful, it was persuasive. It was also, she now had to admit upon rereading, utterly charmless. Marius was right. Her test-blog had all the charisma of a heat-pump manual. It had no beating heart.

Who would be moved to comment on a blog like hers, as unspiced as a hospital-tray lunch? Daphne was not as blog-blind as Marius seemed to think. She understood that having no comments on a blog was more shaming than having nasty ones. It meant that your musings and observations were so vapid that even the professional commenters who lived only to revile would have nothing to sink their fangs into.

If the blog didn't fly, Daphne wouldn't get booted out of her apartment. She would still be paid her stipend, would still get her year-end bonus, presuming, that is, she stuck it out till the finish line. But she didn't want to be remembered as the experiment that flopped; the blogger so tone-deaf that she was only addressing herself in the mirror. It was Daphne's dream to see her adopted neighbourhood teeming with vacationers as a result of the postings she spun out at her keyboard. Subterranean tourism venues were hot concerns, each one jockeying for the lion's share of travellers. Daphne wanted Montreal's Underground City to wipe the floor with the Diefenbunker, the Paris catacombs, and even her beloved Cappadocian caves. She looked forward to the day when every underground merchant and restaurateur would reach out to shake her hand when she passed, un grand merci for all the extra loonies and toonies she had caused to drop into their tills. What she wanted was to see the whole complex thrive under her stewardship, its remote corners brought to light, its hidden treasures unveiled. She wanted, quite simply, to succeed.

Daphne opened up her laptop and dragged her impotent document into the trash. For good measure she trashed it from the trash. If it hung around too long her computer would start stinking of dead fish. She would start fresh. But not till tomorrow. Right now she had to find some way to divest herself of the leftover embarrassment of her meeting with Marius where she had tried to pass herself off as God's gift to social media. Her old standby method, she decided, would work nicely. She'd sweat it off.

Running was out of the question. The waves of daytime crowds cluttering up the passageways of the Underground City would oblige her to dodge and weave, preventing her from running flat out. Even at a slow jog, she'd be a menace to her subterranean community. Until she tracked down the quieter corridors of the complex where she might safely put in a few kilometers without mowing anyone down, a run was verboten.

Daphne had to free her endorphins from house arrest by some other means, so she fished around in the box of swag the agency had left her for the key fob that allowed her free entrance to the Y.

By temperament Daphne wasn't a gym person. She preferred to exercise in solitude, watching the scenery go by. Going round and round in circles on an indoor track held no appeal. It was too reminiscent of the pattern of her life. So rather than trying to replicate underground her former fitness regime, she decided to shoot off in a different direction altogether. Maybe a few laps of the backstroke in the pool could pack the same therapeutic punch as a run. She threw her bathing suit and nose clip in a bag, and headed downstairs.

Daphne touched her key fob to the magnetic reader that unlocked the turnstile mechanism. It was one of those über turnstiles, floor-to-ceiling, designed to resemble a revolving door, but with stubby parallel metal rods poking out from the central column in place of the glass. Just as Daphne was starting to push on it to make her way into the Y, a body materialized out of nowhere and jolted into her back full force, slamming her so forcefully up against the bars it knocked the breath clear out of her. If whoever it was behind her shoved her any harder Daphne would come out the other side sliced like a loaf of rye. The cruel momentum of that push propelled them both forward until the turnstile opened up into the foyer of the Y and Daphne's intruder sprinted off. If anyone were to ask, Daphne wouldn't be able to provide much of a description. It was a woman. That much she knew. Her back had recognized the anatomy. And she had a youngish look. The only distinguishing feature Daphne could swear to was hair so blue it looked as if it had been dyed in Windex. Other than that, she was a blur.

The spandexed greeter behind the reception desk witnessed the two-for-one blast entrance. "It's the homeless people," she said to Daphne, shrugging her shoulders. "They like to come in for the showers. We put in those jump-proof turnstiles to stop them, but they just found another way. Are you okay? Still got your wallet? Your virginity?"

Daphne patted herself down. "Yes to both, I think."

"Bruised any?"

"I don't think so. It's more the shock. It felt like I was being tackled by one of the Alouettes."

"Well, what can I say? Welcome to the Y. A first-timer?"

"Yes."

"I didn't think I recognized you. I'm Sofia. At your service."

"Good to meet you, Sofia. I'm Daphne. Could you please point me in the direction of the pool? If I don't go right now, I might chicken out."

"Daphne? Not Daphne that underground lady?"

"One and the same."

"This is awesome. I've never had anyone famous come through on my shift before. I'm the one who filled out all the paperwork to get you the free pass."

"Well, thank you. I guess."

"Don't let that bad start turn you off. It's a great place we've got here. Come on, let me show you to the pool, give you a bit of a tour on the way. You deserve the VIP treatment after that."

Sofia put up a back-in-five-minutes sign and the two of them set off to explore the highways and byways of the Y. Daphne's appreciation for the offer of a guided tour didn't take long to wither. Her docent nattered on with no apparent need to take a breath. There might have been a mote of dust she neglected to point out in their endless travels, a fellow employee whose peccadilloes she forgot to divulge, but Daphne thought it unlikely.

"Shouldn't you be getting back to the desk upstairs?" Daphne asked, pouncing on a rare pause in Sofia's monologue. She was desperate to shuck her chaperone, all her early enthusiasm for the pool waning by the second. "Won't people be needing you up there? I'll be fine on my own. What are the odds of me being jumped a second time in the same day?"

"Relax. There's no hurry. I'm totally at your disposal," Sofia assured her. "I work through my breaks all the time so they owe me."

Daphne was starting to worry that her Velcro tour guide would go so far as to share her lane in the pool. Even once Sofia eventually delivered Daphne to the change room, she clearly felt no pull to return to her post, leaning against one of the nearby lockers while Daphne undressed, continuing her exposition on her place of employment. If Daphne had known that her body was going to be under such close scrutiny, she would have put on her doctor-appointment underwear, her special reserve bra and panties, the ones with no stains or rips.

"What's that thingy on your ankle?" Sofia asked. The question was inevitable, but Daphne wasn't keen to enter into a discussion about personal surveillance with the Y's on-staff yenta.

"That?" she extemporized. "It's a heart monitor."

"Oh, my auntie Roz has one too," Sofia said, "but they put hers on the inside."

Their comparison of coronary accessories had nowhere to go; Sofia appeared not to be overly engaged by the topic, but Daphne sensed that for all her guide's apparent disinterest, she was filing the detail away in her data bank from which it would be withdrawn with a flourish later to hand off to the next person in the underground chain. Even though Daphne disliked being the subject of gossip, gossip was publicity of a sort, so she accepted her fate.

It was the lifeguard who finally took Sofia off Daphne's hands in a rescue every bit as appreciated as if she'd been flailing in the deep end. Marc-André, who turned out to be well acquainted with Sofia, invited her up into the lifeguard chair to check out the view, as he chastely put it. An infraction no doubt, but his laxity granted Daphne her freedom. She swam her laps, got her heart rate up, and made her escape from the pool unescorted. In the locker room, she kept her eyes peeled for anyone blue-headed towelling down, but all the women she encountered had hair out of the normal colour palette.

Daphne tried not to let the incident turn her off. It wasn't as if she had never had misadventures while she was out running; road-rageous drivers, bikers, dogs. Twice she'd been doored. But no one had ever laid hands on her, let alone pummelled her. She should have felt sorry for her mugger, she supposed, young and homeless as she was, but she had trouble rustling up much sympathy for the person who had soured her first real outing as an inhabitant of the Underground City. Was it an omen? she wondered. Her grandmother was big on signs. To Nora, everything was larger than itself. Daphne could imagine what cosmic warning Nora would extract from Daphne's Y run-in, in the unlikely event she would ever worry her with it. Her granddaughter's year, she would say, was doomed.

CHAPTER 15

S O TAKEN ABACK was Marius to see someone other than Daphne open her apartment door to his knock that the rules of politeness that normally governed his behaviour escaped him.

"Who are you?" he said to the tiny older woman in front of him.

"I'm Ethel. Who are you?"

"I'm Marius."

"What are you collecting for, sonny?"

At the sound of a masculine voice Daphne poked her head out of the kitchen. "Oh. Never mind him," she said to Madame Marcil. "He's my inspector-general, here to make sure I'm not sharing the premises with undesirables. Or desirables even."

Ethel shrank into herself. "We wouldn't want to get Daphne into any trouble. Me and Nora, we've just been invited for dinner. That's all. We're not permanent boarders or anything. We'll be heading home soon. Leaving Daphne here all alone. Like always. But if you have to see for yourself, you're welcome to come in and take a look," she said, swinging the door wide.

It rankled Daphne to hear her grandmother's friend kowtowing to Marius of all people, as if he were a policeman at the door acting on a drug tip. She'd be sirring him next. "I think he's seen enough," Daphne said, putting a comforting arm around Madame Marcil, and giving her a squeeze. "He doesn't need to come in. I'm fairly sure he won't be putting me on report. Although you might want to lift up a corner of the duvet so he can confirm that I don't have anyone hiding under the bed."

As much as he wanted to resist the generous sentiment, Marius couldn't help but sympathize towards Daphne in her testiness. If he were the one on the receiving end of pop house inspections, he'd snark too. So, when she moved to shut the door in his face, he made no protest. In fact, he obligingly got his nose out of the way so it wouldn't make contact and mar the finish. But before Daphne could close the door completely, Nora came out of the kitchen and addressed the young man in the hallway. "To whom do I have the pleasure of being introduced?" she said. Nora was using her Queen-Mother voice to counteract Daphne's manner, which she found severely wanting.

"This is Marius, Grandma. The spot-check guy? From the contest? Nanny cams and all that? Remember?"

"Oh, right. I'm Nora," she said, performing the other half of the introduction that her granddaughter had omitted and holding out her hand. "Won't you come in and join us?" Despite her antipathy towards the contest's Big Brotherisms, if someone showed up at your door at dinnertime, you welcomed them in. Nora wasn't blind. She could size up that her granddaughter was anxious to cut this fellow down to size for whatever crimes he had committed against her, but in Nora's personal code of ethics, hospitality always trumped spleen.

"I'm sure Marius has someone else he's meant to be snooping on," Daphne said. "We wouldn't want to hold him up in his appointed rounds."

"But it's a celebration. Of course he should come in and join us. There's plenty. Besides, it would give us another opinion later in the blind taste-test of those baguettes you got." Nora opened up the door to a more welcoming angle and pulled Daphne's minder in. "Here," she said, steering him towards the table. "We'll put you between me and Ethel." Nora calculated that buffering him between the two village elders would be the safest seating plan, but Marius continued standing. He took in all the balloons static-attached to the walls.

"Whose birthday is it?" he asked.

"Nobody's," Nora said. "Birthday balloons were the only ones I had in the house. I figured they'd work just as well to celebrate Daphne's first successful month of blogging. We're very proud of her."

Nora's pride was well-founded, not merely a case of grandmotherly boosterism. Lately the blog had mellowed out, as if it had been tippling margueritas, and every day the vocabulary was sounding less and less Oxford donnish. After her first few flat-footed efforts, Marius despaired that the agency's chosen candidate would ever be able to find the common touch. Holding forth seemed to be bred in her bones. But round about week three something shifted and the blog found its feet. Daphne settled into a warmer, more familiar tone with a cheeky little underscore. This led him to postulate, despite his experience with Ms. Down-Under, that her sense of humour had not been excised accidentally in the same surgery that had removed her appendix.

His job required that Marius monitor the blog comments, which were now starting to roll in, the majority of them positive he was relieved to note, with lots of repeat visitors putting their two cents in. Daphne was actually acquiring a modest following. At the office, Larry was floating. "So, our girl, she's everything we thought she'd be, isn't she?" he said. "I had a gut feeling she was the one." Larry's gut was notoriously unreliable. Marius might not have been on staff very long but he'd witnessed his boss scarfing back Tums the way barflies nibbled salted peanuts. This was not a man who should have been using his gut as a compass, but in this case it seemed to have steered him in the right direction. Even if it was way too early to judge if the blog was having any influence on tourism traffic, the mood around the office was optimistic.

It was thanks to Marius that Daphne's blogstyle came down to earth, not that she had the courtesy to let him know he was in any way responsible. After he had taken his butcher knife to that first test blog, she'd struggled to find the right tone, but every new draft she churned out still sounded like a *Britannica* entry. Then she recalled Marius suggesting that she frame the blog as if she were sitting around chatting with a friend, which gave her the idea to resurrect Belle.

Imaginary friends are meant to be relegated to the trash heap of childhood at about age seven or so, and in that little Daphne was right on Piaget's schedule. When she crossed the threshold into Madame Thomassin's grade-two classroom, Belle, her imaginary BFF, did not matriculate with her. From what Nora could make out, her granddaughter's confidante and constant companion had gone *pfft*, and she stopped setting a plate for her at the table. But in truth Daphne had never really driven a stake through Belle's heart. She'd merely set her on the back burner of her life. Belle was ready to be snapped back into service now that she was needed as Daphne's invisible addressee, for Daphne's newest and ultimately successful approach to blogging turned out to be epistolary. Daphne would sit down and write a breezy letter to Belle describing some wonder of the Underground City, and then, after reading it over, would go back and redact the salutation. Voilà. What was left, if not yet pitch perfect, was at least pitch presentable.

That a celebration was well deserved, Marius had no doubt. Daphne's liftoff might have been clumsy, but she finally did manage to fly. He couldn't be part of the feting, though. He had to maintain an arm's-length distance with his supervisee. It wouldn't do for him to sit down at the table with the family; it wouldn't be proper. That was his story and he was sticking to it. The truth was that he didn't want to sit at any table where he was only being tolerated. He wasn't that desperate for a free meal. He'd go home and eat in front of his laptop as usual. At least, unlike Daphne, it was always happy to have him for company.

Marius extricated himself from Nora's clutches and left the three women to themselves. In the quiet of his apartment, he sat down with a beer and flipped open his laptop. He clicked on his bookmark for the *Daphne Down Under* site and scrolled down to her first successful blog, the one where she'd first managed to smother her dry tone under a layer of sparkle. He reread what she'd written:

You know what it's like when one of those cravings comes over you that takes control of your tastebuds and demands that you do its bidding? Well today, after doing my taxes, I had to have something sweet at all costs, preferably chocolate, or I was going to go into meltdown mode. Luckily, I happened to be near Place Ville Marie where there are enough bakeries scattered around that you can get a sugar high just passing through. I decided it might be fun to set up a little competition for myself, to sample the wares at two different pâtisseries and see which one came out on top.

So first, I took my tastebuds to Matinale. It's just been open for a few weeks. I've been dying to try it out ever since I learned that their baker jumped ship from the much-ballyhooed Duc de Lorraine. Well, let me tell you, even before I'd sampled its wares, I was completely seduced by the place. Its funky décor tickled me; vintage coffee pots everywhere you look, no two chairs or tables alike. It's like the place was designed especially with me in mind—I'm a sucker for mismatchery.

After a lot of dithering at the counter I ordered myself an opéra, a showy rectangle composed of layer upon delicate layer of almond sponge, buttercream, and chocolate ganache, with a little look-at-me gold leaf on top. Ooh, trust me on this, it was like biting into a cloud—if clouds came in chocolate that is. It was absolutely orgasmic! And the coffee I washed it down with was perfection. I walked out of there completely sated and with one stamp on my new loyalty card.

It was going to be hard for any other PVM pastry shop to top that experience, but I was determined to give another place a crack at it, at least. I decided to go for an establishment that's the polar opposite of Matinale, which landed me at Sur l'Ardoise. No shabby-chic there—its aesthetic is all sleek lines, restricting any frills and curlicues to the contents of the pastry case. And what a pastry case it is, each individual offering a work of art. You almost feel guilty biting into one—it's like defacing the Mona Lisa! But I couldn't let a little guilt hold me back—I was on a mission.

I scanned the pastry display and my eyes glommed onto the Paris-Brest— two perfect circles of choux pastry cuddling between them a piped filling of chocolate cream. Oh, the depth of the chocolatiness—it was to die for. And did I detect a hint of rum in there? I licked my fingers at the end, cloddish, I know, but I couldn't bear to have any of it go to waste.

I sat and sipped at my excellent coffee and mulled over which pâtisserie would be awarded the Oscar in my little competition. Well, after much deliberation, it ended up in a tie. Even-steven. I couldn't possibly choose one place over the other. It would be like trying to choose one of your children over the other. So I added both of them to my Daphne-Down-Under map where you can find all my underground gems marked. Try either place out when you're in the vicinity. You won't be disappointed. Guaranteed.

Marius was proud of Daphne. She'd actually broken down and used an exclamation point. Twice! The post was a bit skimpy; she could have puffed it up with some more detail, but he gave her a pass. She was definitely coming along.

CHAPTER 16

Daphne was struggling to wend her way through the lunchtime throngs without having to resort to elbowing. The passages she had to negotiate were more than normally choked because it was pouring outside. On wet days, no one who worked in any of the office towers that sprouted up from the underground complex felt any compulsion to duck out to run a quick errand or grab lunch. It wasn't worth getting drenched when they had a whole world at their feet. Instead, they left their coats hanging in their cubicles and took the elevators down down down to spend a relaxing hour taking in the window displays of the Underground City while nibbling on their sandwiches, the lot of them moving at a Sunday-stroll pace.

And if the passageways weren't already clogged enough thanks to the rain, Complexe Desjardins was playing its part in gumming them up to gridlock proportions by hosting one of its notorious blockbuster events in its atrium. This week it was a full-fledged rodeo. The tile floor of the Grande Place was bedded down with a hundred tonnes of soil shipped in specially from the Townships to give the cowboys on horseback a nice cushy footing.

Complexe Desjardins had quickly become one of Daphne's favourite haunts in the Underground City, the single part of the network with chutzpah. No one could accuse Complexe Desjardins of thinking small. Where other malls might be satisfied setting up a rinky-dink petting zoo with a pair of scrawny chickens and a few comatose sheep doing their farewell gig en route to the abattoir, Complexe Desjardins was aspiring to nothing less than an indoor version of the Stampede. Yee-haw! Whenever

72

the blog part of Daphne's brain was shooting blanks, she had only to stroll over to Complexe Desjardins for inspiration. Even if there was nothing special going on at the Grande Place—no human chess board, no Tubafest, no Global Breastfeeding Challenge, no kick-boxing demo—it was never a wasted trip. She could always pick up a chocolate-yuzu éclair, the citrusy specialty of the pastry chef at Ô'Gâteries, and her day was made.

Daphne was anxious to get home to her laptop to compose her rodeo letter to Belle, but it was slow-going what with all the rubberneckers. She was nearly back at her apartment, formulating the sentences in her mind as she walked, when a familiar-sounding laugh caught her ear. Its honk straightaway made her think of her grandmother. Nora's laugh was so realistically goose-y that anyone in hearing range automatically scoped out the sidewalk ahead for guano. Her laugh wasn't ladylike, it wasn't dainty, it was more of an assault. She hawked it out as if she were trying to Heimlich up a cherry pit lodged in her windpipe. Daphne looked around, curious to get a glimpse of the other unfortunate who shared her grandma's laugh issues. She'd always thought Nora had that market cornered. A second honk followed soon after the first, so raucous this time its source must have been in the midst of squeezing out a golden egg. When Daphne's radar finally succeeded at homing in on the sound, her eyes lit not on the stranger she'd expected, but on Nora herself, who was seated at a square table with three Asian men, in the thick of a hot game of mah-jong. The tiles were whizzing across the tabletop at such high speed they were leaving contrails.

"What are you doing here?" Daphne asked when the tiles came to rest at the end of the game.

"Oh, Daphne. What a nice surprise. I'm playing mah-jong."

"I can see that. I mean *here*. What are you doing *here*?"

"They've been letting me play ever since Henry, he's their usual fourth, has been away visiting family back in Guangdong." The word rolled so smoothly, so authentically off her grandmother's tongue, it was as if she'd grown up in Canton. Her pronunciation was impressively layered with diphthongs. Who was this foreigner who had taken over the body of her grandmother?

"Let me introduce you." Nora gestured around the table. "This is Anthony," she said, lightly touching the arm of the man sitting on her left. "He's been kind enough to give me some after-hours coaching so I can fit into their style of play. Over there is Joseph, Anthony's brother-in-law, and this is Luke. May I present my granddaughter, Daphne." The gentlemen were somewhat older than her grandmother, courtly in their manners. They all stood. Caps were tipped. Hands shaken.

"So it's you who's living in the Underground City for a year," said Anthony, the tallest of the group. "What a challenge. It's an honour to meet you."

"You know about me?" Though Daphne craved notoriety in her new role, she didn't quite grasp that she already had a measure of it. She had always been a great success at failing, and now that she wasn't she didn't quite know how to handle the feeling. It disrupted her psyche. The time had come for her to find herself anew. It was a more common phenomenon for this blossoming to begin in one's teens. Daphne was tardy to the process.

"Of course they know about you," her grandmother said. "You're famous. They've all been following your blog."

These senior citizens didn't fit the campaign's target demographic, but anyone who tripped her site's hit counter, whatever their age bracket, was fine by her. She felt the buzz of a debut author at a signing. Daphne thanked the men for their interest and then turned her attention back to her grandmother.

"So you play together often, do you?" she asked.

"Three times a week, maybe four," Nora said.

"That often. You don't say."

The others around the table couldn't have been faulted for assuming that the conversation between the two women had died out with Daphne's last comment, but in fact a back and forth was still going on between them; one that didn't require the crutch of voices. Their mental braille was an entirely reliable system of communication, no nuances missed simply because the words were silent. The exchange wasn't pretty. At its close, Daphne reactivated her lips to address her three new acquaintances. "It was a pleasure to meet you, gentlemen. I'll leave you to finish your game," and without another glance in her grandmother's direction, she merged into the milling crowd and headed towards home.

"I'm in for it now," Nora said to Anthony once they were on their own.

"What do you mean?"

"She's in a sulk. A good one too."

"She looked fine to me."

"How could you be expected to pick up on it? You've barely met. But trust me. She's about to blow."

"Why would just seeing you here set her off?"

"It's hard to explain. Family stuff."

"Try me."

Since he was pushing for it, she gave him the abridged version. "It's just that, well, I didn't exactly tell her I was hanging around here. With you."

"Do you need her permission?"

"No, it's not that."

"Then why would she object? It's not like we're playing for money. It's just a friendly game."

"Oh, it's not money. She wouldn't say boo about that. I've been known to drop a buck or two at the tables in my time."

"What then? You can tell me. The others don't need to know. It'll all stay between us. If you share whatever it is that's troubling you, maybe I can help. I hate to see you so unhappy."

His gentleness in coaxing wheedled it out of her. Nora was a pushover for a soft approach. She'd had paltry experience of it in her life. Her ex and tenderness had always maintained an arm's-length relationship.

"Okay, fine. If it's full disclosure you're asking for. Here. The fact is, I didn't always pop in to see her when I was here. Sometimes, once I got to know you and the guys better, I'd just come play mah-jong with all of you and then go about my business. Here I was, in the neighbourhood, just an elevator ride away from her apartment, and I didn't drop in. Now that I say it out loud, I can't believe I did that. What was I, under a spell?"

"I always assumed you went up and visited with her before we started the game," Anthony said. "I thought you were close."

"We are! I Skype with her every morning. Never miss. I guess I was stupid enough to figure that that counted as a real visit. She likes me to use technology, Daphne, and I was so damned proud of myself that I could do it. Before all this contest stuff came along, my idea of technology was a garlic press. But I was wrong to let the computer take the place of a real visit where I could give her a buss on the cheek that would actually leave lip marks and not just pucker up in front up some screen. I'm an idiot. I mean it's not like she can come over and see me whenever she wants, can she? She's the one who's the prisoner. I should have rung her bell every day. Every single day. Daphne bruises so easily. Always has. What was I was thinking?"

"Maybe you were putting yourself first for a change."

"That's no excuse."

"Go up now. Make amends," Anthony urged her. "You'll feel better."

"I hate to conk out on our lunch."

"It's not a problem. Go. Make up with her. That's the most important thing."

"You sure?"

"Absolutely. The restaurant will still be there tomorrow." They separated uncertainly; the protocols of the goodbye not yet settled on. Was a handshake too distant? A two-cheeked kiss too forward? Was nothing too, well, nothing? It was one of many delicious new problems Nora was having to deal with now that her life too had branched out underground.

■ ■ ■

It had all happened accidentally. At the beginning of her granddaughter's tenure as doyenne of the Underground City, Nora would just sit on her bench with her dépanneur lunch balanced on her knees and watch the foursome play after she had gone up to touch base with Daphne. Nora and the players always maintained the fiction that she wasn't really taking in the game in any meaningful way, that she was just passing the time. But then one lunchtime, one of the men made such a boneheaded play, she couldn't help but snort. He turned around to face her, for the first time directly acknowledging her existence. Nora was mortified. But all he did was laugh. They all did. And from that moment on she was adopted as part of their group. It gave the four retirees a charge; it was as if they were on centre court at Wimbledon, with a sun-visored audience in the stands that knew its craks and bams. Nora moved swiftly up the ranks from mascot to kibitzer to player, and now that she'd been drafted, her commitment to the Underground City intensified, even if her priorities within it shifted. But right now, her priority was to sort things out with Daphne.

Up in the apartment, they didn't waste their breath on preambles.

"You spend your time with strangers instead of me?"

"They're not strangers. They're my friends."

"You've known them what? A month? Two?"

"Something like that."

"And me? How long have you known me?"

"I'm sorry, Babka."

"How could you do that? You'd explode if I came to the old neighbourhood and visited Madame Marcil but not you."

"I was out of my head. There's no other explanation. I never meant to hurt you. It was just nice to have adult company for a change, and I got carried away with it."

"What, I'm not adult enough for you?" Yet again Nora had stuck her foot in it.

"Okay, since you're going to make me say it, adult *male* company."

"I wasn't aware that you were craving adult male company."

"Me neither, but when it showed up out of the blue I liked it."

"So it's Anthony, is it? Your pick of the litter?"

"Well, we do go out for lunch once in a while after, the two of us, but we're just friends."

"He's not attached I take it."

"Of course not. What do you take me for? None of them are. They've all lost their wives."

"And I suppose it's gotten to the point that it's serious. 'After-hours coaching.' Give me a break. Is that what passes nowadays for 'let me show you my etchings?'"

"I don't like what you're implying, girlie."

"If the shoe fits."

Daphne's tone, let alone her insinuations, was beyond the pale. If ever she deserved a dressing-down, now was the time, but Nora was hardly in a position to take the moral high ground. Her only option under the circumstances was to rise above her granddaughter's cheek, and try to make peace.

"I told you. We're friends. Period. Meeting with Anthony and the guys, well, it just gives me a reason to put on some lipstick when I get up in the morning. Come on, Daff, let me off the hook. I messed up. That I admit. I confused Skyping for real human contact. A rookie mistake. But it's not like you to begrudge me my bit of fun." The ice mask was crackling slightly around the edges so Nora pressed her advantage. "Let me take you out for lunch to say sorry. Somewhere I bet even you haven't seen yet."

"That I doubt very much."

Impugning Daphne's authority as queen bee of the Underground City was a savvy strategic move on Nora's part. It hit Daphne where she lived, forcing her agitation to morph into self-righteousness. How could her grandmother presume to have unearthed a restaurant on Daphne's home turf that she herself had yet to discover? It was a logical impossibility. On Nora's tepid forays into the Underground City, her eyes were always riveted on the ceiling, scanning for that first crack. She couldn't have noticed anything at ground level. Daphne would let Nora play Sherpa if she was bent on it, but when they ended up, as they inevitably would, at an eatery Daphne had already scoped out in her own meanderings, she wouldn't hesitate to bask in an I-told-you-so moment.

That moment never came.

Daphne's grandmother led her to a dépanneur not five minutes from the apartment and paused in front, looking very satisfied with herself. Even by convenience store standards it was unprepossessing.It was one of the great ironies of life that dépanneurs were inevitably such sad little places. Considering they trafficked in most of life's pleasures—tobacco, sugar, alcohol, trans-fats, lottos—they should have been as bright and filled with laughter as the ball pit at Ikea.

"So this is it?" Daphne said. "We're here? You're going to treat me to Twizzlers and a Pepsi for lunch?"

"Patience is a virtue, virtue is a grace."

"Yeah, yeah, I get it."

Nora led her deeper into the dépanneur where the hot-table was still in full swing, even though the lunch hour was drawing to a close.

"Jamie," Nora said to the server, "could you please fix up a nice plate for my granddaughter? She's never been here before. Something that shows off a little bit of everything?"

"This is your granddaughter, Nora? Very pretty girl."

"You know these people by name?" Daphne said.

"I have been coming in a fair bit lately. It's reasonable, and the food's great. Wait till you taste."

They settled in on a bench and attacked their lunches. Daphne noted Nora's smooth chopstick skills. She no longer harpooned the morsels of food, but pincered them up with aplomb.

"I've got to hand it to you," Daphne said, "this food's fantastic."

"Grandma knows best."

"So I guess your Anthony led you to this place."

"Nope. I found it all on my ownsome. You think you're the only one with a nose for what's good down here?"

"I'll have to subcontract you."

"I'm available."

They sat watching the underground world go by, the last remnants of their dispute dissolving, and that's when Daphne spotted her, the thatch of blue hair unmistakable. Her Y invader was right there in front of her, circulating among the vacated tables, searching out leftovers to appropriate for her lunch, skimming the tabletops busboy style. It was slim pickings. Most of the noontime crowds were house-trained and dumped the uneaten dregs of their meals in the trash. The woman Daphne had in her sights seemed to have her standards, though, and stopped short of rooting around in the bins. She was very thin, Daphne noticed with some surprise; when she was riding on her back through the revolving door, it had felt like she had more mass to her. Her clothing hung off her bones, suggesting that her body had once been more heavily upholstered. She was younger than Daphne had taken her for that day when she'd glimpsed her shape retreating into the distance at the Y. She couldn't have been more than twenty.

Despite the fact that she had semi-mugged her, Daphne couldn't help wondering where she set her head down at night. Not outside most likely; she'd be scruffier if she lived rough. Besides, she had no belongings with her, no cardboard to bed down on, no plastic bags. She must have uncovered some hidden nook in the Underground City that she used as her private sleeping pod. It couldn't have been easy for her to ferret out such a spot. Management of the various interlinked complexes that comprised the Underground City was adamant that it not become a mecca for vagrants, and instructed its security guards to show no mercy. Daphne had often seen them conducting their *raus-raus* rounds in her after-hours strolls through the complex, ejecting the homeless. Did this poor young thing spend her nights in a fitful half-sleep, fearing that any moment a muscle-bound uniformed arm would invade the niche that she'd carved out for herself and snatch her out? It was hard for Daphne not to see in this person with whom her path had literally collided, a parallel self, a fellow permanent resident of the Underground City, but one forced to live a secret life, not an open one, a hounded life, a life bereft of the barest necessities and pleasures.

Daphne was not what you'd call a bleeding heart. When solicitations from charities arrived in the mail, she dumped them directly. She never bought a copy of *Itinéraire* from the homeless hawker she passed at the foot of the metro escalator every day, never tossed a spare coin into anyone's cup. Why should she? Even with her new regular paycheque, she could still barely make ends meet as she struggled to pay down her debts. Daphne was well acquainted with the poverty line. Her grandmother hung her laundry from it. But suddenly she saw things differently. No, she hadn't been flush growing up, far from it. Still, at the end of the day she always had a meal on the table, a roof overhead, and someone happy to take her in. Maybe her grandmother was right. The constant pressure of the city of Montreal from above was affecting Daphne's thinking down below. Now she knew what she had to do.

CHAPTER 17

THE PASSAGEWAY THAT was the unlikely home to the chic and shiny Tunnel Espresso Bar was one of the dreariest in the Underground City. Its retail tenants never hung around too long, their leases scribbled on the backs of envelopes, their stock fallen from the back of a truck. In the outside world, a comparable street would lie in the armpit of a highway on-ramp, a shopping destination of last resort, its single hipster outlet trying desperately to signal to its confreres, "come on in, the water's fine."

Daphne had specifically chosen this coffee spot for a touch-base meeting with Marius because it offered no seating, meaning their rendezvous couldn't drag on. Also in its favour, the place served an espresso so volatile it could be used to blast out tree stumps. Though no inspectors had ever applied their measuring tapes to confirm it officially, in all likelihood it was the tiniest commercial outlet in the Underground City, not to mention a geometrical oddity, in that it was wedge-shaped like a serving of camembert. For a barista, it was an ergonomic dream gig, all the tools of the trade within arm's reach. But Ludovic, the proprietor and sole employee of this hole-in-the-wall, wasn't satisfied by mere proximity to his knobs and levers. It wasn't enough that his porcelain cups and saucers were stacked right under his nose, the glass pastry domes at his elbow. He bolted a rejigged turntable to the floor, a relic from his DJ days, and on this revolving platform he stood all day long, pirouetting in his domain, never obliged to take a single step. At peak hours, he spun around so fast he looked like a nascent bud vase on a potter's wheel. Why he bothered to install this rotating redundancy into his nano workspace, no one really knew. It might have been that he was genuinely bone lazy, or maybe the spinning made his greying ponytail flip pertly around in a way that fed his vanity. As to whether he was a genius or a loon, his regulars in the Underground City were as yet undecided, but among the same group polled, there was no dispute that he was the man with his finger on the pulse of the network. Occasionally he even served as Daphne's Deep Throat. This supplementary work he performed for her pro bono. It was the least he could do after she'd profiled his establishment in her blog with the result that he had to treble his weekly cannoli order to respond to the new demand.

"Daphné, ma belle, the usual?"

"Oui, Ludovic, s'il te plaît."

Marius had yet to arrive, so Daphne rested her arms on the counter and chatted with Ludovic while he wielded the controls of his baby. She loved to watch him at work in his cockpit. His giant Italian espresso machine, Rocky, he'd nicknamed it, packed enough punch to caffeinate a small village. When he had it operating at full throttle, all the lighting fixtures dimmed in the skyscrapers above. Rocky was too wide by half for the shelf accorded to it. It loomed over the pint-sized premises like a predatory animal. Ludovic alone could make it say uncle.

"Ludo," she asked him while he steamed her milk and poured it into a pitcher, "you ever see a girl with blue hair pass by?"

"Sure, lots. Blue is the new blonde, haven't you heard?"

"You're a big help."

"Give me a break. I need a little more to go on than that. Got a mug shot?"

"Nope. I wish I did."

"Well, what colour blue? Tell me that at least."

Daphne mulled it over, trying to visualize the precise shade in her mind's eye. "Cyan, I'd say."

"Cyan. What the hell? Is that a Crayola colour?" Ludovic's English was excellent, perfected in his years on the police force before he'd taken his pension to devote himself body and soul to coffee, but Daphne's descriptor was not a word he had butted up against before.

"It's turquoise-y," she clarified, "maybe the colour of windshield washer fluid, or Listerine."

"And?"

"And what?"

"More of a description if you please."

"I'd say she's maybe twenty or so. Thin. Shorter than me a little. Curly-headed. Clothes a bit ratty. I'm thinking maybe she's homeless, but I'm not sure."

"French? An Anglo?"

"I don't know. We've never actually spoken."

"Well, based on what you've given me she doesn't ring any bells, but I'll keep an eye out for you."

"Thanks, Ludo, I'd appreciate it. You have my number, right, if you need to get in touch?"

It seemed only fair, if she was soliciting Ludovic's help, that she regale him with the full story of how she and Ms. Blue-Hair had their meet-cute in the Y revolving door, but with the arrival of Marius at the coffee bar she left the threads of the tale dangling. He didn't count as a member of her inner circle. Or her outer circle for that matter.

It was a lawyerly dictate that Daphne submit to periodic meetings with a duly designated representative of the contest to document that she was not being subjected to undue pain and suffering due to her artificially confined circumstances. So far, the only pain and suffering she had experienced derived from the meetings themselves.

"How are you doing?" Marius asked her.

"As you see me, alive and well."

"What do you recommend?"

It was a coffee place. He needed her advice?

"Everything's good. Didn't you read my blog?"

"Touché."

Marius ordered an allongé and a mini clafoutis from the whirling dervish behind the counter. He had to hand it to Daphne. Her funk detector was highly tuned. It could scent out the offbeat even in the mall-like sameness that was the Underground City. The odd time that it wasn't operating up to its full potential, her severe allergy to chains moved in to pick up the slack.

"No problems you need me to deal with? The wi-fi issue's been taken care of?"

"It's fine now thanks. Four bars."

"And the e-deposits?"

"No hitches anymore there either."

These meetings bothered Daphne more than the anklet, which she was gradually learning to think of as no more than a mispositioned wrist watch. Marius was only there to provide her with support, and his interventions did smooth the road for her, no doubt, but she was unaccustomed to such aggressive helpfulness and her instinct was to fend off the attack with her arms crossed in front of her face. She'd always preferred to be a solo operator. Then you were beholden to no one but yourself.

Ludovic was listening in on the pair discreetly. The reason Rocky had cost him a fortune was that he'd sprung for the optional audio buttons, the ones that pumped up the volume on the conversations the coffee operator deemed worthy, and damped down the others. Stasi patented. Since he felt protective of Daphne, he made it a point to monitor her exchange with the red-headed dude who'd joined her, but there turned out to be nothing of interest to glean, all evidence of her normally voluble self effaced. Still, the low level of chat was in itself information of a sort and he tucked it away. So microscopic was the small talk going on between the two of them that Ludovic was starting to drift off. He had just about decided to switch channels to eavesdrop on some suits talking stocks, when he snapped to attention, grabbing onto the counter to stop himself from revolving.

"Heads up," he barked at Daphne, his head tilting in the direction of Place Ville Marie. "Blue blue blue blue blue at three o'clock."

Daphne didn't react. She could make no sense of the barista's blather. The string of nonsense syllables flowing out of his mouth made him sound like he was under water. She stared at him uncertainly, wondering if he could be having a stroke. Ludovic tried again, more slowly this time, and more literal. "Your blue-haired girl. Isn't that her over there? Heading towards Place Ville Marie?"

Daphne whipped around and took off in pursuit, but she'd lost precious seconds trying to make sense of Ludovic's first bungled tipoff. If she wanted to catch up with her quarry she'd have to run. What she would say once they were face to face Daphne had no idea, but she didn't let that detail slow her down. It was her shoes that did. Her slingbacks with their slick soles weren't cut out for trailing fugitives, and Daphne lost sight of her where PVM hooked up with Central Station. The crowds massing for the 11:00 a.m. Via trains to Toronto and Quebec City effectively swallowed her up. Daphne stood fuming in front of the ticket booths. If she had been wearing her old reliable Nikes she would have nailed her for sure, but how could she have imagined that morning when she'd dithered over her footwear that she would end up doing sprints?

When Marius caught up with Daphne, he bent forward, his hands on his knees, straining to catch his breath. Clearly running was not a major element of his fitness program.

"What's up?" he asked her once his lungs were back in operating order.

"Nothing, nothing. I thought I saw someone I knew but I lost her in the crowd."

"You were really moving."

"Why did you follow me?"

"I don't know. I was worried, I guess. You took off so fast, like someone fired a starting pistol."

Marius genuinely was worried. If it was true that Daphne was trying to catch up with someone she knew, why didn't she just call out to her instead of taking off through the Underground City like a bat out of hell? Maybe Daphne was not alive and well. Maybe living underground for so long was in fact affecting her sanity. He wondered if he should report her behaviour to the medical team they kept on retainer, but he decided against it for the time being. He didn't want Daphne to risk disqualification due to a misdiagnosis on his part; he didn't want them to think her unstable. Instead, he decided to keep closer tabs on her. If she was losing her grip, it was safer that he be the first to know.

CHAPTER 18

ANY ACTUARY WORTH his salt would have advised Anthony to proceed otherwise. If Anthony was sure about what he wanted, he should not have been inching forward. At his age, he should have been leaping. But that wasn't his way. Before Nora stumbled into his life, he'd figured that the next time he would have a woman lying by his side would be in the cemetery. Not that he and Nora were anywhere near the lying stage yet; oh, that delightful *yet* on which he hooked his hopes for the future.

And if *he* wasn't a leaper, neither was Nora. The finish line was still far enough in the offing, at least in their minds, that they could savour the slow unfolding of their relationship. A sideline observer of said relationship might more accurately label that unfolding as *glacial* not merely *slow*. Never did they phone each other to whisper sweet nothings. They hadn't even exchanged cell numbers. And certainly never did they cross each other's thresholds. There were no dinners, no movies, no Wednesday night line dancing in Parc Sun-Yat-Sen. It was only over the mah-jong table that they met; no other assignations prearranged. Their games did often segue into a leisurely lunch in the neighbourhood, but that was the extent of their liaison. So far, the two of them only existed to one another across a table of one kind or another. Still, the amount of headway they had made while seated was, by any measure, considerable.

Which was why Anthony was now flummoxed. It had been weeks since Nora last showed up to play. Such a lapse was unprecedented in the brief history of their acquaintance. Could she be ill? Had some other misfortune befallen her? He berated himself for never having gotten her phone number or address. Was there ever a suitor as inept as he? His marriage had been arranged, even if in a loose-ish North American kind of way. At the time, Anthony had fought against his parents binding him up in their old-crone customs, him of all people, the first native-born Canuck of his family. Why had they schlepped across the Pacific if not to embrace modernity? But now he realized his parents had been right. At the rate he moved, if they'd left him to his own devices back then, any courtship he'd have engaged in would still be dragging on.

His thoughts circled back to Nora a hundred times a day. It started first thing in the morning with his parakeets pecking at the seeds in their cage. To his ears, it was the exact same sound as Nora's fingernail tapping against a mah-jong tile while she was trying to decide whether or not to discard. Who would have thought that such a tiny flick could arouse in him such longing?

Since Anthony had no way of contacting her via traditional means, yet again he cursed himself as an imbecile, the only option open to him was to approach Daphne to find out why her grandmother had dropped out of sight. This inquiry had to be undertaken with the utmost delicacy. It would be cruel to alarm Daphne needlessly if his imagination was just working overtime. It wasn't as if she had the option to race back to the family homestead and check up on Nora to ease her mind. If he bungled this, he'd land on the blacklist of the Elman women, there to remain till doomsday.

The intelligence gathering plan Anthony ultimately settled on amounted to bumping into Daphne casually, just an accidental-on-purpose encounter where they could chat about this and that, until eventually, as if it were purely by-the-way, he'd nudge the conversation over to the subject that was consuming him. In his mind it made sense. His strategy was neither pushy nor intrusive, just a simple polite inquiry, not too much weight attached to any one topic among the general clutter of the conversation.

He set his scheme into motion immediately. Anthony made it a point to arrive early at the mah-jong table he and his friends usually commandeered and to leave late, giving ample opportunity for Daphne to wander along. For days he maintained the stakeout. She had to pass by sometime; her apartment was just upstairs. But Nora, it seemed, wasn't the only one who had gone AWOL.

If Daphne was never anywhere near her apartment at midday, it was due to her new side-project, which required that she range far afield in its execution and always at the lunch hour. Poor Anthony had no way of knowing that if he didn't expand his perimeter, he would never cross paths with her.

■ ■ ■

Since the sighting with Ludovic, in her daily comings and goings underground, Daphne had caught one further glimpse of her blue-haired alter ego. The woman was circulating in the food-court at the Eaton Centre, appraising the table tops, trying to cobble together a lunch from left-behinds. She had a nervous energy to her, darting from one table to the next, snatching up bits of cast-off edibles and jamming them into her mouth. Here finally was Daphne's opportunity to make contact; she wasn't that far from her. Daphne slalomed her way through the forest of tables, heading in her direction, but the woman must have had a sixth sense that she was targeted in a stranger's viewfinder and slipped away. She seemed to have a gift for rendering herself invisible.

Daphne inspected the table where just seconds earlier her prey had been standing. It was copiously littered with lunch debris. A large loutish party must have just departed, one that didn't know the meaning of cleaning up after itself. What was it like, she wondered, to be reduced to scraping up the leavings of strangers to fill your belly? She decided to find out.

Daphne hadn't yet eaten lunch, but she was already salivating over the excellent one she had in store. That morning, before she'd been distracted at the food court, she'd stopped at Cantor's in the train station to pick up some potato-and-onion knishes to go. Cantor's was the one lonely spot in the entire subterranean complex that tipped its hat to Eastern Europe, at least so far as she'd discovered, its shelves jam-packed with pumpernickels and kuchens and babkas. That regional snub was a mistake in Daphne's view. One of these days she'd have to blog about the geo-political bias of Underground City kitchens, but in the meantime, she just clutched her precious cache of knishes and scuttered along towards home.

The paper bag the bakery provided was too flimsy to contain the potent odour of onions that had been caramelized in non-PC chicken fat; such a glorious overabundance of chicken fat that Daphne could have sworn she heard her knishes cluck. The lingering warmth of the ovens was radiating through the bag, the fat saturating the brown paper to grease up her fingers. Even if those knishes were likely to shave a month off her lifespan it would be worth it. But her view of her lunch bag took an about-face after observing her doppelgänger forced to make a smorgasbord of slops. Though it grieved her to do it, Daphne balled up the bag with its contents untouched and dumped it in the trash. Instead of feasting on what she now saw to be a meal of privilege, she would graze from the scraps and bits before her.

The trays were a muddle of soiled napkins, oozing ketchup packets, chicken bones, and various undefinables. Was that powdered sugar dusting that muffin top or dandruff? Daphne was hardly a thin-skinned civilian; she had waitressed before. She'd seen what slobberies paying customers were capable of, the indignities they could inflict on a smoked-meat sandwich and a coke, but back at the deli it had never been a question of ingesting any of their handiwork, of sneaking a discreet bite of a pristine pickle that had survived the carnage. She just piled all the refuse up on her tray and shouldered it back to the kitchen, leaving it to the dishwashing crew to deal with the toxic waste she offloaded at their stations.

Now though, dealing with it was her affair, and dealing with it amounted to making it her noontime meal. Daphne seated herself. The chair was affixed to the floor so she couldn't back away. Its position forced her to get up close and personal with the leavings before her. At first, she could barely force herself to reach out and touch anything without her gag reflex exercising its authority. She spent a good fifteen minutes scrutinizing stray fries and pizza crusts for the imprint of strangers' bridgework. She did manage to pick up a pita, completely intact, both sides apparently pristine, but once she conjured up an image of the barbarians who had occupied that squalid table, their spit spray misting over their meals, even it didn't make the grade. And who knew what orifices their fingers had been rooting around in before they touched that food? For all her earlier resolve, Daphne's total intake at lunch added up to exactly zero grams. Nor did her battered appetite rebound by dinner.

It didn't matter which Tupperware container of leftovers from her fridge that she opened, the baba ghanouj, the hummus, the spicy lentils; all of it had a regurgitated look. If she never ate again, it would be too soon.

The following morning, over a breakfast of nothing, Daphne's digestive system gave her a good talking-to. Eating scraps, it admonished her, was not going to help Ms. Blue-Hair in any way. If she genuinely wanted to improve the circumstances of this stranger, she would need to take a more constructive approach. In the end, both Daphne's stomach and the homeless woman would thank her for it.

This advice struck Daphne as sound so she decided to act on it, developing a new routine. She took to buying full lunches at various food courts around the Underground City and leaving them on the tables, intact. On ambitious days, she packed bag lunches in her apartment. Nothing fancy, cheese sandwiches on multi-grain, celery sticks, an apple, and a juice box. It was the kind of Birkenstock lunch any savvy fifth grader would trade away in a heartbeat for a bag of chips and some Oreos, but Daphne was determined to keep her offerings healthy. These bags she scattered hither and yon, throughout the various food courts in the Underground City. She started with just three or four in a day, but over time, she upped her production.

Whether her intended recipient was the one to profit from her free-lunch program, Daphne had no way of knowing. A certain amount of faith was involved and Daphne was now calling on reserves of it that she didn't even realize she had. It was like making a contribution to any charity. Who knew if the money contributed ever connected to the swollen-bellied orphan across the globe? Who knew if the funds went to mosquito nets or a Mercedes, trees or guns, vaccinations or villains? In the end it was all a crapshoot, but Daphne couldn't stop herself. And even if the woman who had awakened Daphne's latent generosity was not the one gorging on Daphne's food donations surely other homeless people in the Underground City were. If traffic was up underground, and Marius had recently relayed to her this piece of excellent news, it probably had less to do with her blog and more with the fact that Daphne was conducting her own subterranean World Food Programme.

So busy was Daphne breaking in her wings in her new role as food fairy of the Underground City that it barely registered that her grandmother was quieter on her end than usual. The Skypes had become clipped, the phone calls intermittent, and the visits few and far between. It was only when Anthony arrived at her front door and spilled out the brimming worries he could no longer contain, that she realized how wrapped up in herself she'd become.

Anthony had trashed his original plan which was, not to understate it, a dud. Time was fleeting, Nora still wasn't appearing, and he was having no success in engineering an accidental run-in with Daphne. His anxiety for Nora's well-being had reached such a pitch that drastic measures were called for. He knew where Daphne lived. It took no special detective work on his part. He pushed the buzzer next to her name on the listing in the lobby, identified himself to her over the intercom, and she summoned him up instantly. Why had he been diddling around with intrigue?

"To what do I owe this pleasure?" she asked as she let Anthony in the door. She led him into the kitchen to put on the kettle for tea. Daphne had a row of assembly-line lunches going on her counter, twinned slices of bread ready to be serially mustarded and filled, packets of juice, veggies, and fruits. All were marshalled in front of a parade of open bags. Anthony had three kids, he was familiar with the drill. He briefly wondered what Daphne was playing at, behaving like a mom for a family of eight in an apartment that could barely sleep one, but he swept aside his curiosity. He had other more pressing business.

"It's your grandmother," he blurted out when she put the mug of tea in his hand. For the briefest of moments she assumed he had come to ask her for Nora's hand in a nice twist on tradition. "She hasn't been by to play for ages now, hasn't even stopped by to check in. I haven't heard from her at all. In all this time. We didn't have an argument. There's nothing wrong between us. I'm worried." The earnestness of his inquiry seized her attention, drawing it away from the unfinished sandwiches languishing cheddarless on her counter top.

Daphne cast her mind back over her own recent interactions with her grandmother. Then she interleaved their skimpiness with Anthony's concerns and stepped back to look at the stack of clues they formed. And that's when she spotted it. It was nearly invisible to the naked eye, but there it was, the first hairline fissure, the harbinger that her underground world was gearing itself up to collapse on her head.

CHAPTER 19

T HE ALARM BELLS were clanging in the hallway of Daphne's building, a piercing, insistent nee-nee-nee in response to the smoke that was swirling through the corridors. Her neighbours poked their heads out of their apartments at the sound and decided that this was not merely a case of a tenant's bacon overstaying its welcome under the broiler. The smoke was too thick and widespread for a run-of-the-mill kitchen contretemps. They were already setting off through the emergency door at the end of the hall that led down to de la Gauchetière Street, their ears peeled for fire trucks tearing up from the caserne on St. Urbain, which was reassuringly close by. There was no wild stampede, no flames were crawling up the walls, but they headed speedily out of the building, coatless, only their babies and electronics in hand.

Daphne watched them sprinting towards the door that led beyond the invisible fence that circumscribed her world. As soon as she joined the evacuees and passed through it to the great outdoors, her anklet would signal the breach to the gearheads who monitored her movements and her down-under career would go belly-up. At least according to the letter of the law. But what did they expect her to do, hang around and fry? If this didn't count as extenuating circumstances, what did? The contest lawyers would have a hard time maintaining that she should have stayed on-site while the smoke alarm was bleating. No way was she going to hold out on her balcony all alone until a firefighter flung her over his shoulder and hauled her away by force. She closed the door of her apartment behind her and followed her anxious neighbours towards the glowing red *sortie* sign at the end of her hallway.

What would happen once the anklet picked up that its wearer had vaulted the moat and was outside the confines of the Underground City? It had never occurred to Daphne to inquire. Would it send a punitive electronic shock up her leg, a taser-ish jolt that would have her top and bottom teeth clattering against each other like castanets? Or would it emit its own alarm, adding to the clamour? There was only one way to find out.

At the foot of the metal staircase Daphne hesitated at the door, prepping herself mentally for whatever strain of abuse her anklet had in store for her, but the lineup of people behind her, chafing to get the hell out, had no sympathy for a dawdler and bulldozed her through. No jolt, no sound. Her ankle adornment turned out to be nothing if not discreet, sending a simple silent alarm to tip off her handlers that their blogger had gone rogue.

The plaza across the street from her building, normally occupied by Tai Chi practitioners, was now crowded with her neighbours nervously scanning the building for sparks shooting from the roof. Daphne didn't join the group. She had other plans. Now that she was out, she was out. What did it matter how far afield she went? Here she had the perfect opportunity to hightail it over to her grandmother's house, get to the bottom of her recent reclusive behaviour, and scurry right back to her apartment. Just a quickie visit to put her mind and Anthony's at rest. Daphne decided not to hail a cab; no point being too showy about her absence from the Underground City. She could run the distance easy.

For the first time in months Daphne stepped down onto pavement instead of terrazzo. Her running shoes appreciated the roughness of the surface that gave their waffled soles a good solid grip, and they took off all zippy as if their underground hiatus had never taken place. Maybe she'd pay for it tomorrow, but rather than easing up from a trot, Daphne shot off at full speed right from the start. Her ankles, which occasionally needed a spritz of WD-40 at the beginning of a run, didn't complain, and her lungs felt pumped up to full. All systems were go.

Well, almost all. An attack of guilt was hampering her progress some, fuzzying up her focus, and attached to that was the worry that the long arm of Google would red-flag her for her research into smoke bombs and land her in jail, which she deserved, she supposed, for inconveniencing all those innocent people who shared her building. She had been careful, though. The bomb she fabricated at her kitchen counter didn't belch the tarry kind of smoke that seeped into the upholstery, stinking it up for good. It didn't leave sooty marks on the walls or ceilings, or aggravate the alveoli of asthmatics. It was innocent theatrical smoke, closer to the mist side of the smoke spectrum, although she was careful to pack it with enough oomph to set off the alarm. But after you opened a window or two for it to dissipate, at least according to the website, there remained no trace. She had tried to be a responsible neighbour.

The smoke bomb solution she only settled on as a last resort, once she had already exhausted all the other means at her disposal to find out what was up with her grandmother, and her panic level had ratcheted up to high. A phone call, the first and most obvious step, had yielded nothing concrete.

"So, Grandma, what's up?"

"Same old, same old."

"Nothing special going on over there? It's just that you haven't been by much."

"Oh, I'm on the DL again. My knee's been acting up. Nothing serious but I'm giving it a rest, hot packs, keeping it levitated, the whole bit."

"You mean elevated?"

"Isn't that what I said?"

"So your knee is also why you've been calling me less often? It keeps you from picking up the phone, does it? I could have sworn you used your hand for that."

"Have I been calling you less often? I don't think so."

"I've got the record of the phone calls right here on my phone. Or should I say the non-record of your phone calls."

"You don't have to get all nit-picky with me, you and your fancy iPhone. It's like I'm being stalked."

"And when I call *you*," Daphne pushed ahead, "you wind up the phone call before it even gets started."

"You're dreaming. You probably just caught me while I was busy with something."

"You seem to be awfully busy with something lately, that's for sure."

"Daff, don't waste your time looking for problems where there aren't any."

"You promise me you're okay?" Daphne asked.

"Fit as a fiddle."

"It's just that I'm alone here, having conniptions."

"Babka, relax."

"Me? Fat chance."

Daphne was certain that the result of that conversation, which laid out all her gripes, would be a more communicative grandmother, but in fact the opposite was true. The phone calls continued to drop off in frequency and length, mere hi-byes with nothing of substance padding out the strategic middle. The rare Skypes were even more worrying. Nora was distracted on the screen, always looking off to the side as if the kidnapper holding her hostage were positioned in the wings signalling her what she could and couldn't say. And what were those noises Daphne picked up in the background? It had to be her grandmother's soaps going on TV, what else could account for the crying, but it sounded suspiciously live to her.

For the first time since she'd moved in underground, Daphne railed against her constraints. What the situation demanded was a boots-on-the-ground approach. She had to march up to her grandmother's door, throw it open and confront her. But life wasn't fair, at least not distance-wise. Here Daphne was, not all that far from her grandmother's house, but she might as well have been on Saturn. Anthony was the obvious candidate to sub for her, that lovestruck puppy masquerading as a senior citizen, but he was off to Vancouver to see his daughter, knocking him off the list of possibles. He hadn't wanted to leave under the circumstances, but Daphne insisted that he not trash his ticket. His daughter was counting on him to babysit while she was in hospital delivering grandchild number four. Daphne would handle everything on the home front she assured him, and keep him apprised. He'd trusted her and she didn't want to let him down.

Ethel Marcil would blunder in and do the job with her usual rumble-in-the-jungle finesse. She'd be thrilled to be asked. But she would inevitably spill to Nora that Daphne had been machinating behind her back. She was a good soul, Ethel, but she had a tendency when given too much responsibility, to stir the pot. Which left Daphne to the last choice on her list, the one person in her emaciated Rolodex she really didn't want to be approaching for any favours.

"You know I'm not supposed to be your enabler," Marius said when she put it to him. "I can't go out and do things you can't because you're underground. It defeats the whole purpose."

Daphne's invitation to her apartment for dinner had taken Marius by surprise. Was it implying a new détente? Except for the occasions of his spot inspections, they always met on neutral territory, their meetings engineered by Daphne to have a short shelf life. But if this meal was an indicator of an easier rapport with his charge, Marius was glad of it. He wasn't one for holding grudges. He was more than ready for their earlier tensions to dissolve. Daphne, on the other hand, seemed to cling to her grievances. She watered them, aerated them, and dosed them with Miracle-Gro to make sure they stayed healthy and strong. Maybe it had finally sunk in, though, that he was just following orders in all this, that she didn't have to place all the responsibility for the snarls in her underground life squarely on his shoulders. But, ninny that he was, he'd misread the cues.

"Can't you just phone her?" he said.

"I did. Over and over. But she cuts off the calls before I have a chance to find out anything. I can't force her to talk."

"She doesn't come by to see you?"

"Not anymore. You can see why I'm frantic. Suddenly she's turned into another person and I'm stuck in here. Please, just this once, could you? It's totally not like her to be behaving so hush-hush. Something is up. I know it. And I can't find out what it is from here. You could just go there and say it's some kind of official visit. Very quick, over before you know it. And then you could come back and tell me what's happening over there. She's very deferential to authority. I know she'd open up to you." Was she really begging?

"I'm sorry. I know how important this is to you, but it wouldn't be ethical. Don't you see? I wish I could, really I do, but you'll have to find someone else."

"There is no one else."

That this was true Marius had no doubt. Hadn't they selected her in the first place because she wasn't burdened down by family? But if he did what she was asking and anyone at work were to catch wind of it, he'd be sacked. The contest, Larry's baby, had to remain untainted. From the rumours Marius had caught wind of, it was all that was keeping the agency afloat.

Even if it did gall Marius that Daphne was trying to buy him off, he felt for her family-less state. He had more relatives than he knew what to do with, cousins once removed, twice removed, thrice removed; a cast of thousands. If his car needed a boost at 2:00 a.m., one of them would pull up on the shoulder with the cables. If he needed a loan of a few bucks, a bed to crash on, or a spare kidney, there they'd be. He could barely imagine what it must be like to go through life so unconnected. But in this matter his hands were tied. She would have to work it out on her own.

CHAPTER 20

T HE DOORBELL STARED at her accusingly when she bypassed it in favour of her key. After all this time away, it would have been proper to ring so her grandmother wouldn't go toes-up when Daphne materialized unannounced in the kitchen. But with her decision to set off the smoke bomb, Daphne had effectively given *proper* the boot, so she went ahead with her plan to take her grandmother by surprise. It wouldn't do to afford Nora enough time to get all her excuses lined up in a row. She unlocked the door and headed in.

Daphne poked her head into the living room but Nora wasn't there. Nothing about the room had changed in her absence, she was relieved to observe. It was still a cozy jumble; a pair of Crocs abandoned heel to heel under the coffee table, a few days' worth of newspapers resting on top anchored by a mug, and the green zigzag afghan balled up in the corner of the couch, ready to be deployed when *Antiques Roadshow* came on.

Housekeeping wasn't much of a preoccupation for Nora. Her lifelong cleaning philosophy was validated by the fridge magnet Daphne had given her for Mother's Day years before and still had pride of place on the freezer door, *A clean house is the sign of a wasted life*. Nora *neatified* the rooms, as she phrased it, on an as-needed basis. When the cobwebs landed enough dust on them that they looked crocheted, Nora made a few passes with the Swiffer, and when the carpet had a bit of a crunch to it, she lugged the vacuum out of the hall closet, but the house as a whole never lost its lived-in look.

A lingering smell of cooking floated about. Daphne pegged it as Nora's signature spaghetti sauce. On the domestic front, if Nora could be said to apply herself anywhere, it was in the kitchen. Fancy cooking wasn't her thing but somehow she had a gift for taking low-born ingredients and elevating them above their station. Daphne nearly lost track of her mission at the familiar scent of tomatoes and garlic hooking up in the Crock-Pot. The homesickness she had been keeping at bay all these months threatened to overwhelm her. All she wanted to do was cuddle up on the couch under that pilled afghan and let the Underground City go on about its business stag. Back when she was little and a TV show she was watching had a scary bit, she'd pull the afghan over her head for protection and watch the program through the holes. Daphne had the sinking feeling that whatever she was about to witness in this house, she'd rather see it through the holes too.

From her vantage point in the living room, Daphne could easily scan the rest of the rooms on the first floor which turned out to be similarly Nora-less. No grandmother materialized upstairs either, when she scoped out the bedrooms. The bathroom? Open-doored and vacant. Daphne stood in her old room, staring out the window at the tiny fenced backyard, trying to take in the enormity of her blunder. All the risks she'd taken, the contracts she'd violated, the laws she'd broken, the lives she'd manhandled, and no one was fucking home? How colossally stupid could she be that she had never once considered that a possibility? Where could Nora go with her bum knee, but of course here was the proof that the knee was nothing but a beard behind which the real excuse for her withdrawal was holed up.

What a fool Anthony had been to put his faith in her. Her grandmother had probably filled his ear with tributes to her smarts, and he would never doubt Nora's judgment, even though he might have guessed it was just a case of grandparental grade inflation. As a grandfather himself, many times over, he should have recognized the syndrome. Daphne understood it was churlish to blame the victim, but the failure of her undertaking had her completely unglued. She recalled how downcast he had looked that day, leaving her apartment so reluctantly, how she had showered him with reassurances that she would get to the root of it all and now, thanks to her, he was stuck worrying at a distance of four thousand kilometres and she with nothing good to report.

Daphne dragged back downstairs relying heavily on the railing for support. Her arms and legs felt rubbery. All the grit that had been keeping them operational since the moment she'd set off the smoke bomb had drained out onto the floor of her old bedroom as if someone had pulled out a stopper. The reading on her energy scale was at empty but that didn't exempt her from finishing the job of scouring the house from top to bottom. If she didn't do it today, she wouldn't have the chance again until she got sprung on day 365. Unless, that is, she had the good fortune of a real fire breaking out in her building, and she could slip out once again using the alarm for cover. With the last dregs of strength she had left on call, Daphne steered herself towards the stairs to the basement. Her last hope was that Nora would be down there doing laundry, though the chances of that were slim. It wasn't Sunday. Nora wasn't big on regimentation, but for some reason lost to the mists of time, her Sunday laundry mornings were sacrosanct.

The lights in the basement were on. Daphne could tell from the position of the switch at the top of the stairs. This was a good sign. Nora didn't believe in adding to the coffers of Hydro-Quebec unnecessarily. Whenever she left a room, she flicked off the lights. It was a compulsion with her, a penny-pinching tic that she'd always tried to get Daphne to adopt, though without much success. This minor electrical discovery so buoyed Daphne that she was able to take the basement stairs at a jog, convinced that at the bottom her reunion with her temporarily misplaced grandmother would be staged.

At the foot of the stairs she stumbled over a bundle of laundry and nearly fell. That bundle then began to cry. What Daphne had taken to be a pile of folded clothing resolved itself before her eyes into a baby. A woman dashed over from across the basement and scooped him up and into her arms, sheltering him against her bosom as if she feared Daphne was planning on eating him for lunch. The crying was infectious, it seemed, and a little girl sitting on a folding lawn chair dropped the picture book she was holding and joined the chorus. A tall man who had been sitting in the webbed lawn chair beside hers gathered in the second crying child and moved forward to envelop the mother and the faux-laundry baby. The four of them clung together opposite Daphne.

If her limbs had been able to execute her instructions the way they normally did, Daphne would have raced back up the stairs and out the front door shrieking for help, but she found herself paralyzed. She couldn't even reach into her pocket for her phone to dial 9-1-1. She regretted now that she hadn't confided in Marius, however foolish that would have been. At least then, one person on the face of the earth would know where she had disappeared to and could send out a search party when she failed to return. But she hadn't trusted him that far, and this was the result. She was trapped.

Daphne flashed a quick glance around, praying that an escape plan would jump out at her, when she noticed that the basement was completely transformed. When had the basement, of all places, that infinitely expandable receptacle for the detritus of their lives, ever been this immaculate? Air mattresses, neatly made up, were pushed up against the walls. The summer picnic table was unfolded and set for lunch. The shelves had been cleared of all the half-empty paint cans and the fodder for the garage sale they had always intended to hold; the outgrown skates and the suitcases short a wheel. In their place were neat stacks of diapers, linens, dishes, and folded clothing.

Her gaze steered back to fix on the strangers in front of her. They drew back in fear when they felt her focus drilling into them. What did *they* have to be afraid of? Daphne wondered. Couldn't they see the reciprocal fear in her eyes? No one spoke. With the shock of their appearance, Daphne had forgotten the combination to her voice box and the two adults seemed to have suffered likewise. They wouldn't have been able to hear each other at any rate. The persistent crying crowded out the possibility of any other sound prevailing.

If only she could run her day in reverse, retracing her route to go back and lock herself up in the Underground City where life now made sense. All those boundaries and restrictions she'd chafed at before? Bring 'em on. She was sheltered there, safe. It was the outside world that was burbling with dangers. Daphne had read about ex-cons who couldn't get the hang of life on the outside and reoffended just to go back in the joint where they knew the score. Those guys had a point. But for her there was no putting the genie back in the bottle. The clock was running on her self-granted humanitarian leave. She couldn't piss away the time wishing she was back underground. The stakes were too high, higher than she had ever suspected. Her grandmother was well and truly missing. These home invaders had stashed her who knows where and were using her house for a squat. Daphne's fried brain was struggling to come up with its next move when the door to the basement bathroom opened and Nora came out shaking her hands dry. She took in the scene in all its particulars and turned immediately not to Daphne, but to the strangers.

"It's just my granddaughter, Daphne," she said. "Don't worry. Everything's good. It's all good." Nora shifted her attention to Daphne. She gave her a hug and then pulled back to perform a status check on her granddaughter's face. "What is this, Daff?" she asked, giving her a hug and then pulling back to perform a status check on her granddaughter's face. "You've quit the contest?"

Daphne withdrew from her embrace, nettled at coming in second behind these interlopers.

"No. For your information, I did not quit. No one knows I'm gone. I only have a few minutes. I have to go right back or I risk losing it all. I snuck out so I could see what's up with you. You've been so silent. I've been worried sick. Anthony's frantic. What is all this? Who are these people?"

"Oh, this is the Demel family. From next door. The McLeans' old place. I told them they could stay down here. Just temporarily. Their papers aren't quite in proper order and they don't want to be ordered back to Côte d'Ivoire."

"What? You're sheltering illegals in our house?"

"It's not as simple as that."

"Yes, it is," Daphne said. "It's just that simple."

"Daphne, I used to lay in bed and hear Yvonne sobbing through the shared wall. For hours on end it would go on. When she finally told me what was happening with her family, the threat hanging over them, well, what would you have had me do?"

"Direct her to the closest church basement. That's what they're for."

"That's not very charitable of you."

"Charity has nothing to do with it. I'm being pragmatic. In a church they're protected. It has, I don't know, legal precedent, whatever. In your house, if they're found, they're dead in the water, and you too probably."

"No one's going to find them."

"Of course they'll find them. It wouldn't take a bloodhound. They're right next door for God's sake."

"That's the beauty of it, don't you see? Who would expect to find them hiding so close? Besides, it's not forever. Just while they're trying to get things regularized."

"You read about cases like this all the time. It could take years. Those kids'll be old enough for university before they see the light of day. Don't they have a lawyer?"

"Since you mention it, that's one of the issues we're working on."

"Meaning?"

"Meaning we're working on it."

"So for now they have no legal counsel other than you? Wow. They're in great shape."

Daphne gestured around the basement at all the supplies her grandmother had laid in to accommodate her guests. "All this costs money. How are you paying for their upkeep?"

"I manage on the money you send me."

"My money? You mean the money that's supposed to be the start of our nest egg? You're telling me it's already gone?"

"No. Not gone. Just a little shrunken is all. We get by. But what does it matter anyway? You're going to collect the big payoff at the end of your year, right? Assuming you go back, that is. We'll be on easy street. It's just some belt tightening for the time being."

Daphne thought she might pass out at the thought of all the extra bodies that would now have to be supported on her dime, a dime so precarious that it might be cut off as soon as that very afternoon if her contest bosses took her absence amiss.

"It's you I have to thank," Nora went on. "You're the one who put the idea in my head."

"Me? What are you talking about?"

"All safely tucked up underground like you are. I thought, why not?" A shadow came over Nora's features as the Underground City rose up in her memory.

"Poor Anthony. This all happened so fast. Suddenly I had a house full of people. There was so much to take care of. So much to get organized. I didn't have a second to spare to go let him know what was up. He deserves better than me."

"Poor Anthony? Poor Anthony she says. What about poor me?"

"Daphne, I'm sorry I dumped so much worry on you, but as you can see, I'm fine, we're all fine. You can relax now."

"Right. Why not? Everything's just dandy, isn't it?" All the steam pouring from Daphne's ears brought up the humidity level in a basement that was already too damp. "I don't get it," she said. "Why couldn't you be up front with me? Why all this undercover stuff?"

Nora had the good grace to look uncomfortable. "I guess deep down I was afraid you might not approve."

"Well, you got that one right. No one with a grain of sense would approve. It's madness. What about Madame Marcil? Is she on your side?"

"She doesn't know. Nobody does."

"Finally, a bit of good news. So at least it's contained. We can still undo the damage. Find them some other place to stay. I'll start looking into it right away."

"There will be no undoing of anything," Nora said, drawing herself up to her full five foot one. "They're staying." It was Nora's that's-final voice, the voice that brooked no opposition. Daphne could have kept banging away at her but there wasn't much point when Nora was in brick-wall mode. Her childhood had taught her that much.

"This isn't happening" Daphne said. "Am I in some alternate universe? My grandmother is going to get arrested for harbouring fugitives, and after what I've done today, I'll probably end up being her cellmate. Plus, as a nice add-on to all that, we're going to go broke. I went through all this to help get us back on our feet, and you've wrecked it."

"I haven't wrecked anything. What would you have done, let them rot?"

"It's not my responsibility. It's not your responsibility."

"I can't believe this is my sweet Daphne talking. You don't even want to hear their story? Maybe it'll bring out a little of the sympathy I thought I had instilled in you."

"I don't give a shit what their story is. There's only one story I care about. Ours. And all I know is that our story can't have a happy ending if it's tangled up with their story."

Nora looked stricken. "When did you get so hard?"

"I'm not hard. I'm sensible. Somebody has to be."

The door from the laundry room opened.

"What, there are more of them?" Daphne clutched at her chest.

"Okay, Mrs. Elman, your two handymen have replaced the bulb above the washer. Any other jobs for me and my trusty assistant?" Marius was carrying a little boy on his shoulders who was giggling away on his perch. He was pretending to pull Marius's hair in a game they had going. Marius reached up above his head to set the child down, and that was when Daphne's feet hove into view.

"I thought you said nobody knows," Daphne said, turning to her grandmother.

"I didn't think he counted."

■ ■ ■

Fury gave Daphne a gear she never knew she had for her run back. Marius struggled to keep up but she was flying.

"It wasn't ethical, you said."

"I know."

"You couldn't interfere, you said."

"I did say all that, I know. But later, the more I thought about how worried you were, I decided I'd just take a quick look, confirm that everything was okay, and then come back and reassure you."

"I wouldn't have had to do any of this if you'd told me you'd go in the first place."

"You look cold." Marius said. Despite her break-neck speed, Daphne was shivering. She wasn't accustomed anymore to dressing for the outdoors, and had no proper outerwear at any rate. "Here, take my jacket." Daphne grudgingly slackened her pace and accepted his offering.

"How did you get out?" he asked her. He could see the tracer still bound around her ankle.

Daphne considered concocting a fictionalized version of her breakout but in the end she told him the unvarnished truth. What was the point of dissembling? He'd find out soon enough about the smoke bomb that set off the alarm. And even if it didn't point directly to her as the perpetrator, she'd been careful to leave no signs, he would eventually put two and two together. "I suppose you'll report me," she said.

"Not unless you feel inclined to report *me* for improper conduct."

Like it or not, Daphne now had an accomplice.

CHAPTER 21

WHEN DAPHNE SHOT out of her grandmother's house, her endgame was already fully formed in her mind. She would get that family of leeches booted out of the basement if it was the last thing she ever did. Her means of arriving at that goal, though, were less clear-cut. With Nora flat-out opposed to eviction it would be a hard sell, but Daphne could send out an SOS to Marius to help tilt the balance of power in her direction. They could go two-on-one, wearing her grandmother down till she gave in. Daphne was relieved to have Marius as a sidekick, even if he had weaseled his way into the position through the back door. This situation with her grandmother was too thorny for her to deal with on her own, especially from a distance.

If not for Marius running interference, the fallout from her Underground City escape would have been a nightmare. The agency was exceptionally testy about Daphne's prolonged absence from the network. Of course they understood that she didn't want to be burned alive. They weren't inhuman. But Daphne was out gallivanting long after the fire department sounded the all clear, which led to all sorts of sticky questions. Marius fielded them so elegantly the agency let the matter drop, satisfied in the end that their underground girl had behaved with the utmost propriety. But just because Marius was willing to paper over the details of Daphne's French leave, it did not follow that the two of them were joined at the hip on all its aspects.

"They strike me as a very decent family," Marius said as he and Daphne had made their way back towards the Underground City from her grandmother's house, settling in midway between a walk and a run, a pace that split the difference between their preferred strides.

"Very upstanding I'm sure," was all he got out of her.

"We had the chance to talk a lot before you showed up. About what brought them here, I mean. Christ," he said, "it was a living hell. No family should have to go through what they've been through."

"All families have their grief," she said.

"You don't think they've had more than their fair share?" Marius wasn't prepared to let her get away with her pat answer even if she had charged out of the house before giving them the chance to lay their history out before her. "How many families have you ever met that had to flee for their lives?" Her silence gave him the answer that he would have expected. "Their story, it's heartbreaking. All I can say is they're lucky they landed on such a caring person as Nora."

"She's a chump." The word landed cold on Marius's ears.

"You can't really believe that," he said. Daphne didn't know what she really believed. Too much had dropped down on her too quickly. She wasn't yet prepared to be generous. Instead, she did what she often did when she was angry or confused, she lashed out. Usually, Nora was the one to lasso her in, but this time she wasn't available with the rope.

"Maybe if I were to tell you exactly what happened to them before your grandmother was good enough to take them in, you'd think otherwise," Marius said, his tone taking a page from Daphne's book.

"Don't tell me! I don't want to know!" She raised her palm traffic-cop style in front of Marius's face to insure that he would put on the brakes. The best way for her to steel herself against the castaways in her basement was to keep them as strangers, their problems as unknown to her as those of any of the other poor sods she passed randomly in her daily travels, dragging their wheeled metal carts of hard luck tales behind them. Only then could she make the kinds of decisions that would keep her little family of two from going down.

Marius knew Daphne to be tetchy. Not only that, she had it in her to be uppity, stubborn, and standoffish. She was not what you would call an easy person. But for all the tightness of her character, he had trouble accepting that she was so thoroughly lacking in compassion for the family her grandmother had taken in. It was all a hunch of course.

She had certainly never shown herself to be warm and fuzzy towards him, but he could see she cared deeply about her grandmother, which led him to suspect that there was a pool of sympathy at her core that she just chose not to dip into for all and sundry, or more accurately for any and sundry. And that inkling that Daphne kept concealed within her unstoked embers of empathy helped him decide to go along with the embargo she was demanding. He wouldn't foist the harrowing details of her grandmother's guests on her, at least not until the initial shock of her visit home had worn off. She deserved that much respite. Their full story would catch up with her soon enough. He stayed mum on the subject until they reached the entrance to her building at the Underground City, where he left her alone to come to grips with the new reality of her life.

A good dose of unconsciousness was all Daphne craved when she got back up to her apartment. Even from as far away as her front door, she could feel the bed winching her in. Sleep wouldn't solve her problems, but at least it had the virtue of staving them off, and so wasted was Daphne after her morning on the lam, so pummelled by circumstance, she was sure that if she neglected to set her alarm she would sleep straight through till the end of her term in the Underground City. Her body was as depleted as if she'd run an ultra, not just a few poky kilometres. Her legs were cramped and her brain was silt. So what that it was the middle of the day. She dropped down onto the mattress fully dressed and pulled the comforter over her. She made one last check of her email before surrendering to oblivion, and that iPhone reflex was what did it, terminating her brief period of denial.

The single unread email at the head of her inbox came from her grandmother. Daphne sat up in bed, her fatigue zapped out of her. Here was the apology. What else could it be? It was less shaming to apologize in writing than by phone. Her grandmother had caved, and it had taken no time at all. Daphne hadn't expected remorse to come on her so fast. So much for that family. *They were hist- they were hist- they were hist-tor-y.*

Except that they weren't. The email turned out not to be written by her grandmother. It came from the father of Nora's basement lodgers, using her account.

Chère Mademoiselle Elman,

I understand your hesitance to open your home to us. It puts your family at risk, a situation I understand intimately. I know our problem is not yours to deal with. Nor is it your grandmother's, but she has been selfless enough to shelter us in our time of need. She will be blessed for her kindness in the hereafter.

Please allow me to explain. We come from Côte d'Ivoire. I was a doctor there. During the civil war in 2010 when violence erupted in the city, my wife Yvonne and I decided to flee to the countryside where we had family. I thought it might be safer. I have punished myself every day since over that decision. The fighters came to the village during the night with their guns. In all the disarray we managed to escape and hide in the bush with several others. We could see them burning houses behind us as we ran. We heard the screams but we had to close our ears. There was never enough to eat or water to drink but at least I thought the fighters would not follow us into the bush. I was wrong.

Again they came in the night. The shooting, the panic that followed, I will not describe. My uncle, the one who had agreed to take us in, was among those who were shot and killed. Many of the other villagers who had fled with us were injured. When they came at my daughter Grace with a machete, I tried to come between them. They sliced my shoulder open. I fell. They left me for dead, and then finished their work on poor Grace, our eldest. Somehow my wife and my other two children managed to survive. I had to be brave for them, though at times in my grief over Grace I thought that it might have been better if had I died of my wound.

I was very weak and had lost a lot of blood. There was no medicine or bandages. They patched me up as best they could. All my decisions up to that point as to how to keep my family safe had been as poor as they could possibly be, but I made one final one that I hoped would be the right one. I decided that we would try to cross the border to a refugee camp in Liberia, and there we might be safe. We travelled by night and at last we made it to the camp. We were luckier than most of our fellows who were languishing there. I had a cousin in Canada who was willing to sponsor us. He worked for the government and pulled strings. It was like a miracle. We were able to be put on a plane quickly and brought here.

We have been very happy in Montreal. It has been hard for me to find work, due to my damaged arm, but we were managing. Then we learned that because

109

my cousin who brought us here has since been convicted of a crime, he is no longer permitted to serve as our sponsor and we would be deported. Our legal status in this country was yanked out from under us. We are afraid to go back. They claim that Côte d'Ivoire is now stable, but after what we experienced, it is hard for us to believe. They expect us to go back to the country that is the source of all our nightmares?

I pray that our time under your grandmother's roof will be short-lived, and that an answer will be found to our troubles that will allow us to stay in Canada. Please do not be dismayed with her that she has come to our rescue. She is a great lady.

Emmanuel Demel

Daphne tipped over her king.

CHAPTER 22

I N THE GOOD old days, when her movements were her own to direct, when she could freely point her toes toward any destination and no man nor device would impede her, a state like the one she was in would send Daphne straight to the Botanical Gardens. It was the ideal spot for serious thinking. Not school-type thinking. That she could do anywhere. Life thinking. Big T thinking. And that was the kind of thinking Daphne needed to do now that her visit back to the old house on rue Melançon had butted her off the rails. Except that the space that now confined her was not one that lent itself to rumination. The Underground City was awash with humanity; it had more than 500,000 people tramping through it every day. Most of the quiet niches tucked away among its corridors where one could sit solitary and meditate had long since been discovered and overrun, victims of their own success.

In her peregrinations around the Underground City over the weeks that followed her illicit trip home, Daphne tried out several substitute Zen spaces. She figured she'd have a winner with the libraries. Back when she was in full dissertation mode, libraries had always served her well, time-honoured havens against hurly-burly. She parked herself in a lonely-ish corner of La Grande Bibliothèque hoping for the same serenity the gardens had always granted her, but the quiet that was part of the package the library was shilling turned out to be false advertising. With all the yakking, the security alarms, the ring tones, the notification bleeps, and the leeching earbuds, it was as noisy in the library as the IGA in Complexe Desjardins where Daphne did her groceries. She might just as well have settled herself in for a good think in the vegetable aisle. She x-d the libraries off her list with regret.

The observation tower at the Olympic Stadium put itself forward to her as a plausible candidate. Up at its summit, with only the sky and the clouds as companions, Daphne imagined herself being able to reflect without distraction, like the gods on Mount Olympus, on the problem that was bloating her grandmother's basement, so she decided to try it out. A glass-fronted funicular sped her up to the top. It wasn't a straight vertical climb like an elevator ride up the Space Needle. The Olympic Tower was built on a forty-five-degree angle, an architectural conceit copycatted from Pisa that did not sit well with Daphne. During the slanty ascent, gravity tugged uncomfortably on her stomach contents. She got out at the top queasy, not in the best contemplative mood, but worse than that, she found herself hemmed in by crowds of rowdy children. Zeus probably never had to deal with school groups. This outing had turned out to be as big a write-off as the one to the library. Without even pausing to check out the million-dollar view, Daphne took the next funicular back down. When it landed on ground level with a thump, it sent the blood rushing up to her brain, giving it a jolt in the imagination department. She now knew where she had to go next.

The metro that transported Daphne to Christ Church Cathedral might have looked like an ordinary subway, but in fact it was a time machine. When it dropped her off at the McGill Station and she took the winding stairway up towards the nave, she left the LED lights, the laminates, and the stainless steel behind, exchanging them for burnished wood, limestone, marble, and stained glass. There were other churchy spaces underground, as elaborately vaulted and pillared, but the colleges and universities got their mitts on them early in the game. Their administrators were happy to boast of architectural wonders on their campuses, but once they took them over, they gutted the vocations right out of them. Christ Church Cathedral was the only subterranean religious institution left that hadn't been spayed.

Sitting in the pews of the Cathedral under its great Gothic arches, Daphne felt like a trespasser. She was searching for nothing more than a quiet patch of turf in which she could sort out her life, but since there were no synagogues in the complex, she was obliged to appropriate whatever spiritual space was on offer. Surely, under her extenuating circumstances, sectarian swaps like this were approved of. She adopted a prayerful posture and waited. In the calm that draped over her, Daphne let her thoughts tumble around freestyle, hoping that they would eventually touch down on the solid ground of a solution, but for as long as she sat musing, no solution came. There was no way out. For the foreseeable future she would be saddled with five extra mouths to feed. Illegal mouths. Insatiable mouths. Mouths that would suck down every cent she brought in. Her end-of-the-year prize money? The money that was going to give her a cushion for once in her life? The basement family would reap its benefits, not her, a winning lottery ticket fallen from her pocket that they would snatch up and cash in. Thanks to them, shopping in thrift shops for her clothes wouldn't be a phase, but a lifelong habit, her style as she aged crossing the line from funky to bag lady. Here she'd have spent a year in solitary and would come out as broke as when she went in. It had all been for nothing.

Her business in the bosom of the church was over, a good idea gone sour. She hauled herself out of the pew and in the process knocked her tote bag to the floor. Daphne carried the world in her tote. It was her apocalypse bag, as Theo used to call it. If ever she needed a banana, a fork lift, or a tin-foil hat, it was there. In sheer poundage, it rivalled a bowling bag. When it fell, the sound resounded like a gun shot in the silent premises. At the report, a head shot up into view from one of the pews in front of Daphne to check out the source of the disturbance. And the hair on that head was blue.

Daphne hoisted up her bag and fitted the strap into the permanent dent in her shoulder that gave her posture its trademark tilt. She walked slowly down the central aisle until she came alongside the pew where the muse for her underground lunch project had now resumed her prone position, satisfied that the noise that had startled her represented no danger. Her antennae, which always seemed so sensitive in the food courts where Daphne had previously spotted her, must have been in the shop because Daphne was able to plunk herself down on the pew beside her before she even realized she was being stalked. She sat up, but showed no impulse to run. She had as much right to be there as Daphne did. All she did was give Daphne a cool once-over. Daphne's eyes were similarly occupied so their glances caught up in each other.

"I've seen you around," Daphne said, "underground."

"What of it?"

"Just saying. Maybe you remember me? We made each other's acquaintance at the entrance to the Y. Or almost. Clearly you had a pressing engagement and couldn't hang around for a proper introduction." At that remark, the young woman's eyes darted about, starting to look interested in an exit strategy, but Daphne and her bag had her efficiently wedged in.

"I've noticed you at the food courts a few times too," Daphne said.

"Look, you're not my type, so fuck off."

"You were having quite a feast of leftovers."

"That's not a crime last I checked."

"No, not at all. I'm sure you put together some very healthy meals from those trays."

"So what are you? The health police? It's not stealing. Just because your type can afford to buy your lunch at the counter doesn't mean all the rest of us can."

"True enough. I suppose it's better to be here, snacking on communion wafers."

"What's it to you anyway, what I do or don't do? Now if you'll excuse me?" She stood up to leave but Daphne didn't budge. She was far from finished. The underground authority glanced around the Cathedral like a real estate agent sizing up the window treatments and the parquet.

"Is this where you've been living?" Daphne asked.

"It ain't much but it's home," she blurted out, wishing instantly that she could take that information back.

"They allow it?"

"Let's just say what they don't know don't hurt them."

"I'd be afraid if it were me. I pass some scary types who hang out around here."

"I can handle myself."

Her bravado couldn't hide the fact that she was frightened by Daphne's intrusion into what she had considered her safe space. Sweat was beading at her temples and whatever colour had tinted her cheeks at the beginning of their conversation had faded to chalk. Daphne was ashamed of herself. She had only ever wanted to speak to this person who was her shadow self in the Underground City, but instead here she was intimidating her, so much so that she was shaking. She'd taken a turn for the worse Daphne noticed, since they'd last crossed paths. Her hair was matted and oily and her clothing had grubbed up considerably. A gamey smell wafted off her. She couldn't have availed herself of a shower in a while. The security goon from Guarda the Y had installed at its entrance was apparently earning his pay, doing his bit to keep unwashed the great unwashed.

Where the offer came from, Daphne had no idea. It just spurted out of her. It went against her nature, against clause 3.4(b) of the contract she was living under, and against her recent behaviour chez Nora, but mysterious influences were acting in her brain, reworking its tight-ass circuitry into a more giving configuration.

"Come over to my place tonight, why don't you? Stay over. I can offer you a sofa bed and a home-cooked dinner. And you can wash your clothes if you're in the mood. Mi washing machine es su washing machine. I'll throw a shower into the bargain. What do you say?"

If Daphne was going to go down, at least she was going to go down in a blaze of glory.

CHAPTER 23

SHE'D DONE RISKIER things in her life. Stupider too. But still, this was way up there. She was following a complete stranger home as meekly as a stray puppy just because she'd been offered dog biscuits, fresh sheets, and a wash in a legal shower.She didn't need to be told that this was how kidnappers operated, not to mention serial killers and your other unclassified wackos. In their devious minds they figured out what it was you yearned for the most and laid a trail of it back to where they lived so they could hack you into pieces or whatever, in the peace and privacy of their own home. And she had played right into this Daphne person's hands, if that's what her name really was. Didn't resist for a second.

Who would have thought after all she'd faced off against that she'd crumble just because she smelled like a litter box? Until she had set herself up as a card-carrying homeless person, she never fully appreciated the simple luxury of being clean. The fact that she was hungry 24/7 was nothing by comparison, even if her daily caloric intake would hardly be enough to keep a chipmunk going. At the beginning, she'd kept the dirt in check using the Y, but once that option was no longer open to her, she did bird baths in public washrooms, a little splash-splash on her pits and bits. They hardly had any effect so what choice did she have? She went ahead and stunk. She could barely stand to be in her own company. And the ranker she got, the fewer decent public places she could hang out in during the day without attracting attention. When Daphne set before her the prospect of endless steamy running water, she was powerless to resist.

She hadn't lasted long on the street before caving in and accepting this help. Well, technically speaking she wasn't out on the street, although the distinction was minor. Whether she was spending her nights on a mat of newspapers at Berri Square, or sleeping in the organ loft of a downtown church, she was equally homeless, equally cut off from her parents. In fairness to herself, taking up this offer of bed, bath, and beyond didn't make her a quitter. If this supposed do-gooder hadn't shown up, she would have continued scraping by. And even if it was totally reckless of her to go home with this woman she didn't know from dirt, it was only for one night. Tomorrow, presuming she survived, she'd slip back into the anonymity of the Underground City.

It bugged her that she couldn't quite peg Daphne. Assuming she wasn't your run-of-the-mill psychopath, then what reason could she possibly have for inviting her home? Was she a defrocked social worker who got off on rounding up strays, or maybe one of those down-and-dirty nuns she'd heard about who dress in Levi's and work in the streets. She mulled it over as they made their way toward the apartment where she would be spending the night. It was a strange walk. All along the route, people who worked in the different shops and restaurants waved at Daphne, called her by name, and came over to shake her hand. It was like walking down the street with Obama.

"You sure know a lot of people."

"It's because I'm Daphne Down Under."

"Who?"

"Of the *Daphne Down Under* blog. I write about what's happening in the Underground City. I'm like one of those embedded reporters, except instead of living in Afghanistan, I live in the Underground City. Everybody down here knows me."

So that was it. She'd been taken in by some kind of dweeby local celebrity, someone not that much higher on the famousness scale than Jungle Jerry, the dork in a safari suit who used to bring snakes and raccoons and other low-end wild animals to assemblies at her school. It seemed a pretty safe bet, then, that her hostess for the night wasn't a maniac. Still, she would have to be cautious. It was risky to have a blogger of all people taking a particular interest in her. If she needed any further encouragement to keep her mouth shut for the duration of her visit, here it was.

"I suppose you have a name?" Daphne asked her as they walked.

"Archie," Chantal replied. It was as good a name as any. She appropriated it as they were passing a comics rack outside of Multimags. She liked the idea of having a street name, a spiky new handle that split her off from her old identity.

"And do we have a last name?"

"Doesn't everyone?"

"Okay then." She was a tough nut, this one. Daphne held back on the third degree. She would wait until she had her guest fully fed and fumigated. Maybe then she'd be more in a confessional mode. They walked on in a stiff silence. Daphne only engaged her visitor once she was unlocking the front door to her apartment. "Eat first or shower? Dealer's choice."

Now that Archie was on Daphne's home turf, she shed some of her lip. "Maybe shower please."

Daphne approved internally of her preference. She hoped that hot water, in liberal quantities, would be sufficient to exterminate whatever creepy-crawlies had accompanied her indigent house guest in, before they decided to explore the residential possibilities of Daphne's cushions.

"Come on," she said. "Let me get you some clothes I think'll fit you." Archie followed her into the bedroom area where Daphne riffled through the drawers of her wardrobe. "Here," she said, handing Archie a pile of neatly folded garments. "You can put these on after your shower. There are some pyjamas and other stuff, some pants and tops. They might be a bit big, but they should be okay. Just leave what you're wearing outside the bathroom door and I'll throw it all in the machine if you like." Daphne couldn't wait to pincer up the offending garments and dump them in the washer on the filthy-beyond-belief setting.

"I'll get to work in the kitchen while you're washing up. Anything you don't eat? You vegetarian or anything?"

Archie was not a meat-eater in fact, but in the spirit of beggars can't be choosers, she had been letting her principles slide since she'd been underground.

"I am actually, but anything you have I'm fine with."

Daphne rooted around in her freezer. "Well, looks like I can offer you mushroom pizza or mushroom pizza."

"Let's say mushroom pizza then."

"Right-o."

"The bathroom's through there. Just help yourself to towels from the cabinet and anything else you need. I'll get going on the salad."

Once Archie disappeared into the bathroom and Daphne heard the latch click, she raced around the apartment, securing her tiny array of valuables. She needn't have hurried. Archie was locked away for so long Daphne could have grown the lettuce for the salad from seed and still had time to spare. When Archie emerged from the bathroom dressed in Daphne's oversized hand-me-downs, her skin rubbed pink, her hair shiny and neatly combed, she looked as if she'd shed a few years down the bathtub drain. Daphne had the strangest urge to tuck her into bed and read her *Goodnight Moon*.

Conversation over dinner was minimal. Daphne's visitor was too busy packing away the pizzas to spare her mouth for talking. Only after ice cream did a bit of a back and forth get going.

"So other than my grandma and her friend," Daphne said, tapping a key on her laptop to wake it up, "that's them on the screen there, you're the first person I've had over for dinner in my stint underground."

"Their loss. You're a good cook."

"Thanks. My defrosting skills are very high."

It was payback time, Archie knew. Now it was her turn to keep the conversation grinding along. She'd brought her manners with her in her back pocket when she'd left home; she just hadn't had much occasion lately to trot them out. Daphne's last comment had the subject of frozen pizza just about tied up, so Archie threw out a question that veered in a non-culinary direction.

"So what's it like being Daphne Down Under?" she asked. She was happy with the open-endedness of the question. It would wind up the metal key on Daphne's back and keep her marching for a good long stretch with just a few encouraging nods and uh-huhs from her.

"It has its moments. I do like having one limited area and learning all there is to learn about it. It appeals to the researcher in me."

"It's not so limited though, is it?" Archie jumped on what she'd said. "It extends really, really far. I spend a lot of time wandering around, exploring. You know what I like best? The Pink Trees. The ones in the Palais des Congrès. They're so weird and gorgeous. I mean the colour! I feel like I'm Alice in Wonderland when I'm walking through them. I like to imagine what kind of animals would live in a forest like that. Turquoise squirrels maybe? Plaid foxes. And you know what else I love? Those giant birds hanging from the ceiling of Cours Mont Royal. The ones with human faces. Wouldn't you just love one of them to lift you up and take you back to where their nest is? What a place that must be."

What was she doing blathering? But she couldn't help herself. Before she ran away she never could have foreseen that being homeless involved taking a vow of silence. Since she'd dug in underground, not a single soul had engaged her in conversation until Daphne cornered her in the Cathedral. Before that encounter she'd developed the habit of deliberately jostling people in a crowd so she'd have an excuse to say *pardon*, and test if her voice still worked. Archie rejigged her earlier resolution to muzzle herself. She'd already made a hash of it anyway. In the revised version she would allow herself to take her voice out for a spin. It deserved it after spending all that time on idle. She would just avoid speaking about anything personal.

"It's hard to beat trees that come in fuchsia. I grant you that," Daphne said. "But that's not my absolute favourite spot. What's your take on the installation at Place des Arts, those wild and crazy metal sculptures, half animal, half human, half sphinxes? It's like King Tut's tomb on steroids."

"That's a great spot all right, but I prefer the little water garden at Cours Mont Royal. You know it?"

"Yep. I've seen it. But not enough bang for your buck. IMHO. Just your ho hum palm trees around a pool. Not an over-excess of imagination wasted on that spot."

"But it has fish. Actual carp or giant goldfish or whatever they are. Where else underground do you see anything besides the human race? To me it's a treat. Like having a pet almost."

Blogging about life underground wasn't the same as talking about it with someone else who semi-shared her experience, Daphne thought. Professor Séguin had a passion for underground cities but only ones that were of sandal-and-toga vintage. Their chats during his occasional visits to the Underground City were pleasant, but scholarly, as dry as a Cappadocian cave floor. She couldn't bounce off his observations like she could with Archie's. Daphne had been right about her all along. She really was a subterranean kindred spirit, someone who saw into the fabric of the Underground City and could appreciate its drape.

Daphne was feeling mellow, a sensation she never thought she'd retrieve since the day she had discovered the family from Côte d'Ivoire scrunched into her grandmother's basement, bleeding her dry. She felt light-headed and relaxed. Happy, you might say. She was enjoying her visitor. From what she could observe, Archie looked similarly laid-back. All her tightness had evaporated. A full stomach worked miracles. They relocated to the couch and put their feet up on the coffee table. Daphne broke out the ice cream again for some supplementary scoops of choco-chic, and the two of them yakked the Underground City into submission.

And that's when Daphne brought it all to a thumping halt. "So how is it that someone like you ended up on the street?" It was exactly the wrong question to ask. She could see Archie pulling up the gangplank. She wouldn't get another word out of her before they went to sleep.

Daphne didn't get it. Here was a young woman who was well-spoken, refined, and personable. Mostly. Why wasn't she in university? Or working? What had chased her away from her home and family to eat dust? Okay, Daphne had learned her lesson. She was wrong to have blundered in with such a personal question. It wasn't proper hostly behaviour. At breakfast, she would institute her inchworm approach, winkling the truth out of her more obliquely. But when Daphne got up the next morning to fix a nice mea-culpa breakfast for Archie, she discovered that her visitor had scarpered.

CHAPTER 24

IT WAS A ROUGH transition from a spa to a mud puddle. It would have been easier never to have left the mud puddle at all. Archie was having re-entry problems. Reacclimating to the grunge of the street was tricky after she'd availed herself of all the bottles of lotions and gels Daphne had jammed in the rack hanging from her showerhead. Archie had shampooed and conditioned and moussed. Three times over. Then she scrubbed the first layer of crust off herself, and worked her way down like an archaeologist through the second and third layers till she hit skin. It shamed her to leave the washcloth behind. By the time she was done with it, it was so irretrievably soiled it looked like a mechanic's rag after he'd rotated tires all day. Archie stuffed it way down deep in the hamper where she hoped it would go unnoticed. After her shower, she rooted around in Daphne's bathroom drawers where she found orange sticks and tweezers and all manner of beautifying and cleansing paraphernalia. Archie flossed until her gums bled and excavated so deeply for wax in her ear canal that the Q-tip came out on the other side of her head. When she left the bathroom, she was aseptic enough for an operating theatre.

At first it was glorious. With her crisp clothes from the Daphne collection and her gleaming hair Archie swanned around the Underground City as if she owned it. The croissant she'd grabbed on her way out of Daphne's fortified her in her travels. She tried on dresses in the designer boutiques that occupied the top floor of the Cours Mont Royal, where the sales people served her cappuccinos in between ferrying outfits back and forth to her dressing room. Then she moved on to Browns where the price of a single pair of boots could have kept her in meals at underground food courts for a year. Archie explored the art galleries near the Palais des Congrès and even took a peek at the free Barbie Expo for old times' sake. By late afternoon, when she was in the mood to rest her feet, she marched right past the liveried doorman of the Hôtel InterContinental and settled into one of its lobby's tufted armchairs. She wouldn't have dared hang out there prior to her Daphne interlude. It was far too posh, all gilt and marble. They would have shooed her away before she had a chance to make their Louis Vuitton guests skittish. But today they left her in peace, assuming she was a member of the tribe. Archie leafed through their magazines while she chomped on a Granny Smith that she took from the help-yourself bowl on the registration desk. She partook liberally of the water out of the glass samovar that had slices of oranges and lemons and limes swimming around in it among the mint leaves. It looked to her as if you were serving yourself water out of a tropical-fish tank, but it gave her a nice citrusy jolt.

Once she had exhausted every piece of free reading material available, Archie resigned herself to picking up her old life and headed back to the Cathedral. She didn't want to press her lobby luck by overstaying. If she could keep her clothes decent for a bit longer, she could spread her business around in other hotels in the days to come, sample their apple varieties. It wasn't the same as spending time in Daphne's cozy apartment, a pair of hand-knitted slippers hugging her feet, but it would allow her to hang on to her dignity at least for a short while before the inevitable underground scuzz started to settle in on her person. She would have been happy to stick around at Daphne's place for a few days more. Archie had enjoyed her company. And her pizzas. But Her Nosiness made that impossible. Why did she have to go and ruin it all?

Archie's sleep space in the organ loft didn't hold a candle to her accommodations from the night before, but at least it was cleanish, quietish, and best of all, a single. She had that much to be thankful for. She unlocked the grille, replaced the key on its hook and mounted the stairs. She always enjoyed her first step into the loft. Even if she didn't take any pleasure in organ music, she loved the organ itself, the sheen of the wood, the majesty of the pipes rising up to frame the rose window. She was hesitant about touching any part of it for fear of accidentally eking out a sound, but occasionally she treated herself to sitting on the bench and skimming her fingers ever so lightly over the knobs and keyboards as if she were really playing this cruise ship of an instrument. The organ was Archie's one daily encounter with beauty in a life that doled it out with a stingy hand. But when she got to the top of the stairs this time, there was no beauty in the view. Once her eyes accommodated to the dimness of the loft, she was able to make out that her space was occupied. Two women were sitting on the floor playing cards. They looked up as she entered.

"Hey, Denise," said the younger-looking of the two, "we got company. Should we put out the hors d'oeuvres?"

"This is my spot," Archie said.

"Was, you mean," said Denise. She returned to the card game as if the issue were settled.

Archie tried to summon up her old street-side toughness, but Daphne's fabric softener had seeped from her clothes into her very marrow. What she needed right now was a voice with hair on its chest, but instead she ended up sounding like a bratty kid.

"It's mine," she said.

The two interlopers looked at each other and laughed. "It's mine, it's mine," they mimicked. The one who had first spoken to Archie ran her finger down an imaginary hotel register. "I don't believe you left a deposit so I'm afraid we had to cancel your reservation."

"Sorry, and have a nice day," said her friend and they high-fived each other in appreciation of their own wit.

"I'm not leaving," Archie said, still trying to dredge up some grit.

The older woman didn't so much stand up, as uncoil. Her greying hair was convenience cropped, stubbled and raggedy as if she'd taken pinking shears to it. The hollows in her cheeks were so deep she could have used them to store the backup chips for her shoulders. A lit cigarette was hanging from the corner of her mouth like an aberrant incisor.

"Maybe you didn't hear what I said."

"I heard you fine," Archie said. The fresh clothes Daphne had given her worked against her again. A good shot of dirt would have given her more street cred. She looked like a daisy that had sprouted up amid the sidewalk cracks, a homeless dilettante.

"Get the fuck out of here, Baby Jane. Your mommy must be getting worried and I'm fed up with the interruption."

"I'm staying."

"Aren't your eyes working?" Denise said. "Do you see space for three here? It's barely big enough for two. Besides, Liz and I aren't looking to have roomies. Get it through your head. You're leaving. Now. Before I regret that I've been so patient." Liz stood up to reinforce her friend's point. They crossed their arms in front of them like twin club-bouncers. Their stare was musclebound even if their bodies weren't; it was a stare that said they would happily stomp Archie under their heels just like they would the roach that was scooting across their discard pile. No skin off their nose.

Archie pitied her sleeping loft. In the space of just a night and a day they had fouled it almost beyond recognition. She couldn't quite fathom how, in such a short time, and with so few belongings to their name, those two had managed to desecrate it so utterly and most probably she didn't want to know. They'd even let their filth spill over onto her precious organ. Archie ached to defend her space but she had to admit to herself that dealing with these types was above her pay grade. They were right in seeing her as a soft target.

"Okay," she said. "Have it your way." She raised her hands up in a sign of surrender. "I'll just collect my stuff and then I'll be out of here." Archie walked towards the back corner of the loft where her bag of belongings was stashed in a cabinet with old sheet music. She hadn't brought it with her to Daphne's. Retrieving it would have revealed the exact location of her hiding place and the trustworthiness of her host for the night had yet to be proven.

"Oh, you mean this?" Denise said and held up a plastic bag from Bureau en Gros. "The management can't be held responsible for belongings left behind. Didn't you read the sign?"

"Give it here." Archie grabbed for the bag but Denise yanked it out of reach. "I'm leaving like you wanted," Archie said, "but that's my stuff. You know there's no money in there, nothing valuable. It's just my junk, that's all. What do you need it for?"

"You want it? Take it," Denise said, brandishing the bag high above her head. Archie leapt for it as if she were LeBron, but couldn't make contact.

"Give it back."

"Yeah, like that's gonna happen."

Denise continued to dangle the bag in the air and Archie sprang up for it time and again. She was prepared to keep on for as long as it took. That flimsy bag, however humble its contents, was all she had to claim as her own in the world. But Denise was tiring of playing piñata. When Archie fell against her while trying to grab onto a corner of the bag, Denise hauled off and punched her in the face for the infraction. The blood started to stream from Archie's nose. Now here was a game Denise could get into. She punched Archie again, in the eye this time, and then in the other eye for the sake of symmetry. Archie wavered in front of her but she didn't fall. Denise took a good look at her punching bag and what she saw rubbed her wrong. To her discerning eye, it was aesthetically unpleasing that the bottom of Archie's face no longer matched up with the top. Except for the blood dribbling down her chin, it was completely unblemished. Denise couldn't have that, so she set her fist to work on Archie's jaw.

It would have been impolite to leave Liz out. She deserved a turn too. Denise locked Archie's arms from behind to keep her upright and pulled her hair back so Liz could have a clear shot at her face, but Liz turned her nose up at the offering. She didn't want any part of Archie's face. It was already pulp. No point overworking it. Liz looked Archie up and down for virgin territory and made her choice. She put all her force behind her and gave a short uppercut to the stomach. When her fist met the bull's-eye Liz found that she liked the give; she had her sweet spot. For the sake of variety she gave the ribs a try, but she didn't like their bony resistance, so she reapplied herself to Archie's pillowy midsection.

"Lay off, bitch, enough," Denise said to Liz, twisting Archie out of her friend's reach mid-punch. "She has to be able to walk out of here. We don't want to be stuck with her." And Archie could still walk. Theoretically. When Denise let go of her she bobbled, but she didn't collapse. By rights Denise should have been happy with the success of their twofer, they'd both had their fun and their plaything was still ambulatory. But it peeved Denise that in trying to teach Archie a lesson, she hadn't once screamed out. Except for some grunts, she'd maintained a steely silence. To Denise, Archie's stoicism meant that their lesson had not been relayed in full.

"You hold her this time, Liz."

"I thought we were done, you said."

"Almost. Just a little goodbye gift. Hold on to her tight while I think about what to offer." Denise appraised Archie while she took a drag. "You don't look so fresh now, do you, little princess? Let's see what you have going on here." She pulled up the bottom of Archie's blouse and admired the bruises that were already starting to bloom.

"Hell, Liz," she said, moving in closer to inspect, "you missed a spot."

"Do you want me to take another crack at it?"

"No. Forget it. If you want something done right…" Denise took the lit cigarette out of her mouth and approached it to a patch of skin on Archie's stomach that was pink and unmarked from their beating. When Archie saw what was coming, Liz could barely hang on to her. Denise hovered the cigarette above Archie's stomach, hemming and hawing. "Now should I put it out here? Or maybe here?" When she settled on the perfect spot she pressed the cigarette down firmly, as if she was stamping a passport, and was rewarded with the howls she was after.

"Shit," Denise said to Archie, "you made me miss where I was aiming for with all your wriggling. Hold still this time so I can get it right." With all the strength left in her, Archie lunged out of Liz's arms, but Denise tripped her and brought her to the ground for a second go, Archie's knees cracking against the floor. The church had excellent acoustics. Archie's screams bounced off the walls to reach every corner. If this had been a concert there would have been no bad seats.

"Now that's more like it," Denise said, tipping her ears to drink up the echoes. They were having more trouble keeping their victim still now. Liz had to sit on Archie's legs. Denise knew that they had gone too far. All the noise might bring attention, but she was drunk with the urge to finish what she'd started. She took another long drag. "Don't move, I told you. You don't want me to make another mistake, do you?"

Liz struggled to hold her down but Archie jackknifed her legs, toppling Liz to one side. Their clash put Denise off her aim, but she landed the cigarette where she could, a perfect glowing circle just above the waist. The singed flesh gave off a nice sizzle, like sausages tossed into a perfectly heated cast-iron skillet.

"Let her up now," Denise said, "but hold on to her this time for Chrissake. I give you one simple job and you can't even manage it." Denise positioned herself in front of Archie.

"Now. Whose bag is it?"

Archie refused to give her the satisfaction of a response. Denise signalled Liz to wrench her arms tighter.

"I'll ask you one last time," Denise said, holding her cigarette just short of Archie's eyelid.

"It's yours," Archie said.

"Whose?"

"It's yours, it's yours."

"Don't you forget it. Let her go, Liz. We're done."

CHAPTER 25

I F SHE HADN'T recognized her own clothes, Daphne might never have twigged that the spectre with the mangled face standing at her door was Archie, blue hair or no. There was no evidence of her eyes; they'd been replaced by mere slits, and blood was seeping down onto her lips from her nostrils. Her forehead was so swollen it had developed a Neanderthal ledge. Archie hadn't even been gone from her apartment a full day, but her posture was stooped as if she'd aged sixty years in the interval.

"My God, what happened to you?" Daphne circled her arm around Archie's shoulders to help her in. She could feel her flinch at her touch. "Here, sit here," Daphne said as she led her to the chair closest to the door. She stooped down in front of her and gently took Archie's hands in hers.

"Who did this to you?"

"No one. I fell."

That first cavewoman with a bashed-in face who told her mother that she'd fallen against a kitchen cupboard could never have imagined that her spur-of-the-moment cover-story would become a classic to be picked up and reused by battered women through the centuries. Daphne chose not to push the point. Right now, *who* wasn't the most pressing issue.

She brushed the hair gently out of Archie's face. "Sit tight. I'll call 9-1-1. They'll take you to the hospital, patch you up good as new."

"No, don't call."

"What?"

"Don't call."

"Why on earth not? You need to be looked at."

"I'll be fine. If you'd just let me rest here for a while. I'll be okay." Her words sounded garbled. Daphne wondered if her complement of teeth was still at the requisite thirty-two after the bashing she'd taken.

"Don't be ridiculous. What you need is serious medical attention. A little rest ain't gonna cut it."

Daphne started to dial the three numbers that she had never in her life had occasion to call. She wouldn't end up dialling them this time either. She only got as far as the *nine* when Archie knocked the phone out of her hand and then yelped with pain. Her shoulder seemed to have a serious objection to the effort she had made to keep Daphne from sending out an SOS. Daphne bent down to pick the phone up off the rug and set it on the table. "Okay, okay. I get the message," she said. "No Urgences Santé." She tried to collect her thoughts. With a tissue she gently dabbed at the blood that was dripping onto Archie's mouth so she wouldn't have to keep licking it away. "Look," Daphne said. "How's this for an idea? How about I call you a cab if you'd rather not take an ambulance. You like that better? You won't have to go in with the sirens blaring?" Daphne reached for her phone again.

"Put it down."

"Archie, be reasonable. I'm no miracle worker. This is more than I know how to patch up. The people at Emergency, they'll know what to do. There's nothing to worry about. I wish I could go with you, but my hands are tied, or my feet, I should say."

"With you, without you. It doesn't matter. I won't go. If you call, I'll leave."

"But why?"

"I have my reasons."

"Have you broken the law? Is that it? Are you trying to avoid the police? You can tell me. I'd keep your secret." And she meant it. Lately, Daphne's life had gotten cluttered up with a whole cast of characters who, when it came to the law, were determined to stay under the radar. At this point, what was one more?

"No, nothing like that."

"Then what? What possible reason could you have?"

"I can't explain, but I won't go to hospital."

Probing into Archie's personal life was a losing proposition. Daphne had found that out on her first visit. The last thing she wanted was to wake up in the morning and find Archie gone again, even if, in her current state, she probably couldn't get off the couch without renting a derrick.

"But I don't know how to take care of injuries like these. I don't have a clue where to start even. I could do more damage than good."

"I trust you."

That was all it took for Daphne to melt. If her underground soul sister was willing to put her mutilated body in her hands, how could she turn her away? Besides, she had the feeling that the line of people willing to come to Archie's aid was short to non-existent. Daphne's own line was hardly a mile long, but at least she had one.

"Okay," Daphne said. "I'm in. But let the record show I think you're making a huge mistake." She reached over to help heave Archie out of the chair. "Come on. Let's get you into my bed. We'll clean you up a bit first and then we'll get you into some nice fresh pyjamas. That should make you more comfortable." Daphne instinctively adopted the royal *we* in trying to inch Archie along. It sounded more motherly somehow, more comforting. Maybe it was some subliminal remnant, dredged up from her brain's history channel, of how her own mother had spoken to her in the womb. Daphne supported Archie to the bedroom where she collapsed onto the bed, the last of her strength depleted by a walk of only ten steps.

Sitting at Archie's bedside with a bowl of warm water and a washcloth, dabbing at her patient's face, Daphne felt like she was in a Jane Austen movie. She wished she could offer a treatment more twenty-first century. It was Archie's poor eyes that worried her the most. The lids were swollen far beyond normal bounds, the skin so taut that when she rubbed it ever so gently with the washcloth she feared it might tear. And Daphne could just make out through the slits that the whites of Archie's eyes were the wrong colour, blood-red. Did hemorrhages like those simply cure themselves over time or did Archie's eyes need emergency attention? It turned her stomach when she went to empty the contents of her bowl down the sink, all the clots circling the drain.

In a quick side trip to the kitchen Daphne sliced two paper-thin slices of cucumber that she then placed on Archie's lids. Somewhere on the web she'd once read a beauty tip that it eased puffy eyes, but who was she kidding? Archie was beyond any quack vegetable cure. The cukes were purely self-serving, masking Archie's ravaged eyes from view so that Daphne could proceed with her task of getting her into pyjamas, her stomach unmolested.

"You okay? I'm not hurting you?"

"No, I'm good."

"Shouldn't take too much longer. Just hold on." Her buck-up words were aimed as much at herself as Archie. Her own land-legs weren't much steadier than her patient's.

She gently started to unbutton Archie's blouse, an action which prompted her to recall the night when Theo had last unbuttoned that same blouse when *she* had been wearing it; the night he had quoted his father spouting at the dinner table about Daphne's future qualifications. Her degree, Theo reported, aping his father's windbag tone, wasn't worth the toilet paper it was written on. Of what practical use was archaeology? Could archaeology pay the bills like his son's precious economics degree? Why was the girl wasting her time?

"And what did you say back?" Daphne had asked.

"Nothing. You can't change the guy's mind once he gets rolling. It's best just to let him rant till he flips over to slamming something new."

"So you didn't defend me? You just let him go on mocking me?"

"It wasn't you per se, it was your field."

"What's the difference? When you attack my field, you're attacking me. It doesn't bother you that he has no respect for me? That he calls me 'the girl'? He might as well be saying 'the help.'"

"Who cares what he thinks? He's a clown."

"I care, as it happens."

"Come on, Daff, chill."

"That's all you have to say to me? Chill? You know, it occurs to me, o my knight in tarnished armour, that maybe the reason you didn't bother sticking up for me is because you agree with him."

"That's what you think?"

"Like father like son."

It was that night that they had broken up for the first time, following a battle royale that dug into some dirty corners. The lingering memory of that blow-up was why Daphne had been happy to pass on that particular blouse to Archie when she needed fresh clothes. At the time, Daphne hadn't considered that its bad aura might survive the transfer of ownership and infect Archie, but clearly it had. Now, as if things weren't bad enough, she felt complicit in Archie's troubles. Why hadn't she just thrown it out?

When Daphne began to pull apart the material, undoing the top button, she saw that the upper part of Archie's chest was largely untouched. Maybe the grimmest part of her job was over. But as she worked her way down towards Archie's ribs and stomach the bruises emerged so abundantly they melded together into one massive trauma. All Daphne could do, in her sorrow and inexperience, was dab and clean, keeping a faux-cheerful patter going to Archie as she progressed. But when Daphne unbuttoned the bottom button and saw the two perfect charred circles that were Denise's signature, she rebounded off the bed as if some maniac were coming at *her* with the business end of a cigarette.

"Are you protecting someone? Is that why you don't want to go to hospital? Because the animal who did this to you, he doesn't deserve your protection. He should be locked up."

"I'm not."

"Is that the truth you're telling me?"

"I swear."

"You're not involved with whoever did this to you?"

"No. Believe me."

"In any way?"

"No. I told you."

There was a tremor in Daphne's hands when she returned to Archie's side to finish with the bed bath. She gave up on conversation, afraid of what she might learn, and went about her task like an automaton. Daphne's medicine cabinet was pathetically stocked for the situation in which she found herself. All its shelves offered up to dose Archie with were Midol and aloe vera. Her utter helplessness in alleviating Archie's pain pushed her to try one last time to make her see sense. "Here's what we're going to do," Daphne said. "I'm prepared to let you have your way for tonight, but let's say that if you don't show any improvement by morning, you'll go to Emergency. Okay?" She waited for a response. Archie didn't agree. She didn't disagree. The patient was fast asleep.

Daphne kept watch by the bed all night to make sure Archie didn't stop breathing. She was beyond sleep, her unquiet mind torturing her with alternating lashes of guilt and panic and stupidity. Maybe the delay in treatment she'd been railroaded into granting was aggravating Archie's injuries. Maybe Daphne had compromised crucial evidence in scrubbing Archie up. She should have put her foot down, that's what she should have done, insisted Archie go to hospital. The girl wasn't in her right mind to make a decision on her own. Why had she let herself be pushed? By morning, Daphne was so bleary-eyed with exhaustion she could have done with a pair of cucumber slices for herself.

Her injured charge, on the other hand, slept straight through, though her night was also troubled. Heart-rending moans emerged from her lips whenever she tried to shift position, and she shouted out from time to time, in the throes of a nightmare. Daphne would have paid good money to see the action playing out in those nightmares. Horning in on Archie's subconscious was the only way she would ever find out what she had gone through. For sure the conscious Archie wasn't about to divulge the truth of the matter.

In the light of day, the prostrate Archie looked worse than she had the day before, if that was even possible. Her abraded face resembled tartare, her eyes over-ripe plums that had burst under the sun.

"How are you feeling?" Daphne asked her when she finally showed some signs of life towards noon.

"Peachy."

"All evidence to the contrary."

"You've been sitting here all night?"

"Where else would I be?"

"I'll be out of your hair soon, I promise."

"Don't worry about that. Let's just concentrate on getting you better."

"Could I have something to drink please?"

"Sure, sweetie, here, sip some water." Daphne held the straw to her lips and Archie took a long draft. The novice nurse didn't know what to make of her request. Extreme thirst. Was that a good sign? A bad one?

"You hungry?" she asked. "You should probably put something in your tummy." Archie tried to shake her head *no*, but even that much exertion was too much for her and she shrank back into the pillow.

That midday flirt with alertness was just a tease. Archie fell into a dead sleep and didn't rouse again till evening. Daphne profited from all those bedside hours struggling to figure out what she could say once she awoke to persuade her to accept treatment. It wasn't an easy assignment Daphne set herself; this wasn't a no-account marketing blog she was composing; it was life and death. She had to strike the perfect balance between compelling and un-pushy, and after hours of mental redacting, she nailed it. It was a gentle speech, nicely low-key. But when Archie snapped awake at seven thirty, clutching her stomach, gripped with pain, Daphne just spewed out the unexpurgated version. "I don't give a shit what you say. You're not going to be taken out of here in a body bag while I have anything to say about it. You'll go to Emergency if I have to tie a rope around your ankle and drag you there myself."

What Daphne hoped was that after all those hours in bed with only the pain for company, Archie might change her tune, but apparently her stubborn streak survived the beating unscathed.

"I'll leave if you want, but I won't go to a hospital." It was an empty threat. Archie could no more walk out of Daphne's apartment than the fridge could. Daphne could have called Urgences Santé and had her carted out on a gurney, but she was resistant to cutting the cord. She sat quietly for a bit, considering her options.

"What if I told you," she said, "that I could have you looked over by a doctor, but you wouldn't have to go to a clinic or the hospital, no paperwork, no nothing. Would you agree then?"

"Who would be willing to see me that way?"

"Leave it to me," Daphne said. "I have friends in high places."

■ ■ ■

"Did you get a car?"

"Yeah," Marius said. "I have a Communauto parked out front. So what's this mysterious favour?"

"I just wanted you to drive my friend to my grandmother's house. She's feeling a bit under the weather. I didn't want to put her in a cab."

If that was so, she could have said as much on the phone. It was hardly a state secret. No, there had to be more to it than her needing a simple shuttle service. Even now that he was Daphne's co-conspirator, involved up to his elbows in her unauthorized escape from the Underground City, she still was only willing to parcel out information to him on an as-needed basis.

"Okay, if she has to go, let's boogie."

Daphne led him into the bedroom where she had Archie dressed and propped up against some pillows. All the manhandling with armholes and zippers had been too much for her and she fell back to sleep. When Marius first set eyes on Archie, he thought he might gag. Her skin looked like she had put it on inside out.

"Jesus, Daphne, why did you bother asking me to come? You should have called 9-1-1 right off."

"She won't let me."

"Why not?"

"She has her reasons."

"And you listened to her? What are you, crazy? Why didn't you use the sense God gave you?" In his shock over the gargoyle occupying Daphne's bed, he forgot to walk on eggshells with her like he normally did.

"You're right. I know. But I'm stuck."

"Why would you have me take her to Nora's? What can she do for her there?"

"I thought Emmanuel could take a look at her."

"Emmanuel?"

"He's a doctor."

"I know, but what'll he use if he has to do stitches? Your grandmother's sewing kit? Besides, she probably needs x-rays."

"Nothing's broken. She can wiggle all her fingers and toes."

"And you got your medical degree where? Remind me? For all we know she shouldn't even be moved in her condition."

"Look, I know it's nuts, but I'm at my wit's end. I don't know what else to do. She categorically refuses to go to a hospital or a clinic. She won't tell me why. My suspicion is that she doesn't want to have to show ID anywhere. I'm just speculating though. I have absolutely no idea what her deal is. I thought she might be in an abusive relationship, but she swears no. Maybe she just looked cross-eyed at the wrong person, and he lit into her. Your guess is as good as mine."

"What about her family? Where are they? I can take her to them if you want, instead."

"I don't know anything about her family. I don't know if she even has any."

It struck Marius as passing strange that Daphne had a woman who was battered, bruised, and bloodied snoring away in her bed, a woman she referred to as her friend, yet she seemed to know next to nothing about her. "So you two go way back, do you?" he asked.

Daphne was too frazzled to play games. "If you would call the day before yesterday way back, then yes."

"You met her only the day before yesterday?" If Marius had any reason to doubt that Daphne and Nora came from the same gene pool, here was his proof that they did. Each was fitted out with the same type of in-built electro-magnet that pulled in the most wretched of strangers bunking out anywhere in their postal code so they could place them under their protection.

"Strictly speaking, yes. I mean we only exchanged names then. But I sort of knew her before."

"How do you sort of know somebody?"

Daphne let it all hang out, describing her first literal run-in with Archie at the Y and her subsequent sightings of her scavenging at various food courts. "I don't know what it was, but I felt some kind of weird kinship with her. I know that sounds crazy but I wanted to help her if I could. It was like a compulsion. If you knew me better, you'd appreciate that that kind of behaviour is very un-me, but somehow I couldn't help myself. Anyway, I never actually caught up with her or spoke to her, just spotted her here and there until that day you and I were having coffee together at the Tunnel Espresso Bar. You remember? When I took off running after somebody? Well, that was her."

"Yeah, I remember all right. You were jet-propelled."

"For all the good it did me. I lost her in the crowd at the train station. But then, out of the blue, the day before yesterday, I caught up with her at the Cathedral and she agreed to come over for supper. We hit it off. Then boom, the very next day after I take her under my wing, some freako beats her up, and she finds her way back here. Don't ask me how. She can barely put one foot in front of the other. I just want to cry when I picture it. Some bargain-basement guardian angel I turned out to be."

That narrative was enough to bring Marius onside. He finessed Archie into a wheeled desk chair, trundled her out to the car, and delivered her to a safe house that was already bursting at the seams.

CHAPTER 26

They didn't have to play open anymore. Emmanuel and his wife Yvonne were quick studies. Every night after the kids were tucked in, they cleared off the table, shifting all the legal paperasse, the schoolbooks, and the Lego constructions to their temporary second home in the green laundry basket so they could make room for the mahjong game. It had gotten so they all looked forward to the ritual that let the four of them wind down at the end of the day, shoving aside their various worries while they focussed on nothing more consequential than which tile to discard.

The mah-jong set Anthony had brought Nora home from Vancouver in his hand-baggage was probably over-the-top, considering the stage in their relationship. It was an antique set, imported from the motherland. The mahogany box with brass fittings didn't have the usual North American attaché-case profile. It sat upright on the table, and had five slim, satin-lined drawers, one above the other. Its profile suggested an heiress's jewellery box, meant to house pearl necklaces and cameos rather than game tiles. When Anthony caught sight of it in the shop, among all the lower-level tchotchkes surrounding it, he was helpless to resist.

"Oh my God, Anthony," Nora said once she had undone the wrapping. "It's so beautiful. You shouldn't have. It must have cost the earth."

He had wanted to say something romantic back, something flowery and suave like, "you're worth the earth and the stars and the moon to me." Instead he'd said, "not really." An opportunity missed.

Anthony was the only outsider Nora invited into her confidence about her basement visitors. To him it made perfect sense that his open-hearted Nora would rush to the aid of a family in distress, welcoming them into her home whose address he was at long last privy to. When Nora showed off the gift she'd received from him to Emmanuel and Yvonne, they expressed an interest in learning how to play mah-jong and Anthony and Nora accommodated them. Around the table they established a quiet communion, and the Demels took that first tentative step towards reconstructing out of local materials the extended family that they had lost.

"It's Grace's birthday today," Yvonne announced one night at the mah-jong table, while they were rebuilding their walls.

"Grace?" Anthony asked.

"Our eldest. We lost her to the war back home." Emmanuel sat across the table from her, holding her gaze. "She was such a good girl," Yvonne continued. "Always helped her mother. And an excellent student. The schoolmasters all praised her. Never without a book. She was going to be a teacher when she grew up." Yvonne's next sentence she directed to her husband. "Do you remember that time she walked into a wall she was so engrossed in her book? How embarrassed she was?"

Now that she brought it up, Emmanuel did remember, but his mind, when it came to Grace, was fixed forever on her last day, the day he failed her utterly. That one blood-spattered memory effaced all the others.

"It's a terrible thing to outlive your child," Nora was able to say from misery born of experience, though her son was a grown man when he was taken from her, already a father, master of his own decisions, even that cursed final one. Nora had a hole in her heart just like Yvonne did, a hole that corresponded exactly to the shape of a lost child; a hole whose edges never knit together no matter how long ago the loss. At least, Nora thought, Yvonne had her other children to give her a reason to carry on whereas she had lost her one and only child. But Nora didn't offer that up to the table. This wasn't a competition.

A hush settled over them. No one wanted to suggest resuming play. It seemed impertinent. They stared unseeing at the jumble of tiles, their respective ghosts flexing their muscles, when the doorbell rang.

Nora had never minded the bell. Proselytizers, kids shaking charity cans, peddlers of paint jobs and brick pointing; she didn't begrudge any of them their ten minutes on her threshold. She was always up for a bit of conversation. But ever since Daphne had planted in her mind the idea that Immigration might turn up to round her visitors up and set them on the next plane home, a coolness had developed between her and her doorbell. Would those types ring, though? she wondered as she made her way up the stairs from the basement. Wouldn't they just break down the door like they did on TV?

It was a relief, then, to peer through the peephole and see that it was Marius on the stoop. He was a good sort, Marius. Even if Daphne didn't have the wit to take to this fellow, she'd warmed to him right away. No airs about him. Theo, on the other hand, a typical Daphne pick, was puffed up with enough air to resist gravity. It was too bad the kids were asleep downstairs. They had been captivated by Marius when he came by the day that Daphne had played hooky from the Underground City. He'd goofed around with them like the best of older brothers. Nora often felt a stab of regret on the children's behalf, living in an isolation booth essentially of her making. Maybe Daphne was right; if they were living in a church, at least there would be a community, people coming and going, stimulation, but at the time it had seemed like the best solution, the only solution. Nora stashed her guilt temporarily behind her and opened the door. Her dilemma wasn't about to solve itself now. She was eager to put the kettle on so they could all catch up.

"Daphne sent us," Marius said. He felt like he was at a speakeasy and this was the password.

"Us?" Nora looked down from Marius's face and saw that there sharing the stoop with him was a young woman sitting in a wheeled desk chair of all things. Her face looked like she'd been outmatched in a title bout with Muhammad Ali.

"Daphne thought Emmanuel could look Archie over," he said tipping his head down to indicate his fellow visitor. "She's had a bit of a rough time."

"Of course, come in, come in." Marius jigged the chair up the final step and rolled Archie into the living room. Nora called down to summon Emmanuel and Yvonne. Normally it made her nervous to have them come upstairs; she was worried that they'd be seen, but this was an emergency. Nora had always trusted her neighbours, but now that she had something to hide, her old complacency took a turn. It was probably a side-effect of too many late-night movies about Occupied Paris where neighbours regularly ratted out old friends for no more than a pair of silk stockings or a turnip. Her situation wasn't precisely comparable, she knew, but one couldn't be too vigilant.

Emmanuel stooped down and took one long appraising look at Archie slouched in her chair, and said, "The hospital, I think. That would be best."

"No." Archie and Marius cried out in unison. "That isn't possible," Marius clarified. "Archie needs this to stay between us, if you follow me. That's why we're here." Emmanuel absorbed the pleading look in the orbs that were passing as Archie's eyes and nodded his consent. Nora went around pulling the curtains to while the men shifted Archie from the chair to the couch.

"So, young lady," Emmanuel said, "you have a very unusual wheelchair. Your desk must be wondering what became of it." The corner of Archie's lip twitched up a millimetre, suggesting what might have been intended as a smile, but which torqued into a grimace once the muscles of her cheeks got involved. The doctor took note. The diagnostic part of Emmanuel's brain hadn't had much of a professional workout since he came to Canada. There wasn't any demand for it at the job he'd held before going underground that had him pressure-washing trucks. He was afraid it might have atrophied in the interval, but now that it was called for, it obligingly snapped back into service. Emmanuel kept a gentle patter going while he palpated so that Archie didn't have to be bothered to speak. His hands told him what he needed to know.

It felt good to be a doctor again even if in an hour it would all be over. It was a welcome blip in the alternating boredom and tension that characterized the bizarre half-life he lived with the family members that remained to him. When first he came to Canada, legal and aboveboard, he was prepared to jump through all the hoops the College of Physicians put in front on him to be able to qualify, but with his cousin's conviction those hoops were repossessed, and here he was, holed up in the basement of a woman who he had barely known to say *bonjour* to before all their troubles began. Every morning when he woke up and took in his surroundings, his situation shocked him afresh. He was grateful to Nora, absolutely, but sometimes he wondered how long he could survive in the uncertainty of his circumstances. There were others, he knew, who lived year upon undocumented year this way, but why was he given a life on earth if not to serve? What good did he do, of what benefit was he to humanity? All he did was exist. But at least now he had a patient before him and he would draw on every ounce of skill he possessed to restore her to health.

Emmanuel examined her fully, or at least as fully as he could minus all the high-powered diagnostic equipment that a hospital would have provided, and when he was done, he sat down in the desk chair, rolled himself up to the couch, and took Archie by the hand. He called out to the others who had been waiting in the kitchen to give them a measure of privacy. "You are very lucky, young lady. Very lucky. There are no internal injuries that I can detect. I'm not saying your situation isn't serious, but nothing that strictly speaking requires that you go to hospital. At least not for the present time. My opinion is that the damage should heal with time and rest. I am fairly sure that there will be no complications arising from this..." Only here did he falter. *Accident* was the word he eventually landed on. He turned to the others in the room. "I feel confident that we can bring her out of this."

"So you're saying I won't be taking her back to Daphne's?" Marius asked.

"Not for now," Emmanuel said, his glance brushing ever so lightly over Marius's knuckles. "She does need treatment and I want to keep a tight watch over her for a while, make sure she's stable."

"We'll give her all the TLC she needs," Nora said, looking to Yvonne to second her. "Not to worry."

Yvonne had always acted like a little mouse in Nora's basement. She was a woman living in another woman's house; not her mother's house, not her mother-in-law's house, not her daughter's house, and she felt keenly the absence of any precise role cut out for her. But with the arrival of this stranger, on her beloved Grace's birthday of all days, she now understood exactly why God had placed her there.

CHAPTER 27

E MMANUEL THOUGHT she needed medicines. And she did. Nora thought she needed food. And she did. But Yvonne was the one who knew what she really needed, this friable young woman. Love. She was operating on empty. It was no disparagement of Emmanuel's professional competence that uncredentialled Yvonne was the one to come up with the proper diagnosis. If he had been in a position to run the full gamut of lab tests, the deficiency would have been flagged to him on the results. It was fortunate for Archie that Yvonne's x-ray vision allowed her to see beyond the bruises and lacerations to the nub of what was ailing her.

Under Emmanuel's guidance, Nora, Anthony, and Yvonne worked to nudge Archie's recovery forward, but it was Yvonne who did the lion's share. She stationed herself by Archie's bedside and served as the patient's nurse, orderly, and right arm. It was she who applied the salves Emmanuel had Marius fetch from Pharmaprix. It was she who spoon-fed Archie the protein purées Nora whizzed up in her blender, and mopped up the dribbles that trailed down her chin. If the pain pills did a job on Archie's stomach, it was Yvonne who held the bucket. She did, in short, what any mother would do; any mother within the normal parameters for the species, that is.

Though she rebelled against acknowledging her as such, Archie did have a mother of her own, after a fashion. Elsa. If called upon to show proof of their relationship, Elsa could have produced the appropriate paperwork. And even if Archie were to rise up and challenge its authenticity at the top of her lungs, a cheek swab would confirm that yes, the pair of them did share the same genetic bits and bobs. Biologically and legalistically speaking, there was no denying that she was the woman who had given birth to Archie. But in Elsa's case, *mother* was purely titular. She wasn't given to all those bothersome extracurriculars that went along with mothering: protecting, for example, cherishing and nurturing. So it was a completely new experience for Archie to be properly mothered by Yvonne, a true adept. The unfortunate upshot was that Archie had no desire to recover. Ever. The pain was a small price to pay. She could happily stay cocooned in the basement till the end of time if it meant she could have Yvonne in her corner. But things didn't pan out quite as Archie planned. Her body refused to accept the boss's directive, and made its own independent decision to mend, albeit in slow, halting steps, aided every step of the way by Nora's pit crew.

With the addition of Archie to the ménage on rue Melançon, Nora's busyness level ratcheted up off the charts. Between cooking for a crowd morning, noon, and night, staying on top of all the supplies from the pharmacy and the grocery, keeping the neighbours at bay, Skyping with Daphne, stretching the bank balance with water and bread crumbs, and the thousand and one other balls she had to keep in the air, Nora was a blur in her kitchen command post. Anthony took what he could off her plate but his talents didn't align with her needs. Where Nora most required a second set of hands was on meal prep duty. It was the most onerous and unrelenting of all her activities now that she had an overfull house, but it turned out that Anthony was completely *nul* in the kitchen, an all-thumbs impediment to the smooth assembly and distribution of breakfast, lunch, and dinner. She banished him with no little regret from the kitchen and sent him down to the pleasant anarchy that was the basement to take his marching orders from Yvonne.

The mah-jong king was more than welcome below stairs. Yvonne was in the market for a part-time surrogate to post beside Archie for the times when she was tied up tending to the needs of her own family. Emmanuel pitched in as much as he could, but he usually had his nose buried in one of the fat law tomes Marius had lugged over from the library, hunting for the loophole that would allow his family to emerge into the legal light of day. Anthony stepped into the breach. His assignment was to keep Archie entertained so she wouldn't doze her days away for lack of stimulation. How he was meant to satisfy this assignment, though, she left to his discretion.

Straight-up conversation, Anthony's first choice, went nowhere. Archie was a hoarder, socking away all her chat for Yvonne. He tried rattling on as a monologist but he even bored himself. Board games required more of an attention span than she had yet built up, and when he got them started on a jigsaw puzzle, the pieces kept dropping down into the folds of her bedding, and he could hardly go poking around her to fish them out. He even went so far as to try teaching her the sign language he'd used as a child to communicate with his deaf auntie, but it too was a no-go. Anthony sat next to Archie's mattress, despairing. He couldn't fail at this, his second deployment in Nora's house now that he'd flunked out in the kitchen. She might start wondering why she was wasting her time on such a good-for-nothing, and she'd be right.

For lack of a more inspired choice, he started reading to Archie out of the newspaper that fwapped onto Nora's front steps every morning. He knew it was too geezerish an activity; young people didn't connect with newsprint nowadays, but against the odds Archie took to it. She wasn't much for the news or business sections, but she liked the sports pages and the horoscopes, and was happy to assist when Anthony hit a brick wall in the crosswords. Their sessions together had the perfect rhythm. He'd read a bit, she'd drift off a bit, he'd read some more. It wasn't what you'd call participatory, he was the one who did the majority of the talking, but he could sense that his charge was engaged despite her silence. Which was why he thought he was hearing voices the day a full sentence floated up from the pillow.

"So you're Daphne's grandfather," she said, trying to get the dramatis personae in proper alignment.

Archie's assumption of longstanding coupledom between him and Nora, which he reported upstairs in the kitchen, both tickled them and aroused them.

"It's too bad," he joked with Nora, "that except for our mah-jong games, I'm usually stuck downstairs and you up. If I ever want to see more of you, I'll have to move in."

"Good idea," she said. And so it was settled. For once in his life, the suitor who couldn't shoot straight had stumbled into saying exactly the right thing.

■■■

Philippe, Yvonne and Emmanuel's youngest, was a prodigy. At seven months of age, he already seemed to know how to tell time. In the middle of the night, when the clock struck 2:30, not 2:31, not 2:29, he popped awake, bawling his lungs out for a feed. Most nights, Yvonne lifted him up out of the cushioned bureau drawer that served as his crib and took him back to bed with her. But now and again, if she noticed that Archie was fretful, she snuggled herself in beside her while she nursed and the two of them held whispery conversations. These were Archie's favourite times in the basement, her private tête-à-têtes with Yvonne, Philippe shlurping away in the background.

"His table manners need work, don't they?" Archie said.

"You're right," Yvonne answered. "He'll never get anywhere in life eating like that."

"What do you think he'll be when he grows up, a big guy like him?" Archie asked.

The *what* question was altogether less preoccupying for Yvonne than the *where* question. Sometimes she couldn't help but picture her baby all grown up, taller than his father, the first stirrings of a moustache accessorizing his upper lip, but still there in the basement, sleeping curled up like a snail in the drawer that used to hold Daphne's socks. Yvonne rubbed her lips against his hair. "I don't care," she said to Archie, "he can be anything. I just want him to grow up, that's all."

They were both staring at the baby, that future prime minister or farmer or hedge-fund manager, when Archie asked her next question. She'd been storing it up for a good while. She might have put it to Yvonne when she was ministering to her during the day, there were opportunities enough, but her intuition warned her this was a question that required the shield of darkness.

"Who's Grace?" she asked.

Yvonne stiffened. The baby ingested his mother's distress and started to fuss.

"How do you know about Grace? Did Emmanuel talk to you about her?"

"No, never. It's you. You call me by that name sometimes."

"I do?"

"Once in a while. At night mostly. I don't mind." In fact she loved when Yvonne called her Grace, her voice brimming with tenderness. Even if the name rightfully belonged to someone else, Archie didn't feel as if she was hacking into affection that wasn't earmarked for her. On some level she knew that she and this Grace, whoever she was, were conflated in Yvonne's heart.

"Grace was my daughter."

Was. Archie digested the tense. She had imagined otherwise, a family member separated from them in the chaos of their flight from their home country, some beloved sister or cousin left behind, never to be seen again. But now Archie's mind made the leap from Emmanuel's scars to Yvonne's *was*, and Grace's final agonies revealed themselves to her as if she had been there.

Where did she get off prying? It went against all the rules of the basement which was a don't-ask-don't-tell zone. No one there had any inkling of the ugly particulars of her past prior to the beating, nor did anyone push her to divulge them. And what did she do in return to these people, strangers just weeks before, who fed her, helped her wipe her ass, sacrificed the choicest mattress for her, crowded their own children together so she could have greater comfort and privacy? What did she do? She took a sharp stick and poked it into their intimate sorrow. She'd suspected all along that the name *Grace* was riddled with risk, but she'd gone ahead and plugged Yvonne with the question anyway, granting her curiosity free rein to trample her better judgment. She should never have said the name aloud, shoving the memory of Yvonne's late daughter to the forefront of her mind.

Archie was still a bit hazy on mothers, even with the benefit of the crash course she was getting from Yvonne. She had no way of knowing that the subject of Grace was like a caul that enveloped Yvonne's brain. Yvonne's every thought carried with it trace elements of Grace. So Archie needn't have berated herself for reminding Yvonne of her daughter. A reminder was redundant. In fact her inquiry gave Yvonne the exquisite pleasure of talking about Grace out loud, giving her substance to someone who had never met her.

"You remind me of her," Yvonne said, "a good girl, smart, and kind, but headstrong. I feel like I have a piece of her back in you, Archie."

"Archie doesn't exist," the invalid whispered back in expiation. "My name is Chantal."

It was a start.

CHAPTER 28

"DID YOU FIND the bag?"

"I found *a* bag," Marius said. "I don't know if it's *the* bag." He held it up to Daphne for show-and-tell, a crumpled buff-coloured Bureau en Gros bag indistinguishable from thousands of others around the city that had been repurposed for lunches and poop pickup.

"Did those she-wolves give you any trouble? You look to be all in one piece."

"I lucked out. No one was home. They must have been out pummelling someone else."

"I can't tell you how relieved I am. I was worried sick the whole time you were gone about you running into that pair. And may I just add that you were heroic to take on this assignment?"

"Hardly heroic," he said, but her words made their mark. Daphne wasn't profligate in the compliment department. This was the first time in the history of their acquaintance that she'd ever floated one in his direction. It was a day to star in his calendar.

"So what's in the bag? I assume you already took a peek. Can I see?" That it was a privacy faux-pas to nose around inside the mystery bag that contained Archie's stash of personals, Daphne was aware, but since she was the one who'd organized the rescue mission to retrieve it, she felt entitled to a quick look-see.

"You're going to be disappointed. It's just some junk." Marius rooted around. "A half used-up roll of Lifesavers, a toothbrush, a T-shirt, and a stuffy."

"A what?"

"A stuffy, look." And like some down-on-his-luck magician he reached into the Bureau en Gros bag and pulled out a stuffed rabbit that was missing one ear. The poor bunny had been through the wars. He might have sported a paunch once, but now he was a gaunt little thing, the result no doubt of years of over-squeezing. His colour was up for debate. On the Toys"R"Us shelf, at the beginning, he might have been white, or a sweet Easter-chick yellow maybe, but now he had the off-colour of downtown slush. His fur had fallen out in patches as if he'd just started chemo.

Marius dangled the ear-challenged bunny up in the air between them, holding it by the tips of his fingers so as not to pollute himself by close contact. They considered it, then each other. "So am I to understand," he finally said to her, "that she was willing to face off against those two crackheads for the sake of this crappy stuffy?"

Daphne took the maligned bunny from him, and cuddled it in her arms. She stuck her nose in its belly and took a good sniff. The odour was piquantly sour, but Daphne's sour may have been Archie's roses.

"All I know," she said, "is that Yvonne told my grandmother that Archie longed for some bag she'd had to leave behind, that those women who beat her up had taken it."

"And then Nora told you and you told me. Maybe something got lost in the transmission?"

"I don't think so."

Their thoughts seemed to be moving in the same direction, but Marius took the lead in articulating their mutual worry.

"How old did you say Archie is?"

"I didn't."

"Well how old do you think she is?"

"I don't know. Twenty maybe. Twenty-one. You've seen her."

"When I saw her, her face looked like it needed resurfacing. I'm in no position to judge."

"Well, if you'd seen her in her normal state, healthy, filled out, you would agree with me."

"But you never actually asked her her age."

"No, why would I?"

"Well, what about when you talked. How did she strike you?"

"Grown-up. Mature."

"Mature?"

"Ish," she felt obliged to qualify.

"Daphne," Marius said, tired of dancing around it, "do you think it's possible that all this time we've been harbouring a runaway?"

"No. No way. Archie's no kid."

"You sure? Because if she is, we could be in such deep shit."

This wasn't happening. Why couldn't she be trapped with an ankle tracker in ancient Cappadocia where her biggest worries would have been trying to balance a wine flask on her head and making sure all her goats were milked, not whether the police were going to swoop down to repossess all the various combinations and permutations of fugitives she had in her care offshore. Daphne would have given anything to be living in a cave network back in Byzantine days where they weren't big on blogging. She wouldn't have to be wasting her time churning out daily Internet reports about Underground City rubbish when her future was teetering on a tightrope without a net. What misbegotten protective impulse had ever led her to invite that girl into her life, if indeed she was just a girl. That topic was still under debate.

None of the missing-children sites she and Marius proceeded to pore over together had an APB out for anyone resembling Archie, proof positive to Daphne that their convalescent was above the age of majority. Marius, though, refused to knuckle under simply because they'd come up with nothing. By his tortured logic, overheavy on the negatives, nothing didn't prove that there wasn't something.

"Face facts," Daphne said. "No frantic parents are out there looking for her. No cops. If they were, she'd be listed on one of these sites. It's like I said. She's not a kid."

"There are tons of reasons why she might not be listed."

"Such as?"

"That I couldn't tell you. I'm just going with my gut here."

"It's still that stuffy thing with you, isn't it?" she said.

"Okay. So tell me, then. Why would a grown woman, someone mature like you say, put her life on the line for a stuffy, for God's sake," he said. "Especially one that looks like roadkill."

"You don't get it. Looks don't matter with those things. It's all olfactory, tactile. Don't you see kids all the time dragging around tattered stuffed animals and blankies, gross-looking things they won't part with without throwing a fit? They won't even let their parents put them through the wash. And you know why? Because at night, in the dark, even if they can't see them, they know they're there from the smell and the feel, staving off the monsters, like it says in their job descriptions.

"You don't have to be a kid to want to hold on to something like that, something that's always comforted you and protected you, especially if life has kicked you around the block a few times too many, and I think our Archie qualifies on that score. You could be thirty and still want to keep it near.

"So what I say is this," Daphne went on, "minus any proof to the contrary, we just have to operate on the assumption that Archie's not a minor, and we're not accessories after the fact. No one's going to put us in the slammer." Her mind took a brief unauthorized side trip to Nora's other illicit basement residents. It pulled up a snapshot of the Demels, posed formally as if for an old-timey family photo, tinted in sepia. Yvonne was seated with Philippe in her arms, Emmanuel standing behind, his hand on her shoulder, Bérénice and Paul sitting tailor style at their feet, all of them in prison stripes. "Not for that anyway."

"Says the expert."

"Marius, let it go."

"I can't. And I don't see how you can. Do you remember on one of those sites we saw somewhere when we were trawling through the web it said that there were over two thousand runaways in Canada last year. Two thousand! But on those missing kid sites, there were only posters for a fraction of that number. What about all the rest of those kids? Even if they're not listed, somebody out there must be worried sick about them, wondering if they're dead or alive."

"At the risk of sounding heartless, it's not our concern about the rest of them right now. It's only Archie we care about and she's an adult in the eyes of the law, stuffy or no."

■ ■ ■

It was not solely at Daphne's that Archie was the controversy du jour. In a different underground spot in the city, a set-to between Emmanuel and Yvonne had their blue-maned patient at its core as well.

"You think I don't see what's happening?" Emmanuel said.

"Just what do you see happening?" Yvonne snapped back. She had been hoping to forestall this conversation, but now that it reared its head she wasn't about to back off. They were jammed in the laundry room, their refuge within a refuge, so they could sound off in private, but even doored off from the others they had to keep their voices muted, giving a hushed intensity to their argument.

"You're getting too close to her."

"So that's your assessment, Doctor? You see that as a bad thing?"

"Yes, if I am to be honest. It is."

"I'm simply taking care of her, nursing her as best I can. Bed rest and bedpans."

"No one is faulting the quality of your care."

"Don't patronize me."

"You know very well it's not your nursing I'm talking about."

"What then?"

"You are going to make me say it?"

"Why shouldn't you?" Yvonne said. "Go on. Let me hear it."

"All right, if you have this need to make me say it, I will. It's not Archie you're lavishing your care on. It's our Grace."

"And how is that any different? Do you want me to treat Archie less well, because she's not Grace? Is that what you want?"

"You're putting words in my mouth."

"Because that would be very strange coming from a doctor who advocated treating every patient as if he were a member of his own family. Nothing less would do. Is that not what you always said? But I see now there's a catch. Every patient except Archie deserves the full and proper treatment? If I understood you wrongly, then explain."

"You're deliberately off point."

"Not to my mind."

"I want that girl to be well as much as you do. I want to give someone a better life out of the shambles of ours so our stay in this godforsaken basement will have been worth something." He raised his voice as much as he dared. "I can't believe you'd imply otherwise."

"But that's exactly what we are doing."

"We're healing her, yes. But that's not our present issue."

"The present issue being Grace."

"No, not Grace, you," Emmanuel said

"Me? I'm the issue? I'm the issue?"

"Yes, you. It's you who has transformed her into Grace. You even call her by that name. Yes, I've heard, so don't bother pretending otherwise. To you, she's Grace reborn. And I don't blame you. It's natural that you would want to mother her. But one day soon, either she will have to leave this sanctuary of ours, or we will. Do you think you will be able to tolerate a separation like that a second time?"

Grace had reached out to both of her parents using Archie as her medium, but unlike his wife, Emmanuel programmed his software to block the signal. Refusing to let himself accept that his daughter's essence was there in the room with them, cozily spooning with Archie on her mattress, kept his guilt alive as was only proper. Let his wife revel in their daughter's gauzy presence in the basement, he would not share her illusion. But Yvonne knew him better than he knew himself.

"Will you?"

CHAPTER 29

"IT'S KAPUT, MADAME." The workman delivered his folksy requiem for Nora's roof. "I've shovelled it off and patched it as best I could, but that won't solve your problem anymore. It's too far gone. Those gaps up there are big enough to stick your head through and they'll only get worse. If you don't deal with them pronto, one day soon you'll be sleeping in your bed and you'll hear a crash and next thing you know you'll be looking up at the stars. Unless you'll be dead, of course." The roofer and his tar bucket were frequent visitors to Nora's house over the years layering patches on top of patches like a shtetl tailor, but she'd held back on calling him this time, sensing that he'd finally be hitting her up for the full monty, not some stopgap band-aid job.

When she'd felt a steady drip drip drip of water on her nose during the night, she thought at first she was dreaming. Nora had an active dream-life, although to be completely accurate it wasn't as much dreaming as horizontal thinking. Even asleep, she orchestrated what was going on in her head. She never allowed herself to fall into a deep REM sleep. It was an extravagance she couldn't afford. Only at night in bed did she have the downtime to plot out on the giant whiteboard in her mind how she was going to get through the next day. It was known to happen though, very occasionally, that she indulged herself overnight with the odd fanciful scenario; Daphne walking across the stage in her cap and gown to accept her degree, the Demels getting their papers, Archie landing on her feet, she and Anthony opening up a B & B whose almond-crusted French toast would be touted far and wide by Tripadvisor, but since none of those nighttime flights of fancy had a water feature attached to it, she came to the realization in short order that the dripping she felt was not a figment of her imagination, but in the here and now.

Anthony offered to do the manly thing. "I'll go up there. Shovel off the snow. That should help."

"Like hell you will." Nora's normal composure was unravelling as she envisioned the scrim of mould that would soon be horning in on the floral pattern of the upstairs wallpaper. "All I need is for you to fall off and break a leg. One patient in this house is all I can handle. Just set out the buckets to catch the leaks."

Emmanuel volunteered next, despite the burden of an arm that only inconsistently did his bidding. The gesture was appreciated but Nora refused. If she wasn't going to send a seventy-plus-year-old up to the roof, she certainly wasn't going to send up Emmanuel. The doctor was not geographically cut out for snow removal, especially the high-altitude variation that was traditionally undertaken without guy-wires or protective gear, simply bullheaded confidence, a beer, and a shovel. But since, out of the theoretically vast pool of potential local snow shovellers, Nora could come up with no candidates who would undertake the work gratis, she broke down and called the roofer.

His verdict came at a bad time. Was there ever a good time? Nora's fridge and furnace, hoary the pair of them, had long been in a friendly competition as to which one of them would last the longest, and now it looked like the furnace was going to claim the title. Just a few days before Mother Nature attacked Nora's roof with a hole puncher, Nora's fridge, its Alzheimer's progressing faster than she'd anticipated, had forgotten how to keep its contents cold. It happened just before the weekend, natch, when it was full to the brim with the weekly Friday grocery haul which represented a serious outlay. The service man couldn't come till Tuesday, but ironically, the same weather that had done in her roof came to her aid in this instance. Anthony helped Nora drag all her food out to the front porch where they stacked it up and packed snow all around it as if they were on a winter camping trip. With the temperature in the negative digits, all her edibles would survive nicely. Except that when Nora went outside the next morning to get some milk to wet her All Bran, everything they had carted out front was gone save for a half empty jar of half-sours.

Nora's quartier was a bit ragged around the edges. She knew that realtors referred to it neutrally as *in transition*, leaving it to the clients to make up their own minds as to whether it was upwards or downwards. Sure, the odd car disappeared from an alleyway from time to time, the occasional bicycle went walkabout, but Nora had never felt anything but safe in her home, her possessions, such as they were, entirely secure. That her opinion was not shared by the newer residents of the neighbourhood was clear, with their alarm signs sprouting up out of their front gardens like some new variety of tulip. And now it looked like they might be right. She had been the victim of a barefaced robbery just outside her front window by a pickle-hating thief whose boot prints revealed that he wore Sorels, size eleven, and that he over-pronated. Anthony's podiatric sleuthing in the snow served no practical purpose, even if he was trying to be useful in tracking down the burglar. She couldn't turn his forensic evidence over to the police and have them sniffing around. Too much was at risk. She'd just have to swallow the loss and restock. A trip to the supermarket, and all this would be behind her.

No such luck. Restocking turned out to be the least of her worries. When the appliance guy showed up and asked the fridge to cough, he looked up into Nora's face with compassion, as he always did when he had to pronounce the dreaded c-word. A compressor was a big-ticket item, but it was that or spring for a new refrigerator, he said. Your pick.

It got so Nora couldn't stomach the sight of a repair van. Whenever she passed a parked one in her travels, she had the urge to pull out a key and run the tip of it across the paint job. Not that she would ever act on it. The repairmen weren't to blame, she knew; time was the guilty party. Nora's house had served her well, but it had now reached the stage where it belonged in a retirement community with 24/7 nursing care and emergency call-cords in the bathrooms. And things would only go downhill as far as house expenses went. She couldn't work up the nerve to open the oil bill that had come in the mail the previous morning. Back when it was just herself and Daphne at home, they'd always spent the cold months swathed in sweaters, their noses and fingertips perpetually numb, the thermostat on the cheapskate setting. But with the arrival of the Demels and Archie, Nora had been cranking up the furnace to its topmost limits to combat the basement's natural dampness and chill. She couldn't expect her guests to shiver away the winter in Frostbite Falls. Weren't they already suffering enough?

"Your granddaughter is right, you know," Yvonne said. "We should go."

Nora's below-stairs visitor had made a rare expedition into the kitchen after dark so the two of them could have a heart-to-heart. Yvonne and Emmanuel were not unaware that Nora's already pinched circumstances were exacerbated by their presence in the basement, and they felt it deeply. Not that Nora ever expressed to them the slightest regret over welcoming them into her home. If Emmanuel had not chanced to overhear her on the phone with Daphne trying to explain away her most recent overdraft, they would never have had an inkling that her circumstances had become so dire.

"If we resettled in a church, if we could arrange that somehow, it would lift a burden off your shoulders."

"Don't you go worrying about my shoulders. They're plenty strong. Besides, having you here is no burden. Just the opposite. Daphne's taking her good old time supplying me with great-grandchildren. At the rate she's moving she might never get around to it. So in the meantime I'm happy to be the unofficial grandmother to your brood."

"But you can't deny that having five extra people in the house to clothe and feed and support is a strain."

"Archie makes six extra. With Anthony seven. Where would you have me draw the line? I work on the cheaper-by-the-dozen principle. Or the-more-the-merrier principle. Whatever you want to call it. Everyone stays."

"If there were only some way we could contribute," Yvonne said. There was a saying back home, "a small house will hold a hundred friends," but it didn't give any tips about sustaining them once they were there.

"How can you honestly say you don't contribute? Didn't Emmanuel save Archie's life? If he hadn't been here, who knows what would have happened to her, poor thing?"

"Her life wasn't in danger, Nora. We both know that. He patched her up. Daphne would have come up with another solution if we hadn't been here. She and Marius would have dragged her to the hospital, or a clinic. Something."

"Knowing Archie the way you do now, do you think she would have put up with that? Even in the state she was in? Stop running down what you've done. You pull your weight. You help me in any way you can. I have no complaints. Besides, I'd be so lonely if you left. Anthony too. This is where you belong."

"You have to think about your future, Nora. This situation with us. It's untenable. You and I both know it. It could drag on for years. And even after all that, we know the likely outcome."

"No." Nora refused to accept Yvonne's dismal assessment. "We'll find a lawyer who can dig you out of this. You just have to hold tight. It's only a question of finding the right person."

"Nora, the law is against us. The chances of our being allowed to stay, even with the best of lawyers working on our side, is minute. We would be the last to blame you if you asked us to move on. Be reasonable."

"Sometimes in life it doesn't pay to be reasonable. This is one of those times."

CHAPTER 30

ARCHIE WAS LEARNING what a gerbil on its wheel felt like. She'd done so many circles around the periphery of the basement that she thought she'd need Gravol to keep from throwing up. It was the new regime Yvonne had cooked up for her with Emmanuel's encouragement. They didn't like the way Archie seemed too content to vegetate, conversation her only exercise. From Archie's perspective, though, she wasn't vegetating; she was storing up her energy in the manner that a squirrel hoards acorns, readying herself for the day when she would be forced to resume her underground life. She didn't want to squander any of her strength beforehand, so she was content to loll around in bed, letting her body restore itself on a low flame. Not so Yvonne, who transformed herself from nurse into Archie's drill-master in chief.

"Up. Out of bed, my lady of leisure," Yvonne said. "Time to get your legs used to supporting you again. They've probably forgotten what they're for after all this time." She whipped the quilts off her. "Allez, oust."

Archie pulled the covers right back up and tucked them in all around her in a prim, old-lady gesture. "I don't think I'm ready."

"You are," Emmanuel said, standing next to his wife to bolster her request with some clinical clout. "Would I have you getting up before I thought you were able? I'll be right here beside you if you have a problem. No one will let you fall."

Falling was the least of her worries. In fact, she would have welcomed a tumble that ended her up with a sprained ankle, nothing major, just enough of a wrench to require that she extend the period of bed rest Emmanuel and Yvonne now seemed bent on snatching away from her.

It wasn't falling that worried her; Emmanuel had it backwards. It was healing. A clean bill of health would knock her out of Yvonne's orbit. She'd be like Pluto, expelled from the legitimate family of planets to continue in life as an independent contractor, and that thought was terrifying to her. The beating and the burns were mere pinpricks by comparison.

Archie might have been able to finagle a delay out of Yvonne, but there was no contradicting the doctor who was less of a soft touch, unfailingly solicitous, yet still somehow remote. Archie's wiles, not highly sophisticated, had no impact on Emmanuel. His edicts in the basement regarding her treatment carried the weight of law. There was nothing for it but to submit as they hoisted her out of her bed and helped her put on her shoes. For Archie's inaugural exercise session, Yvonne supported her on one arm and Emmanuel the other. It was Anthony's idea to play music in the background to give them a beat to aim for. On their first circuit they shambled and stumbled around the room like a troika of vodka-stoked Russian circus bears doing a folk dance. Archie fell back into her bed after only two laps, depleted.

The good doctor, clearly a bit rusty, had underestimated just how damaged his patient still was. Archie had no wind to speak of and her knees wouldn't always lock when they were meant to. Her disobedient arms and legs behaved more like flippers than limbs, and she complained of dizziness and electric-type shocks zapping up through her body every time one of her feet made landfall. The upright position was disagreeing with her in the extreme.

In the outer world, if only he had access to it, Emmanuel might have sent Archie for physiotherapy, gotten her limbered up in advance of forcing her out of bed. He might have even, with the full panoply of Canadian medical specialists at his disposal, sent her to have her head poked at a bit, letting the experts trowel out the issues that were lurking just out of reach and impeding a speedier rehabilitation, or so he surmised. But with the constraints imposed by their circumstances, he had only his own professional opinion to go on, and he remained staunch that the time had come to get Archie's motor running. Every morning without fail, just after breakfast, two adults out of the four the house had on call propelled Archie around the basement, less on her own steam than theirs, until gradually her tours of the basement stopped feeling like a forced march and she started to lose her wobble.

In this venture they were aided by the mini Demels who cheered Archie on as she made her way, clapping their hands to the music and providing backup vocals. When she'd first arrived the children didn't know what to make of the intruder who had parachuted into their tiny domain, silent, almost sullenly so, her cuts oozing, her face misshapen and mottled. These kids were no strangers to blood and injury; they'd seen abominations to the human body no child should ever have to witness, but it did not translate that they were inured to them. Archie's moans tripped their nightmares, their shrieking woke the baby, and the bedwetting, only recently under control, started up again. This unanticipated spillover from Archie's presence had Yvonne putting out fires all over the basement, night and day, and she was exhausted. If asked, the children grudgingly assisted their parents in Archie's care, mostly by fetching and carrying for them. At all other times they kept a safe distance.

But as the swelling receded and Archie's face began to regain human proportions, their curiosity got the better of them. Archie was immobile, after all, they had enough evidence of that. She couldn't leap out of her bed and grab them like the witch in a fairy tale, and in the unlikely event that she were to find the energy to pounce, their mother and father were never more than a few steps away, even if they did spend a considerable amount of time in the laundry room with the door closed, rustling about. The dryer really was temperamental, like their father said.

Bérénice in particular found a certain punk glamour in Archie with her outré blue plumage, and she made a study of her from afar, or at least as far afar as she could manage in the restricted confines of Nora's basement. The longer she surreptitiously watched her, the more Archie struck her as no more than a wounded exotic bird, not a bogeyman after all. A chip off her mother's block, Bérénice determined that Archie needed her own special brand of care. In a fit of bravery that stunned her younger brother Paul, she stepped directly up to the patient's bed and offered to give Archie a manicure using nail polish from a half-dried-up bottle Nora had given her from Daphne's cast-offs. Archie silently stuck out a hand whose nails were bitten down to the nub and over the towel that served as a manicure table, a tentative closeness built up between them. Bérénice began to pamper Archie, treating her as she would a doll, dressing her up with jewellery hand-fashioned from the oddments Nora dug up for her to play with. She took the broccoli rubber bands rescued from the kitchen and glued macaroni onto them, transforming them into bracelets, and reworked Daphne's tangle of abandoned earbuds into necklaces. Bérénice fussed endlessly with Archie's hair, gelling its curls into submission, then brushing it into whimsical shapes, and ornamenting it with plastic beads and ribbons. If someone were to put a lit candle on top of one of her hairstylings, Archie's head could have been used for a buffet centrepiece.

"Are you pleased with my work, Madame?" Bérénice asked her at the end of every salon session, holding up a hand mirror.

"Yes, it's just how I wanted it," Archie said, patting her hair. "You're very talented."

"How do you know? You never look in the mirror," the junior hairdresser said, put out. "All you do is feel it."

"I'm not too big on mirrors these days. But I promise that once I have my old face back, I'll look myself over in the mirror and see that you're a genius."

"Well, I think you look beautiful right now."

"That's a coincidence," Archie said, sealing the friendship, "I think you do too."

Not to let himself be outdone by a girl on the bravery front, Paul began to make his own clunky overtures towards Archie. His routine was to hover his hand over the bed, and when Archie moved to grab it, he yanked it away, a game of speed and agility that he always managed to win. He graduated to showing her his treasures out of his Van Houtte's tin. It didn't take long before Archie had herself two devoted groupies who, like their parents, did their bit to move her cure along.

■ ■ ■

There could be bursts of joy in Nora's basement, discrete moments when laughter took over the space, the odd burp of silliness and fun, but what the basement had never beheld since the Demels first pitched their tents there was any sense of forward motion. The family was no closer to a way out than they had been at the beginning of their stay at Nora's. A whiff of hope always floated around the space but in the way of most hope, it had no real leg to stand on. Archie remastering the vertical position changed all that. Here at last was distinct, measurable progress, on one front anyway. Emmanuel was of the belief that progress was like lightning, it wouldn't strike twice in their tiny environs, but to Yvonne the reverse was true. If progress had gone to all the trouble of tracking them down, buried away though they were on a nondescript cul-de-sac that a Montreal taxi's GPS had difficulty zoning in on, then maybe it would hang out for a while spreading its good cheer.

Whoever's intuition was correct was beside the point. What counted was that Archie was improving, and that gave them all cause to celebrate. They were proud of every step she took towards recovery and Skyped Daphne constantly to keep her in the loop. At the end of every session, all eight of them scrunched together in front of the monitor and wished Daphne a communal goodbye.

It was this documentation of Archie's upswing that marked the beginning of Daphne's downswing in her career underground. Her imagination started to fail her. The Underground City was meh compared to the *Archie Show*, which had all the highs and lows of human drama packed into its episodes. How could that tumorous undergrowth of concrete, steel, and retail be as engrossing as a family in all its variety, for wasn't that odd-socks group in Nora's house a family after all?

Daphne's blogs started wilting like she'd left them out in the hot sun too long. This time around she didn't need Marius to bring that fact to her attention. A chimpanzee could see that her words were so limp they hardly had the strength to cling to the page. Her assignment of finding 365 subterranean items of interest to blog about was mission impossible. Despite her best efforts to convince the public otherwise, the Underground City was a royal yawn, a mall with a gimmick. Its unique situation gave it airs that it didn't deserve. The complex wasn't Atlantis, it wasn't the Space Station, either of which would have provided her with endless raw material about enclosed habitats for her blog. Montreal's Underground City was nothing more than a hypertrophied shopping centre with the odd university and government building stapled on to lend it the gravitas that Victoria's Secret could not.

The trouble with the Underground City, one of them anyway, and recently Daphne had a lengthy list accruing, was that it was too wholesome. Sometimes you just craved a dingy, raucous bar where you could sit and drown your sorrows with like-minded losers, a bar with the friendly smell of leftover vomit in the bathroom stalls. But the Underground City, so unrelentingly clean, didn't know from biker bars. The only drinking spots it had on offer were prom-queen bars, pre-theatre, dandified spots designed to the hilt, serving herby-fruity cocktails and artisanal beers in mason jars. Daphne didn't care for those hipster bars that only hired pretty boys to pull the pints. She wanted one where the bartenders needed dental work and her shoes stuck to the floor every step she took, a Cheez Whiz bar not a chèvre bar. But she was out of luck.

Daphne was suffering from a crise de panique. It wasn't writer's block, her old nemesis, come back to plague her; it was more like writer's remorse. What had possessed her to take on this lunatic writing challenge that came provided with a built-in shackle? Before those schmaltzy group Skypes started coming through, Daphne hadn't allowed herself to wallow in her loneliness. She got up every morning, put one foot in front of the other, and did her job trying to fabricate come-hither notices to unsuspecting tourists. But now all she wanted was to be in on the action back on rue Melançon, to be part of the bustle. The contrasting un-bustle of her little studio apartment grated her nerves raw, though it had never bothered her before. Her meals, usually taken leaning against the kitchen counter watching the microwave tray revolve, now seemed pathetic compared to the rollicking affairs at the table in Nora's basement that had expanded to include Archie now that she no longer needed a bed tray. Daphne should have been back at her grandmother's, part of all the kerfuffle, lending a hand, helping Archie come back to herself, but instead she was stuck on the wrong side of the screen, on the outside looking in.

In every Skype Daphne put Archie under the loupe. From what she could observe from the jumpy images that Bérénice captured as chief videographer, Archie was probably improving at a fast enough clip to be moved back to her apartment soon. Nora's was only ever meant to be a pit stop, the ER to Daphne's rehab. Daphne missed having her old underground compadre around, even though she herself wondered how it was possible to miss someone so much that she barely knew. She'd broached the subject of Archie's repatriation with her grandmother, but Nora waved her off, feeling no pressing need to redress the imbalance that had seven extra people fizzing up her place, while her granddaughter was hosting a grand total of zero.

"Couldn't you use the room?" Daphne asked her yet again, appealing to Nora's practical side. "The Demels could spread out a bit if she were gone. They wouldn't have to live so scrunched, especially with someone who's not even part of their family. Without her there they could have their privacy, walk around naked if they wanted."

"Oh, Archie doesn't take up that much space, a little sprig like her. And I don't think the Demels are walking-around-naked types."

"They're probably afraid to. They can't afford to rile up their meal ticket."

"Watch yourself."

Daphne didn't.

"Not to be crass, but it would be a savings for you."

"What kind of savings are we talking about? A few pennies? It's not like I heat the place just for her."

"She eats, doesn't she?"

"She'd eat at your place too. And isn't all the money coming out of the same pot? I don't get it. What's behind all this? Why are you hustling to have her go back to your place? Wouldn't you get into fifty shades of trouble having someone stay over with you long-term? That *is* what you told me, isn't it? Correct me if I'm wrong."

"It wouldn't be for forever. Just for the last little bit of her convalescence. To give you some respite."

"Clean out your ears, girlie," Nora said. "I already told you. I don't need any respite. Don't make out like you'd be doing me a favour taking her away. I never asked you to. She's fine right where she is."

Disrupting the equilibrium at her grandmother's had no real arguments going for it. Nora was right. Archie seemed happy and well looked after. Daphne lobbying for more complications in her underground life was illogical, but somehow when it came to Archie, logic never prevailed.

Improper or not, Daphne felt a certain degree of ownership towards Archie. She'd been the one after all, in her tortured reworking of their first meeting at the Y, who had discovered her, who then drew her in, fed her, clothed her, and eventually took the steps that saved her life. Of course that was the *Cole's Notes* version, the one that glossed over certain salient details, like how Daphne had stalked Archie in the Underground City, how she'd set her spy Ludovic on her, how she'd nearly badgered her to tears in the Cathedral. Still, Daphne's motives had never been anything but pure and now she was experiencing an irresistible urge to have the underground stray back under her wing.

Daphne wanted to be the one, herself and no other, to untangle the tendrils of Archie's secrets, to find out what calamity could possibly have pushed this young woman to nuke her future and opt for a life of poverty and squalor. It wasn't idle curiosity that motivated her. Daphne thought that in understanding what factors had acted on Archie, she could come up with the antidote, one that would allow Archie to walk around without sneaking looks over her shoulder, to eat off plates that hadn't first belonged to someone else, to live above ground and up to her potential. This was Daphne's mission, but one that she couldn't enact long-distance. A mission this delicate required the intimacy that they had been starting to build up before Archie vanished from her apartment.

Maybe Archie didn't realize that the persistent pain in her shoulders came not from the beating, but rather from being at the centre of a tug-of-war between Daphne and her grandmother, and neither one showed signs of letting go. Nora had an agenda of her own regarding Archie, which was in direct conflict with Daphne's. She had observed the interplay of her basement visitors with a scientist's eye. They were, she concluded, like bees in a hive. Each one had a particular role to play in keeping the community viable. And Archie's role, contrary to what a less seasoned entomologist might presume, was to prop up Yvonne so she could go on living, not the reverse. To prevent the basement dynamic from imploding, Nora was prepared to hold on to Archie for as long as she could.

In their game of duelling agendas, Nora had the slight edge over Daphne with Archie on-site and her granddaughter hog-tied to the Underground City. Neither one of them, though, for all their good intentions, ever considered the possibility of Archie taking responsibility for her own life. Somehow each of the Elman women felt she had ownership of her, and at worst, if an amicable agreement could not be reached between them, they would work out a joint custody agreement as to where their disputed property would spend alternate weekends.

CHAPTER 31

THE URGENT TEXT summons wasn't a surprise. It had been weeks since Ludovic started tinkering with a new coffee concoction that he was naming after Daphne, and he probably wanted her final go-ahead before officializing it on his chalkboard bill-of-fare. The last she'd heard, he was infusing his strongest power-brew with a breath of cardamom, and topping it with a skim-coat of almond-milk foam that he then decorated freehand with a flourishy letter D. Not for Ludovic those cappuccino stencils that allowed barista pretenders to decorate milk-foam with the shape of a leaf or a heart or a letter. He spat on such unprofessionalisms. If he couldn't doll up the foam freestyle to his desired design, he didn't doll it up at all.

When the text came through, Daphne headed straight towards the espresso bar. She was in desperate need of a boost. With her Archie issues weighing her down and her blog struggle compounding the load, she'd been dragging around the Underground City looking like the *before* picture in an ad for Red Bull. A megadose of caffeine from Rocky was just what the doctor ordered. But when she settled herself in at the counter, it wasn't an espresso Ludovic slid across to her; it was a folded piece of paper.

"What's this? I have to take a test now before you'll serve me coffee?"

"Open it up," he said, "but it's for your eyes only." He signalled with a discreet tip of the head the customers chatting on the far side of the counter.

"Come on, Ludovic. I'm not in the mood for games."

"I'm dead serious here, Daphné. Open it."

Daphne unfolded the sheet and glanced down at the colour photo centred on the page under the banner that cried out in ultra-bold caps with no softening serifs, *MISSING*.

It was a head-on shot of a girl in a trim navy blazer with a Hogwartsian emblem on the pocket. She'd been posed for a speed shot by a school photographer trying to cycle through three hundred kids in the few hours allotted to him. No time for niceties. He hadn't bothered to fluff out the girl's dark curls that were still sleep-flat on one side and the camera caught her eyelids at half-mast, but the photo, for all its slipshoddiness, somehow managed to capture the outlines of the fence she'd constructed around herself. It was unmistakably her Archie.

But the particulars beneath the picture begged to differ. This girl's name was Chantal. Chantal Clark. And when Daphne did the calculations, twice, from Chantal's stated date of birth, both times did she come up with the same mathematical impossibility. Fifteen. That Archie had adopted an alias Daphne always assumed, its confirmation no shocker, but the fact that she was just a few notches out of childhood, as Marius had suspected, plugged the breath in her throat. It made her want to reach for her puffer although she hadn't needed it in years.

"It's her, isn't it?" Ludovic said. "The one you asked me to keep an eye out for?" But a reply was superfluous. That Daphne's skin was bleached whiter than the bistro apron he kept tied around his waist gave him all the confirmation he needed.

"Where did you get hold of this?"

"Some dude dropped it off. Her dad, I'm guessing. We had a bit of a talk, him and me."

"I don't get it. What kind of a half-assed search is this he's doing? Why hasn't he plastered these over the whole Underground City if he suspects that she's here? Why hasn't he contacted the police?"

Ludovic shrugged his ignorance. "He seemed to want to keep it low-key."

"Low-key! That's bullshit," she said, brandishing the sheet of paper in the air despite Ludovic's warning. "What father worth the title doesn't try every means at his disposal to get his missing kid back? Huh? He should be crying out her name from the rooftops, not prowling around down here like a rat. He deserves to be shot, that guy. Drawn and quartered would be too good for him." She was raking her hand through her hair, readying herself for another salvo.

Daphne's voice had forgotten it was out in public; it was shrill and penetrating, and had an edge to it that was veering towards the unbalanced. Ludovic's other customers eyed her covertly, weighing which way it was likely to turn. The ones who had been prescient enough to order their coffees in to-go cups didn't linger to find out. They drifted away to finish their coffees in peace at their desks. The other unfortunates, sipping out of porcelain, sidled as far away from Daphne as they could and stared into their cups. No one wanted to catch the eye of a potential loon.

The questions kept splurting uncontrollably out of Daphne's mouth. "Why isn't her picture on any of the missing kid sites? Tell me that. There's no website either. Why did he wait so long to start up a search? Does he want to find her or not?"

"Whoa, Daphné. Calme-toi."

Daphne had a wonky pressure valve when it came to the subject of fathers. Paternal infractions that she observed, even those of the lowest order, were guaranteed to provoke a flare-up. It had not always been so.

■ ■ ■

Daphne's own father died before she had the least awareness of him. Whatever knowledge she possessed of the one parent who outlived her birth came second-hand, funneled-down memories from Nora that Daphne subsequently sponged up and made her own. By Nora's accounts, Jacob was a model father, a hands-on dad who, in the few short months he had with his daughter, showered her with love and attention, as attested to by the ranks of framed photos that shrouded the wall above Nora's buffet. Nora always said he'd loved Daphne to death. His own death as it turned out.

An accident it was, a tragic accident out in the oil fields of Alberta. The freshly-minted widower had left his baby girl in his mother's care so he could follow that well-trod path out to the True North's personal land of milk and honey to rack up some serious cash. He would come back as soon as he could set them up comfortably. Except that he never did.

The bare bones of all of this Daphne knew. Her grandmother had never hidden it from her once she deemed her old enough to hear the particulars. To pile irony on top of injury, her father's death had nothing whatever to do with the oil patch, laden with dangers though it was. He drowned, Nora told her, on an off-day with the guys; swam out too far in the river, cramped up, and before anyone realized he was in trouble, it was too late and he was gone.

Whatever ultimately possessed Daphne to google her father she couldn't really recall. She was nearly an adult when she idly put the name *Jacob Elman* into the search engine in a late-onset flicker of curiosity, expecting nothing more than a death notice or two, but instead references to him streamed down the page in the thousands. Clearly her father had forgotten to brush up on the bio Nora had ghosted for him, the one she'd read out from to Daphne, because the Jacob Elman of Internet notoriety had no more worked the oil rigs in Fort Mac than his mother. His true occupation, if it even counted as an occupation, was *environmental activist.* Daphne's father was dedicated body and soul to bringing the tar sands to its knees.

His early protests had been of the banner-and-bullhorn variety, a pesky fly buzzing around the Goliath that was the oil industry, piddling in the kiddie pool of activism, playing the game by its rules. But by the time he reached his mid-twenties, the rules fit him more like a straitjacket. He abandoned his timid comrades, leaving those wimps behind to wave their placards and hold their interminable consultations while he upped his tactics, up so far in fact that he acquired an impressive rap sheet; breaking and entering, theft, destruction of property, reckless endangerment, and possession of explosives. The organization under whose name he'd operated from the beginning cut him loose; a touch of vandalism it could stomach, it was part of the game, but his flirtations with violence sullied a reputation that was already shaky.

Answering to no one suited Jacob. Bosses were a redundancy when you had right on your side. He increased the frequency of his commando raids on oil sands installations, inflicting greater damage with every sortie. In some circles he was hailed as a folk hero, a man whose principles were in the right place, a mash-up of Mother Teresa and Jesse James. Not the oil companies though. Jacob kept them, and law enforcement, on the run, but they could never track him down. Then, just months after his wife's sudden death, he broke from his previous pattern, coming out into the open.

The driver of the truck claimed not to have seen him, the naked man wrapped in chains, kneeling directly in the pathway of his left front tire. Granted, the truck was an oil sands behemoth where a single tire weighed in at five thousand kilos and stood as high as a steeple. And maybe the dipper, loaded with ore, really was blocking his sightlines. As a defence it had seen some success. It was the same one pulled out by the drivers of those old-style dog-nose school buses, the ones that had the unfortunate habit of mowing down kindergarteners crossing the street invisibly in front of them. It succeeded this time too. The inquest found the truck driver innocent of any wrongdoing, although the optics of squishing a protester did cause a public outcry that gave the oil company's PR directors a run for their money. For a while. Then the rape of the environment resumed apace.

That was it. Daphne never forgave him. One ill-conceived troll of the Web was all it took to shift her over from revering the memory of her father to reviling it. She didn't blame Nora for lying to her; she understood her motives. All her fury she reserved for her father who cavalierly put his life on the line for the sake of what, the stinkin' environment, when she was squalling in a crib back in Montreal with no other parent on the face of the earth to call her own? He allowed himself to be killed, practically begged them to run him over, and they obliged him ever so politely, and then sent his flattened body home for burial rolled up like a yoga mat. The fact that he was trying to minister to the planet left her cold. Shouldn't his own daughter have counted to him more than climate change? Couldn't he have done like everyone else and let it be the next generation's problem? Did he figure she didn't need a father? Her resentment festered in all the years that followed and spilled over to tarnish her opinion of fathers in general. Nothing less than all-out devotion to the child would do, and Archie's father (she refused to think of her yet as Chantal), conducting such a flaccid search for his missing daughter placed him, in Daphne's hierarchy, on the lowest and most populous rung of fatherdom.

"Did you tell him anything?" Daphne asked Ludovic.

"Do I look like a stoolie to you?"

"Sorry, Ludo. No offence. Look, can I have this photo?"

"Sure. It's yours." Daphne started to go but Ludovic called her back for a final whispered consult.

"Is she okay, this kid?"

"She's fine. Trust me."

"I do. Do you think I'd name one of my coffees after a bum? But listen to me, Daphné, and listen hard. This kid's a runaway, and the outlook for them ain't good in this world. I've seen it first-hand plenty of times. I didn't like the look of this guy. He had a stink about him. But I would hate to think that by my silence I'm playing a part in throwing this kid from the frying pan into the fire. So you better be damn sure she's fine. Damn sure."

"She is, Ludovic. I guarantee. You don't have to worry about her."

"You're sure?"

"Absolutely."

"If you need my help, you know where to find me."

"Thanks, Ludo. You're a real friend."

"I hope that's what I am. My brain and my old badge keep telling me I'm an idiot."

"Don't listen to them. I swear to you I won't let any harm come to that girl. She will be safe and cared for. I'll do the right thing by her. On my life."

■ ■ ■

"You free?" Daphne asked Marius when he picked up.

"I'm in the middle of something for Larry. Can't it wait?"

"Aren't you supposed to be on call for me round the clock? Isn't that what the contract stipulates? I can quote chapter and verse if it's slipped your mind. You've gotten kind of laissez-faire about your responsibilities to me, wouldn't you say? I should be able to snap my fingers and you're here. 'Can't it wait?' he says? I don't think so."

"Okay, don't get yourself in a snit. I'll be there right away." Even when Daphne had called him to play ambulance for Archie who was bleeding all over her bedsheets, she hadn't sounded this desperate for his presence.

"Are you all right?"

"Obviously not, or I wouldn't be calling you to get the hell over here."

"What's wrong?"

"I'll tell you when you get here."

"Sit tight. I'm on my way."

When Marius pulled up to Daphne's building, he caught sight of her pacing back and forth in her apartment lobby, slinging envious glances at him through the front windows into the outdoors where he had the privilege of circulating freely.

"What?" he said. "What's happened?"

"You'll see upstairs."

"Is it your grandmother? The Demels? Is somebody sick? Anthony?"

"Wait." She revealed nothing, the ride up in the elevator taken in absolute silence giving Marius's imagination time to craft new disasters beyond those he'd come up with on the way over.

In the apartment, Daphne directed him to sit down on the couch and then placed the paper with the picture of Archie down on the coffee table before him. Marius took in the photo and the details, and then did the same mental math that Daphne had. She sat down beside him. "You were right all along," she said as they stared at the paper together.

"Which gives me zero satisfaction."

"Imagine," Daphne said, "just a kid, having to live that way, all on her own devices. I know Montreal's not Kabul, but still."

"I know what you mean." Marius had four younger sisters, each more annoying than the next, but all the accumulated years of brotherly resentment towards them vaporized when he pictured them on the receiving end of fists and lit cigarettes.

"They're sure offering a sweet bundle as a reward," he said. "You could set yourself up for life on that kind of money."

"It looks like money is one thing her family's not short of. I wonder how they came by it?"

They sat on the sofa, numb the pair of them, stumped as to what move to make next. Out in the hallway they could hear Daphne's laughing neighbours, blissfully unencumbered by crises, gathering their gaggle of children for a trip to the park, while their dilemma had them set on mute. It was Marius who finally roused himself to fill the breach.

"I say we call the number. What choice do we have? It's the only ethical thing to do." Marius made this incursion into devil's advocacy to turn the conversation in the direction it needed to go.

"No, you've got it all wrong," she said, her reply right on target. She picked up the picture and looked into Archie's eyes as if seeking confirmation of her instincts. "Calling is exactly the not-ethical thing to do. What do you think, that Archie, or Chantal, or whatever her name is, was living underground as some kind of perverted lifestyle choice? That a lovely young girl from a well-off family preferred to live in filth and danger? I don't buy it. Something drove her out of her home, however ritzy it might have been. There's no other explanation the way I see it."

"We could report it to the police ourselves, I guess," he said, "if it weren't likely to get Nora and the rest of them in the soup." Marius hoped he could perk Daphne up a bit with his "if it weren't" construction. He knew she took him for an "if it wasn't" kind of guy, but she was way too down for grammar to lift her spirits.

"Are you serious? I can't believe you're even suggesting it. You know how hyper Archie is about getting her name in the system anywhere. She wouldn't even go to a hospital when her guts were practically hanging out because she would have had to identify herself to someone in authority. You can't have forgotten that. Plus, like you said, there are the others to consider. So until we find out why she left home, no police, no calling the number, no telling anyone what we know. Total cone of silence. Deal?"

"Deal."

"If I could just get her back here," Daphne said. "I'd know better this time than to use the sledgehammer approach. I'd work her over gently, on little cat feet, open her up a tiny bit at a time. The trouble is that my grandmother won't give her up. She's turned herself into Archie's personal bodyman. I know I'm the one who asked her to keep Archie safe, but this is ridiculous. I've created a monster. She won't even let *me* get close."

"Uh-uh. You've got it wrong I think. From what I've seen the times I've been over there, it's not Nora who controls the keys to the keep. It's Yvonne."

"Yvonne?"

CHAPTER 32

T HEY'D NEVER BEEN left alone at night before. During the day, Nora and Anthony would occasionally pop out together to run errands, leaving their clandestine lodgers to their own devices for an hour, maybe two, during which they all kept obediently to the basement. They weren't barricaded down there; it wasn't like they were Anne Frank, but they chose to stick with what was safe and familiar. It was a different story after dark, though darkness to them was not ruled by the clock. Ever since the first major snowfall of the season walloped in so early, blocking the basement windows with drifts, it was as if they were living in the Arctic Circle, on the back side of the sun. It used to be that Nora's aged verticals, even if they were always kept closed, allowed slim rods of daylight to sneak through into the basement, marking the walls in a pattern reminiscent of prison bars. But it was only now that the natural light was blocked absolutely that they truly felt like they were in prison.

The residents of Nora's basement never allowed themselves to overly indulge in fantasies of a life above stairs, a life beyond their present limits. At least not out loud. Emmanuel tried to keep a lid on speculative conversations when they flared up. They could only lead to frustration. But this night, with the confluence of Nora and Anthony's absence and weeks of unremitting darkness playing mind games on them, they all got to feeling twitchier than usual, like teenagers whose parents had left them home for the first time unsupervised, inspiring in them an urge to test the boundaries. They didn't want to go upstairs and break into the liquor cabinet, nothing so boorish. The desires they expressed were homey, so modest and innocent they wrenched Emmanuel's heart. His wife wished only to look out a window and see the sky; his children nothing more than to go up the stairs, out the back door, and into the fenced backyard for a frolic in the snow.

"We'd be absolutely quiet, Papa," Bérénice said. "No one would hear us. We'd just make a map in the snow with our feet like we used to. That's not very noisy."

When the Demels had their first experience playing in the snow, that had been their family game. They stomped out trails with their new clompy boots and fashioned a map. It was their father's idea, in his inexperience with snow, to do something intellectual with it. Paul and Bérénice only later picked up from the kids on the street that the main purpose of snow was not cartography. They were meant to pack it into balls and whomp each other. Still, mapping remained their favourite winter game.

"How does that sound to you, Paul-Paul?" Emmanuel said.

Poor Paul was in over his head. He wanted desperately to go play in the snow in the manner his older sister described, but he'd intuited since they'd made the move to Nora's basement that he wasn't meant to give vent to such desires. He was a sensitive little boy, Paul, who understood on his level the seriousness of their predicament and tried his best to live up to his parents' expectations. He would never even dare ask to go up beyond the basement's third step (the parentally imposed limit to his jumping distance), let alone go outside into the real world. But now his sister, whose cues he usually took, was freely voicing such a traitorous notion. He was with her all the way. He just couldn't make himself say it. It took all his boyish strength to properly answer his father.

"We shouldn't, Papa."

"But you would like to, non? Have a little run outside in your boots?"

With those two innocent-sounding questions, Paul lost his compass. Who was this man who looked like his father, walked like his father, and even had the voice of his father, but clearly wasn't his father? His own father would never egg him on in such a way. His own father was forever reminding them that their safety as a family depended on total obedience to the rules of the house. They had to be disciplined, his papa said, brave, united. Sometimes Paul secretly wished that he could go upstairs and keep Mamie Nora company in the kitchen while she cooked like he used to do at home with his mother. He could curl himself into a little ball under the table so no one could see him through the windows and tell her more riddles. She hardly ever got the answers, not even to the chicken one, but she always asked for another from his endless supply. This desire he kept strictly to himself. Not even to Bérénice did he confess his kitchen fantasy. Going upstairs, even wishing to go upstairs, was the worst crime his imagination could come up with. But bypassing the upstairs altogether to go outside, actually outside into the fresh air, was a sin outside his comprehension. It was mammoth. Like murder. Was this a test? One that his sister had already failed?

"Well, my Paul-Paul? What do you say?" his father pressed him.

His glance skittered from his sister to his mother and then back again, but their expressions gave him no guidance, so he managed his confusion the only way he knew how, by bursting into tears.

"Emmanuel, stop," Yvonne said. "You're torturing him, can't you see?"

"I'm just asking our boy a simple question."

Yvonne reached over and took Paul in her arms. "It's all right, my darling boy. It's just a game we're playing. You can say whatever you want to Papa. It's not real," but his hiccupping breaths prevented him from participating any further in this game that for him held no charm.

Of all the things his children could have been wishing for, friends, school, a home of their own, freedom, safety, daylight; they yearned solely for a simple romp in the snow. Their glorious imaginations had been stunted, shrunk to fit the parameters of their cinched life, stretching only as far as the back door and a tiny virgin patch of snow. What miserable excuse for a father was he that he couldn't indulge his children in their simple craving?

Yvonne secretly shared her children's longing to go outside. She had grown to be on chummy terms with the Canadian cold. Based on their initial encounter, she never would have imagined it happening. The Demels' plane had touched down on an ice-slicked tarmac in Montreal plunk in the middle of a fiendish snowstorm she now understood was of an intensity to make even blizzard-blasé Montrealers cower. They arrived with virtually no belongings to their name. All that they had in quantity was advice, thanks to Emmanuel's cousin Léon and his wife Priscilla, God rest her soul.

"Don't even think of buying tomatoes in the winter." Priscilla instructed her cousin that first night. "You might as well eat a ball of wax out of your ear."

"Please, my dear," Léon said. "Must you be so coarse?"

She waved off his dig as was her custom. Maybe his minions at the office thought he walked on water, but she knew his father had driven a donkey cart. "I'm just telling it like it is, as they say up here. And they have an aftertaste, don't they, chéri? You'd think they were irrigated in petrol."

"Let's not exaggerate," her husband countered. "The markets are filled with many fine foods. We wouldn't want to give our cousins the wrong idea. It's just that at this time of year…"

"Exaggerating? Me?" She barrelled on in the absence of any opposition of consequence. "And what they call *fresh* here? Maybe it was fresh a week ago when some peon threw it into a bushel basket in Mexico. But now? They even have a category, don't laugh, that they call *fresh frozen*. Can you credit it? In my opinion those two terms cancel each other out. Wouldn't you say?" She looked to her presumed new ally Yvonne for agreement, but her husband's cousin was still too dazed by the drifts blocking the view out the windows to weigh in on Priscilla's vocabulary conundrum. She sat mute, the ambient chill of her cousins' living room mocking the light dress that she wore.

From the shortcomings of Canada's food supply, Priscilla moved on to the ins and outs of Canadian outerwear, about which she was conveniently also an expert. "Down coats. *Point final!* Never polyester. They're pricier, yes, but for the kind of warmth you'll be needing, nothing surpasses them. And boots? The highest quality. Name brands. That goes without saying. You mustn't let yourself be lured by knock-offs. You wouldn't want the children to lose a toe." Yvonne hadn't been expecting risks like this. Canada was a country where you could lose body parts as easily as a few coins out of your pocket?

"And grippers to slip on over the boots are a good investment."

Would it never end? "Grippers?" Yvonne asked, trying to make some sense of the spiked leather thongs that dangled from her cousin's fingers. They looked like medieval torture equipment. "Boots aren't sufficient?"

Priscilla was a firm believer in the belts and braces model. "Oh no. Not if it's glare-ice. You need the extra traction. It's like putting chains on your tires," she said, another Canadianism that mystified Yvonne. "Otherwise your feet could shoot right out from under you. I've seen it happen. You don't want to be laid up with a fractured coccyx because you skimped, do you?"

Yvonne feared she would never learn the ropes. As she was first settling in to her adopted country, it took her so long getting the children sealed up properly to go outside she felt as though she was dressing astronauts for space flight. So many mysterious layers, so many snaps and zippers and grippers and hooks and mitten strings. It was exhausting to go out to the corner with them just to pick up some eggs, those same eggs Priscilla scorned for their insipid yolks, but what could she do? Her family had to eat.

Somewhere along the way, though, Yvonne and sub-zero came to an understanding, thanks in large part to her children who served as matchmakers. She came to marvel, as did they, at snow's constructive qualities, missing in other climatic manifestations. You couldn't build with rain. Wind was elusive. But snow, like marzipan, was mouldable into an infinite series of fanciful shapes. Many a wintry day she would join her children in the vest-pocket backyard of the house Léon had found for them, as they trampled and rolled and sculpted the snow to match whatever image they had in their minds. To Yvonne, it had the same satisfaction as baking a loaf of bread, with the added challenge of having to do it wearing oven mitts. And the frigid air, far from being the demon Priscilla made it out to be, angling to snip off unsuspecting fingers and noses the minute your back was turned, revitalized her, rebooting all her systems that had been sputtering on *doze* ever since they'd buried Grace.

So when her children tried to make a case with their father for sneaking out into Nora's snowy backyard, her heart went out to them, even though it could never happen. What had possessed Emmanuel to encourage them? She would have to speak to him later, once the children were asleep. In her view it was better to keep their urges on a short leash, as cruel as that may have been.

"You know what I could really go for?" Archie piped up, in a helpful redirect. "A soak in a tub. With bubbles maybe."

The bathroom they all shared was basic. Its minuscule footprint didn't run to a shower let alone a tub. The sink was practically sitting on the toilet's lap. As soon as her neighbours moved in, Nora rigged up a pseudo camp shower in the laundry room near the utility sink. It had started out in life as a garden hose with a spritzer on the end, but with a few creative drapes over the exposed pipes that criss-crossed the basement ceiling and an old plastic painting drop cloth tacked up to contain the spray, it did the job. She was rather proud of how she had acquitted in one of her first challenges as house mother, but the consensus downstairs was that the shower was not a DIY triumph. Nora had no way of knowing, never having actually availed herself of the apparatus, that taking a shower was a test of fortitude. The arrangement was minimally private and maximally uncomfortable. The temperature flip-flopped wildly between glacial and scalding, the water pressure was limp-wristed, and a nasty puddle tended to accumulate at the floor drain if anyone was so rash as to linger under the spray for more than a few minutes running, a puddle that threatened to lap over into the living area.

"Who would know?" Archie went on, embellishing her proposal so as to draw her loyal little chum Paul out of his funk. "I could be up and back before they come home, no one the wiser. I'd use our towels from down here and would dry everything off and tidy it all up just as I found it. Do you think they have a rubber ducky up there to keep me company?"

Her chatter was having its anticipated effect. Paul's snuffling was slowing down, but some of her bath blather accidentally overshot her intended target.

"A nice soak in a tub with Epsom salts would do you a world of good," said Emmanuel.

"Hold it, Emmanuel. I wasn't angling to go upstairs. Really. I was just..."

"It's very soothing," he went on as if she hadn't spoken. "A good natural remedy. Works wonders on stubborn aches of the type that keep plaguing you."

"Come on. It's only old ladies who dump that stuff in their bath water. You'll have me eating prunes next."

"Don't denigrate the wisdom of your elders. There's a reason they use it. It relaxes the muscles and helps with swelling too. You probably wouldn't be so stiff if you followed their example. It's the magnesium. That's the magic ingredient."

Hearing Emmanuel's paean to the health benefits of Epsom salts, it started to slip Archie's mind that a few minutes before she'd actually had no interest in taking a bath at all.

"Would it really help, do you think? Those night-aches make me crazy."

"It couldn't hurt."

"What are you doing encouraging her?" Yvonne said. She didn't like him bringing their pie-in-the-sky session down to earth.

"All I'm saying is that medically speaking, with all her lingering soreness, a bath would be very beneficial."

"We could have her move around more," Yvonne said, "work out the kinks that way."

"There's not much scope for moving around any further down here. We all know that. It's too cramped to do her any good."

"Well, it may not be a dance floor, but look how far she's come."

"We can do better."

"Better how? Tell me what more she needs and I'll do it."

"I think," he said, looking into each of their eyes in turn, "that in this one instance, a trip upstairs could be justified."

"Upstairs, Papa?" The u-word on his father's lips revved Paul's tears up afresh.

"Emmanuel, I'm fine down here," Archie said. "Let's not rock the boat."

"Papa, you always said…"

"I know what I said, but the situation has changed."

"Changed how, Papa?" Bérénice asked him. "What's changed?"

"Don't, Emmanuel," Yvonne said. "Think of Nora. All she's risked to keep us. It would be spitting in her face."

"I'm sure Nora would be in complete agreement if it's a necessity for our patient's well-being."

"Yet you only bring it up when she's not here to disagree."

To this he had no reply. Emmanuel loved Nora dearly for all she had done for him and his family, but it was at times difficult for him to reconcile that his saviour was also his captor.

"You would go behind her back?" Yvonne continued.

"In this case I would have to say the situation dictates that we must." He stood up to indicate that the decision had been made. "You go up with Archie. Make sure she can manage. Leave me in charge of the children. We'll survive for half an hour."

"Emmanuel, what are you thinking?"

"I'm thinking that we will survive for half an hour."

"You know that's not what I mean."

"Yvonne, you'll be able to see out a window. Go up. Say hello to the stars from me."

"Where is your head? It's too big of a risk."

"You'll be fine."

"Not for Archie and me. For you and the kids. Do you think I can't see where you're really going with all this?"

"Leave us, Yvonne. It's something I need to do."

CHAPTER 33

"I'LL MISS THIS when I leave," Archie said, as she closed her eyes in the tub, the water up to her chin.

"Miss what?" Yvonne asked her. "All of us or just the bath?"

"You know what I mean. Being with you. Talking. All that."

"I didn't know that it was in your mind to leave."

"Not tomorrow, but sometime. I can't stay here forever crowding you guys."

"We don't feel crowded."

"Philippe sleeps in a drawer. To me that's crowded."

"For the time being he's fine in there. What's that expression Nora always uses? Snug as a bug in a rug. There's no rush for you to move on our account."

"I know, but I have to think about the future. Even if it is far away."

"Where will you go? When that future comes, I mean."

"The Underground City. Where else?"

"How can you be thinking of going back there? The very place where they did those horrible things to you."

"It'd be different now, don't you see? I know how to work the system. It'll be easier. I'll be the one to get the best sleep spots."

"That's the sum total of your aspirations?" Yvonne said. "For *you* to be the one entitled to sleep on the hot air grate?"

"Why shouldn't I be comfortable?"

"If you were my daughter, I'd whip you out of that place so fast your head would spin."

If you were my daughter was the worst formulation she could have chosen. Archie was operating under the assumption that she had already become Yvonne's daughter, that it was a done deal, accomplished through some fancy twist of transubstantiation or nuclear fusion, or maybe just sheer force of will. As far as she was concerned, she and Yvonne were blood, so when she heard Yvonne's statement that placed her quite clearly outside the Demel family circle, she was crushed.

"Well, I'm not, lucky you," Archie said, slinging attitude towards Yvonne as she had towards Daphne when first they met, letting the shards land where they may. "The purity of your family is intact. They won't be polluted by me." Archie's unprecedented insolence stung Yvonne speechless as she barrelled ahead. "'My daughter' you called me all those nights. Remember? 'My daughter.' I should have known then that you were bullshitting. That you never saw me at all, only Grace. I was just a handy substitute in the dark.

"You think you're so special. So compassionate. That you're the only person other than Daphne who wants to rescue me from the Underground City. The only one who cares if I'm rotting down there or not, beaten to a pulp or whole. Well, you're not as it turns out. My real mother, that bitch who gave birth to me, would agree with you one hundred percent. She'd want to get me out of there too, but not for the same reasons as you. It must make you so proud to know that you're two of a kind."

"And what reasons would those be?" Yvonne forced herself to ask, though she could barely choke out the words. Never before had there been any mention of a mother, or any other family member for that matter. It was an opening and Yvonne had to grasp it, even if it did come as part of a flak storm aimed squarely at herself. What had happened to her poor Archie? She sounded possessed.

"I don't have to tell you," Archie said, downgrading from vulgarity to mere snottiness.

Yvonne had the tongue-lashing coming, she supposed. This out-of-bounds evening she and Archie were spending together, totally closed off from the others and at risk of imminent discovery by the very person who had gathered them in had her stressed to the hilt. In the calm familiarity of the basement, such a thoughtless remark never would have escaped Yvonne's lips. Down there she would not have lost sight of Archie's essential fragility, despite the brave face she glimpsed her strapping on every morning like a goalie mask.

If one of her children had lashed out at her in that way, they wouldn't have gotten away with it. In pride of place on the Demel family coat of arms, in flourishy capital letters, sat the phrase *respectez vos parents*. But of course, wasn't that the issue? Just where did Archie stand in relation to the Demel family? Was she in or was she out?

"I am not your real mother," Yvonne said. "Nothing can change that. I am only the person who loved you and cared for you when you needed it. I am only that person. Nothing more."

A slap would have suited Archie better. She had crossed a line, a line that could not be uncrossed. Punishment was what she'd deserved. Kindness was what she was handed. And that was too much for her to bear. She was flooded with regret over the tantrum she'd thrown. If not for that, her safe haven could have stayed open to her for months yet, allowing her to string out her recovery until she was strong enough to pump iron, basking in Yvonne's care all the while, but she had slammed that door closed on herself.

"I'll leave," Archie said. "Tonight."

"What are you talking about? You can't."

"It would be best, I think, for everybody."

"Your body still has lots of healing to do. If you leave before you're ready, it could set you back."

"I'm fine enough."

"I know I have no right to keep you, but I pray you will see good sense and change your mind."

"I've decided. It's time."

"In the space of ten seconds, you've decided something so important?"

"Please thank Nora for me, and Anthony. Say goodbye on my behalf. I'll probably be gone before they come home."

"That I will not do. If you want to leave without thanking them for all their generosity towards you, then go, but I will not relay the message if you walk out." Archie had started to get up out of the tub, ready to put her half-cocked plan into action, but with this refusal she faltered. "And the children, don't forget," Yvonne continued, guilty of piling on, but unrepentant. "They would be devastated if you disappeared with no warning. They have had to deal with too many abrupt disappearances in their short lives."

It wouldn't be easy for Archie to walk out of this house on the bad side of everyone she cared about in the world, but when had things ever been easy for her? Easy was for other kids. If Yvonne weren't right there in the bathroom to prevent it, she would just sink down under the water and let it be over. Fini. But Yvonne *was* there, still pushing her to stay, her finest arts of persuasion invested in what she said next. "Not to mention how your leaving would break my heart."

"How can you be saying that after the way I just spoke to you?" Archie cried out to her. "You can't mean it."

"You know," Yvonne said, "I've always had in mind an invention, a very useful tool. It would make me rich, I think. I still have to work out the mechanics of it, but the principle is that it would have our mouths operate on a delay. You could say something, but the words would not go out there to be heard until our brains did a mine-sweep of them and then gave the go-ahead. We could both use it, I think."

Yvonne squatted down by the side of the tub. "Archie, my dearest, I don't hold what you said against you. Sometimes, when anger overtakes us, we say things we wish we could eat back up. You are not alone in that. But to give in to that anger, to run away because of it, well, it's not a very grown-up way to act."

For so many years Archie had been running on fumes that what she now had left in the tank wouldn't be enough to power up a barbecue. Her body was depleted in almost all the essential fluxes and humours. The only natural substance it had left in abundance were tears, so she gave in and let them flow, taking a page from Paul's book. She had been holding them back for so long, that even before they finished falling the level of water in the bathtub had risen by an inch. Her heaving sobs made speech difficult, her breath catching in her throat, her sentences curdling, but she seemed desperate to reply to Yvonne who could only grasp a word here and there.

"What?" Yvonne asked her. "I don't follow you. Grown what?"

Every attempt to clarify was aborted by further eruptions of tears. Yvonne sat helplessly by, unable to piece together the message Archie was struggling to relay, until, in a lull between sobs, she hawked it up in

Yvonne's face like an accusation. "Why should I be acting like a grown-up? I'm not one."

Yvonne's gaze bore into her, wondering how she could have failed to see. More likely, she had just made up her mind not to see. When Archie first materialized on Nora's doorstep, slumped in her improvised wheelchair, Yvonne found it difficult to pin down her age; the signals were wavery. But at the time, between the contusions and the burns, it seemed unimportant, a detail. In appearance she was womanly and Yvonne let it go at that. Even if Archie's behaviour over the weeks that followed occasionally contradicted her curves, Yvonne closed her eyes to the mismatch, never asking the question that would settle the issue once and for all. She and Daphne had that in common. Yvonne hadn't wanted to open herself up to the inconvenient truth that she could be sequestering someone else's baby. Now that period of willful ignorance was at an end.

"I'm fifteen," Archie said.

Upon hearing that number, such an unripe and vulnerable number, Yvonne's neat basement universe was upended. She would have to build up a new one, based this time on the reality she had been keeping at bay.

"Let the cool water out and turn on the hot," Yvonne ordered Archie. She waited until a fresh nimbus of steam settled over them. "This is going to take a while I suppose. No point in us being cold." She hoicked herself up from the floor and sat back down on the toilet seat. "I'm listening," she said.

■ ■ ■

"I always figured our family was normal," Archie began. "When you have nothing to compare it to, what do you know otherwise? Your family is your family. You accept. I thought this was how it happened at everyone's house, that your father brought men home from work to babysit you while he went out with your mother to a restaurant or a play. Manager types, these guys were that came over, in suits and ties. As if there was a dress code. My mother referred to them always as colleagues. 'One of your father's colleagues is coming tonight,' she'd say. I knew what that meant. I never thought to wonder how it was that my dad had so many colleagues. I'd been to his office. It was just him and a secretary. I never thought to wonder lots of things. I was such a stupid, stupid kid.

"It was all so proper on the surface. You would laugh. My mother left out snacks in the kitchen. Yeah, she did. Cookies. Told them how late I could stay up. Then, once my parents left the house, Mr. Human Resources Director or Mr. IT Boss would babysit me. In my room. In his own way.

"Babysit, yeah. That was the word we used at our house. Me even. Babysit. Can you believe it? You know later, way after it all started, in English class one year, we were studying metaphors, similes, that kind of writing stuff. *My love is like a red red rose*, like that. We were supposed to come up with examples. Then, our teacher taught us another term like those other ones, a *euphemism* she called it. It was a word I'd never heard of before but it clicked to me right away. Here all this time I'd had a definition in my mind hunting around for a word, and there it was. I thought to myself, I could raise my hand and give an example of a euphemism that would knock those sheltered little babies in my class right off their seats. But I didn't, of course. *Never talk about home at school.* That was rule number one. Also rule numbers two through ten. It was like they'd carved it in my forehead so I'd see it every time I looked at my reflection and not forget. As if.

"These colleagues of my dad's, they kept coming to the house. Not every day or anything. Not like that. You could never predict. Two times a month, maybe three. Whenever a stretch of time went by longer than usual, I'd treat myself to imagining that it was all over, that his supply of babysitters had finally run out. But then one day I'd overhear my mother say to my dad, 'Arn, I need a night out.' And that was it.

"I wanted it to stop. I did! But at the beginning, in my eight-year-old brain or however old I was, how did I know what to do? I fell for it totally when my parents told me that these visits from the colleagues were what allowed us to have the things we had. Dummy that I was, I took it to mean that if I didn't go along, we wouldn't have food to eat or clothes to wear. We would be poor. I didn't want to be poor, so…

"Later, when I was older, I came up with something that worked, at least for a while. I'd do the bulimic thing, not that I knew that it had a name back then. I'd stuff myself, and then I'd puke. Make it seem like I'd been sick. Would you believe that I thought I invented doing that? Me personally? I didn't have any idea that anyone else in the whole world had ever done anything so gross. Why would they? I thought it was only me alone sticking my finger down my throat. That there was nobody out there as disgusting as me. But it ended up making things worse. See, normally my parents didn't lay a hand on me. But now that I was getting in the way of the program, that changed. So I had to quit.

"It all became such a routine thing in our house that after a while, when I was, I don't know, maybe thirteen, my parents didn't even bother to come in to check up on me when they got home, even if checking in did amount to a joke. When my quote unquote babysitter heard the front door open, he would put his suit back on and straighten his tie in front of my mirror. He'd leave my room and they'd have a little nightcap, the three of them. I could hear the glasses clinking, and then my parents would go straight to bed. I could have been lying there dead for all they knew, but they must have been worn out after their evening at the restaurant or wherever. So it was straight to beddy-bye for them. Couldn't have them waking up with bags under their eyes, could we?

"That it went on for so long was my own fault. No. Don't give me that look like it wasn't." Archie refused to allow Yvonne to cut her off with a contradiction. "I mean it's not like I was living in a cave. I had the web, I had TV. I knew what was happening to me. They didn't keep me locked up or anything. I went out, I went to school. I had every opportunity. But I chose not to tell a teacher or someone else in my class. I chose not to report them to the police. My parents called the shots and I protected them, even though I knew exactly what they were. And it's strange, you know. They trusted me, let me go about my business. They knew that I'd never blab. That I could go out in the world and they'd be perfectly safe. And they were right. So what does that make me?

"Anyway, what finally changed everything was that I got pregnant. Last year. That definitely was not part of their plan. I was so terrified of telling them that I kept putting it off. I never did actually. Tell them that is. I just kept it to myself, hoping I was reading the signs wrong. That it was all a mistake. But eventually my mother started to suspect and bought one of those test things. And what do you think? It said, *Yes, your daughter is off-the-charts pregnant but what did you expect you twisted, subhuman excuses for parents who deserve to rot in hell?* That was not a good day, let me just say. They went ballistic, blamed me. I was careless, stupid. Did I realize what I'd done? The consequences? What could happen to all of us because I'd delayed telling them, and now what were they supposed to do, so late on? I'd never been so scared of them. But the thing is, I was even more scared for the baby. It didn't take a genius to know that they'd make me get rid of it. But there was no way I was going to let them. Never. That baby was mine, and I was going to take care of it. Whatever it took. The way parents are supposed to."

The internal resolution Yvonne had made to keep silent until Archie's memoir caught up with the present splintered with this last detail. "You wanted that baby? To keep it?"

"It sounds sick, right? But I did. I didn't know who the father was and I didn't care. He was nobody. Invisible. Like he never existed. Getting pregnant, it woke me up somehow, like one of those hypnotists you see on TV had snapped his fingers in front of my face. It made me brave for the first time. I'd followed my parents' warped agenda my whole life, never strayed, barely even considered it, but now that was over. I was going to run away. Anywhere. Just so long as it got me away from them. That was my plan. But before I could get myself out of there, they showed up at the house with some doctor they'd dug up, if he really even was a doctor. He looked too young. I refused flat out to go through with it. They couldn't believe it. You should have seen their faces, their house-trained little puppy finally turning out to be a pit bull. That doctor guy was probably wishing he'd never agreed to come, whatever they were promising to pay him. He hadn't bargained for a biting kicking crazy. But he stuck it out, and they got their way. As always. They took my baby away from me. So, I had two choices then, the way I saw it. I could either slit their throats while they slept or get the hell out of there. You know which one I picked."

CHAPTER 34

A POLICE CRUISER was idling in front of her house, the flashers off. Nora spotted it from the cab window. Their taxi driver pulled over to drop them off at a respectful distance behind. "Sorry I can't go any closer, but the police, they get grumpy when we get in their way. I don't want any trouble. This one time, on Gouin Boulevard, I was clear across the street, at a taxi stand, parked all legal, eating my lunch, when I hear these sirens…" Nora didn't linger to listen to his full rant against the excesses of the SPVM's finest. She left Anthony behind to settle up while she flew out of the cab to intercept the two officers who were making their way up her walk, the beams of their bazooka flashlights already playing around her front door as if Céline were about to emerge to sing her second set.

"Is there a problem, Officers?"

"We had a report of a break-in, Madame."

"A break-in? I don't understand. I didn't call you."

"And you are…"

"Nora Elman. This is my house." She fished around in her purse, grabbed the first piece of ID that came to hand, and brandished it in front of the policeman's face, though no one had doubted her claim to ownership.

"But you weren't here tonight."

Nora's guilt at abandoning her post led her to take the uninflected statement as a rebuke. It was against her better judgment that she had given in to Daphne's invitation and let herself mellow out for just a few hours over some wine and conversation in the Underground City, but that smidgen of relaxation had cost her. Nora was of the opinion that as long as she remained in a constant state of anxiety about the world crashing down on her head, it wouldn't. Worrying was, in effect, a cosmic insurance policy, but tonight she had stinted on the premium and see what happened?

"No. We weren't," she said, her head hanging at the perceived dressing-down. "We had dinner out with my granddaughter."

"Our dispatcher says a neighbour reported suspicious activity. Movement inside the house."

"A neighbour? Which neighbour? Who?" Although the answer to that question should have been obvious. There was only one neighbour who would bother to keep her house under surveillance. Nora turned to look across the street and sure enough Ethel Marcil was steaming her way over, her flannelette nightie peeking out from under the hem of her winter coat.

"It was you who called the police?" Nora said.

"Of course it was me. Who else? I was getting ready for bed and I looked out my window and I saw someone moving around in your house. You told me yesterday that you and Anthony would be out tonight to go see Daphne at that race thing, so I knew something was fishy. I called 9-1-1 right away."

If she was expecting appreciation, she wasn't about to get any. "Ethel," Nora said, "you can't see the nose in front of your face. Isn't it me who has to read all your pill bottles to you?"

"That's near, this was far. I'm telling you, someone was definitely upstairs. I saw shadows." She pointed towards the bathroom window.

"Upstairs?" This positional detail threw Nora even further off balance than finding the police parked at her curb.

The policewoman interrupted their back and forth over the degree of Ethel's myopia to get them back on track. "Do you want us to go through the house, Madame, check around back? You don't want any nasty surprises."

There would be surprises all right, guaranteed, but they would be on their side, not hers. Nora knew exactly what they would find; a houseful of illegals plus one questionable who had inexplicably made their way upstairs to make shadow puppets for Ethel Marcil. All the alcohol Nora had downed at dinner was numbing her faculties. She couldn't muster up a single plausible excuse to keep them from searching her house that wouldn't have a suspicious ring to it. Who but the guilty denied access to the police? Damn that Ethel.

Anthony joined the huddle once the cab drove off in an exaggerated arc around the squad cars. "It must be our house guest, Officers, my niece from Chilliwack. Or my great-niece I should say. She's been driving cross-country, bunking out with relatives along the way." He looked to Nora for support. Even a nod of agreement would have helped, but she was sluggish on the uptake so Anthony plowed ahead on his own. "We weren't quite sure when she was going to show up with all the snow and everything. She hasn't been keeping us informed the way we would have liked." He shrugged his shoulders as if to say, "Kids, what can you do?"

"What house guest?" Ethel said to Nora. "You never said anything to me about anyone coming to stay." Their conversation had taken a sharp detour away from the immediate subject of prowlers and break-ins over to the snags of friendship. Anthony was now the vessel into which Nora deposited most of her confidences, a position Ethel formerly held, and it left her feeling on the outs.

"Didn't I?" Nora said. Her friend might have been miffed, but she couldn't stop to placate her now, not while she was struggling to come up with some credible detail that would belatedly shore up Anthony's fabrication.

"No, you didn't. Not one word," Ethel went on. "How did she get in? I have your spare key behind my oatmeal canister where it's been sitting since the beginning of time. What did she do, Miss Chilliwack, crawl in through a window? Go down the chimney maybe?"

A neighbour like Ethel was a blessing. Except when she wasn't. Like now. The policewoman parsed the interchange between the two women. It altered her previous assessment. The fluency of the great-uncle's explanation now struck her as overly glib especially when paired up with Madame Elman's obliviousness vis-à-vis the niece. Officer Lyne Geoffrion was fresh out of the academy, every scrap of her training still crammed into her memory bank, hungry for an outlet. All the ex-cops who taught in the program had hammered away at their students to trust their instincts, and Lyne's instincts, though wet behind the ears, told her that something was off with this couple.

"If we can just have a brief word with your niece," she said, going with her hunch, "we'll be out of your hair in no time."

Lyne's partner, Victor, had over twenty years experience under his belt as certified by his ample midsection. He raised his eyebrows at her unorthodox request but let her have her head. How else to learn?

Nora looked away from the policewoman to the older officer, hoping he would contradict his bushy-tailed junior, but she was stuck with a case of bad cop–bad cop. The decision held. The fictional niece would have to be produced. Nora wrung her hands on the walk, undone. It was left to Anthony to take the keys out his pocket and open the door to their Magic Kingdom one last time before it got condemned.

■ ■ ■

No stars would dazzle for Yvonne tonight. Unmoved were they that she had made a special trip upstairs, fraught with peril, to have special one-night-only access to their display. After listening in on Archie's story through the bathroom window, the constellations had no oomph left to twinkle and closed up shop. Yvonne stood to one side at the window, partially shielded by the flimsy curtain. There was no point anymore in looking upwards. So she looked down.

The view below the window was harsher still. A police car was racing down the street, unheralded by sirens or flashers. It jolted to a stop directly in front of Nora's house and the officers shot out. The duplexes on Nora's street sat cheek by jowl. The chunky neighbourhood raccoons had difficulty negotiating the gap between adjacent homes, so for a few seconds Yvonne was able to delude herself into thinking that the police might be heading next door, but as soon as they exchanged a few strategizing words outside their cruiser, they started with purpose up Nora's front walk. Yvonne watched helpless as the agents of her family's ruin closed in. Again. No rifles or machetes this time, only flashlights, but she wasn't duped by the apparent innocence of their equipment. So this was it then. The end.

In this, the last moments of what passed for her freedom, Yvonne pictured Emmanuel and the children out in the snow, mapping to their hearts' content. She hoped they had left a large enough swath of untrammelled snow in Nora's backyard so they would have room to make snow angels on whose wings they could fly up over the fence and off to safety. As for herself, she was earthbound. There was nothing left for her to do but watch the worst unfold. From her perch on the upper floor she observed Nora come rushing out of a cab to plant herself between the officers and her front door like the blast wall in front of an embassy. She showed them some card out of her wallet, but the piece of plasticized officialdom had no police-repelling powers. Ethel Marcil, Nora's across-the-street neighbour, came over to join her friend on the front walk, still in her nightclothes. From what Yvonne could make of her gesticulations, Nora was more agitated with her than with the police. Had she a hand in this business? Last to come up the walk was Anthony, the rock of the household. He seemed to be trying to bedazzle the police with some story he was spinning, but the police were impervious as Yvonne knew they would be at the last.

"What's so interesting out there?" Archie asked her. She saw Yvonne's trembling fingers twisting and working the curtain pull until it resembled a noose. At her question, Yvonne knelt beside the tub, leaving the scene on the sidewalk to play itself out without an audience. The mother in her briefly considered shielding her wannabe-daughter from the truth for the few minutes that remained before the roundup began but their recent conversation nudged her towards frankness.

"The police. Parked out front."

"Coming here?"

"I believe so."

"What can we do?"

"Nothing, my darling. It's over."

"It can't be. They can't take you away."

"We all knew it would probably happen some day, and it's happening now."

"It's not fair. You didn't do anything."

"I'm sure that isn't how they see it."

"But I need you." All the love cupped in that statement counterbalanced its selfishness.

"Be strong. You have Anthony and Nora to lean on. They're here for you. They only have your best at heart."

"It's not the same with them."

"They're better for you than I am. They can come and go. They aren't trapped in a basement, with no status, no connections, no freedom. Trust them. Believe me on this. If ever again in your life you come across people as fine as they are, you can consider yourself more fortunate than most."

"I don't want fine people. I want you." Yvonne couldn't find it in herself to laugh.

"Listen to me." She reached into the bathwater and took Archie's hands in her own. "You'll tell Nora what you just told me. Everything."

"I can't. I can't say it again."

"You have to."

"No. To repeat it… It's too hard. I won't be able to do it."

"You have to promise me that you will."

"Even if I did, she wouldn't understand the way you do."

"Give her more credit. You can tell her. And she'll deal with it, she and Anthony. And there's Daphne too, don't forget. If it weren't for her, you wouldn't even be here now. We never would have crossed paths. Oh, my Archie, you're an exceptional young woman. Nothing you've lived through has sullied you. Right now you have everything to look forward to if you'll only let them help you along the way."

"I'll follow you," Archie said, her signature stubbornness transcending its previous limits. "I'll get the money somehow and I'll follow you. I'll get on a plane."

"Archie, my love, we don't have much time. Don't waste it talking nonsense. You're not going anywhere but out into the world to live your own life. A good life. And it will happen, I promise you. You don't need me."

"Don't you want me?" It grieved Yvonne that it was even a question she had to ask.

"Of course I do. More than anything. But your place isn't with us, across the ocean, far away from everything you know. Even you understand that, deep down. It's here. This is where you have to make your way."

"But I'll never see you again."

"That is the way of things in this life. I'll miss you every minute of every day. We all will. Don't ever doubt that. Grow up and make us proud. It will be Grace's legacy. You owe it to her to survive and thrive."

Even that, the last arrow in Yvonne's quiver, couldn't stopper Archie's flow. She clearly had a headful of protests yet to vent, but they both froze when they heard the front door open. Yvonne expected the pounding of police footsteps to come next, but instead all they heard was Anthony's voice floating into the house. "Archie, could you come to the door for just a minute please?"

"Me?" Archie said. "It's me they want?" Now it was Yvonne's turn to panic. Despite all she had said, with the tables turned, she wasn't ready to have this girl torn from her. She couldn't live that agony twice. If only the mirrored medicine chest above the sink had supernatural properties that would allow Yvonne to open it up and push Archie through the back panel, not necessarily as far as Narnia but at least to Daphne's apartment where she would be tucked up out of harm's way. Yvonne's eyes raked the spartan bathroom, desperate for it to deliver a hiding place behind the tiles or inside the pipes where she could stash Archie safely away. The instant Yvonne's back was to her, Archie leapt out of the tub and made a sarong of her towel. She didn't dare pause to dry off or dress. If she dragged her feet, it would give the police an excuse to muscle in and hunt her down and there was too much at risk in the house. She had to leave. Now.

Archie got as far as the upstairs landing and looked down at Anthony and the two police officers waiting for her at the threshold, Nora hovering behind. As determined as she was, her bare feet refused to carry her downstairs. She stood paralyzed on the second floor, suffering already from acute Yvonne deprivation, when her imagination jumped in to the rescue. It hastily cobbled together an alternate backstory for the scene in which Anthony was still at the foot of the stairs, smiling up at her encouragingly, but he was wearing a suit instead of his usual roomy-cut jeans, and had a boutonnière in his lapel. The banister was garlanded with blooms. When Archie looked down at herself, she wasn't clad in terry cloth anymore, but in white satin. The train of her gown was trailing behind her, royally long, held up off the carpet by Bérénice, or was it Grace? Strains of music hung in the air, all flutes and violins. Classier music than the Willie Nelson that usually accompanied her practice walks around the basement. The rest of her housemates were also in attendance in her daydream, seated in the first row of folding chairs next to Marius. Even Daphne had managed to make it somehow.

Everyone on the first floor was clearly happy, awaiting Archie's arrival for the proceedings to continue. This matrimonial rejigging of events gave Archie the will to descend and place herself in Anthony's hands to give her away to whatever came next.

Archie had only made it down the first two steps when Victor raised his hand to her in a *stop* gesture and shouted up, "It's okay, Mademoiselle. Sorry to have disturbed you. You can go on back up. We won't be needing to speak to you after all." He turned to address Anthony and Nora. "We'll be going. Apologies for the mix-up."

So rock-sure had Lyne Geoffrion been that Anthony's family story was manufactured to cover up something shady in the house, she would have wagered her pension on it. Even with the evidence right before her of a young woman on the landing, she wasn't ready to let go of her theory. The interrogation of this *niece*, who she still thought of with air quotes, would reveal the exact nature of the family's illegalities.

Lyne tailed after her partner, humiliated that he'd left her hanging out to dry. "Apologies? What are you saying, *apologies*? We should question the niece."

"For what crime? Taking a bath?"

"They're hiding something."

"We came to investigate a possible break-in and that we've done. We have no call to be interviewing the inhabitants of the house as if they were suspects in a crime. It's beyond our purview."

"I know in my gut something's up with them. That niece story is a crock and you know it. They might look like they're an innocent old couple…"

"Probably because they are an innocent old couple. Look, Lyne, it's my duty as senior officer not to let you turn into one of those cops who shoots first and thinks later. You took some leeway, I let it go, but you've got to know when to stop."

"I'm thinking a grow op," she persisted, hoping to bring him around. "Smallish, but still."

"They could be supplying every stoner between Montreal and Trois-Rivières for all I care," he said, her enticement falling flat. "It's not our business, at least not now. Lyne, how many ways can I put it to you? You can't let yourself get carried away with your authority. In our line of work, there's nothing uglier. Come on. We're leaving."

PHYLLIS RUDIN

Nora gave an amiable wave as the police drove off, a rictus plastered to her face. She shooed Ethel away home, and then she and Anthony came in and shut the door behind them. Archie still stood near the top of the stairs dripping water and guilt onto the stair runner. Yvonne came out in timid steps from the bathroom holding Archie's clothes in a bundle. No one made a move to speak. It had been a long time since the house had been so silent. It felt wrong. But the quiet soon corrected itself. Emmanuel and the children, oblivious of the danger they had so narrowly escaped, trundled in from the backyard, and all the giggles they had been holding back on outdoors as promised burst out to fill the kitchen. Their laughing fit cut out, though, when they caught sight of Nora, home ahead of schedule and witness after the fact to their wintry gambol in Verbotenland.

Nora surveyed her clan. One group was damp from the snow, the other from the bath. The shock of finding them so wantonly out and about, even with Ethel's foreshadowing to cushion the blow, shook her to the core. Her basement guests had shown contempt for the rules of the house; rules which were only designed to preserve their own safety, rules that they themselves had had a role in creating. If their cabin fever was so acute, couldn't they have thrashed it out with her? They could have come up with a solution together. But no, instead they had bided their time like Andy Dufresne, holding on until the coast was clear and then *bam*!

Anthony put his hands on her shoulders from behind. "Breathe," he whispered in her ear.

"I am."

"Human breathing, not fire-breathing." With the benefit of his respirational prodding Nora tried to will herself into composure. "Don't jump to any conclusions that you won't be able to go back on," he cautioned her.

"Does it look like I need to jump?"

This kick in the teeth nearly succeeded in knocking the do-gooder wind out of Nora. Until this moment having responsibility for her gaggle of basement visitors pumped her full of energy. She bounded out of bed every morning and pounced on her to-do list, delegating what jobs she could, but tackling most of them herself, and on full throttle. Anthony always honoured her with a snappy salute as he received his allotment of tasks for the day from his Generalissimo Nora. She had never felt so alive. But with this turn of events, the thought of having to cook up even one more batch of her Soupe Mystère as Bérénice had dubbed it, that murky root vegetable concoction that varied its ingredients daily, but somehow always burbled up into the same shade of mud-puddle had Nora exhausted in advance. So limp was she now that she could not even open her mouth to question or berate.

The heavy dose of muteness reverberating in every direction did a job on Paul. He was a very resilient little boy normally. He could handle the family's isolation, he could handle the privations, but plunge him into an atmosphere where tension and uncertainty reigned, and his coping mechanisms rusted right up. In the space of just a few hours his equilibrium had been tested twice. The first time he responded with tears, but this time, as he had so often been adjured, he used his words. He ran up to Nora, heedless of the puddles his boots tracked across the kitchen, and rested his head against the pillow that served as her stomach. He was in the habit of seeking refuge there whenever he needed a grandmotherly cuddle to carry him through. "Papa said Archie needed a salty bath so she wouldn't ache so much and wake up hurting during the night, so Maman took her upstairs, even though she didn't want to. Then Niecy asked if we could please please please go outside without making a single noise, and Papa said that just this once we could. And we didn't make a noise, not once. Did we Papa?"

"No," Emmanuel said, not looking at Paul but at Nora who was cradling his son's head. "You were the best of children."

Nora's charges were sodden, they were cold, they were aching, they were lost. Her vocation, momentarily waylaid, tipped back into its groove. "Okay, everyone," Nora said, "back to the basement. Chop chop. Dump all the wet stuff in the laundry room. Anthony, fetch us extra towels from upstairs, the big beach ones from the top shelf, the ones with the sea horses on them. I'll get the milk heating for cocoa in the microwave." She waited till all the others had traipsed downstairs and she pulled up the rear. Order once again reigned in the house on rue Melançon.

CHAPTER 35

"I WAS TOO SOFT," Nora said, shaking Anthony just as he was on the verge of drifting off.

"You're just right soft," he said, snuggling closer in against her and kneading a paddle of slackish flesh at her thigh to prove it.

"Be serious."

"I am."

"Seriouser," she said, underlining her demand with an I-mean-business smack.

"Okay, okay," he said, downshifting from frisky mode to earnest. "Go ahead. I'm all ears."

"Was I wrong to let it all be bygones? Should I have come down harder on them?"

"No. Of course not. Everybody just needed to let off some steam after being cooped up for so long, that's all. It was a freakish, one-time thing they did. You were right letting it go." It was Anthony's naive impression that they'd chewed the subject bare before finally dropping into bed well past midnight, but clearly Nora thought there was still some meat left on the bones.

"But they walked all over me. I should be angry, right?" Nora often doubted the essential rightness of her own emotions. She liked a second opinion to insure that she wasn't heading down the wrong path. Anthony sometimes wondered how she had ever known whether to be happy or sad before he came along. Marie, his late wife, had never needed him to give a green-light to her feelings before she went ahead and felt them. Uncertainty wasn't part of her makeup. She instantly knew which side she came down on on all manner of subjects, and seldom backtracked. It was a point of honour with her. Her surety was admirable until over the years it settled into an irritating cocksurety. Anthony found Nora's insecurity endearing by contrast. It was satisfying to him to know that he had a role to play in stabilizing the emotional temperature in the household, for if ever there was a house that needed a steady hand on the thermostat, it was Nora's.

"They didn't walk all over you. They were wound up too tight and the rubber band snapped. So they took a little trip outside. They took a little trip upstairs. You don't want them to think of you as their jailer, do you?"

"But what if the police had come in in the end?"

"But they didn't. Why agonize over what never happened?"

"I can't help it. I keep picturing them being dragged away."

"Nora, we've been over this how many times. They're good people trapped in a terrible situation."

"But to take such a risk. What were they thinking?"

"*They* probably don't even know what they were thinking exactly. They were just living for once. Like regular people. Doing what they felt like doing. Just like we do every day. Come on. Let them off the hook."

"I did, didn't I? As far as they know, everything is like before."

"I mean in your mind let them off the hook. They'll sense it if you haven't. It would be cruel to keep them here without an open heart."

"You're right. I know you're right."

"I feel a *but* coming."

"But nothing," she said, grappling for the words that would properly express the muddle she was slogging her way through. "When you come right down to it, I guess you could say I feel towards them like they were my own family. It's not wrong to get upset with your family, is it? To want to wring their necks sometimes? God knows I find Daphne's neck tempting from time to time."

"Yeah, I couldn't help but notice that tonight," he said. "Look, I'd be the last person to say it's wrong. You know my family drives me round the bend half the time. But the people we have in our basement aren't in the same ballpark as some wayward granddaughter or deadbeat brother-in-law. They aren't even on the same planet. They're broken, Nora. I don't know why I even have to be saying all this. It's not like I'm telling you anything you don't already know. They need you to be with them like you were before, on their side, a hundred and ten percent. Otherwise the kindest thing we could do for them would be to set them up somewhere else."

"I would never." He could feel her whole body heaving with affront.

"Why not?" He decided to push her further towards the edge to see if dangling her there might crystallize her thinking. "You have an out here, and you know what it is. A legitimate plan B." She jerked her head around to face the wall, as if by not seeing him mouth the words she wouldn't be able to hear them either.

"Come on. Don't be that way. Look at me," he said, taking her chin gently in his hand and turning her back towards him. "You could put them in a church. Yvonne has lobbied you for it herself, so no one would think any less of you for doing it. I could deal with all the details if you wanted. Find the right place for them, make the arrangements. Set them up safe and sound. You wouldn't have to be the one. I'd handle everything. As for Archie, well, we could farm her out to Daphne. You heard her after the race. She's on the bandwagon again, wanting Archie back at her place. You could always take back what you said at dinner tonight and let her go. We'd be just us chickens after. No worries beyond our own."

"You've got to be off your rocker. How could we ever look each other in the eye again if we did that? Talk about a knucklehead suggestion. Everybody stays, but you I'm putting on probation."

■ ■ ■

The foot race was Larry's brainchild. Even if he had nominally ceded control of the Underground City portfolio to Marius, who had proved himself eminently capable, Larry couldn't let go. The account had too much heft on his ledgers. Every week he showed up at Marius's cubicle, plunked his bottom on the corner of his underling's desk, and recounted his latest idea aimed at increasing the sizzle factor in the Underground City. So far Marius had been able to fend off every suggestion with a few well-considered objections. But when Larry announced his wildest idea, the one that would drop a logistical bombshell square on his ex-intern's head, that was when he decided to withdraw Marius's right of rebuttal.

They would host a race, Larry said, a race like no other race ever seen before; a subterranean run, under a roof from start to finish. Like the Montreal Marathon. But not. Think of it. No pollution, no hills, no dog shit, no potholes, no snow or slush even though it would be in winter. Instead, sleek ramps and corridors, climate-controlled. Some revolving doors and escalators tossed into the mix to separate the men from the boys. A way-out urban experience. Intense. Larry was of the opinion that an underground event, something with splash and hoo-hah as he'd put it, would amplify the blog. "We need something 3D," he'd said to Marius, "not just something flat on paper. Well, I know that the blog isn't on paper, but you get my drift. Something not virtual. Something with real movement and sweat and noise and crowds whipped up to spend. Something mega."

Which was how Daphne came to be standing at the head of a phalanx of 1,000 runners, "Y.M.C.A." thudding out of the loudspeakers, onlookers pressed against the yellow danger tape. Pinned to her T-shirt was a dossard bearing the number one. Based on her previous race performances in the outer world, the organizers should have assigned her a back-of-the-pack number, one that wouldn't see her trampled when the starting horn blew, but in deference to her position as big kahuna of the Underground City, Daphne was accorded a bib that put her ahead of everyone, even the Kenyans.

Runner number one wasn't aiming to break any land speed records. She was just out to enjoy the scenery, even if that scenery was old hat to her. It did gratify Daphne to see that the runners around her, less familiar with their surroundings, were lapping up the quirky route, many of them snapping photos with their smart phones along the way, even if their pauses would bollocks up their finish times.

She had to give Marius credit. Larry had demanded unique and that was what he'd delivered. But just because the route was sheltered from outdoor hazards, it didn't translate that it was easy. An indoor circuit generated its own brand of urban obstacles. The tile floors around the water stations were dangerously slick from all the spills; the mop brigade couldn't keep up. And running down moving escalators was not a skill Daphne and her fellow runners had ever trained for. Gravity, which during a normal outside running race, didn't get all show-offy, seemed to be pulling runners into fancy aerobatics as they jumped off at the bottom, the lucky ones anyway. The others just stumbled off the last step and ran knock-kneed for the next couple of meters as if they'd had a few too many. It was just the kind of race Daphne loved, edgy and unpredictable. Not that she had raced extensively. She was more of a fun-run kind of gal.

Around the 3K mark her ankle developed a bit of a shimmy, fallout from an old injury, but she ran through it, energized by the crowds, and made it to the end, if not speedy at least strong, leaving nothing back on the course. Planted somewhere in the throng, cheering Daphne on, were her grandmother and Anthony. She had invited them to watch the race and then meet up with her and Marius afterwards for dinner. Daphne had reserved them a table in a restaurant facing the lobby of Place des Arts, a resto for concert subscribers who wanted to arm themselves with some solid cuisine du terroir before facing off against a few hours of Mahler. She ordered a Bordeaux for the table as soon as they sat down. Nora peeked over her granddaughter's shoulder at the wine list. She had palpitations when she caught sight of the price.

"Maybe we should just get a carafe?"

"It's okay, I can manage it. You're my guests."

"This is nice," Nora said as she sipped the wine the waiter brought to their table along with a platter of nibbles. "When's the last time we were all out together?" It was a strange comment as the four of them had never even been in a room together let alone out for a social evening. Various combinations and permutations of Daphne, Marius, Anthony, and Nora had shared the same airspace here and there, but never once as a foursome. Daphne cast a sidelong appraising glance at her grandmother, one that tried to calculate how many marbles she might have lost since they'd last sat down together and had a good long talk.

"We've never all been out together," she reminded her. "Or in, for that matter."

"Oh, that's right. What was I thinking? I lost track. You can wipe off that worried face, Daphne. I'm not losing it. It's just the wine going to my head. Speaking of which, I'd like to propose a toast. To Daphne's fantastic finish in the race."

"Grandma, 834th place is hardly worth celebrating."

"It's nothing to be ashamed of. You got a medal."

"Didn't you notice? Everybody got a medal. Even that last-place guy who collapsed across the finish line. Your registration gets you a medal and a T-shirt. It's part of the deal."

"It doesn't matter," Nora said. "To me, completing five kilometres of running is an accomplishment."

"I'm with you there," said Marius. "I'd be lucky to not die after running 1K."

"I probably couldn't even walk 5K, let alone run," Anthony said.

As they were all holding up their glasses expectantly, a look of unironic pride on their faces, Daphne gave in to popular opinion so they could clink and move on.

"My lucky shorts failed me. They should at least have got me 500ᵗʰ place."

"You have lucky shorts?" Marius said.

"Don't laugh. But I think I've put them through the wash too many times. They seem to have lost some of their mojo."

"Maybe that's what I could use," Nora said. "Lucky shorts."

"What for, Grandma? You and Anthony planning a little jaunt to the casino?"

"No, not that. For home and everything. A little magic would do us some good."

"New problems or same old same old?"

"Newish I guess you'd say. It's the lawyer."

"That pro bono guy you found?"

"If you want my opinion, he's worth every penny we pay him."

"That good, huh?"

"Worse." But before Nora could unfurl the full list of Maître Teasdale's shortfalls and work herself into a lather, Anthony cut her off.

"No doom and gloom tonight," he said, pounding his fist against the table like a gavel to give his pronouncement all due authority. "We're meant to be celebrating." Everyone would benefit, he judged, from a night on vacation from their various troubles. He steered the conversation into what he presumed was less touchy territory.

"So, Daphne, how's your dissertation coming along?" Daphne would have preferred sticking to the stinko-lawyer line of conversation for she had nothing good to report. It was more of a wishertation at this point.

She had so many other concerns tugging at her skirts for attention; Archie, her grandmother, the Demels, the blog, that the dissertation had sunk to the bottom of the pile where its chance of resurgence was slim and none. The spate of emails from Professor Séguin checking up on her progress she left unanswered, to her shame. What was there to say, that life had overtaken her and the dissertation would just have to wait its turn? She was so far removed from it that at this point she could barely remember what it was about.

"Well, I've been pretty busy with work and everything. The blog. You might not think so, it being so short and all, but it's a real time sponge."

"Have you gotten any new chapters out to your professor for review since you've been here," Nora asked her, "any at all?"

"Not yet actually."

Nora couldn't prevent her lips from pursing. *Not yet* in Daphne-speak was synonymous with *it-ain't-gonna-happen*. It was just as she'd feared. Daphne was never going to finish. That was the long and short of it. For all her talk of how this year in isolation would give her the freedom to buckle down and write, it was just so much hot air. Her granddaughter would emerge from her underground stopover a whiter shade of pale and not a single step closer to her dream of a steady university teaching job. The last thing Nora wanted was for Daphne to follow in her footsteps as a worker bee, but she could feel it coming. The fates seemed to have decided that higher education was just too high above the likes of them.

Marius tried to come to Daphne's rescue. "She's been uncovering all sorts of weird and wonderful stuff for the blog. Creating lots of buzz. They're very happy at the office. Larry is over the moon. Just wait till you see her blog about the *No Pants Montreal Metro Ride*. You'll get a kick out of it."

"Don't look at me like I'm nuts," Daphne said to her grandmother. "It's a thing. Not just here. Internationally. One day a year, all over the world, in cities where they have a metro, Paris, New York, Moscow even, people gather on the platform, students mostly, dressed like usual except they aren't wearing pants. Then they get on the cars as if everything is normal. They sit down, do their Sudoku, listen to their music, work on their laptops. It's a giant improv. Check it out on the web if you don't believe me."

"And you let that take precedence over your dissertation?" Nora asked, wearing her what's-the-world-coming-to face. "Writing about idiots who ride the metro naked?"

"I can't help it. It's my job to cover what's happening underground, and that's a big happening as it turns out."

Anthony was in agreement with Nora that the event was demented, those kids participating would all catch their death, but he tried to jolly her out of her agitation. "Nora, we're just a pair of old farts. We can't judge what young people are prepared to get up to."

"She's practically writing a porn blog," Nora said, looking to Anthony for backup.

"Grandma!"

"How do you hold your head up?"

"Let's not get carried away," Anthony said, his hope of keeping the evening off the negative rapidly dimming. "It's her job, like she told us."

"We've always done honest work," Nora said to her granddaughter. "Maybe we weren't rich, but we always did honest work."

"What? You're saying I'm prostituting myself?"

"I'm just saying, Daphne Elizabeth, that you shouldn't let your paycheque from those people blind you."

"*You* haven't minded taking advantage of that paycheque. Doesn't it keep you in food and whatnot for all your *guests* shall we call them?"

Nora maintained a smoldering silence.

"Well, doesn't it?"

Marius had botched the evening but good. He was keenly aware that this dinner with Nora and Anthony had a subtext; it was more than just a post-race fête. Daphne was planning on using it as a platform to launch a new pitch for Archie's return, one lubricated with sufficient wine to make it more palatable to her grandmother than the previous one when Nora had turned her down flat. So much for that idea.

"You're blowing this all out of proportion," Daphne went on. "I've done absolutely nothing to be ashamed of. If you're ashamed of me, well, that's your issue, not mine. If you don't want to take what you see as tainted money, that's your issue, not mine. Just say the word and I'll cut off the flow."

"Threats don't become you, girlie."

Anthony made another stab at pacification. "Nora, we're out for a nice evening. Let's not ruin it."

"It's not me ruining it."

"Believe what you please," Daphne said.

"Don't delude yourself," Nora said. "You're losing your kwan under here."

"Where do you get off accusing me? My integrity is as intact as it ever was. Who died and made you judge and jury?"

"You think I don't have eyes to see?"

"Maybe you should use those eyes to look in the mirror."

"Enough," Marius broke in, his tolerance for sniping having reached its limit. "It's over." No one had ever heard Marius raise his voice. They didn't even know he was capable of it. "We're wasting a rare opportunity here to relax and enjoy ourselves. You think that's nothing? We're together. We're healthy and we're safe. I can think of a few people we all know who would give anything to be able to go out for a simple meal in a restaurant, to be able to sit and chat in a bright, cheerful public place and not have to spend the whole time looking over their shoulders. Maybe what we need is a little perspective here." His rap on the knuckles raised the civility bar back up to where it had been at the beginning of the evening. Or nearly.

Daphne looked out over the table and pictured an altered configuration of chairs, one with Emmanuel at the head of the table and Yvonne at his right, Philippe in a high chair jammed between them, gumming away at a piece of baguette. Bérénice and Paul would sit next to each other, on Emmanuel's left, all dressed up for the outing. Archie would be stationed beside Paul, helping him cut up his chicken, her stone façade long relegated to the garbage. It was that image that pushed Daphne to purge all the leftover spikiness from her voice, even though she normally was slow to unrile.

"So how are the Demels getting along?" she asked, in a show of reconciliation.

"Oh, they're hanging in there," Nora said, making a comparable effort to shuck off some of the aftereffects of their clash so they could meet in the middle.

"I don't know how they handle it," Marius said. "Futureless like they are."

"They have a future all right," Anthony said. "The question is, is it a future they can stomach? Futures are a scary thing, any way you look at them."

"It kills me to think of them getting sent back," Nora said.

"Let's not get ahead of ourselves. For now they're safe and sound tucked up with us," Anthony said, not wanting to let the conversation take another nosedive. "There's a solution out there. We just have to find our way to it."

"Let's drink to that," Daphne said, and they raised their glasses again. Soon it became a habit. They toasted over and over to any grain of hopefulness they could dig up in their lives. A new bottle had to be brought out before they'd even thought of food so they could continue to trinquer. Fuelled by those toasts, the evening, which had gotten off to such a rocky start, settled into a comfy looseness.

"How's Archie coming along?" Marius asked.

"She's getting there, knock wood," Nora said. "It's been a slog, but she's getting there. Looks-wise she's much improved. Her face isn't really black and blue anymore. It's a nice overall shade of yellow. Her prettiness is peeking through. I always knew it was hiding out there somewhere in the background."

"True enough," said Anthony. "It's not the bruises that are the issue anymore. Or the ribs. And the burns are pretty well healed, not much scarring to speak of. She got off lucky there. It's her legs now that need work. Emmanuel wants her to walk more, build them up, but, well, you know the situation. Not much scope for mileage where she is, poor little soul, like a calf in a pen."

Dearest Anthony. He had given Daphne the gift of an opening, and just at the point when she had chalked off the evening as a writeoff. Here she still had a chance to go for the gold.

"Well, if you think it would help any," Ms. Disingenuous said, as if the notion had just then dropped from the sky, "I guess it would be okay if she came to stay at my place. Just for a bit. Not be too showy about it. We could walk all over underground, get her legs back in shape, and then she could go back to you for the finishing touches. It sounds like it's just what the doctor ordered."

Marius might have brokered a truce, but Nora refused to initial the codicil that pertained to the transfer of Archie. She answered to a higher authority on that issue. "No," she said. "Absolutely not. You need to focus on your dissertation. You have enough distractions already. Better that Archie stay put. We'll manage." A waiter hovered at Nora's shoulder, his pad flipped open and ready. "Shall we order?" she said. The subject was closed.

CHAPTER 36

WHATEVER HACK APHORIST coined the phrase *a problem shared is a problem halved* didn't know Archie. Or maybe his math skills weren't as strong as his writing skills. Archie seemed no lighter for having split the weight of her past with Yvonne. If anything, once the initial euphoria she'd enjoyed at getting her story off her chest wore off, she seemed more burdened than ever, crawling deeper and deeper into herself. Seeing her history through someone else's eyes for the first time made her feel dirty in a way she never had before, when she alone knew the full account of her day-to-day.

How could it be, she now asked herself obsessively, that she had never reported her situation to anyone who might have helped? Why had she rolled over and played dead for so many years? Yvonne might not have asked those same questions of her aloud during her bathtub recital, but Archie perceived her initial blip of shock at how she had handed over her childhood on a silver platter. Archie's situation wasn't like the ones in those cop shows where kids like her were held captive in a stinking crawl space to be used by their piggy parents who had the mental capacity of a broom. She came and went like any kid in her neighbourhood, leaving the house for school every morning with her backpack and her lunch, wearing a uniform clean and pressed. Yet she'd never used her freedom to extricate herself, just trudged straight home every afternoon like a kicked dog who didn't know any better than to return to the owner with the trigger-happy foot. Although there had been that one time.

■ ■ ■

When she was around twelve, school trundled off a busload of girls to a gymnastics competition in Ville Saint-Laurent. Even though Chantal was congenitally klutzy her parents signed her up for gymnastics year after year, her sole extra-curricular activity. She wasn't going to be competing. This was too high-level a tournament for her low-level talents. Coach Galucci always shook her head over Chantal, comparing her flailing tumbling style to popcorn in a popper. It was only at bench-warming that Chantal showed any true skill. She cheered on her teammates when they were out on the mats, but otherwise just sat on the sidelines guzzling Gatorade as if she too needed her electrolytes replenished.

Seated next to her on the bench was Karine, a year or so her senior. Though they had been acquainted a long while, coming up through the balance beam ranks together, they weren't really what you would call friends. In fact, Chantal had no friends to speak of; friends being frowned upon by the parental unit. So closed-mouthed was Chantal, in class and out, as unyielding as a swollen cupboard door, that even her classmates who made a career of kindness gave up on her as a project and left her to her own company.

Karine had the perfect anorexic build of a stellar gymnast plus the requisite sproing. There were times in her floor routine at practice when Chantal wondered if Karine was ever going to come back down to earth, or just stay suspended in the stratosphere until she had to pee. But there were other times, most times, when she just went through the motions, her jumps so listless they would barely get her over a crack in the sidewalk. The coach could never predict which Karine would show up on which day, so she rarely put her forward in competitions like this one where the trophy was so splendid, practically outsizing the Stanley Cup.

The two benched girls were watching the wobbly floor exercises of their teammate who had been plunked into the roster in place of Karine. She wasn't a total write-off, but her ups were more commanding than her downs. She had a strong takeoff style, like Superman off to fight the good fight, but she inevitably landed with all the grace of a gutter ball. Feeling uncharacteristically outraged on her passed-over teammate's behalf, Chantal turned to Karine and said, "It's you who should be out there, not

Nadja. You're a hundred times better than she is." It was the first time Chantal had addressed her outright on any subject more personal than chalk or towels and it took all her nerve to do it. Karine was as friendless as Chantal, but she seemed to be above wanting friends. Whereas Chantal's circumstances dictated that she be alone, Karine carried a force field around her that said *approach at your own risk*.

"Like I give a shit. Let the little turd have it if she wants it that bad."

"It doesn't bother you?"

"Are you kidding? It's not like gymnastics means anything to me. I'm only here because my parents force me. They want me to come? Fine. I'll come. But don't expect me to do any more than the minimum."

"Don't they get mad at you?"

"You think I give a flying fuck about that?"

Chantal was warming to Karine. She had always admired her aggressive style on the mats, but now that admiration grew to encompass the comparable stamp on her character. So much was she in awe of Karine's take-no-prisoners style that a few years later, when Chantal would run away to the Underground City, it was Karine's persona she adopted. Her own simpy character would never let her survive there. That much she understood.

"It's my parents who make me come too," Chantal volunteered. "I would never have picked gymnastics either." Admitting just that much was a huge departure for her, a front pike into unknown territory.

"I figured as much, seeing as how you suck at it." Chantal wasn't in the least offended by Karine slamming her. It was no more than the truth. "So why do they make you keep on with it then?" Karine asked. "Are they blind or what? Why don't they let you take your ass over to Robotics where you belong?"

Chantal could have just spit it out right then, as naturally as you please, that her parents needed their clumsy daughter to participate in gymnastics because it would help explain away, should anyone ever get suspicious, the frequent black and blue marks that dotted her landscape, the ones that derived from less socially acceptable sources. But when it came right down to it, she couldn't say the words. Her habit of toeing the family line was too ingrained. Not even to save her own skin could she open up. That was the moment she realized she deserved whatever she got.

■ ■ ■

Archie didn't know if Yvonne had gone on to share the story of her past with any of the others in the house, but even if she had kept it to herself, the rest of the crew would soon catch the drift. They had all been living in such close proximity for so long that a hive mind had developed. Thoughts, though unspoken, leapt like lice from one head to another. And once the rest of them learned of her background they couldn't help but find her disgusting, despite all of Yvonne's assurances to the contrary. Her story would take up too much space, and space in the basement was at a premium. It would press on her. She wouldn't be able to breathe. Her initial reaction in the bathtub had been the right one. She had to prepare herself. She had to leave. The anonymous Underground City, where no one knew what a piece of filth she was, would welcome her back, no questions asked.

Step one in her exit strategy was to make herself less noticeable, to look like more of a cog in the Underground City than a bug, at least at the beginning while she was still presentable. Archie had dyed her hair blue a week before leaving home in her first show of defiance after her parents had sicced that butcher on her to scrape out her unborn baby, but now she understood the hair colouring had been a mistake; she would have been better served to fade into the woodwork. In her last days under their roof, though, she couldn't resist the compulsion to go blue. Another sort of girl might have cut herself to prove she wasn't a cipher, to assert she was alive and kicking and calling the shots, but blood-red wasn't for Archie. Blue dye had been her gateway drug but now that blue, faded and growing out though it was, had to go.

The big coupon-cutting scissors that Nora often left down in the basement after one of her clipping extravaganzas were sitting on the table. Archie picked them up and handed them to Bérénice handles first, "All the blue round the bottom," she said, "off." Normally an eager enough beautician, Bérénice looked unsure. "Your parents won't mind," Archie said, tipping her head towards the closed laundry room door behind which Yvonne and Emmanuel were having one of their confabs. "You're doing it with my permission."

"Those scissors are awful big," Paul said to his sister.

"I'm not a little kid. I can handle big scissors. Just because you're not allowed," Bérénice said, although Archie could see she was waffling. It was Bérénice who had suggested going out in the snow on the night of Daphne's race, and the spillover from that suggestion had not been pretty. She didn't want to be at the root of any further squalls.

"You could cut part of her ear off," Paul said. "What would Maman say then?"

"How clumsy do you think I am?"

"I don't think we're supposed to use those scissors when she's not here."

"Maybe he's right," Archie said. "I can do it myself. I wouldn't want to get you into trouble. Just hold up the mirror for me. That would be legal, I think."

Bérénice was torn. "It'll look awful if you do it yourself. You won't be able to see behind you to get the back right."

"Well, if that's my only choice."

"Why can't Anthony do it for you?" Paul asked. Anthony was the household's resident barber. Even with the slight tremor in his right hand he acquitted himself quite nicely in the role. Bérénice treated Paul to an older-sister look that expressed the requisite disdain. He was starting to clue in that this was to be a sub-rosa haircut, one with no direct adult participation or foreknowledge. Archie could have had Anthony do it, Paul was right, but she didn't want to get into the whys and wherefores of her request. She wanted to spin her cut as a surprise, just a simple updating of her look, nothing more.

Bérénice took the scissors from Archie's hand. "Sit down. I'll do it." She started spreading newspapers on the floor around the chair as she had seen Anthony do.

"I'm telling," Paul said, and headed toward the laundry room using his pouty walk.

"You do and you'll be sorry." It was an idle threat and Paul knew it. So unversed was his sweet sister in the language of intimidation that she could not even come up with any specific torment to dangle over his head as an experienced bully would have done. Still, her amorphous threat stopped him in his tracks. If this hidden haircut was important enough to Bérénice for her to make a stab at blackmail, he would stand by her.

219

When Yvonne came out of the laundry room with her husband, Bérénice was just finishing up on Archie, removing the sheet she had draped around her as a smock. Her assistant stylist, Monsieur Paul was scurrying to gather up the blue wisps that had escaped the newspapers. In trying to keep the sides even, Bérénice was guilty of a bit of over-snipping, with the result that Archie now had a tousled pixie, not even close to the style Bérénice had intended, but her client declared herself wholly satisfied with the results when the mirror was held up to her. Too short or no, she had her old chestnut hair back and was glad of it. Yvonne was lavish with compliments to both the cutter and the cuttee, but she would have uttered the same claptrap if Bérénice had chopped Archie's hair down to the nub POW style. All that mattered to Yvonne was what the cut presaged in the grander scheme of events, and she was afraid she knew what that was.

CHAPTER 37

IN 1989, WHEN the Berlin Wall was being hacked to pieces, the Underground City acquired itself a goodly chunk of the ex-barrier at fire-sale prices, airlifted it to Montreal, and mounted it on a plinth at the Centre de Commerce Mondial near the reflecting pool. The tourists loved the graffitied hunk of concrete; it was a selfie magnet. Daphne's relationship with it was more conflicted. To her it was the spirit and symbol of her confinement, a twelve-foot-high reminder that she was stuck in an inverse gated community, one designed to keep her in not out. There were times when she could have sworn she heard it mocking her as she walked by. "What are you kvetchin' about, toots?" the wall would say. "A year in captivity ain't nothin'. I kept my people shut up tight for twenty-eight years. Now that's what I call barricaded. Your stint here? Piddly shit." Was she losing it?

Daphne tried to make maximum use of her quarantine to distract herself from her worries, filling every spare minute to overflowing so Archie would be stuffed into remote corners of her mind rather than blanketing it like a flag on a coffin. If there was a line to stand in, she stood in it; an appointment to be made, she booked it. As a result, she was sublimely up-to-date in the paperwork department. Her passport, though useless in her clipped-wing state, was spanking new; ditto her driver's license. In offices and anterooms all over the Underground City she pulled off a number tab from the dispenser and waited patiently so she could renew all the cards that accordioned out when she opened her wallet. Nora would not have recognized this version of her granddaughter for whom a deadline had always been a moving target. Cosmetically she had never been so cossetted, scheduling herself for every procedure on offer. Daphne made liberal use of the freebie coupons the contest had provided to get herself threaded, manicured, pedicured, waxed, massaged, and exfoliated. The petite jellyfish tattoo on her left hip, regretted even before the ink was dry, she had lasered into oblivion. Good riddance. She even went so far as to have her fingerprints taken when she stumbled into a crowd of people milling about, waiting for the ID agency to open.

From morning till night she kept herself tied up in an endless flurry of make-work assignments, but manic busyness didn't do the trick. Daphne's Archie worries were as resistant to tampering as a childproof cap; there was no outmaneuvering them, no outrunning them. They were a fact of life and she had to deal with them. Her thoughts kept creeping without her consent towards the phone number on the Missing poster, the only lead she had. She had done everything she could with that number short of dialling it. She had plugged it into every search engine on the Web to see if it led her anywhere, and when her efforts flopped, she appealed to Ludovic to put a squeeze on his old police connections. If life were a TV show she would have had a name and address to connect to that number in no time flat, but the Montreal police force, as free with its illegal favours as it usually was, seemed to have some residual grudge against the retired cop-turned-coffee-entrepreneur and wouldn't cough up any of its insider knowledge his way.

At the other end of that phone line was a family that wanted Archie back. Archie's parents were a spectral, malevolent presence in Daphne's imagination; the precise nature of their misdeeds unknown to her. Daphne's creative gifts usually dressed in hiking boots. They were sturdy enough for a blog, but not nimble enough to visualize the snarls of depravity that infested the Clark household, for all that she sensed the ugliness there that drove Archie from the scene. She should have considered herself lucky to be spared.

Yvonne had no need to rely on her imagination. Archie had made her a gift of the truth, even if it was a poisoned gift. From Archie's description, she could picture in living colour the girl's parents, could see right through their packaging, anatomically correct in all respects save for the mounds of smoldering ash where their hearts belonged. She lined the two of them up in her personal pantheon of cruelty alongside the other monsters she had come up against in her life, rampaging thugs and killers, yet she had trouble deciding where Archie's parents ranked in relation to those others from her past, who among them was entitled to top spot. It was a close contest. Yvonne didn't consider herself a vengeful person—sorrowful, wounded, angry, all of the above, but vengeful, no, not until now. So much so that if Archie's parents were lined up before her doused in gasoline, she could have struck the match and walked away whistling.

It was Yvonne who shouldered the burden of the story that Daphne was longing to hear. Instead, Daphne had to be satisfied with snippets of information that trickled out to her, usually via Marius, who was not afflicted by her mobility issues. It was his assignment to serve as Daphne's eyes and ears on rue Melançon. Ever since Daphne's failed attempt after the race to effect Archie's transfer, she had him make more frequent forays out to her grandmother's house to gather intelligence, after which they would reconnoitre at La Fabrique du Bagel, a lunch spot just beside the Berlin Wall. It seemed an appropriate site for their debriefings.

La Fabrique was Daphne's latest café fétiche in the Underground City, an eatery that not only made bagels on-site, but also hosted bagel seminars where attendees could learn to mix and work the dough, and then hand-roll bagels the old-fashioned way, all their efforts followed by a tasting. Her blog on Bagel College a month earlier had racked up a whack-load of comments and La Fabrique was duly grateful for the increased patronage it drummed up. She was already consuming one of her favourites combos, brie and pears on a black-seed, when Marius plopped himself down to join her.

"I bring tidings," he said.

"Of comfort and joy?"

"'Fraid not."

"Figures. When do you ever bring me good news? Okay, I'm fortified by lunch. Sock it to me."

Marius gobbled down the remains of his sandwich before beginning his report. "So I was able to grab a few minutes alone with Anthony at the house. According to him, something's about to go down."

"Speak English please, not gumshoe."

"You know Archie cut her hair?"

"Yeah, I saw it on Skype."

"Well, apparently Yvonne thinks this is significant."

"More significant than cutting her toenails? It's a haircut. What's the big deal?"

"Yvonne thinks she's preparing herself."

"For what?"

"She thinks it's a sign. That's she's gearing up to leave."

"Leave? For where?"

"Back underground Yvonne thinks."

"Why now? Did something happen?"

"That I couldn't tell you. I'm just reporting what Yvonne thinks via Anthony."

All those "Yvonne thinks" ticked Daphne off. She wanted to be the one doing the thinking on Archie's behalf. Hadn't her thinking been right on the money when Archie appeared beaten up and bleeding in her apartment? Hadn't she worked her connections to rush her to a doctor and to safety? All Yvonne had to do was play nursemaid, and now she was presuming to read Archie's mind?

Daphne was stewing, and that, Marius knew from experience could easily drag on. He tried to snap her out of it so they could attend to present business. "We can't just let her slip back into being homeless," he said. "Even with a divining rod we might never be able to track her down a second time. If she's bent on dropping out of sight, you know she'll manage it and if she runs into the wrong kind of people again, well, that'll be it," and he ran an illustrative finger across his throat.

Marius was right. At four-million-plus square metres, the Underground City was so vast, its passages so labyrinthine, its borders so amorphous that Daphne wouldn't be able to count on bumping into Archie again, especially if she was determined to lie low. She was a resourceful girl, Archie, and could find herself a new foxhole to call her own, one far from Daphne's usual trade routes and there she would install herself until all her potential dribbled out of her, leaving behind a husk.

"So, chief," he said, "what's the plan?"

"The plan?" Daphne didn't have a clue.

CHAPTER 38

"YOU READ THAT article on the front page, did you," Anthony asked Nora, pointing, "at the bottom there?" They were catching their breath on the sofa, swapping sections of the *Gazette* back and forth, as they did every morning after the bustle of preparing breakfast for the multitudes.

"The one about that family from Pakistan? You bet your sweet life I read it. I had to take an extra Benzapril after, it got me so riled up. Can you believe it? It's not enough that the poor woman has a heart attack and has to leave the safety of the church and her family to go to hospital, but then they swoop down on her in her hospital room to deport her. They actually come to her bed! It made me sick. I'm surprised those goons didn't just pull the plugs on all her machines and let her drop dead on the spot." Nora brushed her palms against each together. "Problem solved."

"At least the doctor had the guts to stand up to them saying she was too sick to fly. He made them leave her be. So there's one hero in the story anyway," Anthony said.

"He was a good guy, the doctor, granted. I'm not taking anything away from him. But it's only a reprieve he gave her. She can't stay in hospital forever. They've got her tagged as a drain on the health system, so once she's recovered, out she'll go like so much rubbish."

"Did you see where it says that her daughter's a Canadian citizen? I would have thought that would carry some weight."

"Nope. Separating families doesn't give them a single twinge. Remember that story we saw on the *National* a few weeks back where the parents got deported to I forget where, but they chose to leave their children who were born here behind? Teeny kids they were too. I can't even begin to imagine all the agony that went into that decision. I'm glad it wasn't me had to make it."

That was a news bite that still gave them both shivers, cutting as it did uncomfortably close to the bone. Little Philippe, snuzzling peacefully in Daphne's ex-sock drawer beneath their feet, was a proud graduate of the maternity ward at Hôpital Saint-Luc, and by virtue of his local birth was legally entitled to a maple leaf on his diaper. He alone among his family could claim Canadian citizenship with all its inherent rights and privileges, though in practical terms all it meant was that he would be allowed to wave bye-bye to his family from behind the wire fencing if they were ever picked up and manhandled onto a plane bound for Côte d'Ivoire.

"Maybe all this public attention will shame the government into leaving the lady be. It's happened before," Anthony said. "The people make a big stink and the officials back down."

"*This* government? Don't make me laugh. They don't know the meaning of the word *shame*. Some of the heartless things they do to these poor people who've tried to escape every kind of horror back where they come from, it makes you wonder if they're really human or some kind of robots, even if I don't want to be giving robots a bad name. I don't get it. Someone voted those Conservatives in. God forbid those fools might do it again." Anthony had never actually gotten around to telling Nora that he had voted Conservative in the last election. It was one of those details, like your credit rating or your shoe size, that had just fallen by the wayside in all the flutter of a new relationship. It didn't seem worth fessing up now.

The closet Conservative levered himself up out of the couch cushions. "Well," he said, "guess I can't put it off any longer." Delivering the reassembled newspaper downstairs had turned into the low point of his daily routine. If only he were able to snip out the offending stories before the Demels saw them he wouldn't mind playing paper boy, but he could hardly hand them a newspaper shot full of holes. He and Nora had batted about cutting off their *Gazette* subscription and then spinning the move to Emmanuel and Yvonne as a cost-saving measure, but in the end they decided that imposing a news embargo on the house's lower level wasn't their call to make. Anthony would deliver the paper unredacted every morning and the Demels would learn what they would learn, however chilling.

Nora kissed the paperboy on his way and gave him a gentle shove in the right direction, relieved that in the apportionment of tasks that had developed between the couple, this particular job had not devolved to her. She escaped to the dining room where the next batch of jobs awaited her, leaving Anthony standing forlornly at the top of the basement stairs. He knocked on the door frame to announce himself and when he got the go-ahead, descended and handed Emmanuel the folded paper before they sat down to their ritual second coffee together. If the Demels nursed an urge to kill the messenger he wouldn't have blamed them.

The newspapers didn't hold many surprises for the Demels. They wouldn't be stuck in a basement in the first place if they weren't already acutely aware of what could happen to families like theirs, families where the guillotine blade of deportation was suspended above their necks just itching to make a basket. All the articles in the newspaper did was hammer home the truth that in the current political climate, setting one eyelash outside your sanctuary was asking to be rounded up. Emmanuel berated himself mercilessly after the fact for perpetrating the spectacular folly of a backyard winter excursion with the children when danger loomed everywhere, even in their tranquil quartier. Of this he already had direct experience. Sometimes danger slithered right into your own living room through the same trusting mail slot that normally opened its flap to nothing more sinister than supermarket circulars and takeout menus from Pizzadélic.

■ ■ ■

Emmanuel had known it couldn't be good news when he came home from his shift at the garage to find the slim buff-coloured government envelope on the carpet. He was halfway expecting it after the cousin who had sponsored the family to come to Canada, the cousin who had pulled every string to get them out of that refugee camp prestissimo, was slapped into prison. Emmanuel could still hardly credit it; his bespectacled cousin Léon, an educated, introspective, generous man with a high-power government job, a fancy home in Baie d'Urfé, a wife. Well, no wife anymore since he had bashed Priscilla's head in and left her to bleed out on the floor and then called the police in on himself. But Emmanuel's halfway expectation of doom fought for precedence with the halfway hope that in the vast bureaucratic bowels of the Canadian government the Demels' connection with this murderer who did not share their surname would slip by unnoticed. The envelope dashed that hope.

It had come to the Board's attention, the letter stated, that Monsieur Léon Suma, having been convicted of murder in the second degree, was no longer eligible to serve as the Demel family's sponsor under the Immigration and Refugee Protection Regulations (P.C. 2011-1316). In consequence thereof, the family's application for permanent residency was nullified. The letter went on in flawless legalese to detail what avenues remained for the Demels to pursue, but Emmanuel had difficulty focussing on any of the words that came after *nullified*. On subsequent readings, once his heart stopped galloping in his chest, the word *appeal* jumped out of the text. So there was a process apparently. They were not going to be expelled tomorrow. They could appear before the Board, which would no doubt judge them a worthy, law-abiding family that would be a credit to their new country, and it would have the opportunity to reverse the initial decision. But in the end, after all the appeals had spun out, the Board did not take advantage of that opportunity, and another envelope arrived at their door, a thicker one this time, that contained a departure order and a notice to appear.

There was no power on earth that would convince Emmanuel to take his family back to the country that had brutalized them, so he arrived at the decision to treat the *notice to appear* as a *notice to disappear* with surprising ease. An election wasn't that far off, he reasoned with himself; maybe a kinder, gentler new government would repeal the draconian immigration laws that had scooped his family up in their net and be willing to revisit their dossier in a more humane light. It was an insane plan, he knew, one with infinitesimal odds of success, but it was a gamble he was prepared to take. What alternative was there? The family would go underground.

If the decision was clear; the actual mode of execution was murky. How does an ordinary law-abiding person go underground? How do you find an under-the-table job or sign a lease or pay your rent or school your children if you are a non-person? How do you bank your meagre savings or get a driver's license or even a library card? How, without proper ID, do you get a vaccination or medication or even get buried? What Emmanuel and Yvonne needed was a guidebook, but of all the thousands of people who had already slipped into that netherworld of the undocumented, none had stopped to write one up. How would they collect the royalties?

Enter Nora.

■ ■ ■

Something was up next door. Nora started to hear crying all night long through the dividing wall and it wasn't coming from little Philippe. These wails were powered by more mature lungs. The Demels were quiet neighbours, a significant upgrade from the McLeans who had preceded them in the adjoining house and kept the bass thumping strong enough to set Nora's knick-knacks jiggling on their shelves. With the Demels, Nora seldom heard anything louder through the wall than the sound of children shouting in play. But sobbing. This was a new development. She hoped she hadn't pegged Emmanuel wrong. He had always seemed to her a gentle man, but who knew what went on behind a couple's closed doors? More likely they had had bad news from home. A death in the family perhaps. But she couldn't let crying like that go uninvestigated. What if it did have a more sordid source?

After her sixth straight sleepless night, Nora set herself up on her front stoop in what Daphne called her crouching-tiger position, waiting for Yvonne to emerge. The women had more than a nodding acquaintance, less than a friendship. Their relationship had been lolling in the slough between the two for too long, Nora felt. This seemed like the proper moment to scootch it forward. After sitting on her steps for so long she was beginning to wonder how she would crank herself back up to vertical again, Yvonne finally stepped outside. Nora invited her to sit beside her on the stoop for a few minutes, the weather was so fine. Yvonne hesitated.

She was too distraught to stop and make neighbourly chit-chat, and her list of jobs for the day was long enough to trip over, but how could she refuse this older woman who lived all alone and was clearly craving company. She would sit for a few minutes and talk about the weather, but whether the météo forecast rain or snow or locusts or frogs, it was all the same to her. There was only one subject that consumed her, and on that she was sworn to secrecy. She and Emmanuel had a pact. Not a soul must know of their plan to slip off the map. It was too risky. They could trust no one. But with the motherly warmth of Nora's thigh against her own on the stoop it all came spilling out.

"You can come live here with me," Nora said. So they did.

CHAPTER 39

Normally Daphne approached her blog research in tabula-rasa mode. She went into every underground event with her preconceived notions stashed in off-site storage so her reportage would be unbiased, her observations fresh. Her loyal public, whose tastes she had gradually become attuned to, expected nothing less, and she strived to accommodate them no matter the lengths it took. The first major test of her mettle took place at the Foods of the Future Salon where she had been invited to sit down to a plate of grasshoppers simmered in a raspberry vinegar reduction. Even as her throat seized up against eating a member of the buzzy kingdom, she'd closed her eyes to the mandibles and dug in. No one could accuse her of lacking in the openness department. But when it came to the Salon de l'occulte, she balked. Crystals, tarot, palm readers, clairvoyants, neo-Paganists, Druidry, wicca, and Ouija. It was positively medieval. In Daphne's value system, using her blog to promote this salon was on a par with using it to hype leeches.

Though there existed no Hippocratic oath for bloggers to govern her conduct, Daphne forced herself to take the high road. It was her job to bring in the bodies, whatever her personal animus for the subject. So maybe she wouldn't give it her absolutely top-tier treatment, but no one, apart from Marius perhaps, would be able to notice that she'd skimped. And surely, though she wanted to give them more credit than that, there were those among her followers who, instead of getting together for a chick flick and Mojitos on a dateless Friday night, might prefer a good séance. Who was she to be so judgmental? Wasn't she a professional? Daphne set her blogger's hat firmly on her head and got down to work.

To the venue, she assigned top marks. The occult expo was being held at the Palais des Congrès, the city's main conference centre in Old Montreal, an ultra-modern glass box that thumbed its nose at its nineteenth-century neighbours in the 'hood. The light pouring in through its massive stained-glass window panes mottled the exhibit space with colours. All the tinted surfaces Daphne found a bit disconcerting. It was like attending an event inside a Jell-O mould, but they did give the salon an appropriate otherworldly glow. Cubicles advertising free consultations were set out in front of a stage where guest speakers would later be spouting their transcendental drivel, but at the majority of them, Daphne observed, the visitors' chairs were empty. The lonely exhibitors sat at their assigned spots passing the time with their noses pressed against their smart phones.

Daphne relished her power, aware that once she depressed the key that would shoot her sketch of the salon out into the blogosphere, all those visitors' chairs would have butts to fill them. But for the moment, if she was to give a proper review, she would have to choose one to sit in herself, allowing the supernatural a fair shot at bringing her into the fold. The phrenologist she rejected out of hand, even if Nora had adjured Daphne time and again when she'd first accepted her job underground to have her head examined. The palm reader likewise. Lifespan discussions spooked her out. Discounting her grandmother, Daphne came from a long line of short lines. The blogger flitted from booth to booth, but didn't light, like a persnickety hummingbird. After she had made the full circuit twice without making the choice her vocation demanded, she took herself in hand, opening the catalogue of exhibitors, and taking a blind stab at the listings pin-the-tail-on-the-donkey style. Booth twenty-eight, her index finger decided on her behalf. Elyse Spinelli. Psychic Consultations.

The woman wasn't dressed like a clairvoyant should be, all flowing and drapey, but Daphne recognized that she was guilty of letting the movies influence her notion of the vestimentary norms of psychics. This exhibitor wore a pastel smock and had her half-glasses hanging on a chain around her neck. With her yoga pants and white Reeboks she looked more like a mammogram technician than someone who pottered around in the unknown. Her ordinariness disappointed Daphne; she had been hoping for a bit more razzmatazz. It would be hard to twist a catchy blog out of someone so determinedly unflamboyant. She could have walked on past to the adjacent booth where an astrologer tricked out like a chandelier was trying to catch her eye, hoping to hijack her neighbour's wavering client, but Daphne stuck with her first inclination and sat down opposite the plain-Jane clairvoyant.

The psychic's no-frills demeanor nudged Daphne towards straight talk. "I thought you're supposed to be behind a curtain, something velvet maybe with a gold fringe. Certainly not sitting at a cubicle."

"Oh, cubicles are where it's at nowadays," she answered. "All that other stuff, crystal balls and turbans, they went out with the dodo. Today it's more Ikea-style clairvoyance. Simple and clean. The client at the core."

"So we're referred to as clients now, are we?"

"You mean instead of marks?" The clairvoyant laughed at herself. "Like I said, we've had to move with the times."

"I suppose I owe it to you before we start to tell you that I'm a doubter," Daphne said.

"You do give off those vibes."

"You're reading me already? Colour me impressed."

"A five-year-old could have figured that much out from your body language. It's a dead giveaway. I don't deserve any special credit for that one. But whether you're a doubter or not, it doesn't matter. Not as far as I go anyway. I can still do my work with skeptics. It just takes a bit longer. I like the challenge though."

"So you get a lot of skeptics, do you?"

"A fair number, especially at an event like this, free, open to the general public, people who just happen to be passing by and decide to give one of us a whirl. They sit down for a quickie consultation, and next thing you know they've decided you're a fraud because you can't tell them if they're going to get the job they applied for, or if they'll get into this or that university. See, it doesn't work like that. It's not strictly an on-demand kind of thing. Sometimes you just come up empty on the questions they care about."

"Your contacts in the never-never are asleep at the wheel?"

"Something like that."

The way this woman was serious about her work in an unserious way appealed to Daphne's sensibilities. If ever she crossed paths with a troubled soul in the Underground City who was in the market for a psychic, she'd be happy to give this Elyse a plug, although it was probably premature for Daphne to give her seal of approval after an acquaintance of just three minutes.

"Well, you don't have to worry about any backlash from me," Daphne said. "I'm not actually here to dip into your professional talents. Not for me personally anyway."

"Let me stop you right there," Elyse said. "A psychic consultation second-hand, it's never a winning proposition. For things to go well, I need to speak to the actual person who's affected."

"No, that's not what I meant. Sorry if I wasn't clear. You see, I blog on events in the Underground City. I'm here to gather material so I can push the salon to the outside world, try to increase the foot traffic. Maybe you've heard of me? The blog's called *Daphne Down Under*."

Elyse shook her head. "No, I can't say I've come across it. But that doesn't mean anything. I don't follow many blogs, or any actually, but from the look of things, this salon can use all the publicity it can get. If I can help out in some way, I'm happy to do it."

"So you don't mind a bit of an interview?"

"Interview away."

Daphne settled more comfortably into her seat. "Okey-dokey, let's start with your gift. Is that what I should call it? Is it inherited?"

"Hardly. My father and mother didn't have a psychic bone between them as far as I could tell. She didn't clue in that he was cheating on her till the day he walked out the door, and he couldn't land a bet on the ponies to save his life." The exhibitor hesitated. "You don't have to put that part in your blog, if you don't mind. Not the specifics. Unless you count that as interfering with the press. I'm just telling you by way of clarifying. Can you just say something like 'it wasn't inherited'?"

"Roger that. Not a problem. How *do* you account for it though?"

"Honestly? I have absolutely no idea how I came to be this way, if it skipped a generation or two or came to me through a radon leak in the basement. All I know is that I've always been able to sense things that other people can't."

"Even as a child?"

"For as long as I can remember."

"What did you do with it? With your ability I mean?"

"Nothing much really, when I was young. My mother wanted me to keep it under wraps once she realized what was going on. She didn't want people seeing me as a freak."

"So she wasn't stage-motherish about it."

"Just the opposite."

"I suppose that was a good thing."

"I think she got it right."

"When you got older, though, what made you want to take your talents to the public?"

"By then, some of my friends nudged me into it. They thought I was wasting an opportunity to make some difference in the world. It sounds highfalutin', I know, but that's how I started out, on a very limited basis. Trying to make people's lives a little easier."

"So the motivation was humanitarian."

"Yes, essentially. Small scale, but yes."

"Tell me, what kind of things do people want to know through your interventions?"

"Lots of them want to contact the dead, but that I don't do."

"Don't or can't?"

"Let's just say it's too messy. They can find someone else if that's what they're after. I'm not their gal."

"What are you their gal for, then?"

"Oh, it's hard to generalize, but lots of times I'd say they've got something buried deep down that they're trying to bring up to the light of day so they can deal with it head-on."

"And you, what do you do to make that happen?"

"I guess you'd say I help them clear off the cobwebs."

"How does that make you any different from a psychiatrist, then, digging down into people's psyches?"

"Look, I don't make any claims to be a replacement for a doctor or to put myself above doctors. I wouldn't want your fans to think so. In healing, there's a place for all of us. It's just that I can often see to the root of the problem, read it right through the client. Not always, mind you, but many times."

"So they don't need to shell out for twenty years of analysis. You cut to the chase."

"In very vague terms."

"And I suppose too there has to be some *otherworldly* element to their issue." Daphne's tone carried with it a bit of a smirk. She couldn't help herself.

"You shouldn't assume that at all. The problems my clients suffer from are usually very concrete. Very much of this world. *I'm* the otherworldly element in the equation. These people, these troubled people, have chosen to take a paranormal route to help them with what are very normal problems."

Daphne absorbed the explanation which messed with her preconceived notions of psychics and their johns. Blogging had certainly expanded her horizons.

"If I'm not being too personal," she went off script to ask, "can you earn a living at this?" As soon as the question left her lips Daphne wished she could have swallowed it back. She sounded like she was channelling her grandmother. "Sorry, that question was impertinent."

"No, it's a perfectly reasonable question. Some people think that I can use my gift for profit. Like insider trading. But they're wrong. If I did try to, I'd starve. I've always kept my day job."

"And what's that?"

"I'm a research botanist."

"A scientist? Who'd have thunk? And you have no trouble reconciling the two sides of yourself?"

"None whatsoever. There aren't sides. They're all me."

Even if Elyse had no trouble reconciling the yin and yang of her character, Daphne did, and the longer the interview went on, the more confusing things became, but she supposed that was the nature of the beast. She tried to divert the focus away from Elyse herself to the business end of the operation. That was what her readers craved after all, the nitty-gritty.

"Have you had any great successes?"

"Meaning?"

"You know, predicting things that are spot-on. Making connections for people, or discoveries that change their lives."

"I like to think that my interventions have helped people who've needed it, but I can't really give you any concrete examples. That's not for public consumption I'm afraid."

"I'm not asking you to name names or anything. Just to give my followers a little taste of what you can do."

"Not a chance. One of my clients might recognize himself or herself in the description. I can't risk it. Anyway, their problems would probably seem small-beer to your readers, but take my word for it, they're big to them. Really, all I do is give my clients whatever information I can and they do with it what they will. It sounds rather undramatic, I know, but that's the way it is. Sorry if I can't give you something sexier to put in your blog, but it's kind of a muzzy business. Even I don't know how it works."

Something sexier would certainly have helped. This blog, Daphne could see already, had a major hole in it that generalities wouldn't plug. What it was missing was a grabber, a specific example of Elyse's powers to use as the lede. Without that, the blog wouldn't fly. Surely this psychic had some juicy anecdote she could share. It wasn't like Daphne was looking to pen a rival to *Blithe Spirit* in five hundred words, but there was no doubt that a story on that order, of a medium hired to exorcise the ghost of a first wife from the house where she's driving the second wife batty would pull in the readers like nobody's business. Daphne tried to wheedle just one such tale out of her, but Elyse was unbudgeable, and with her refusal to spill any psychic beans, the interview fizzled to a close. Daphne hadn't really gotten all that much for her trouble, but she could pad what little she'd gleaned to fill in the corners. It was a writing skill at which she was becoming more adept. "Thank you for giving me so much of your time," she said, reaching out to shake Elyse's hand. "I'll send you a link when it's up."

"Not so fast," the psychic answered her, not letting go of Daphne's hand. "My turn."

"Fair's fair," Daphne said, though she didn't feel that an interview subject was necessarily entitled to a quid pro quo. "Shoot."

"I wouldn't have held you up," Elyse apologized, "I know how busy you must be, but I sense that you're burdened by some overwhelming worry. Maybe I can be of some help?"

Overwhelming didn't do it justice. Daphne would have called her worry soul-crushing, but why quibble over vocabulary when a child's well-being was at stake? Daphne didn't really see any reason to open herself up to a stranger about the whole Archie affair. There were too many shades of illegalities interwoven into the story; too many other lives abutting Archie's that couldn't stand up to scrutiny. No point attracting attention. Besides, Daphne knew full well what her worry was; she didn't need a psychic to trowel it out. And it wasn't as if this Elyse had been especially forthcoming when Daphne had attempted to winkle some woo-woo case studies out of her for the divertissement of her readership. The way Daphne saw it, they were quits.

The psychic's shopworn approach lowered Elyse even further in Daphne's esteem. Probably every last member of the International Brotherhood of Occult Workers kicked off a session with some variation on "you seem to be worried." Who goes to a psychic when all is well? She had expected more originality out of Elyse somehow. If this was truly an A-list clairvoyant, couldn't she siphon Daphne's worries out of her even without her cooperation? Hadn't Elyse stated outright that this was what separated her from the shrinks? Why then, did she have to ask questions about them point-blank? Even if Daphne didn't feel inclined to talk about them directly, her worries were so abundant that they seeped out of her pores. Daphne's dermatologist would have been able to swab them up and read them under the microscope and this Elyse couldn't? Either the psychic's highly vaunted ESP was taking a siesta or the woman was a fraud, and as much as she had taken to her during the interview, Daphne couldn't help but presume the latter.

"No. Things are fine in my life. Just your joe-normal run-of-the-mill worries. Nothing out of the ordinary," Daphne said, the lie pouring smoothly from her lips.

"So everything with you is right as rain. That's rare, in my experience."

"What can I say? I'm at a good place in my life for once. My family is healthy, my job's secure. Everything's copacetic."

"Hmm. I would have sworn you were unsettled in your mind. You're saying that nothing is keeping you awake nights?"

"I sleep like the proverbial baby."

Sleep. Daphne vaguely remembered the concept. You put your head down on the pillow and shut your eyes while your body switches off the breakers to your brain granting you a few blessed hours of respite from whatever it is that's grinding away at you. But lately, sleep only toyed with her, letting her drift off just long enough for the Archie nightmares to kick in.

"Nothing with your sister, perhaps?" Elyse prodded.

The woman was really off base, taking potshots in the dark, hoping to hit the target. Maybe she was mixing Daphne up with some other client who came from a more extended family.

"I don't have any siblings," Daphne said. "I'm an only child, the daughter of two only children."

Elyse put on her glasses to check Daphne out on a more high-powered setting and whatever it was she gleaned through that look decided her to put the brakes on the interrogation. "Well," she said, "I won't pry any further. I can only be happy for you that all is well with you and yours."

In a farewell show of politeness, Daphne helped herself to a wad of business cards that she now knew she would dump in the recycling the second she got home. She stood up and headed off towards her apartment. Even if Daphne was convinced it was all bunk, somehow Elyse's probing had made her brain feel like a sponge that had been wrung out. She couldn't get to her Tylenol soon enough. But before she had gotten more than a few cubicles beyond Elyse's station, the psychic called out to her. "Oh, and Madame?" What could she want now? Hadn't they tied everything up? Daphne grudgingly turned and walked back to booth twenty-eight and Elyse stood up to face her. "That young girl you're so worried about? The one you're afraid might run off? Good luck with her. I hope it turns out all right. Poor kid. She's suffered enough."

CHAPTER 40

THERE WERE STILL a few residual ice crystals on the phone line whenever Nora and Daphne spoke to each other since the day of the race. For all that Marius had manipulated them into making nice that evening at the restaurant, for all that the two women had made the appropriate kissy noises in parting, they weren't yet rubbing along as smoothly as they used to. As a grudge-holder Daphne was without peer, but then she'd learned at the knee of a master. Neither she nor her grandmother liked to be the first to let go. It was a question of pride. This time around, though, exceptionally, Nora was prepared to do whatever it took to defrost relations. If her new life as a den mother had taught her anything, it was that bonds of friendship and family were too precious, too fleeting, to let them crumble prematurely due to misplaced pride.

She had the perfect vehicle for a reconciliation—a birthday party. Her granddaughter loved to be fussed over. A party for Daphne, Nora was sure, would mend the rift. There was just one minor logistical problem that splattered the planning; or maybe, on further reflection, Nora would have to call it a major logistical problem, namely, that Daphne would be unable to attend. When she had originally come up with the idea of a party, Nora thought she would hold it at Daphne's apartment, an intimate affair, with just herself, Anthony, and Marius as guests, maybe Ethel Marcil parachuted in to make the mix less volatile. Ethel's presence would keep the conversation safely off the hot-button topics since she was still in the dark that her neighbour's basement had a secret vocation.

It was Nora's knee that put a kibosh on that idea. All those millions of trips she had been making up and down the basement stairs since the

Demels and Archie arrived took their toll on the already-rickety joint. Her left knee now had the same circumference as her head. She pampered it as much as possible, bumping down the stairs on her bum to spare it any extra strain, as her in-house physician had advised. It was undignified, but it allowed her to stay enmeshed in all the below-stairs intrigue that had become as vital to her as breathing. Dragging all the way over to Daphne's was a higher level of exertion than her leg could tolerate for the moment, so she made the executive decision to switch the party venue to her basement where Daphne could attend via Skype. Granted, it was a bit unorthodox, hosting a party with the guest of honour in absentia, but they had probably done it that way for Nelson Mandela all those years. And wasn't it the thought that counted?

The change of location, as anticipated, did not go over well with the birthday girl. "Let me get this straight," she said. "You're having a party for me and I can't even be there?"

"Daff, my knee hurts like hell."

"I believe you. So why don't you just scrap the whole idea? It's crazy anyway. Lots of extra work, lots of standing, and for what in the end?"

"No. We can't not celebrate your birthday. It's out of the question. Every year since you were born we've had a party, every single year, even that year you had strep, remember? I don't intend to interrupt that run now."

"You have my permission. Let it go. I'll get older whether you have the party or not. Just forget it. I'll go out for bulgogi. Celebrate by myself. It'll be fine." The guilt message Daphne shot out, even if it was in Korean, stung Nora as intended, but her grandmother pushed on regardless.

"But you won't be alone. I have it all figured out. Marius will be there with you keeping you company. Oh, Babka, the kids are so much looking forward to it. They have all sorts of things in the works. They've been so busy with the preparations. It would be a huge disappointment to them to have to cancel."

So that was it. This party wasn't for her at all. "Okay, whatever," the grinch answered. She wouldn't stand in the way of their fun, but no one could force *her* to have any.

■ ■ ■

What they needed for this party was Smell-O-Vision, Nora reckoned, an old idea but a good one. With all the flaky technology available nowadays, she was surprised that no one had revived it. If only Daphne could virtually dip her head over Nora's burbling stockpot and take a sniff, her attitude might take a positive turn. So crabby was her granddaughter still at this idea of a ghost party that Nora was starting to backpedal in her mind. Maybe this long-distance feting of Daphne's birthday really was a monumentally bad idea.

Back when Daphne had been in kindergarten and it was one of the kiddie's birthdays, the teacher let that child select six classmates who would be allowed to sit on their stools at the special blue table and have cake with the birthday boy or girl while the others in the class sat in enforced silence in a semicircle on the floor and watched the anointed ones stuff their faces. Daphne always came home sobbing after those parties, so seldom was she picked. Nora wanted to strangle that teacher. Mademoiselle Jacobs was her name, she had never forgotten it. How had that troll ever been put in charge of a classroom of impressionable children when she didn't have enough empathy in her to fill an eyedropper? That memory gave Nora pause. With this party she was planning, was she just creating an updated version of Daphne's childhood trauma but on big-people chairs? Nora tried to stifle the thought. There was nothing she could do now. The train had left the station.

In the run-up to the event, everyone was called on to pitch in where they could. Bérénice stepped up to be in charge of decorating. Nora found her a couple of time-worn happy-birthday banners to hang up where she saw fit to perk up the room, but no matter where Bérénice positioned them, she was dissatisfied with the effect. The two lonely banners left too many pipes and ceiling studs peeking through. *Understated* was not a decorating philosophy Bérénice could get on board with. It violated her personal aesthetic. To remedy the deficiency, she rooted around in Nora's extensive stash of holiday odds and ends accumulated from Dollarama over the years and found banners that wished partygoers Happy Halloween, Happy Chanukah, Happy New

Year, Happy Graduation, and Happy Sweet Sixteen, which she strung up alongside the birthday banners in a style that could best be described as ecumenical. But even with the amplified decor, she eyeballed the ceiling with a moue of disappointment. The basement, in her estimation, had not yet had enough of a facelift, did not yet shout out *partay*.

Bérénice conscripted Papi Anthony to go through the rest of the house to find further suspendibles to supplement the banners, but he was not an inspired scavenger, returning from his assigned task with only a chain of garlic lifted from its hook in the kitchen and the leggy philodendron from the dining room window. He, in turn, enlisted Nora, who contributed some glass-bead necklaces from her jewellery box that she thought might catch the light. When pressed by their daughter, Yvonne put her rosary on temporary loan and Emmanuel his stethoscope. The house was squeezed dry of everything dangle-worthy, but Bérénice was insatiable. To fill in the perceived decor deficit she hunkered down into assembly-line mode with Paul. The two of them churned out chains out of coloured-paper rings that they hung anywhere they could to fill in the gaps until streamers criss-crossed the ceiling as thickly as jungle vines. Tarzan could have swung from one end of the basement to the other without ever having to touch down on terra firma.

And that was only stage one. Yvonne would have to give her daughter the less-is-more lesson some other day. Bérénice and her brother expanded their line to create paper lanterns, pompoms, crepe-paper spirals, and party hats, all with glitter applied as thickly as Shake 'n Bake. If the glimmer emanating from the handicraft didn't make you want to shield your eyes, it didn't make the cut. The siblings were striving towards nothing less bedazzling than the opening ceremonies of the Olympics with a side order of Cirque du Soleil.

This extreme decorating was overcompensating, not that Bérénice had the self-awareness to so name it, for the aversion she still harboured towards Daphne. She had only met her face-to-face once, the day she'd stormed down the stairs unannounced into the basement, striking terror into her entire family. Even her father was trembling. It had turned out to be a mix-up, Nora's granddaughter was no immediate danger to them after all, but the fear she had sparked at the foot of the basement stairs that day never left Bérénice. It tangled up with her earlier memories of horror fomented on a distant continent until they were all one and the same. Daphne may have been innocent, but to Bérénice she was tarred by association. Happy birthday to you!

The local elves eventually declared their arts and crafts marathon complete and Nora made a final tour d'inspection, checking the last-minute details. The table was set for nine. Taking her inspiration from Eliyahu at Passover, she had allotted Daphne a place setting of her own, even though her granddaughter would be attending in a parallel universe, one adorned with the same frills and catered with the same menu as the home team. Separate but equal. Anthony had made the supply drop to Daphne's apartment the day before, putting Marius in charge of the setup, with detailed diagrams provided by Bérénice so that Daphne's personal surroundings would be properly partified.

The hostess gave a nod of approval to the assembled guests. It was time. With all due ceremony she placed her laptop at the head of the table, at Daphne's designated spot, and got the Skype session running. "Testing, testing," Nora said, in full-on emcee mode. "Can you see us? Do I need to fiddle with anything?"

"Leave it. It's good. I can see everybody." Daphne was the only one among them who had an unobstructed view. This was thanks to her grandmother who had convinced the reluctant party-stylist Bérénice to do a bit of pruning in deference to the sightlines of the guest of honour. Daphne was able to take in most of the basement through the laptop monitor and was stunned by its transfiguration. Her dim, homely little cellar, whose webby recesses had spooked her as a child, now looked like it had been redesigned by Elton John. Every surface sparkled. Despite herself, she was starting to get caught up in the proceedings. It was hard to stay grouchy when so many people were devoting themselves hand and foot to her pleasure.

Everyone was dressed up. The invitations that Bérénice had hand-lettered and decorated, overpowering the basement with the tang of Magic Marker fumes, stipulated formal attire. Emmanuel groused a bit to his daughter about having to put on a tie. One of the few advantages of being in hiding, possibly the only one, was that every day was dress-down Friday.

"Papa, you have to wear a tie. Pretend we're going to church like we used to."

His daughter's request started Emmanuel thinking about what had become of that man who used to put on a suit and tie every Sunday. Relegated to the same trash heap as the man who used to wear a lab coat making hospital rounds, and the man who wore a hooded rain suit and rubber boots at the truck depot. How many more men would he cycle through in his lifetime, how many more uniforms would define him until the day he was measured out for his shroud at the end times of all uniforms?

"Will you, Papa?" Bérénice pushed him, interrupting his ruminations.

"All right, ma beauté," he said. "I'll wear one if that's what you want, but you'll have to help me tie it. You know my arm doesn't always cooperate."

"I'm happy to, Papa," she said, and jumped into his lap eager to make herself useful. The knot Bérénice came up with after a cat's cradle of winding and looping was far from the traditional Windsor. It was a lumpier affair, of the type that would be used to hitch a dinghy to a dock. It stuck out from her father's neck like a prosthetic Adam's apple but she was satisfied with the result so her papa was too.

As for herself, Bérénice had on her ballet recital outfit with the tutu that her mother had stitched up from a cloud of pink tulle. This was back in the days when they lived in the house next door to Nora's and she attended Saturday morning lessons in a mirrored store-front studio that still gave off occasional whiffs of the butcher shop that formerly occupied the premises. When Yvonne would rush her daughter to pull on her leotard so they could get to ballet school on time, Bérénice invariably corrected her. "It's an *académie* de ballet, Maman," she would say, "*une académie*." Those lessons were an indulgence the Demels could scarcely afford, but Bérénice was such a dance-a-holic that Emmanuel put in overtime hours to cover them. It cheered Yvonne to see Bérénice's prima ballerina outfit revived for the party rather than preserved like a museum piece, a relic of a dead life.

Towards Paul's chosen outfit, one that he had pulled from the bottom of Nora's carton of holiday whatnot, Yvonne felt less favourably inclined. To her, a moose costume did not fit the tenor of the event Nora was aiming to create. Besides, it was sized for a teenager, far too big for her Paul-Paul. The antler headpiece had a 747 wingspan. At a normal party, all the guests arriving from the outdoors with their wraps would have mistaken it for a coat rack. If Yvonne did give in and let him wear it, Paul would require a double space at the table to accommodate his moose-y breadth.

"You'll trip all over yourself," his mother said, trying to ease the garment away from him. "Besides, don't you want to dress like Papa? You can wear your nice grown-up shirt and the red snap-on tie. I have it all set out for you. You'll look like a little man."

"I don't want to look like a man. I want to look like a moose."

"But you always loved that outfit."

"You're letting Niecy wear her ballerina costume."

"That fits her. This costume is for somebody much older than you. Taller. Daphne won't even know you're inside there. She'll think you weren't polite enough to come to her party and sent some moose instead. A moose she doesn't even know."

"I want to wear this." He clung to the costume with his dimpled fists, rubbing the plush against his face. His thumb, Yvonne noticed, which only in recent weeks had stopped making regular pit stops in his mouth, was starting to retrace its former trajectory.

"You'll be big enough to wear it next year," Yvonne said, hoping against hope that this basement would be a distant memory in a year's time. "We'll have another party then. We'll all wear costumes."

"No. Now." Her equable little boy had to decide on this moment to take a stand, just in advance of the party. The tears were brimming. Nora and Anthony were standing nearby. Wasn't someone always nearby? They were trying to look otherwise occupied, but it was obvious that they were absorbing every word of the exchange. Disciplining your children was hard enough without an audience, but parenting in a fishbowl had become her new reality.

"Fine," she said, packing the word with enough tone to relay to her son one last time how un-fine she really felt, but he chose not to pick up on her undercurrent and slipped away to transform himself into a creature of the Boreal forest.

The most recent addition to the basement group had no dress-up clothes to choose from at all. If Archie were forced to rely on her personal wardrobe for the party, she would have to attend the event naked. All of what she wore day-to-day came from Daphne's remainders, the subpar clothing that didn't make the cut for the move to the Underground City. No one downstairs would have been surprised to see her attend the party in pyjamas, or, if she happened to be in the mood to make an upgrade towards formality, in sweats. And no one would have blamed her. When it came to apparel choices, because of her lingering aches and pains, Archie got a pass. Which was why, when she stepped out from behind her privacy curtain wearing a dress, they were all struck dumb.

"I found it in that pile of Daphne's things you gave me to sort through," she said to Nora. "It fits. Sort of." Archie tugged at her skirt to cover more of her legs. She was unaccustomed to being so exposed, but she was willing to make the effort for Daphne whose connections had managed to wedge her in to this refuge even though it had a no-vacancy sign in the window.

No one quite knew how to react at the appearance of this stranger, a girl on the cusp of womanhood, a girl who looked like she was meant to look, blooming with the possibilities of youth. Daphne's first instinct was to clap her hands at the transformation, but she was afraid of getting Archie's back up with too much attention. She'd been burned before. Yvonne felt like crying at the butterfly that had finally punched its way out of its chrysalis that had been misfitted for so long as a straitjacket. It was Anthony's temptation to give a wolf-whistle, an ironic one of course, but he worried it wouldn't be taken in the spirit he intended, so he removed his fingers from his lips just in time. The others felt similarly torn, not wanting to draw too much attention to the new Archie for fear of making her burrow back into herself. Even Bérénice knew enough not to make a fuss. Into the midst of this muffled crowd padded Paul, his mascot outfit now fully done up. He looked around with an assessing glance, his antlers rotating like an antenna trying to pick up a signal. Great folds of plush hung off him as if he were on the wait-list for a tummy tuck at the vet. "We all look beautiful," he said. His blanket approval of everyone's wardrobe choices was just the ticket. It spread the compliment out evenly, with no one in its direct line of fire. That boy had an innate sense of a room. He would make a good politician some day.

The festivities got off to a clumsy start. No one quite knew how to mingle with a virtual guest of honour. What was the etiquette? Should they go one by one up to the screen to pay obeisance? Or should they just party on with Daphne staring over their shoulders like a cyber third-wheel? A holographic image of Daphne would have been an improvement over the Skype version. It could have circulated among them. But the pooled technological expertise of the residents of rue Melançon was hardly up to such refinements. It was Skype-Daphne or no Daphne, so everyone just stood around awkwardly and watched the birthday girl smile out from the monitor, a smile that Nora could sense was becoming increasingly forced.

"See," Anthony said to Nora in an undertone, "you should have listened to me when I told you I could borrow the karaoke setup off my cousin Val. That would have loosened things up."

"No. Daphne would say it was déclassé."

"Okay, so if we're not having karaoke, then what? We have to do something to shake things up. This party is not getting off the ground."

Nora was not a seasoned party-giver, but she'd thrown a few in her time, and they'd been successful as far as she recalled. She had figured that this party would take off by spontaneous combustion in the way of those others from her past where she hadn't needed to goose the festivities along artificially. She'd figured wrong. This miserable excuse for a party was dying a slow painful death before it was even born, and it fell to her, as instigator of this bi-locational mess, to resuscitate it. Nora cased the room for inspiration and her eyes lit on the helium balloons Anthony had sprung for at Party Etc. She yanked one down from the ceiling and called Bérénice over with some urgency. She undid the knot and held the balloon's opening up to Bérénice's lips. "Inhale," she said. "As much as you can."

"Huh?"

"Breathe in. A good deep breath. Hold it, and then run straight over to Daphne and wish her a happy birthday. Can you do that for me?" Bérénice was an obedient girl. It would not occur to her to refuse Mamie Nora so she did as she was instructed even if the request did strike her as bizarre.

Nora's emissary went up to the screen and passed along the message to Daphne as directed. Bérénice had never before experienced that peculiar displacing sensation of having her voice temporarily hijacked and replaced by that of a cartoon duck. Parties back in her home country didn't stoop to this particular type of icebreaker. There, guests would talk, they would eat, they would sing. They didn't snort up recreational gases. Different strokes. Her initial stab of panic at hearing her voice shrink-wrapped was instantly dispelled when Daphne hawked up a belly laugh. Paul, on hearing the familiar pitch of his sister's voice go falsetto through the magic of balloons, sped straight towards Nora for his kick at the can. All the adults in both venues took their tokes too, until everyone was doubled over laughing. As much as Anthony enjoyed the quackfest, he did wonder how Nora could call karaoke déclassé while giving her imprimatur to this. In his estimation, helium squeaking was on a par with armpit farting, but as party Exlax it was working so he kept his quibbles to himself. He still had a ways to go in comprehending the thought processes of the Elman women.

"Okay," Nora said to Anthony, her voice back at the x-axis after its helium spike, "everyone's good and loosey-goosey. Let's dig in now before they all sober up."

"Good plan."

"Marius," she shouted out to the screen, "could you please serve her highness while I take care of things on our end?"

"Aye aye, mon capitaine."

"Madame, if you please." Marius shook out Daphne's napkin maître-d'hôtel style and placed it in her lap. "For your dining pleasure," he said, as he set the plate down in front of her.

"Grandma, you made me lasagne? From scratch? You went to all that trouble?"

"It's your favourite, isn't it?"

"It is, but the last time you made it yourself instead of getting it as takeout you said that you didn't love me enough to make it again."

"Don't go quoting me back at me. You know I didn't mean it. Just enjoy."

"Well, thank you."

"You're welcome. Everybody. Dig in. Don't stand on ceremony."

And they did, with gusto. In the midst of all the mealtime hubbub, they were somehow able to knit Daphne, though she was nothing but pixels, tight into the bosom of the group.

"It's almost like a normal party, isn't it?" Marius asked Daphne, as they sopped up the last dribbles of sauce from their plates.

"Let's not get carried away."

"But it's nice, right?"

"I'll give you that much," she conceded. "It is. Very nice."

"My compliments to the chef, Grandma," she shouted out to the screen, holding up a plate so clean it looked as if she'd licked it.

"Thank you, Babka, but hold your horses. You haven't tasted the cake yet."

"Bring it on, then. Is it what I think it is?"

"You betcha."

Nora dimmed the lights and Marius lit the candles on the cake. "Maybe," he said for Daphne's ears only, "we should move closer to the smoke alarm. That way we could spend the party with the others."

"Very droll."

"Don't forget to make a wish."

As a child, when Daphne closed her eyes to blow out the candles, she always wished for the same thing, that somehow she could zip through the secret passageway she imagined only opened up on birthdays to meet up with her parents. The way she pictured it, her feet would reconfigure themselves at the ankle into a propeller like the pert little red one on the hind end of the Yellow Submarine, to power her through the cosmos to wherever it was her parents were waiting. When she popped out at their end, her feet restored, they would shower her with hugs and kisses and then lead her to a reserved table in their celestial visitors' lounge where they would have coconut-fudge birthday cake together and catch up. But as the years passed, and Daphne grew savvy enough to understand that a wish for a time warp was a wish wasted, she hardened herself up and her wishes grew correspondingly more practical, which is to say imprinted with dollar signs. Not that Daphne was greedy. She didn't wish to win the lottery. Sixty million, who needed that? All she hoped for was a little windfall dropping from on high to ease the path for a while. And that remained her pattern. Until this year.

Now she wished only to have her propeller put back into commission so it could speed her towards a solution for Archie. All she wished for, longed for, prayed for was for Archie to be happy and secure, for her to live her life freely, out in the open, under the eyes of guardians who would cherish her. As a wishly sidebar, she wanted all of this to transpire without simultaneously putting the rest of Archie's entourage, those unwitting harbourers of a minor on the lam, in harm's way. There was a risk, Daphne realized, that her multipronged wish might be adjudicated as multiple wishes that she was trying to stitch illegally into one, resulting in disqualification, but there was no way for her to claw back on any of the elements, each of them essential, so she made no edits and went ahead and blew out the candles with enough force to put a burn mark on the computer screen. Maybe this was the year her wish would get the attention it deserved.

As the strains of "Happy Birthday" died down, Bérénice tugged on Nora's hand. Nora nodded her head to her and then tapped her knife against her glass to get everyone's attention.

"And now we move on to the entertainment portion of our program."

"There's entertainment?" Marius said to Daphne. "Nobody told me that part."

"Maybe they hired me a magician," Daphne said, "or someone who does balloon animals. I always wanted one of those but we could never afford it."

Nora went on, "Our own Mademoiselle Bérénice Demel is going to present a scene from *The Nutcracker* as originally interpreted at the Chambord Académie de Ballet. Music please, maestro?" Bérénice handed Anthony an album that he placed on the turntable of the basement's venerable record player and set the needle gently down. At the foot of the table, in the five square feet that passed for a stage, the ballerina began her performance.

Originally, as the climax of the party, Nora had planned to do a Daphne-This-Is-Your-Life, with posterized photos and old film footage extracted from their geriatric camcorder, a whole sons et lumières devoted to her granddaughter. But no matter how Nora shuffled and reshuffled the images, the story they spelled out was a downer. First, one parent drops dead and then the other; an academic career distinguished enough, though hardly at the Ivy League, a string of underperforming boyfriends and underpaying jobs, all consummated by a bizarre year of bondage underground. Nora scrapped her plan. It was a no-brainer. Bérénice on toe shoes would froth up the party better than any dismal Daphne retrospective.

Nora leaned back against the wall and snuggled up against Anthony to watch Bérénice cut loose on the spin-cycle. The evening was drawing to a satisfying close. All that was left after the performance were the presents, and when did things ever go downhill over presents? The hostess, not normally one to accord a thumbs-up or thumbs-down before the final credits rolled, was already declaring the party an unqualified success.

"We did it," she whispered in Anthony's ear, giving it a surreptitious victory lick in the bargain.

"I'll say. Look how happy she is. You two are back on track again. All your work was worth it."

At last, for the first time since she and Daphne had sparred post-race, Nora could relax. All was right with the world.

CHAPTER 41

BÉRÉNICE WAS DANCING her heart out, months' worth of coiled-up energy unleashing itself through her limbs. In the absence of Madame Lydia, who ran her académie like a mini-Bolshoi, Bérénice took the liberty of tacking the recital routines of her former fellow ballerinas on to her own to prolong her time in the sun. Her adoring audience was glued to her every move. Only Daphne's attention flagged. The kid was cute, no denying, but even cuteness can wear thin, unless you're a parent or a grandparent who is contractually obliged to ooh and aah till the final pirouette. The blogger's eyes drifted free of the main event and ambled around the basement until they lit on something so startling she required independent confirmation of her sighting. Her jab to Marius's ribs was as subtle as a cattle prod.

"What the hell?"

"Look," Daphne whispered, pointing to a hint of movement just barely discernable through the tangle of streamers trailing from the ceiling. "Look. There."

Marius followed her finger to the designated spot. "Is that Archie? What's she doing?"

"What's she doing? She's going upstairs. That's what she's doing. And she has a bag with her."

"You don't think..."

"I do too think."

Daphne's understanding of the cuteness factor was flawed. It was an urban myth that parents are so enthralled by their adorable performing offspring that they become a literal captive audience. Yvonne was endowed with a set of periscope eyes of the type common to good mothers, allowing them to screen dangers lurking fore and aft, so that even though she appeared to be wholly absorbed in her daughter's routine en pointe, she picked up on Archie sneaking up the stairs behind her. There was only one possible explanation.

Without a tick of hesitation, Yvonne abandoned her natural-born daughter capering about on the makeshift stage and silently raced up the stairs to catch her remotely born daughter and drag her back from her impulses. And it might have all worked out had she not misgauged the velocity of the runaway, who, despite having been hobbled for so long could still move at a surprisingly good clip. By the time Yvonne made it up to the first floor, her quarry was already gone, out on her own in the great wide world, a world that was just waiting to stomp her flat. Through the window she caught sight of Archie towards the end of the block. It seemed a hopeless distance for Yvonne to cover in time, but if she ever expected to live with herself, she had to try.

Yvonne struggled in pursuit. Even though it was a span of no more than ten double-wide houses that separated her from Archie, it felt to her nonetheless like she was on a journey to a remote galaxy, one that required her body to recalibrate to the change in atmosphere. Unlike her husband and children, who had copped an opportunity to slip outside for a taboo romp in the snow, who had experienced the reviving jolt that cool air brings, she herself had never once set foot outside of Nora's since the day her neighbour had gathered them in. As a result, her respiratory system had gradually reconciled itself to the constrictions imposed upon it the way a baby in an overcrowded orphanage learns to do without being held. The basement's never-ending dampness made her lungs feel as if a mushroom colony were sprouting inside them, fighting for territory with the oxygen molecules. Her unselfish breaths she kept purposely shallow to leave more air to the others. Yvonne husbanded her energy to get her through the days underground. But now, outside, taking in the fresh cold air in enormous, unrestricted gulps, it came back to her what it was like to have your body firing on all cylinders.

"Archie. Wait."

Archie whipped around at the sound of the voice she thought was cut off from her forever, the voice that had no business being outside.

"Yvonne, no!" Her shriek was piercing enough to cleave the low cloud cover. "What are you doing out here? Go back in where it's safe."

"No. You're not leaving alone. If you're determined to go, I'll be by your side."

"Have you lost your mind? You can't be out here. Go back." Archie's frantic eyes raked Nora's cul-de-sac in case that same overzealous police officer who had been so bent on taking her in was staked out in the shrubbery, hoping for a second go.

"I won't," Yvonne said. "Not unless you come back in with me."

"No way. That's not happening."

"Well, that's settled then. Let's go."

"*We*, as in you and me, are not going anywhere. *You* are going back to Nora's and where I'm headed once you're safely back inside is no concern of yours." Despite Archie's explicit stage directions for Yvonne, she refused to budge. "Who *are* you?" Archie said. "I don't even recognize you. Have you forgotten about your kids? Your real kids? What about them? You're totally okay to just dump them and run off?"

"They have their father. Who do you have?"

Archie let her bag fall to the ground. She strafed her nails through her hair. "Don't do this to me," she said to Yvonne. "You think I'm too dumb to see what kind of game you're playing? I see it all right, and it's not fair."

"*Fair*, she says. What's fair in this life? Do me the favour of enlightening me. Do you think it's fair that I lost my beautiful Grace? That I saw her butchered in front of my eyes? Do you? Don't turn away while I'm talking to you. Do you think it's fair that what's left of my precious family is locked away to rot in some cellar that might as well be a grave? Do you think it's fair how you were abused by those beasts who dared to call themselves your mother and father? Do you?"

Yvonne had always taken care to cushion Archie, wrapping harsh truths in bubble wrap, not wanting to add to the girl's stock of bruises seeing as how she already had a bumper crop. But Yvonne had undertaken this trip outdoors so precipitously, she had forgotten to put on her kid gloves before leaving. "Don't just stand there," she barked. "Answer me."

Archie reared away from this new version of Yvonne, the one with prickers. How could she respond? There was no adequate answer for the torrent of unfairness that had pelted down on the residents of the basement, herself included, before Nora offered them protection under her umbrella, and in the absence of an answer, all Archie could think to do was to make a run for it. It had become her go-to solution of late, even if all it did was shift the deck chairs. The girl's sidewise glance tipped Yvonne off that she was gearing up to bolt so she reached out and clamped onto Archie's arm in a death grip. In leaving Nora's house Yvonne had put her whole future on the line. She no longer had the time or inclination for pussyfooting.

"You won't talk? Fine. Then you'll listen. But you aren't going anywhere until I'm through with you."

"Let go of me," Archie said, writhing to jerk her arm free. "It would be easier on everybody, you especially, to have me gone."

"You think that we're not already bound together in all this? That I can separate myself from you, knowing what I know? Then you have it all wrong. As soon as you told me the horror story of how you grew up, it sank its claws into me. It's *our* problem to deal with now. Not yours alone."

"Look. I'm capable of taking care of it by myself. If you would just get out of the street before anyone sees you, I'll handle it. Cross my heart. Go back to Nora's and I'll handle it. Deal?"

"If you think this is a negotiation, my girl, you are sadly mistaken."

"How many times do you need me to swear to you that I'll handle it?"

"And this is how you'll handle it? By running away? By going back to being a street person? You call that handling it? I refuse to let you grind your life away in that hellhole again. I know that's where you're headed. There's no point pretending otherwise. I don't suppose you need me to remind you that you were lucky to come out of that place with your life."

"Yeah, real lucky."

"What is that supposed to mean?"

"Nothing."

It wasn't *nothing*. The undertow of Archie's words tugged at Yvonne. She could feel that waft of rock bottom. It prodded her to reach back towards her old softness. Now that she had accidentally sussed out just how frayed was the tether anchoring Archie to the world, the whip, she deemed, was no longer the proper instrument to the task.

"Archie, daughter of my heart, you don't have to pretend you can deal with it alone. No one could. It's too much. It's too big."

"I've handled bigger," Archie said. "You think I can't stand on my own two feet? I'm here, aren't I? I know you want to save me, and for that I love you. Never in my whole life have I had anyone like you. That's exactly why you have to go back to the house. Right away. Before it's too late. I have to do that for you. Let me feel that I've done one right thing in my life."

"Forget about me. I'm not the one who matters. The time has come for you to think about you and you alone. To liberate yourself. To dig yourself out once and for all from under the weight of those two monsters who enslaved you. Why wouldn't you need help to come out from under all that? And not just from me. Trained help. Professional help. And I'll get you there. I promise you."

Archie yanked her arm wildly in one final effort to free herself both from Yvonne and from the burden of help that was being foisted onto her. "What if you have it all wrong?" she cried out. "Maybe deep down I'm a monster too. How couldn't I be, with them as my parents? Can't you see? It's better that I hide myself away. Not inflict myself on anyone. I have to leave."

"That's what you think?" Yvonne said. Archie, in her abject posture, looked more than ever like the child that she was. How had she ever presumed otherwise? "But you're not anything like them."

"How can you be so sure?"

"You think after all this time I don't know you?"

"You might think you know me, but you only know the surface-me. Sometimes it feels like there's this whole other person hiding inside me, a stranger, who's going to break out one day and I'm terrified of what she'll be like. My genes must be made up of pure poison. I have it coming down from both sides. I'm a ticking time bomb. Can't you get that through your head?"

Where was Emmanuel when Yvonne needed him? She had no clinical experience in talking down a hopeless teenager from the brink, a teenager whose mental health was on life-support, and whose self-image came back at her out of a shattered mirror.

"Archie, Archie, Archie. Nowhere is it decreed that you are bound to be like your parents. Some people, the strongest of people, can break off the chains of their origins, and I am here to vouch for the fact that you are stronger than anyone I have ever come across. Somehow, miraculously, in the complete absence of any models to fashion yourself after, you forged yourself into a fine upstanding person, a loving person. And you did it under no one's influence but your own. I have faith in you. Why can't you?"

"You're just talking. You don't know anything."

"Archie, think sense! Murderers don't always beget murderers or thieves, thieves. You can control your own destiny. You're capable of it. You just need some help in getting there. Won't you allow me to help you?" Yvonne stroked Archie's hair in that way she had, tucking the rangy curls behind her ears. She placed a hand on either side of Archie's head and tipped it gently forward so she could bestow a kiss on her crown. It was a re-enactment of their bedtime routine. Most nights that kiss served to smudge the blackboard of Archie's memories enough to allow her to drift off to an untroubled sleep, a gift of inestimable value. Yvonne stooped to pick up the bag Archie had dropped and then cradled her arm around her. "Come, my love. It's time."

The urge to abandon herself to Yvonne's ministrations, to be veiled once again under the mosquito net of her protection cracked Archie's earlier resolve. She had convinced herself that she could walk away, that she could pick up where she left off underground, but now that it came down to it, she allowed herself be guided homewards. Clinging together, they walked back down the street.

"Hey," Archie said, when they failed to turn in at Nora's front walk. "We haven't been gone all that long. Did you forget where we live?"

Walking back towards Nora's with Archie in tow, Yvonne scrapped her initial plan. It struck her as too timid. If all she did was get Archie into the house again, there they would all be, back on the same old treadmill. If ever there was a time for someone to step off, it was now.

"Archie," Yvonne said, turning to look at her. "You're not going to like what I'm about to tell you, but you have to trust me on this. We're not going back inside."

"What?"

"I know how happy you've been at Nora's," Yvonne said, reflecting on the irony that the happiest period of this wretched girl's life was the time she'd spent in recovery from a savage beating, "but your body is nearly healed. It's time for you to move on. I'm taking you to the police where you can tell your story, start off-loading your past. We'll find you whatever help you need to get you beyond this."

At the sound of the word *police*, Archie snapped out of the Yvonne-induced trance into which she had briefly let herself fall.

"The police! Let me get this straight. We're going to go into a police station and identify ourselves? Just like that. And what are you going to say? 'Please, Mr. Policeman, I have this poor girl here who's been abused by her parents for years. You should go lock them up and then throw her into care.' 'And who are you, Madame?' they'll ask. 'Me? I'm just your garden-variety illegal. If you would be kind enough to give me a lift back when we're done here, you can round up the rest of my family for deportation while you're at it. Why make a special trip?' And you want me to feel responsible for that? No fucking way. Go back in and let me do what I have to do."

"Archie, going to the police, it's the right first step."

"There are five of you in your family and only one of me. Do the math."

"That makes you disposable? You're telling me you're prepared to make yourself into a human sacrifice?"

"You seem prepared to do it. Why not me?"

It was the immovable object versus the unstoppable force, Archie's brief flirtation with surrender quashed by the higher imperative of keeping the Demels safe. That translated into six degrees of separation from the police, or as many as she could secure them. She would not be derailed a second time, however seductive Yvonne's nearness. The two dug in on the sidewalk in front of Nora's house as if they were wearing the grippers Priscilla had been touting.

"Our time is running out and we both know it," Archie finally said, hoping to break them out of gridlock. "In a few minutes, once Bérénice has danced herself out, they're going to look around and notice that we're missing and all hell is going to break loose down there. You can bet Nora won't be able to persuade Emmanuel to stay inside while she goes out to look for us on that shaky leg of hers. He'll be up those stairs so fast he'll be a blur. And if the kids see that Emmanuel is panicky, how do you expect them to feel? They'll follow him for sure, sobbing their eyes out, running around in circles hunting for you under some bush, with Anthony right behind them, trying to keep a lid on things like he always does. And then there we'll all be, outside where we shouldn't be. A spectacle. Nora's across-the-street neighbour, what's-her-name, the one who's always sticking her nose in other peoples' business, she's sure to notice the commotion and she'll butt in like she did that other time. That can't be a good thing. So before they all come pouring out the front door, here's what I'm proposing to you, and you've got to decide fast. I'll go to the police if that's what you want. I'll do it. For you. But only on the condition that you go straight back in to Nora's."

Yvonne recognized it for the empty promise that it was. Never would Archie reach out on her own to solicit help getting her house in order. This solitary mission to the authorities she was offering, this limited-time-only promo, was a mythical journey. Yvonne's damaged little Archie was too cowed to seek out the police. Year upon year of pounding exploitation had trained her to always cast her eyes downwards, never up towards the light. If Archie was to go to the police, she would have to be led. Of that there was no doubt in Yvonne's mind, but she needed more time to stroke her into acceptance, time, as Archie had astutely pointed out, that they didn't have. Every carrot, every stick Yvonne had in her stash to get Archie to come around was already depleted. All, that is, save one.

Yvonne turned on her heel and started walking up the street, following the same escape route Archie had taken when she'd first left the house.

"Where are you going?" Archie called after her. "Didn't you hear what I said?"

"I heard you," Yvonne said, pausing briefly.

"So?"

"Hearing and believing are two different things. I refuse to go back into that house without having done right by you. If you're not coming with me, I'll go report it on my own if that's the best I can do."

"You think I'm going to follow you, don't you?"

"I don't know what I think," Yvonne said, and it was no exaggeration. She was beyond thinking, beyond reason. Instinct ordained that she walk, so she walked, every step taking her closer to unleashing the chain of events guaranteed to bring her family down. Would they ever understand? Would they ever forgive her? No point conjecturing. She had chosen her path, or more aptly her path had chosen her. Yvonne stepped up her pace. Let it be over.

"Yvonne, stop." She heard the call but ignored it. There were times when movement was the only answer.

"Yvonne, wait up. Please."

The voice Yvonne heard coming up behind her had a breathless edge to it, layered over with a wheeze, the kind of gasping inhalation that often accompanied tears. For all the physical pain Archie had had to endure during her interlude at Nora's, pain that at times overcame her in great waves despite Emmanuel's best efforts, Archie never gave in to crying over it. Until the night of her family exposé in the bathtub, the valves on Archie's tear ducts seemed to have been stuck tight in the what-good-would-crying-do-me position. But now it sounded like she was at it again. It took Yvonne's last remaining reserves of strength not to turn back around so she could stroke Archie's back in there-there circles.

"Yvonne, I need to talk to you. Wait, I…" but the voice cut out, sapped by coughing.

Yvonne couldn't help herself; she looked behind her.

"You go back inside where it's safe, Yvonne," Daphne said to her, struggling to catch her breath as she used her sleeve to wipe away the sweat that was pouring off her forehead. "I'll take over from here."

Daphne was certain that she'd set a land-speed record getting from her apartment to her grandmother's street, a notable achievement considering her stride was fettered by the pencil skirt of her party outfit. At the ankle-tracker HQ, her bell must have been ringing off the hook. As she was running over, Daphne pictured an old-fashioned brass bell of the type that hung from the wall in the servants' dining hall at Downton, tinkling gently when Lady Edith rang for her morning fix of Earl Grey, but the ear-blast of an air-raid siren was probably more on the mark. Gentle or piercing, it made no difference. Either way she was screwed. Even the fanciest footwork on Marius's part wouldn't be able to walk things back for her this time.

Yvonne and Archie both approached her as if to confirm that she wasn't an apparition.

"How can you be here?" Archie asked her. "Won't this get you get thrown out as the blog lady?"

Daphne shrugged. "It was getting lonely down there anyway," she said, deflecting any sympathy that might have been forthcoming. Idle chat, especially about her decision to abandon her post, was dangerous right now. It could cause her to reflect on what she had done, and from reflection to regret was just a skip and a jump. What this situation required was for her to look unremittingly forward. "So," she said, moving them all along, "now that I'm here in the flesh, let's deal with the nitty-gritty. Yvonne, you get inside." The ex-underground lady was in take-charge mode. "And you, Mademoiselle," she said, turning to Archie. "You are not going back underground again. Not on my watch. You're coming home with me and we'll sit down calmly and talk it all out."

Yvonne was in no mood to be taken charge of. Daphne's soft-shell agenda was not hers. For better or worse, Yvonne had manipulated Archie to the brink. The last thing she wanted was for Daphne to grab Archie by the belt and yank her back from the guardrail, when what she really needed was a good shove to tip her into the lifeboat. There was only one place for Archie to go, and it wasn't to Daphne's for a placid yak yak yak over birthday cake. If Archie didn't go to the police now, when Yvonne had her all primed, the moment would never arise again, making a mockery of everything Yvonne had attempted since she and Archie had left Nora's house on their respective mad missions.

"You can't take her home with you," Yvonne said.

Daphne did not take kindly to her generosity being rebuffed. Yvonne wasn't the only one who had burned her bridges today by bolting into the forbidden outdoors. You'd think she could have a little more fellow-feeling.

"I beg your pardon?"

"I said she can't go home to your place."

"And why not?"

"Because she has somewhere else she needs to go. Now."

Daphne looked to Archie to see if she was onside with Yvonne serving as her spokesperson. The girl stood frozen between the two women, willing, to all appearances, to let them duke things out over her head. The old scrappy Archie Daphne had come to know in the Underground City, the Archie who had a mouth and a half, was nowhere in evidence.

"Archie?" Daphne prodded her, hoping to rouse the earlier version, but she was rewarded only by further silence. Did things ever go in a straight line when it came to Archie?

"I don't get it," Daphne said to Yvonne, since she was evidently destined to speak to Archie through an interpreter. "She hasn't been anywhere in all these months. She's been stuck in my grandmother's basement, her every need looked after, and now suddenly you're telling me she has an appointment? What? Did she miss her manicure?"

"Not quite. You caught us on our way to the police." This was a slight distortion of the truth since Archie had yet to sign on, but Yvonne wanted the full scenario out in the open for Daphne to chew on.

"The police." Daphne echoed. It was more of a statement than a question. The destination did not entirely surprise her. It mortared in some of the gaps that the Missing poster had only hinted at even if it did not complete the whole wall.

"Why the police?"

"That's not my story to tell," Yvonne said. "Archie?"

Archie looked desperately from one woman to the other, strangers to her not all that long ago, who now were both prepared to see their own lives shattered so she could flourish. They stood at an impasse on the street, the seconds ticking by. Archie checked out Nora's front door. It was still closed, but that wouldn't last must longer. Bérénice had to be winding down. Any minute now she would be lifting her head from her final bow, only to discover on scanning the tiny group in attendance that her mother had abandoned her.

Archie threw her arms around Yvonne in an embrace so crushing it was as if she were trying to fuse them into a single body. She forced herself to release her, and then, with a burst of resilience dredged up from her near-empty cache, she spun Yvonne around and pushed her back towards the house. Archie turned to Daphne. "I'll tell you on the way to the station."

CHAPTER 42

To all my loyal followers,

With today's blog, I bid you farewell. I know I promised that we would be keeping company with each other for a full year, but what can I say? Life intervened.

I've heard from so many of you during my tenure, from near and far. You should know that I consider all of you to be my friends. I thank you from the bottom of my heart for your comments, questions, tips, corrections, encouragement, advice, and marriage proposals, (okay, only one marriage proposal). It has been my honour to be the one to shine a light on the hidden corners of the Underground City for you. I might have been living in a space whose physical boundaries were confined, but my world felt infinite thanks to all of you.

I owe each and every one of you an explanation for bailing out before reaching the finish line. How to put it? You see, an opportunity came along for me to do some real good. How often do you have a chance to put yourself out and do some good? I'm ashamed to say that in my life, whenever a situation like that came along I'd look the other way, hoping someone else would step up. But you, my readers, who have been so kind and generous to me, you taught me to behave otherwise. So I followed the example you set for me, even if it meant that I would have to break my commitment to you all.

I can only hope you will understand and forgive. Together you and the Underground City transformed me. And for that I humbly say merci.

This is Daphne Down Under, signing off.

CHAPTER 43

"SO, YOU HAPPY sleeping in your old bed, Babka?" Nora was snuggled up beside her granddaughter, elated at no longer having to deal with the virtual Daphne.

"Happy enough."

"A rousing endorsement."

"Sorry, Grandma. That came out wrong. You know I'm glad to be back home with you. But everything's still such a mess."

"What do they say? *You can't make an omelette without breaking eggs.*"

"Well, right now I'm ankle-deep in eggshells, but I don't see any omelettes forming."

"Archie's the omelette, you ninny! Archie's the omelette! She's safe and sound thanks to you. And so is Yvonne. And by extension, the others. You don't give yourself enough credit, Daff, for all you've done."

"So why do I feel like there's an elephant sitting on my chest?"

"Daffy, what you went through, it wasn't easy. None of it. First Archie, then your home and your job snatched away, your whole life turned upside down in the blink of an eye. It makes sense that you'd find it rough to recover. You really went through the wringer."

"It was so hard to let her go, Grandma."

"I know, Babka, I know," she said, stroking Daphne's hair, an uncharacteristically tender gesture for Nora.

Daphne rolled away from her grandmother and buried her head in her pillow. Nora was making no headway in raising Daphne's spirits, probably because they were both sharing the same funk, but she tried a new tack aimed at giving them both a boost.

"I tell you what. Dust yourself off and come downstairs. Have a chat with the Demels. Being with them always does my heart good. They'd love to see you. Come on—" Nora tugged on Daphne's pyjamas "—you've been holed up here in your room too long. A little company would do you good."

"Leave me be, can't you? I'm not ready. I'm still too whupped."

"Daff, you can't just sleep it all away."

"I can try."

■ ■ ■

Accompanying Archie to the police station and serving as her mouthpiece had robbed Daphne of nearly all her strength. Being sacked effectively zapped the rest.

The contest brass acted quickly. As soon as the Tourism Board received confirmation that Daphne had split, they shot a lawyer letter out to her confirming that their agreement was terminated and she would have to vacate her apartment forthwith. Daphne had known it was coming, though it did surprise her that they acted with such dispatch. She would have packed up amicably, but those bastards didn't even give her a chance to be amicable. They'd actually sent bailiffs to escort her out. As if she would have resisted. She was a blogger, for God's sake, not a terrorist, but they perp-walked her down the hall in front of her ogling neighbours all the same.

Worse was yet to come. Back under her grandmother's roof, Daphne slung the garbage bags stuffed with her Underground-City belongings into a wobbly pyramid in the corner of her room, and promptly turned her back on them. Nora offered to help her get them unpacked, but Daphne shooed her out and shut the door behind her. The only thing that mattered to her now, the only task that could command her attention, was composing her final blog, the blog that would explain to her followers why she had been compelled to abandon them, and then to beg for their forgiveness. Everything else could wait. She sat down on the floor with her laptop and the words shot out of her, a short missive, heartfelt and true. It said just what she wanted to say on her first run-through; never once did she hit the backspace key. Maybe now, unburdened, she could close this bizarre underground chapter in her life and move on. Daphne reread her words one last time, nodded to herself with satisfaction, and clicked *post*.

Nothing happened. Her blog just hung there on her screen, as if the conveyor belt that normally was on call to zip her raw text over to the *Daphne Down Under* website had been commandeered for another job. She clicked *post* once more. Then again and again, with a similar result, meaning no result. Her blog just stared right back at her. She let the software rest up for a few minutes; her manic clicking had probably confused it, and after a brief interval her patience was rewarded. A new window popped up. Only it wasn't the usual window, the one confirming that her entry had been successfully posted. Instead, it read *unauthorized*.

And that was when Daphne blew. The thought that her family of followers would assume she had simply dumped them for a juicier opportunity was more than she could take. She stormed out of Nora's, headed straight to the Tourism Board headquarters and let rip. The contest overseers were unequipped to deal face-to-face with an unhinged blogger. All their previous transactions with their Underground City employee had taken place either virtually or via their minions at the ad agency. Wasn't that what minions were for? But now they had an axed and ranting employee right in their office. How had she made it past that rottweiler Louise at reception? In the end, they caved. It wasn't worth antagonizing this loon any further. She could probably find out their home addresses. They agreed to let her to write one final blog, as long as they would be permitted to vet it, and a defused Daphne left the office for Nora's, a one-time-only password in hand.

■ ■ ■

"Come down," Nora urged Daphne again, yanking the duvet off her granddaughter in an effort to chill her into acquiescing. "Talk to them. It'll bring you out of yourself."

Nora's desire to get Daphne downstairs had an ulterior motive to it, as Nora's desires often did, her thoughts running not linearly, but in layers. It was her hope that having Daphne in the basement would help cut the tension between Emmanuel and Yvonne. They had been keeping their distance from each other lately, she'd noticed in her trips downstairs, and their interchanges were brief and brittle. Nora could easily intuit the *why*; the timing gave it away. It could all be traced back to Yvonne sneaking out of the basement to try to rescue Archie. Her husband understood what she had been meaning to do in abandoning their sanctuary and endangering them all, but in the gap between understanding and forgiving was the world. They were a solid couple. This Nora recognized by having been part of an un-solid couple herself in her younger days. Emmanuel would come around. Eventually. He was not an unfeeling man. But she calculated that shoehorning Daphne into the basement might speed up the reconciliation. And when Daphne did eventually drag herself downstairs for a late-night visit, the Demels concealed their crispness under their natural hospitality.

"So the parents?" Yvonne asked as she set a tisane down in front of Daphne.

"They're in custody. The police can work fast when they want to. Archie gave them all the information they needed to swoop right down on them."

"They believed her then. Took her seriously," Yvonne said. "I was afraid they might not be able to go ahead just on her say-so, that it's been too long and there would be no way to prove anything."

"Trust me, it was more than enough, what she told them. Just don't make me repeat any of it. I don't have it in me."

"What will become of them? Did they say?"

"The arraignment's not till Tuesday," Daphne said, "but if it were me deciding, I know what I'd do. First, I'd stake them to the ground and let the crows peck out their eyes, and then I'd feed what's left of them through a meat grinder, and then I'd take the remains and toss them under a…"

"Shhh, Daphne, enough," Nora said.

"What, you think they don't deserve it?"

"I do, but ixnay in front of the ids-kay."

"Aren't they asleep?"

"In theory."

"Sorry. I got carried away."

Yvonne went to check on Bérénice and Paul and came back satisfied that they were out cold, and not eavesdropping on the adults.

"And our Archie?" she asked, when she sat back down. She couldn't bring herself to use Archie's real name, the name chosen for her by her parents, so she stuck with her a.k.a.

"Well, you've heard already, I guess, that they've plopped her in a group home," Daphne went on. "That's always the first step apparently, when there's no family."

"I've heard those group homes can be tough places," Nora said.

"Don't worry. She'll get along fine," Anthony said in his chipperest tone. "Wasn't she essentially in a group home here? She's used to it. We got her all broken in." His feeble effort at a pep talk failed to instill any pep in the assemblage.

"Will they be able to place her somewhere?" Nora asked. "In a private home, I mean?"

"Far from the madding crowd? I suppose there's a chance," Daphne said. "But realistically, do we think they'll have much luck finding a foster home for a fifteen-year-old when at eighteen she's legally allowed to be on her own? My guess is they'll just let the clock tick down. Besides, there're probably hundreds of kids ahead of her waiting. Thousands for all I know. I think it's probably safe to say she'll be stuck there for quite a while."

"Maybe it's not so bad," Nora backtracked, trying to convince herself. "I mean I'm just basing it on movies and TV. Maybe those homes are absolutely fine. I mean it's possible, right?"

"Do you think she'll get it into her mind to run away?" Yvonne said.

"Why would she?" Daphne asked. "Before, she was running away from her parents but they're locked away."

"Maybe not running from, but running to," Yvonne said, her voice laced with longing. "Back to us maybe?"

"She wouldn't do that," Anthony said. "No way. Not after all you've gone through to get her to where she is."

"But if she's unhappy there?" Yvonne asked.

"She won't be happy there," Nora said. "It's just a fact. Not happy like she was here. That's for certain, even if the place they put her in is a palace. But Archie's a stoic little thing. She'll stick it out. She knows it's for the best. You and Daphne drilled that into her. No more running. No more hiding."

"What's killing me," Daphne said, "what's absolutely killing me, is that if I still had my apartment and my regular paycheque, I could probably get them to release her into my care, but I can hardly let them do a home inspection here, can I? So that possibility's dead dead dead. And it would have been the perfect solution, right? She could have lived with me. I would have taken care of her. She could have come over here to visit. All good."

"You? A foster mother?" Nora said.

"Yeah. What's so shocking? You don't think I'm capable?"

"It's just that you've never shown any interest in, well, you know, kids."

It was true that Daphne had never been the motherly type. All the other girls in her high school class babysat or worked as camp counsellors to earn a little spare cash, but Daphne avoided any employment possibilities that put kiddies in her vicinity. Maybe her mother dying in childbirth had put her off children for good. Or maybe it was always being singled out as the only motherless kid at school. Whichever, she and children were not a match made in heaven.

"I'm sure you could do it. The idea just comes as a surprise to me, that's all. Aren't you the same person who told me that a woman doesn't have to have a baby to be fulfilled?"

"When did I ever say that?"

"Don't tell me you don't remember. It sure stuck in my mind. I felt like I'd gone back in time and was talking to Gloria Steinem."

"Well, times change, people change," Daphne said. "You don't have to remember every stupid statement I make. Besides, we're not talking about a baby here. It's not the same thing at all."

"Don't get all kerflustered. Anyway, like you say, it ain't gonna happen."

"So that's it, then?" Yvonne said. "She just stays there?"

"The important thing for all of us to remember," Nora said, setting her own misgivings aside so she could rally the troops, "is that she's away from her parents and they're no longer a threat. She has a safe place to live, food to eat, counselling, and she'll be back in school. What else can we do? We have to trust the system."

Emmanuel and Yvonne looked at each other. The system had not been kind to them. It had chewed them up and spit them out. Emmanuel took his wife's hands between his own and gave them the squeeze they had been waiting for.

CHAPTER 44

"LARRY, YOU'VE GOT to look at this," Marius said.

"Later."

"Not later. Now." It was unlike Marius to be peremptory at work. Especially with his boss. His exceptional commanding tone did its job and Larry went over to where his underling was standing with a sheaf of printouts gripped in his hand.

"So what you got there that's so important?"

Marius had spent all morning closing off the underground file, doing the numbers, reading the comments that were posted after the final blog, preparing it all to be wrapped in a black ribbon and buried in the company archives under D, not for *Daphne*, but for *dumb ideas*. But what he found in his morning's work held him back from sealing the file away in the crypt just yet.

"Look here. At this line."

"What is it I'm supposed to be seeing?"

"It's the number of people who commented on Daphne's final blog, minus the crazies."

Larry took in the figure that had a goodly tail of zeros trailing behind it. "That's good, right?"

"Good? It's not just good, it's phenomenal. She always had strong stats, after those first shaky weeks anyway, but this, I'm telling you, she's an underground rock star."

"You're not telling me anything I didn't know. Tourisme Montréal shot itself in the foot getting rid of her. Here she does exactly what they want, brings in the tourists by the shitload with all their barrels of money, gets the locals to shell out more down there than they ever did before, and what do they do? They cut her loose. Those guys wouldn't know a good idea if it came up and punched them in the face. Them and their lawyers. But they're the clients, even if they are idiots."

"She did have a contract," Marius said limply.

"Yeah, but they could have found a way. There are always loopholes, back doors, rabbit holes. They could have saved their asses instead of throwing them all down the drain with the bathwater." Marius didn't quite follow Larry's figure of speech, but he was glad to see his boss getting riled up. Ever since the underground contest was lifted from his books, the normally voluble Larry had been moping about the office. His employees had long hoped that something would happen to get him to muzzle himself but now that it had, they missed the old scrappy version of their boss.

"Didn't I tell them way back at the beginning that the ankle monitor was a crappy idea? Didn't I? That it was just asking for trouble? That you had to have some trust? But no, they knew better. If they hadn't insisted on that damned ankle gizmo, our girl would still be happily blogging away, trawlin' in the bucks for us all. Instead, she's out the door."

"That she is, out the door without a paddle," Marius said, inspired by Larry's freewheeling vernacular.

"So what that she snuck out to visit her granny once. It's not like she snuck out to visit her dealer. She checked on the old broad and came right back. What, we can't afford to have a little heart in all this? That's what I would have told them, but they never even contacted me beforehand," Larry said. "Did you know that? They just went ahead and pulled the plug on her solo. Weren't we a team?"

"Well, strictly speaking, it was within their rights to cut it off without consultation if she didn't abide by…"

"Whose side are you on?"

"I'm just saying."

"Well, quit saying."

"Noted."

Larry was nursing a seething resentment towards Tourisme Montréal for treating him like the little pisher at the bottom of the pecking order, a position to which he had always been relegated by his non-discerning family until he finally showed a talent for making money. He'd thought those days were behind him, but clearly life didn't always let you put your past in the past. He paced back and forth in the hallway in front of Marius.

"You know what?" he said. "Maybe I'll just go pay them a visit."

"Now?" Marius had hoped to light a fire under Larry in showing him the stats, but he didn't think it would work so fast.

"Of course now. What better time is there? Leave it to me. I'll talk them around. Schmoozing is my middle name."

Marius happened to know that it was actually *Arnold*, but he watched his boss go out on his fool's errand nonetheless. The timing was perfect. Larry's call on his ex-client would get him out of the office when Marius needed him out so he could sneak off unobserved. In half an hour's time he had a contest-mandated coffee meeting with Daphne coming up, one that had been scheduled months before. Now that the contest had flamed out, the meeting was moot, but Marius was curious to see if Daphne would show up anyway.

He would miss their regular meetings, which had become more and more collegial over time. Downright friendly in fact. The two of them would dispose of any contest-related issues in the first few minutes and then just gab away until their coffees went cold. Mostly the talk revolved around her grandmother's basement situation, the conversational gift that kept on giving, but over time their own lives sneaked into the mix. Both of them were grateful to have acquired a sounding board, a position that had been vacant for too long on each side.

Daphne was sitting at a corner table when Marius arrived. She had a plate in front of her but she wasn't eating. Instead she was shredding her forlorn baguette into crumbs so tiny they were only fit to be cast to the birds.

"I wasn't sure you'd be here," he said, sitting down opposite her.

"I wasn't sure *you* would either."

Daphne took note of his jacket and tie. "So Larry kept you on?"

"Yeah. He stuck me on the Hamel account, which is punishment enough. So far the best tagline our group could come up with is *cheese if you please*."

"Oy."

"You said it. And it's twice as lame in French. But at least he didn't let me go, and I'm grateful to him for that."

"Me too. I would hate for you to lose your job on my account."

"On your account? Your memory must be failing you in your old age. Wasn't I there when you ran out of your apartment? Didn't I agree a hundred percent you had to go? Starting to come back to you, is it? We were together on this thing. At that moment Archie and Yvonne needed you more than the contest did. Whatever the fallout. For either of us. So don't go blaming yourself for anything."

"Got it. Thanks."

"So how's it going living at your grandmother's?"

"It's rough, way rougher than I thought it would be. All those echoes of Archie all around. You can almost feel her there. But the worst part is that they're always after me to give them all the details of how it went when I took Archie to the police, how everything unfolded out in officialdom. They can never hear it enough. They have to parse every detail. So I end up reliving it, over and over. I don't know how much more of it I can stand."

"What do you expect? You're their only lifeline to Archie now. You can't begrudge them wanting to know what happened."

"I don't. I tell them everything they want to know. The whole truth and nothing but." She ducked her head before adding. "Except for that one part."

"What part's that?"

"The part where I lied."

Marius wasn't sure he'd heard her correctly. "You lied to them about Archie? How could you do that? *Why* would you do that?"

"It's not as bad as it sounds," she hastened to reassure him even though her own ears had already confirmed exactly how bad it sounded. "What I told them was probably 8/9ths of the truth."

In their early days brushing against each other, Daphne's mathematical self-justification would have grated on his nerves. Who else would think to measure in ninths? But now that he had a better sense of her, he didn't hold it against her. He would forgive her the fraction if her explanation for withholding the truth was sufficient.

"And the missing ninth?"

ACKNOWLEDGEMENTS

I spent a lot of time traipsing around the Underground City doing background research for this book. Luckily, whenever I came up for air, I could count on being welcomed by my pit crew, Ron Rudin, David Rudin, and Felicia Gabriele. They provided me with meals, writing and publishing advice, and all-around bucking up, and I am grateful to all three of them. What lonely work this might have been without them around.

Another round of thanks goes out to Kendall Wallis and Hilary McMahon who read early versions of *Tucked Away* and helped me hammer it into shape, to Ann Lambert, and to the crew at Inanna; Renée Knapp, Rebecca Rosenblum, Beate Schwirtlich, Claudia Urlic, Brenda Cranney, and the late Luciana Ricciutelli. They were all a pleasure to work with.

Photo credit: Marcie Richstone

Phyllis Rudin is the author of two novels. Her first, *Evie, the Baby and the Wife*, a fictionalized account of the Vancouver to Ottawa Abortion Caravan, was published by Inanna Publications in 2014. This was followed by *My True and Complete Adventures as a Wannabe Voyageur*, which came out with NeWest Press in 2017. Her writing has also been published in numerous Canadian and American literary magazines. Phyllis has lived in the US and France and now makes her home in Montreal which serves as the landscape for all her fiction. She recently finished her five-year project of walking the full length of every street in that city.